**“So you girls drive all over the countryside,** delivering coffee and doughnuts?” Butch asked.

“Yes,” I nodded, hoping for a faster song which would allow for less conversation.

“Wow, that’s amazing. What a great service for the troops. How close do you get to the front?”

I sighed, thinking of Group F and the *Arizona*. “Sometimes too close.”

“Where are you going tomorrow?”

I looked up at his face, “We’ll stop at a field hospital here in Reims and then two station hospitals on the road to Paris.”

He tripped but caught himself before he could fling me to the floor. “That’s a long drive for one day.”

I pasted a smile on my face. “We just go where they tell us to go.”

I was thankful when Danny cut in and saved me and my toes from agony.

“He’s pretty green, isn’t he?”

I laughed. “Well, he’s young and enthusiastic.”

Joe was a smooth dancer and always made our dances together fun. As the music switched tempo, he never missed a step and certainly never trod on my toes.

“Is this German offensive as bad as it sounds?”

Joe’s face grew serious. “I’m headed to Metz. I was in Paris on administrative duty, but now I’m anxious to get back to my men. It’s been a bad couple of days.”

“Be careful, Joe.”

He smiled again. “Are you worried about me, Ruthie?” He swung me in close, spinning us around.

“I’m worried about all of you, officers and enlisted alike. Don’t go getting a big head, buddy.”

# On the Homefront

by

Barb Warner Deane

To: Sally –
Happy Reading!
Barb Warner Deane

This is a work of fiction. Names, characters, places, and incidents are either the product of the author's imagination or are used fictitiously, and any resemblance to actual persons living or dead, business establishments, events, or locales, is entirely coincidental.

**On the Homefront**


Contact Information: info@thewildrosepress.com

Cover Art by *Debbie Taylor*

The Wild Rose Press, Inc.
PO Box 708
Adams Basin, NY 14410-0708
Visit us at www.thewildrosepress.com

Publishing History
First Mainstream Historical Rose Edition, 2017
Print ISBN 978-1-5092-1520-1
Digital ISBN 978-1-5092-1521-8

Published in the United States of America

**Dedication**

My sincere thanks for all their support, advice,
and hand-holding,
to the best critique partners ever:
Wendy Byrne, Dyanne Davis & Lauren Ford.
My thanks, also, to my sisters,
Kate LaMoreaux, Cim Terry, and Patty Kehe,
my best friend, Jane Klenck,
and all my beta readers.

~

Thanks also to my editor, Nan Swanson,
and all at The Wild Rose Press
for their support and assistance.

~

This book is dedicated, with love and gratitude,
to my husband Chris,
and our daughters, Elizabeth, Samantha, & Miranda.

# Prologue

The sunlight glistening off the bright white marble was almost sacrilegious; how could all that ugliness have created a place so beautiful? In her mind, there had always been a permanent gloom hovering over this hallowed ground; it should be dark and damp. Instead, the sky was crystal blue with only a few wispy clouds, the sun a laser of light brightening up all the dark places in her soul; the grass was so green it was like a warm, lush carpet rolled out to greet them. Irene skipped beside her, their joined hands bumping up and down with each bounce. She was too young to grasp what today meant, what this place represented. To her, it was just a lovely outing with her Granny, to be followed by lunch and the promise of ice cream.

Their drive from Caen to Colleville-sur-Mer had taken less than an hour. Her daughter had insisted that they get a hotel room in Caen, as the trip from Paris was too much for an eighty-year-old, never mind for such a small child. But then, her daughter, who was trailing behind them, didn't understand the need to be here, either, the compulsion to see the headstone for herself, to finally pay her respects. They should have come many years ago.

They stopped at the office to ensure they knew where to go. She'd pictured this spot many times but hadn't done justice to the sheer size of the place and the impact of the white crosses—all the pain, the loss, the heartbreak, but also the sacrifice and patriotism these markers represented. The kind young man in the office offered to take her to her destination, Grave 5, Row 21, Plot B, but she really needed to do this herself, with only her daughter and sweet young granddaughter by her side. She owed it to her friend, to all their friends.

Her mouth went dry. She'd never really understood how many families had been torn apart here, on the beaches below. While the newspapers had shown pictures and the newsreels tried to explain the magnitude of the sacrifice made on those days, now more than fifty years ago, it was never more real than when she stood in the sunshine and tried to count the rows upon rows of brave Americans who had given their lives for the world's freedom.

The lovely gardens, the chapel, and the reflecting pool surely helped to ease the pain of family and friends who traveled to the Normandy American Cemetery and Memorial to pay their respects. The rhythmic movement of the ocean waves in the distance was calming. But the visual beauty of the spot was stilled by the emotional intensity, the somber nature of the memorial, the geometric marvel of concentric rows of white headstones leading out in all directions.

Interspersed among the bright white crosses, every now and then, a Star of David appeared instead. Henry came to her mind. He wasn't here, but he surely could have been.

While many of the monuments had names, many were marked simply "Here Rests in Honored Glory a Comrade in Arms Known But to God." She tried to hold back the tears she could feel welling in her eyes as they passed the headstone of an unknown soldier and saw an elderly woman and a young boy placing flowers at the base of the cross. The woman was speaking French, calling the boy her grandson, and telling him how the Americans and the Allies came to save their country, to rescue them from the Nazis. The boy rose solemnly, turning to look up into his grandmother's face while she nodded her approval. Irene waved at the boy, who turned to smile at her and wave back.

As they crisscrossed over the beautifully maintained lawn, her heart grew heavier. Would she be able to tell her daughter and granddaughter everything she wanted—no, needed—to explain, without her voice cracking or simply failing her? Could she say it in a way the child would understand? She'd waited so long to pay her final respects, to say a heartfelt but overdue thank-you and goodbye; she hoped it didn't tear her apart in front of this sweet young girl.

They stopped in front of the headstone set in a lovely spot near the shade of a tree. She could feel her chest tighten, her eyes begin to burn. All the goodbyes she'd ever wanted to say flew through her mind, the things she'd rehearsed saying year after year, all the times she'd thought "if only" and "I wish." When they'd received the news, it had seemed unreal, too heartbreaking to be true. But standing here, reading the headstone with its date of July 25, 1945, brought the past rushing back to her.

Her friend, who had done so much for all of them, who'd left such a lasting legacy and touched so many lives in so many ways.

She tried to swallow down the heartache that seemed to be choking her, looking out over the English

Channel to try to pull her emotions into check.

"Granny?" Irene looked up at her. "Why are you crying?"

She wiped the tears from her cheeks, kneeled down, and pulled her granddaughter close. "Let me tell you about a dear friend of mine."

## Chapter One
## Lilly

"Good morning, birthday girl." My sister-in-law Ruth poked her head in my door, her rich mahogany hair already up in a victory roll. My own pin curls were falling into my face, as always.

"Thanks, Ruth." I jumped out of bed and looked in my mirror. I didn't look much different, but I was finally eighteen, a woman.

Now to convince my family to treat me like one.

No one gave me enough credit. I was a high school senior, after all. I knew more about life than my parents thought I did. Boys, fashion, local current events, well…gossip, anyway.

I knew there was a war going on in Europe, but it was far away from our small town of Upton Falls, New York. None of the boys I knew had joined up, although some had left school to start working in the aircraft engine factory and other jobs. I missed seeing them at school, especially Johnny Miller and Charlie Michaels, but Upton Falls was a small town, so it wasn't like I'd never see them again.

At eighteen, I was an adult and could do as I pleased. My father didn't even complain when I came to the breakfast table wearing makeup and the nylons Ruth had given me for my birthday. And I could finally go on a real date. Johnny Miller had been asking me out for weeks, and now, if he asked again, I'd say yes.

On December 6, 1941, everything looked as good as it could possibly be in my life. I had a warm home, good friends, and nice, although somewhat old-fashioned, parents. My brother Jack had finally stopped picking on me and calling me "Silly-Lilly," mostly because of his wife. I just adored Ruth, Jack's wife. When they got married a little more than a year before, she became the big sister I'd always wished for.

Not that my older brother Will and his wife, Clara, weren't nice to have around, but Ruth and Jack were different. I was happy when Ruth moved into our old farmhouse after she and Jack were married. Ruth understood what it was like to be young. She had graduated from college and worked as a teacher in town.

Will and Clara were solid. They would probably turn into Mom and Dad someday. Clara had married Will right out of high school, gave birth to Fred a year later, and was expecting their second baby. Clara was sweet and helpful and just a little dull.

Even though Ruth was pushing me to go to college, and I wasn't so sure it was for me, she was always a lot of fun and treated me like an adult.

****

"What are you and your friends going to do tomorrow, honey?" My mother was putting the finishing touches on my birthday cake. I ran my finger along the edge of the mixing bowl and took a taste of the frosting.

"Hmm."

"I know, Lilly. I couldn't get enough sugar to make it taste like it usually does." My mother was a great cook, until we were asked to start conserving food to help the British war effort, and that put a crimp in what we could get at the market.

"It's fine. I was thinking of a small get-together with a few friends."

Ruth ducked into the kitchen and sidled up next to Mom at the stove, helping her clean up and put away the baking supplies.

"This cake looks delicious, Mom." Ruth's own mother had passed away when she was born, so I think both she and my mother enjoyed it when Ruth called my mother "Mom."

"It's not what it used to be, but I think it'll do nicely for dessert after supper tonight. Maybe there'd be some left over to share with your friends tomorrow, honey."

Clara sat at the table, trying to get Fred to eat a little oatmeal. He couldn't take his eyes off the cake.

I shook my head. "I'd rather we went out, Mom, maybe to the drugstore for a milkshake, and then to the show. The new Cary Grant movie, *Suspicion*, is playing in town. It looks dreamy. We could go to the drugstore straight from church tomorrow and then on to the show."

"I guess that would be okay. How many friends are you planning to invite?"

"Only Sue, Dotty, Ginny, and Ava—with me, that makes just the five of us. I don't want a big deal, but a girl only turns eighteen once."

"I can't believe you've turned eighteen already." My mother's eyes looked suspiciously damp. She teared up about everything.

"I can. I've been waiting forever." There was so

much more I could do in my life as an adult.

"I'd like you to be home by six o'clock, though, Lilly. I have a nice supper planned for Sunday night." Mom put the glass cover on the cake plate and set it in the middle of the table.

"I won't be late, Mom. Thanks." I brushed a quick kiss on her cheek. I was so excited for my birthday. It would be fun to have a girls' day out with my friends and enjoy a good movie. Sunday, December 7th would be a great day to celebrate with my friends.

## Chapter Two
## Ruth

That morning was like any other Sunday since I'd married Jack. He woke early to milk the cows, waking me with a kiss when he left before dawn. By the time he was done with the morning chores, I was down in the kitchen helping make breakfast.

Mr. and Mrs. Walker—or Mom and Pop, as I called them—had three children, Will, Jack, and Lilly, which wasn't many for a farm family. They had a tendency to spoil Lilly after waiting nearly eight years for her after Will and Jack. She was the perpetual baby of the family.

The men worked hard in the barns and fields. Mom ruled the house from cooking and cleaning to gardening and laundry, and I helped her where I could. Clara, Will's wife, helped, too, but was busy with little Fred and would soon have her hands full with a new baby besides. Jack and I couldn't wait to have a few little ones of our own.

Once the food was on the table, Mom brushed back a few strands of hair—once russet brown, but now more salt than pepper—and took a deep breath. "Breakfast is ready," she called out the back door, prompting the men to come inside to eat.

"It's cold out this morning," said Pop when he, Will, and Jack lumbered in the back door. My father-in-law always had a smile for me or a wink of his eye, and this morning was no exception. "I guess the Lord wants us to appreciate the warmth inside the church by making it so cold for us outside."

The men stopped at the big porcelain sink in the mudroom to wash up after their work in the barn and then sat at the end of the scarred wood table that stood in the middle of the kitchen. Jack put his still-damp hand on mine and squeezed slightly. "I hope the heat in the Plymouth is working this morning. Otherwise, we'll all be ice cubes by the time we get to church." Jack took a sip of his coffee. "At least the snow is holding off."

We sat at a table loaded down with bowls of oatmeal and scrambled eggs, toast, butter, milk, and coffee. Pop, Will, and Jack shoveled in the food, making up for the hours of work they'd already done. Despite the dark December morning, the cows, pigs, and horses had still needed tending, stalls needed cleaning, and equipment had to be maintained. Clara almost kept pace with their eating, fueling her work of growing a human in her womb.

"Everything is delicious, Julia." Pop took a sip of his coffee and put his mug back on the table.

"Thank you, Earl." Mom smiled shyly. "Do you need more milk, Clara?"

Clara shook her head, "No, but thanks."

Everyone finished eating, and we women gathered up the dishes to wash while the men went to put on their Sunday best. Clara was nearly the size of Dad's old Buick at this point, so I took her dishes and pressed her back into her chair. She nodded distractedly, as she rubbed the small of her back.

"Are you okay?"

"Oh, fine, thank you." She smiled. She would probably smile through a tornado, if we ever had any in Upton Falls.

She wiped Fred's face and hands before Will came along, pulled him from his high chair, and helped his wife waddle to her feet. I grabbed my wool coat, hat, and muffler, and when Jack came down in his Sunday best, we all headed out to church.

****

The Upton Falls Presbyterian Church was a pretty little church with tall windows of stained glass in simple geometric patterns. The light coming in on this cold winter morning didn't quite chase away the subdued shadows in the sanctuary, but the candles on the altar glowed. Thankfully, the new central heating system seemed to be up and humming, and the quiet strains of the organ helped the illusion of being in a warm cocoon.

As the minister led us through the service, I felt the cold build in my hands and feet. When I rubbed my hands together, I happened to notice Clara shifting on the pew, her left hand kneading her back, apparently struggling to get comfortable. Jack and I wanted a big family, but to see her discomfort caused me a bit of concern.

At the end of the service, as Will helped Clara up from the pew, I saw Lilly was already racing off to find her friends and have some fun. Even though she thought she was grown up at eighteen, Lilly was still naïve. She'd led a sheltered and protected life. I grew up in downtown Beacon Heights, a nearby town, not on a farm. My father was always working, so I didn't have nearly as much supervision when I was her age. I didn't get into much trouble, but at least I'd had some freedom, especially when I was taking classes at nearby Keuka College for Women. I'd been trying to talk to Lilly about college, to think about her future, but she was mostly concerned with her friends, clothes, movies, and dating.

We didn't stay long at the coffee hour after church, given Clara's condition. I think everyone agreed that she was just too uncomfortable to stay any longer.

"Let's get you home, sweetheart." Will helped her to her feet and held her coat for her. Once her arms were in it, he pulled it up to her shoulders and placed a quick kiss on her forehead before swinging little Fred up into his arms.

Jack helped me into my coat and then wrapped his arm around my shoulder. He was tall and strong and looked good enough to eat in his Sunday best, not that this was really an appropriate place for such lascivious thoughts.

Jack was the man I'd never even known I was looking for until one day he caught my eye. I'd come to Upton Falls in the fall of my senior year of college, for student teaching, and met him nearly first thing. He was fun and funny, but also sweet and strong. His hazel eyes played well off the golden highlights in his light brown hair. We had fun together, but I also knew he'd be a great father. I couldn't wait to see him holding our baby.

"Let's go, my love." He gave me a discreet kiss as we headed out the door. His mother must have seen, as she lightly rapped him on the arm.

"Jack. Mind your manners. This is the Lord's

house."

He chuckled. "Yes, ma'am."

He never sounded repentant.

We put Clara in the front seat next to Mom to give her a more comfortable ride, but she still seemed to have trouble getting settled, all the way back to the farm.

"I hope we don't get any snow before Lilly gets home this afternoon," said Mom. "Even with her boots on, it'll be a slippery walk from town, and I don't like to think of her getting sick from the damp cold."

"She'll be fine, Mom, don't worry." Jack laughed good-naturedly. He reached over and linked his fingers with mine on the back seat. I was sitting between Jack and Will, not quite as squeezed in as I was on the way to church, when Lilly was with us.

"Maybe we can use the time to work on her Christmas present," Mom said hopefully. There was no way Clara was going to be up to any sewing today. "Do you think we have time to finish her skirt before she gets home, Clara?"

"Can't you see the girl needs to rest, Julia?"

"Of course, of course. We'll have plenty of time to sew another day," Mom said hurriedly. "Why don't you take a little nap when we get home, Clara? I could fix you a hot water bottle. Once you're tucked in, Ruth and I can get some knitting done."

"That sounds great. Thanks, Mother Walker." Clara's voice was so weak, it sounded like she was nearly asleep already.

Back at the house, Jack and I headed upstairs to change out of our Sunday best. It wouldn't be long before Mom and I would need to get to work on cooking Sunday dinner. Once I'd closed our bedroom door, I turned to Jack.

"Clara is struggling today. I don't think it can be much longer before this baby comes."

Jack already had his dress shirt off and walked to me in his pants, suspenders, and skivvies. Circling his arms around my waist, he pulled me to his chest. "If you'd like, we can take a few minutes and work on making one of our own—you know, just to keep up." He started nuzzling my neck.

I giggled, his beard tickling my sensitive skin. "I'm sure no one would notice that we disappeared in the middle of the day." I looped my arms around his neck and laid my head on his shoulder.

His nimble fingers were making quick work of the buttons down the back of my dress, then sliding it down my shoulders.

"Ruth…would you please bring the hot water bottle up to Clara after you've changed?"

Jack's fingers stilled on my back. "How does my mother always know when I'm up to no good?" He chuckled but stepped back.

I leaned in and kissed him. "They tell me that mothers always know." We finished changing and went back to work.

****

By a quarter after two that afternoon, once Sunday dinner was over and we'd finished cleaning up, I tiptoed upstairs and eased open the door to Clara's bedroom just a sliver. I wanted to see if she needed the hot water bottle refreshed or if she'd finally fallen asleep.

She was wide awake, and the look in her eyes was

definitely not relaxed.

"Are you…" I took one look at her and ran to the side of the bed. She was covered with sweat and breathing hard and obviously in a lot more pain than she was when I was last in there.

"It's time; the pains are too strong to be anything else." She reached her arm out for me. "Please help me stand up, and then ask Mother Walker to call the midwife."

"If you're sure." It took all my strength to help her stand. "I'll run downstairs, have Mom make the phone call, and tell Will what's happening."

Instead of agreeing, she started to waddle toward the door.

"Actually, will you help me down the stairs? I need to walk."

Stairs? "Are you sure?"

"Just help me," she snapped. Clara never snapped. At anyone.

I helped her downstairs, although I thought we'd both go flying a couple of times. As we made it to the kitchen, both of us groaning, although for completely different reasons, Mom and Pop were sitting in the living room listening to the radio. They always liked to listen to the broadcast of "The World Today" with John Daly. Pop said it helped keep them in touch with the world outside Upton Falls.

When she saw me holding Clara up, Mom jumped up and rushed to help. "Is it the baby?"

"Clara says yes. She'd like you to call the midwife. Is Will out in the barn?"

Suddenly, Pop was yelling from the living room. "Come in here—all of you!" Pop was not a yeller and not easily startled, so the sound of his voice made us all, even Clara, hurry.

"Listen… We're at war!"

CBS was broadcasting the news that the Japanese were bombing a place called Pearl Harbor in Hawaii. American planes and people were being bombed and shot and destroyed. The war that we were trying so hard to stay out of had come to us. We had no choice about it now.

"Oh, my Lord." Mom sank into her chair, pale and shaking. I could already see the tears in her eyes. "Heaven help us."

Jack had just walked into the kitchen but came rushing to the living room when he heard the shouting. He looked from his father to his mother and then finally to me and Clara. Clara was bent over, wincing, leaning on me. I was trying to hold her up and absorb some of the waves of pain that were tearing her body apart. This immediate agony had to be dealt with before the long-distance—and longer-lasting—crisis in our world could be comprehended.

Jack and I put our arms around Clara, helping her walk toward the kitchen.

"We have to call the midwife, Dad," Jack yelled to his father. Pop didn't seem to understand what the midwife could do about bombs in Hawaii until he turned and looked at us.

Clara and I were standing in a puddle. Clara's water had just broken.

## Chapter Three
## Helen

"Is this good?"

I looked at the cold, deserted bus station and the rickety old bench. What had I gotten myself into? "Of course, this is lovely. I'll just ring my in-laws, and I'm sure they'll be here in a jiffy. Thank you for the lift." I could surely walk from here.

I was grateful that the Smith-Burtons had arranged transport for me from Montreal to Upton Falls and felt lucky that the journey had come off with few complications, but I had absolutely no idea how my new in-laws would take to me suddenly appearing on their doorstep. I couldn't bear to have the driver take me to their home; they might turn me away. Maybe they didn't want a "limey" daughter-in-law.

Walking down Main Street was an eye-opener for me. There was a traffic light, but only one. I passed the town hall and public library, both pretty little buildings of better days. It was quiet, and there didn't seem to be many people about. I missed the colors and vibrancy of London; or, at least, of pre-war London. I wouldn't miss the air raids. Nothing had been bombed or was falling down here, but there was a stillness London had never had.

I double-checked Billy's letter to make sure I had the right house number. The Andersons' house looked like a lovely home. It was painted a pretty, although somewhat faded, light blue with white shutters. The porch swing must be wonderful in the summer, and the roof looked strong in a way bombed-out London might never be again.

I walked through the gate of a little picket fence surrounding the garden and climbed the front steps. I wanted to make a good impression, despite being so knackered from the long day of travel. Maybe I was a wee bit anxious, as well.

A tall, middle-aged woman opened the door. I could immediately see Billy in her striking face and could imagine her now-graying hair was once the soft, chestnut brown of her son's. An even taller, dignified man walked up behind her. They both wore shocked expressions. Not a good sign.

"May we help you?" Her voice wavered. Mabel Anderson looked stronger than she sounded.

"Hello, I'm Helen. It's lovely to meet you both. I know I'm a little earlier than you had expected me to be, but I was able to get a ride from Montreal today, so…here I am."

They exchanged a glance that left me feeling even more nervous. What were they expecting? Two years of wartime rationing, not to mention months of the Blitz, had left me looking older, and certainly thinner, than my pre-war self. I'd always been self-conscious of my height, not only because men preferred petite women, but also because I never seemed to be able to control my awkward limbs. Clearly, they thought Billy could do better.

George Anderson spoke next, his expression curious but also kind. "I'm sorry, miss. This is not a good time, and I'm afraid we can't help you with whatever your problem is."

They made to close the door, and my own surprise nearly let them.

"Wait!" I put my hand out, holding the door from closing fully.

Billy's eyes, in his father's face, glared with indignation. "Now, see here…"

"I'm Helen; Billy's Helen. Helen Anderson." When the name didn't seem to do the trick, I tried another tactic. "Didn't you get Billy's letter? Didn't you know I was coming?"

"Are you referring to our son, William?" Mrs. Anderson seemed more concerned, once I mentioned Billy's name.

"Yes, William Anderson."

"What about him? Have you seen him?" Mr. Anderson pulled the door open again.

"I haven't seen him in a couple of months, but I have his letter." I showed them my letter, without giving up my hold on it. It was my lifeline to Billy, even if I couldn't read it myself.

Mrs. Anderson squared her shoulders, meeting my gaze. "Why do you have a letter from William? He's in England, fighting the Nazis."

"I know he's in England. That's where we met—in London." I was starting to fade quickly. The long drive from Canada, the snowy walk from the bus station, and the strain of trying to be all that Billy thought of me was quickly draining me of the energy I needed to make them understand.

"Do you have news for us? Did William ask you to deliver a letter to us? We haven't heard from him in months. Is he okay?" His mother's expression begged me for only good news. But they didn't understand. If they hadn't gotten Billy's letters, they didn't know I was coming. They didn't know about me. They had no clue why I was there.

"I'm sorry…" I found myself tugging at my necklace, running my fingertips over the smooth silver.

Mabel moaned and swayed into her husband. "No!"

"No, he's fine. I mean, the last time I saw him, he was lovely. If you haven't had a letter from him lately, I'm sure his letters to you are on their way. It just takes time for them to get across the ocean with all those U-boats. The Nazis, I mean." I knew I was rambling, but I couldn't seem to find the words to say what I had to say, until I blurted out, "Billy and I are married. I'm his wife."

They both looked at me, startled and disbelieving. "What?" Mabel's eyebrows drew together, lending her a more sinister, or at least suspicious, expression.

"I'm his wife. Helen," I said proudly, trying to keep my voice from wavering. "My home in London was destroyed—well, most of the houses have been—so Billy sent me to live with you, where I'd be safe."

"Oh, heavens!" Mabel turned her face into George's chest. "It's just too much, I can't stand it," she murmured. "We've gone to war, and Billy could be killed. It's just too much."

Mabel sank into her husband, and he ushered her back into the house and onto the couch. They left me standing on the doorstep, all but forgotten in their surprise. *Start as you mean to finish.* I let myself into the house, tripping only slightly on the doorstep, closed the front door, put down my bags, and took off my hat. This was my family now.

## Chapter Four
## Ruth

"I'm sorry to be leaving you so soon," Jack said, as he packed his small bag with an assortment of clothes, including a warm sweater, plus the airmail stationery his mother had bought him, and the brand new picture of us his father had taken.

"I know. Me, too. I wish it had taken the Army longer to process your paperwork." I sat on the edge of the bed, my heels hooked on the frame. Each time Jack moved close, I moved my right knee to brush against his right leg. I was already aching with the thought of missing him.

Jack came to me, leaned down, and kissed my lips, then brushed a gentle finger down the curve of my neck. "I am going to miss you more than I can say. It's like leaving my heart behind."

Tears formed in the corners of my eyes, but all I could do was nod. Jack was my heart, too, and thinking of him being away for months, maybe years, was killing me.

In the two weeks since Pearl Harbor was attacked, I'd spent a lot of time crying. I'd tried to hide it from Jack, but I was a lousy liar.

I knew Jack and Will would volunteer, but I'd selfishly wished that the war had waited just a little bit longer to darken our doorstep. I felt terrible that Will and Clara had so little time together with baby Robert. I felt guilty that I'd wanted to be pregnant before Jack had to leave. We wanted a family so badly, but fate, and Mother Nature, seemed determined to make us wait.

I tried to clear my emotionally blocked throat. "I understand why you have to go. And the sooner you all go over there and end this thing, the sooner you'll be home."

"I hate leaving the farm when Dad needs my help. I know Granddad is just next door, but I don't know that he has the strength, or the stamina, to be a full-time farmer anymore." Jack sat down on the edge of our bed, his expression serious.

"Well, we could hire some help."

Jack shook his head slowly. "I can't believe my parents would go for it. Besides, what men will be left? Either they're working their own farm or they're going to war. Who could we hire?"

He had me there. While there might be a nearby teenager who could help before and after school, as soon as he turned eighteen, he'd be gone to war, too. It would have to be someone "unfit" to go to war, but fit enough for farm work. And someone who didn't already have a job.

A thought popped into my head.

"What about Leonard?"

Jack cocked his head to one side, squinting his eyes at me. "Leonard who?"

"I don't remember his last name, but you know him. He picks up odd jobs around town; I know he's worked for some of the neighboring farms at harvest time. He was injured in the Great War—his knee, I think. I don't know where he lives, but maybe he needs the work."

"If he's injured, I don't know how much help he'll be."

"Well, he's done good work for the Millers and Engels. Besides, any help would be better than none."

"True," Jack said, standing.

Jack closed up his bag, turned, and held open his arms for me. I poured my love into my kiss and held onto him with all my might. We'd tried to put a lifetime of love, hopes, and dreams into our lovemaking last night and, while it had made me feel even closer to Jack than ever, it also left me feeling already alone.

We walked downstairs to the kitchen, which was uncharacteristically full for this time of day.

Jack's granddad and Pop were sitting at the table, a coffee mug in front of each of them. Mom and Grandma Walker stood at the sink, washing the breakfast dishes, Lilly leaning against the counter. Everyone knew it was time for Jack and Will to go, as the bus to the train that would take them off to Fort Dix was due to leave town in about twenty minutes.

Moments later, Fred bounded down the stairs, followed by Will and then Clara, carrying baby Robert. While Clara had obviously been crying, she had a much more serene look on her face than I'd been able to achieve for days.

Jack dropped his bag on the floor by the back door and stood next to me by the table. Will scooped up Fred, carrying his own duffle to the mud room. Clara slowly walked across the room and back, quietly humming in Robert's ear, jiggling him to sleep.

"Ruth had a good idea, Pop." Jack set the coffee mug down untouched. "She suggested we hire that

Leonard guy, who does work for some of the neighbors, to help you and Granddad with the chores."

"I don't know, Son." Pop shook his head ever so slightly. "I think we'll be okay, at least through the winter."

I couldn't help myself. "But it might be nice to have someone else to do the late milking, don't you think? And besides, I think he could use the work."

Granddad spoke up. "Leonard Kelp. I know him. Good man. He's had some troubles, of course, but he's a hard worker."

I think Pop knew that it would be too much for his father to take up the slack for Jack and Will. Granddad was nearing eighty, after all. It would be better if they had extra help, so neither of them got worn down.

"It might be nice to have someone milking at night." When Granddad admitted to that, Leonard was as good as hired.

Jack agreed. "Sounds like it would be worth it to talk to him, anyway."

His father was proud, and a little stubborn, but always fair. "Do you know where he lives, Dad? Maybe we can have him come take a look around; see if he's available."

Granddad nodded his head, sticking his pipe stem between his teeth and pulling his tobacco from his shirt pocket. "Last I knew, old Leonard didn't have a proper house. He generally lives wherever he can find work, I think."

"He could live in that old tack room off the barn, couldn't he, Pop? Maybe give him room and board as part of the deal?" My father always said I tried to bring home every stray, even if it was a person, but I hated to think that anyone was alone or hungry.

"We'll talk about it later," Pop said, standing. "For now, we better get you to that bus, boys."

Jack and his grandfather stood also. When Jack reached out to shake Granddad's hand, the old man pulled him into a hug.

"We'll miss you, boy. Be careful over there."

Jack gave his grandfather another slight squeeze and pulled back. "Take care of yourself, Granddad."

Jack walked to the sink and pulled his grandmother into a hug next. She looked so tiny and frail next to Jack's six-foot-two frame, but she had an iron will and a spine of steel. She might outlive us all.

"Goodbye, Gram."

"Be well, Jack. Keep your head down and get back to us real soon." As he released her, I spotted the tears in her eyes.

"Yes, ma'am." After Jack made the rounds, Will followed and bid goodbye to his grandparents.

While his father would be driving us to the bus station, his mother was staying home with Robert and Fred. I tried to convince her that Grandma could handle them, and Lilly even volunteered to help, but I think Mom couldn't bear the idea of a public goodbye.

Jack turned to his mother, falling into her embrace like he was a young boy again.

"I love you, Jack," she said, with tears in her eyes. "We'll miss you so much. Please be careful over there."

Jack nodded his head on her shoulder, enveloping her in his giant bear hug. "I love you too, Mom."

When he finally released his mother, I could see unshed tears in the corners of his eyes as he turned to Lilly and pulled her into his arms.

"Be good, Silly-Lilly." I knew he'd go for the comic relief, just to lighten the pressure in the room.

She pulled back and made a half-hearted attempt to swat his shoulder. "I'm too old for that nickname anymore, Jack."

He kissed her cheek and said, "I know, Lil. I'll miss you. Take care not to get too grown up while I'm gone."

She kissed his cheek and hugged him again. "Be careful."

Will stood before his mother and silently pulled her into a giant bear hug. "Goodbye, Mama. I love you."

Julia no longer tried to hide her tears. "Be safe, William, and come home to us."

Will said his goodbyes to Lilly and a confused Fred before taking his sleeping baby into his arms, gently kissing his downy head. "I love you, buddy, and I hate to miss a minute of your life. Take care of your mama while I'm gone."

I didn't want to cry, at least not until the station, but the sight of Will saying goodbye to his infant son was breaking my heart. Clara was holding up well, considering this must be ripping her in two. Will kissed the baby again and handed him carefully to Mom, also gently kissing her cheek. I think Mom was happy to have something to do with her hands.

Will, Clara, Pop, Jack, and I piled into the car and headed to town, where Will, Jack, and all of Upton Falls' newest Army recruits would be climbing on a bus to take them to the Beacon Heights train station and off to basic training in New Jersey. Pop had offered to drive his sons on to Beacon Heights, but the guys said they wanted to say their goodbyes in Upton Falls.

When we got to the bus stop, we climbed from the car and Jack turned to me. His father wandered off to speak to a neighbor whose son was already on the bus.

I threw my arms around Jack's waist, burrowing my head into his chest. Jack enveloped me in his embrace. His hug usually set everything right in the world, but it had the opposite effect today. Today, my world was falling apart.

Jack kissed the top of my head and eased me back so he could look in my eyes.

"I'm going to miss you every minute of every day, baby," he said.

I nodded. "Me, too, my love."

Jack leaned down and kissed me, trying to put everything he wanted me to know into that kiss. I snaked my arms around his neck and kissed him with all my might, all my heart.

He gently eased away, stole a look at the bus. "When I get home, we're going to get to work on those babies, I promise."

I smiled and nodded. "Good."

"I'll write as much as I can," he said, wrapping his arm around my shoulders and walking us toward his father and the bus.

"Me, too. I'll tell you everything that happens at the farm and in town and send pictures whenever I can. We'll all miss you so much, although no one more than me."

When we stopped in front of Pop, Jack removed his arm from my shoulders. As if he was already gone.

Pop shook his hand. "Good luck, Son. Be careful over there."

Jack nodded, pulling his father into a quick hug. "I

will, Pop. I'll come back as soon as I can, I promise."

Pop nodded and pulled his ragged handkerchief from his pants' pocket, quickly blowing his nose.

Will and Clara had a similar private moment, and then Will stood before me, pulling me into a hug of his own. "Goodbye, Ruth."

I hugged him tight. "Take care of yourself and hurry home, Will. Clara and those boys will need their daddy, and maybe a little sister or two."

When he pulled back, his eyes were red, but he was smiling. "I'll see what I can do."

Will hugged his father and kissed Clara once again. He grabbed his bag and headed to the bus.

Jack kissed me one last time, said "I love you," and jumped onto the bus. Pop put his arm around my shoulders. I grabbed onto Clara's hand. I couldn't stop the tears from covering my face.

"I love you, too," I called after Jack. He turned, winked, and waved goodbye from the bus. Once everyone was aboard, it pulled away. Jack and Will leaned their heads out the windows and waved for all they were worth. Pop, Clara, and I kept waving long after the bus was out of sight. We were only one of the many families still waving and watching for the bus that was no longer there.

## Chapter Five
## Lilly

"I can help, Mom. Everybody has to do their part." While stamping my feet would hardly prove how mature I was, I couldn't believe my mother didn't want me to get a job. All my friends were going to apply. I should be allowed, too.

"You are helping, Lilly dear, here on the farm. We all knit for soldiers as much as we can, when we can get wool. And if you want to do more, Mrs. Roosevelt has pointed out the importance of victory gardens and rubber drives. There is plenty for you to do without having to put on coveralls and work in a factory making engines or some such thing."

"I have to do my part. Even Mrs. Roosevelt doesn't expect me to work in a victory garden in the winter. Besides, I could be working at the plant, with all my friends, helping to build engines for the war. You and Clara have Granddad and Grandma to help around here. And now Leonard, too." I turned to Ruth for support. She gave me a nod and then starting feeding Fred while Clara nursed little Robert, off in the corner by the fireplace. "Besides, think of the money I'll make. I can even give some to you and Dad."

The chaos that ensued after the attack at Pearl Harbor had caught us unawares. Not only was that the day my newest nephew was born, but it started the mass exodus of young men from town. Almost every man between eighteen and fifty had volunteered in the days immediately following December 7th. When grandfathers and young boys stepped up to take over family farms, women started taking over jobs for the men who left, whether it was at the post office, the drug store, teaching at the school, or at Nichols Motors, a factory in the next town that had been converted to make aircraft engines. I simply wanted to join most of my friends, and other young women in town, in the work force.

"What do you know about building airplane engines, Lilly? That's hardly the thing for a young lady to do. Older women, maybe, but you haven't even finished high school yet." Mom pulled open the oven door to check the casserole that was baking. She was getting good at altering favorite family recipes. With meat, sugar, and butter already in short supply, we had to make do with more vegetables and potatoes. She was a great cook, but it was hard work feeding eight adults and a toddler on the little she could get at the market these days. Fortunately, we lived on a farm with cows to milk and had last summer's harvest canned and in the root cellar.

"The principal, Mr. Thompson, held an assembly yesterday. He told us that if anyone wanted to take on a job to help with the war effort, he would rearrange our schedules so we could finish the school day early and work the second shift. I can still finish high school while I'm doing my part for America."

Mom stopped and stood still, facing the stove, with her back to me. "You really want to work in a factory, with all kinds of people, and get grease under your fingernails? And what about college?"

She wasn't looking at me, but I could hear the resignation in her voice. I couldn't understand why she was fighting me on this. There was plenty of time for college later.

"Yes, Mom. I really want this. I want to do my part. My life has already changed anyway. Most of the boys I know have already joined up, like Jack and Will, or taken jobs until they're old enough to enlist. All my friends are going to apply; it's not like I'll be there alone."

Mom's shoulders seemed to sag, but she still wouldn't turn to look at me.

"I don't know anything about building airplane engines, but I can learn, just like everybody else. I hate to think of my brothers heading to Europe without enough planes to bring supplies or more soldiers or whatever. If I want to go to college, I can go later. I have to do my part now."

Finally, my mother turned to look at me, shaking her head slowly. "Fine. If you can get your school work done, and you have friends who will ride the bus to Beacon Heights with you, you can take the job." She wiped her hands on her apron. "At least, for now."

I walked over and kissed her cheek. "Thank you."

She looked deep into my eyes. "Be careful, Lilly. This is more than I want for you at your age. Please take care of yourself."

She was such a worrywart, but I gave her a quick hug. "I'll be fine, Mom. Don't worry."

****

After dinner that night, I followed Leonard out into the yard, buttoning my coat. He walked with me across the drive.

"Out for an evening stroll?" asked Leonard.

"No." I chuckled. "I'm walking over to my friend Ginny's house, just for a short visit."

"Did you bring a flashlight? It'll be awful dark by the time you come home."

I pulled it from my pocketbook to show him.

"Good," said Leonard. He started walking toward the barn and then stopped and turned back to me. "You'll wanna be careful out by yourself at night, girlie."

I smiled. "I've walked by myself to Ginny's a hundred times, Leonard. I'll be fine."

He nodded. "Sure, but things are changin' these days. With so many of the men away from their farms, I've been hearin' about eggs being stolen, livestock even. There are some desperate people out there."

I hadn't heard about any thefts. "I'm sure I'll be fine, but thank you for your concern." I started down the lane.

"All right, then." Leonard turned and went into the barn.

I continued on to Ginny's. I wanted to see how the talk with her parents had gone. Ginny was one of seven kids, with two older brothers who had left for basic training at Fort Dix during the last week in December.

Mr. Campbell opened the door for me, calling out, "Virginia, Lilly is here to see you." He gave me a quick pat on the back and sent me in the direction of Ginny's room while he headed toward the front parlor, where I could hear the radio playing.

"Come on in, Lilly," Ginny called from the door. "You two get lost." She was pushing her sisters out the door of their shared room when I got to the top of the stairs. "Go on, scram." She pulled me into her room and shut the door quickly.

"Well?" Ginny flopped down on her bed, and I hopped onto another one. Ginny had red hair, which she loved, and freckles, which she hated. She was petite and cute as a bug, and all the boys followed her around. What made her my best friend, though, was that she was the nicest girl I knew.

"I got the go-ahead; how about you?"

Ginny looked at her door, as if she could see her little sisters holding their ears to it. She leaned in closer to me and said, "They said yes. If I can rearrange my school schedule, and as long as there's a bunch of us riding the bus together, I can take the job."

We jumped off the beds and hugged. The war was terrible, but the chance to take a paying job and be treated like adults was exciting anyway. And with so many of my friends hoping to work there, it would be just like school, only better.

"We can talk to Mr. Thompson tomorrow and get our classes worked out. Then we can probably take the bus over to Beacon Heights after school to apply for jobs." The ad in Sunday's paper had said they were taking applications all week for work around the clock.

"I can't do it if it's the midnight shift, though." Ginny's gaze clouded over as we both sank back onto the beds. "My pap was clear on that. 'No daughter of mine is staying out all night like some trollop.' " Ginny did a pretty good imitation of her father's voice—well, of every father's voice—and we started giggling.

"My mother insists that I ride the bus back and forth with friends; I can't even take a bus alone. Have you heard from Sue, Dotty, or Ava? I wonder if they'll be going over tomorrow, too. It will be so much fun if we get to work together."

Ginny linked arms with me. "Tell your mother not to worry; we're in this together, doll!"

## Chapter Six
## Ruth

*My love,*

*I know you've only been gone for a few weeks, but I miss you and think of you day and night, especially when I'm falling asleep, imagining that you're here with your arms around me. I hope everything is going well and you are adjusting. Do you see much of Will?*

*Have you gotten your orders to ship out yet? How was the end of training? Please be careful and come home to me. I'm proud of you, but miss you. It must be boring for you now, though. In my mind's eye, I see you playing Euchre in the barracks with your buddies. Have fun while you can. When you can give me a hint of where you'll be going, please do. At least that way, I'll know what news reels to pay attention to.*

*Everything is good here. I hope the ground starts to thaw soon so we can get the vegetables planted early. Leonard is working out wonderfully. He was shy about coming to the house for supper every night, but I convinced him that we really wanted him to. Since he can't really cook in the tack room, he relented. He's taken to carrying in the bags when we take a trip to the market and carrying in wood and water when needed. Fred has really taken a shine to him, and they are cute together. Leonard is helping Fred to build toys out of scraps of wood. He seems pretty fond of Lilly, too.*

*Lilly has convinced your parents to let her apply for a job at Nichols Motors, building aircraft engines. She has an interview there tomorrow. Your mother is worried about her, but I think she can handle it. She needs to feel she's doing her part. There are lots of women from Upton Falls going there to work, so I'm sure she'll be fine.*

*Little Robert is an angel baby, as was Fred at this age. Will and Clara really have a knack for this baby business. Clara seems as calm and serene as ever, although I'll never know how.*

*In your last letter, you asked about work. I have to say that, while I still love teaching, I feel removed from the war effort in my classroom. Yes, I get satisfaction from teaching, but I feel like I have more to give to the war effort, if I only knew how…*

****

I was sitting at my desk, finishing Jack's letter, when Lilly eased open my bedroom door. She looked over at me, saw that I was writing, and started to back out of the room.

"It's okay. I'm finished." I patted the side of the bed, and Lilly took a seat while I turned down the Teddy Wilson album I was playing on my father's old Philco.

"I just wanted to sort out what I'm going to wear tomorrow, because Ginny and I are going to Nichols Motors right after school. I want to look, you know…mature. I don't want them to think I'm too young." She was wearing a plaid wool skirt that went to just below her knees, a brown belt, and a white blouse with a Peter Pan collar. She might have been trying a little hard, but she looked nice.

"What do you think?" She spread her skirt out, looking up at me.

"You look quite nice. I'm sure your interview will be fine. They will be lucky to hire you and Ginny. I imagine they need all the good employees they can get."

Lilly sat on the edge of the bed and crossed her ankles. "Ava should be there, too, although I'm not sure about Dotty and Sue. It would be nice to know some people working there, if we get hired."

I nodded.

"From what I hear at school, it seems like a lot of women in town are taking jobs there. The pay is better than most other jobs in the area, and everyone wants to do their part."

Lilly tugged at a loose cuticle on her left index finger. She had a tendency to chew her fingernails when she was nervous, although she was trying hard to break the habit.

"I wasn't sure Ginny could convince her parents, but I didn't think Mom would give me such a fight about getting a job." She looked up at me, somewhat bewildered.

"I think your parents would have liked to say no but realized they were fighting a losing battle."

"I don't know why they think I can't handle it. I'm not stupid, and Nichols will train me for what I need to do." She crossed her arms and stuck her chin out.

I placed my hand on her knee. "Your mother knows you're smart enough to do the work. That's not what's really worrying her."

Lilly dropped her hands to the bed, pulling the worn old chenille bedspread into her fists. "Then why did she give me such a hard time about it?"

"She's worried about you, Lilly. She's worried about the kind of people you'll meet at the factory, especially the men. You're young, and you'll be exposed to language and people who are coarser than your world has been until now. There will be men working at the factory, men who couldn't or wouldn't enlist, and not all of them are nice guys. She just wants to keep you safe as long as possible."

Lilly's chin jutted out in defiance. "Well, it isn't fair. Most of the boys my age are gone, volunteered or drafted. There are so few people in school these days; even some of the girls have to spend more time working their family farms or taking jobs at the factory. Life just isn't the same."

I sat next to her on the edge of the bed, putting my arm around her shoulders. "She knows that, Lilly. She just wanted to protect you as long as possible. That's what parents do. I know Jack and Will would rather be here with us, helping Pop with the farm, but they needed to volunteer. You have to remember how worried your parents are about them. It's hard for them to have to worry about you, too."

She jumped up and gave me a quick hug. "Everything will be fine, just wait and see. I'm going to be able to contribute some of my earnings to the household, which should help take the pressure off Mom and Dad. I'll still graduate, and maybe working in the factory will even help me decide what I want to do after I finish school." Lilly smiled as she turned to leave. "Thanks for your help. See you later."

After she closed the door behind her, I lay down on the bed, just to get off my feet for a while. Teaching full-time, plus helping out around the house and occasionally out in the fields, could be tiring. But as Lilly said, our world had changed, and we'd just have to get used to how things were going to be.

## Chapter Seven
## Helen

"So long, gals. See you tomorrow." Madge turned and headed off toward her side of town while everyone else took their own path. I waved them goodbye and walked up Main Street toward the Andersons' house.

I'd met a number of girls from Upton Falls at Nichols Motors, and we'd taken to sitting together on the bus. I didn't know the girls well, but it was nice to feel a part of their group. I'd been working at the plant now for nearly a month and found it a relief to leave the Andersons each afternoon.

Billy's folks didn't fancy me and made it clear I wasn't the wife they wanted for Billy. It didn't help that they hadn't gotten Billy's letter until I'd been in their house for several weeks. Billy had exaggerated their enthusiasm for meeting me. They let me stay in Billy's room, but they weren't too keen to have me around and didn't invite me to eat meals with them or sit with them in the parlor or listen to the radio. Of course, once I'd started working at the plant, I was gone every evening, except on the weekends, so that saved them from having to eat dinner with me. They just couldn't seem to find anything to talk to me about and really didn't seem to try. They didn't want to know anything about my family, and I didn't want to talk about the Blitz or the fighting going on in Europe, while talking about

Billy always made Mrs. Anderson get weepy.

"Hello," I called softly to let Billy's parents know I was home from work, in case anyone was still awake, so as not to startle them. They always seemed to be surprised to find me in their house.

"Good night, Helen." Mrs. Anderson was always quite formal with me, never inviting me to call her Mum or Mabel. I'd probably be calling them Mr. and Mrs. Anderson forever, even after Billy came home and we were old and gray ourselves. Even so, in my mind, they were George and Mabel.

"Good night." While I put my hat and coat in the hall closet, Mabel walked by me to climb the stairs to bed. She wasn't usually awake when I got home, although George was often still reading the newspaper in his study.

I walked to the kitchen to wash out my dinner pail and thermos before packing tomorrow's dinner. A teacup and saucer were drying in the dish rack, so I guessed Mabel had made herself some warm milk before bed.

I walked softly into George's study, to see if he was still awake, but it was empty. George worked as a banker in the only bank in Upton Falls, putting him in a fairly prestigious position in the small town. Madge had whistled when I told her where I was living. She said the Andersons didn't mix with her kind of folk. They clearly didn't mix with my kind, either.

Since I was alone, I sat down in George's chair and allowed myself a few minutes to unwind with my feet up.

Living with the Andersons was nothing like when I lived at home, or when I lived in with the Smith-

Burtons. My mum and dad had twelve children, with me the oldest, so meals around our house were always loud and chaotic, and there was never enough to eat. Some of the youngest were always fighting over food, and somebody's cup of milk always got turned over. I'd been the one having to help take care of the little ones when my mum was busy having babies, ever since I was eight, so it was my job to clean up their messes. The only one of my siblings I missed was Camilla. Poor Millie had to take over as Mum's helper when I left, although she'd at least made it to age twelve before she had to leave school.

When I moved to London to work as a nanny for the Smith-Burtons, I was happy to take my meals in the kitchen with the rest of the household staff because it was calm and quiet, the only interruptions coming from a member of the family when they needed something. And there was always plenty to eat and no one spilled a thing. It was heaven.

When the Smith-Burtons decided to evacuate their children to Montreal at the start of the war, I was lucky to go with them. Even though I wasn't still living in after Billy and I got married, they kept me on because the kids were fond of me. When we learned that the Smith-Burtons could arrange for my transport to Canada if I would continue to work as their nanny through the trip, Billy saw it as the perfect way to send me to America to live with his parents.

I was grateful to the Smith-Burtons for getting me out of London alive, and to the Andersons for taking me in, even when they didn't seem too keen about it. But other than the girls I was getting to know at work, life in Upton Falls was lonely. I missed Billy terribly. I was safe, and Billy was happy that I was out of England, but I couldn't wait for the war to be over so Billy could come home.

Most of the girls at the factory were older and seemed frightfully clever about everything, from building a motor to styling their hair to music and dances, and they always looked terribly smart. Most of them had been nice to me. Madge even said that she'd go with me to get some proper shoes after the next payday.

I realized after a while that I couldn't keep my eyes open a minute longer, so I headed up to bed. Even though I worked second shift, I would still need to be up early in the morning. Mabel didn't approve of sleeping in, so I had started getting up by seven o'clock even on the weekends, and it was nearly doing me in.

****

When I climbed onto the bus the next day, I took a seat in the front, as usual. Madge, Vera, and Gladys were in the next few rows behind me. Just as we were getting ready to pull out, two young women ran to the bus and hustled aboard. The matron stopped them.

"This isn't a public bus, girls. It goes directly to Nichols Motors. You have to wait for the next bus."

The tall, pretty brunette smiled and said, "No, we're going to Nichols, ma'am. We both have interviews there today."

"Geez, they're getting younger every day. Nothing like a busload of virgins to distract every man at the plant," Madge said, and Gladys laughed, but I saw the girls blush. The petite redhead was cute and looked a bit like a pixie. The taller girl had her pretty chocolate-brown hair pinned in a chignon, clearly trying to look older.

"Well, then," said the matron, "Take a seat, already."

The girls filed into the seat across the aisle from me, looking a bit scared. They whispered to each other.

"So, girls, did Mommy and Daddy finally let you out of the convent? Think you're taking a walk on the wild side, do you?" Vera practically snarled at the girls. She had a bit of a mean streak, especially when it came to getting a bloke's attention.

The brunette turned slightly to look over her shoulder, but must have decided to ignore the jibes. I was hoping that would be the end of it.

"What's the matter, cat got your tongue?" jeered Vera. She moved up a seat, so she was right behind the two girls.

"That won't be the only thing that has their tongues in a few weeks, right, Vera?" Madge let out a throaty chuckle. Gladys poked Madge in the ribs, but it didn't seem to stop the taunting. "Don't think you'll find some soldier to be your beau at Nichols, girls. It's just a bunch of dirty old men and 4Fs who'd chase anything in a skirt."

When the girls continued to ignore them, Vera moved back to the seat across from Madge, and the girls seem to relax a bit, although they looked a little more frazzled.

The brunette looked across the aisle at me and smiled tentatively. "Hi," she said.

"Hi," I replied softly. "I'm Helen Anderson. Don't worry about the girls; it's all in good fun."

The brunette gave a quick glance behind us. "If you say so. I'm Lilly Walker, and this is my friend,

Ginny Campbell. It's nice to meet you."

I nodded at Ginny and gave her a little wave. "So you're looking to work at the plant? On the floor or in the office?"

"Oh, I guess on the floor. That's where all the action will be, right?" said Lilly. "Is that what you do? How long have you been working at the plant?"

"Yes, I've been on the assembly floor for about a month. The work's not too hard."

"You're from England, aren't you?" said Lilly. "I love your accent."

People always had to ask. In a town the size of Upton Falls, there weren't many people who hadn't lived there their whole lives. "Yes, I'm from London."

"Oh, my brothers both got shipped out to England right after Valentine's Day, but we're not sure where they're located. We haven't gotten too many letters yet."

"My husband is over there as well; he's a pilot." I didn't hear from Billy often, but at least more often than his parents did.

"I'm so nervous," said Lilly. "I convinced my parents to let me interview and fixed my schedule at school so I could work second shift. I really hope I get the job. I want to feel like I'm helping, beyond just knitting for the troops."

I smiled. "I know what you mean. I was finding it right hard to not have a job when I first got here; I've been working forever." I smiled at Lilly. "I'm sure you'll do well. They really need more girls."

"I've never had a job before; I just have to get hired. My friends and I all want to get jobs at Nichols."

I fingered my necklace, a thin silver chain with a

simple cross. Billy had bought it for me in London, from a young girl whose whole family was killed in a bombing. She said it was good luck, because she was wearing it and was the only one who lived.

I reached behind my neck and undid the clasp. “Here, take this. It will bring you good luck.” I held the necklace out to her in my hand.

“Oh, thank you, but I couldn’t take your necklace. It’s lovely.”

“Just a loan to help you through the interview. You can give it back to me on the bus tomorrow, when you get the job.” I put the chain in her hand. “Go on, it’s a lucky necklace.”

She smiled. “Okay, just a loan, then. Who can resist a lucky necklace?” She fastened it around her neck and tucked the chain beneath the collar of her blouse. “Thank you so much, Helen. You’re very kind.”

“We can all use a little good luck these days, can’t we?”

Soon enough we were at the plant and got off the bus. “Good luck with your interviews.”

“Thanks,” said Ginny.

Lilly fingered the cross around her neck and said, “Yes, thanks so much. I hope we see you again tomorrow, down on the assembly line.”

As they started to walk toward the office, she turned suddenly. “What happens if I don’t get the job? How can I return the necklace to you?” She had a touch of panic in her eyes.

“Don’t fret. I take the bus every day. You can meet me at the bus stop. But I know it’ll bring you good luck. And good luck to you, too, Ginny.”

The girls waved and got into the queue of young

women at the office door. I knew I'd see her tomorrow. The necklace hadn't let me down yet.

## Chapter Eight
## Lilly

"You don't seem to have much experience, Miss Walker." The plant manager at Nichols was a little scary, but I tried to keep calm. He was old, at least fifty, had black glasses and a serious look on his face, like he never laughed.

"I work on our family farm, especially now that my brothers enlisted. I'm strong and smart, so I'm sure I'll pick it all up quickly." I slid my palms down the length of my skirt, hoping he wouldn't notice how sweaty they were.

"Stand up." He looked over the top of his clipboard at me, the glasses making his eyes look small and beady.

So I stood up.

"Turn."

I turned around.

"Well, we'll give you a try." He signed something and handed me a stack of paperwork. "Take these to the matron and have her get you a uniform." He couldn't have noticed the smile on my face when he turned and picked up the next person's paperwork.

"Thank you, Mr. Ward." When he didn't look up, I grabbed my purse and headed down the metal stairs to find the matron. Ginny and Ava had gone before me, so they were already in a small cubicle to the side of the production floor. Ginny gave me a smile and wink when she saw me coming toward them.

I handed the stack of paperwork to the middle-aged woman standing in front of a battered desk. She was wearing a severe black dress and had her hair in tight gray curls. A pair of reading glasses hung on a chain around her neck.

"Miss Walker?"

"Yes, ma'am." My gaze flew over the room, from the beat-up file cabinets to the shiny black Bakelite telephone on her desk to the stack of uniforms and kerchiefs in the corner.

She looked at my forms, grabbed a coverall and kerchief, and handed them to me. "You're to call me Matron or Mrs. Davis. You start tomorrow afternoon, so be here promptly at three o'clock. There will be a short dinner break. You can bring in your own food or buy dinner from the canteen. You'll be allowed one additional coffee break, when and if we have time, and then work until eleven p.m. Is all that clear?" She looked at me with a tired-of-life expression.

"Yes, Matron."

"Move along, now. See you tomorrow, three p.m."

Ginny, Ava, and I, and about six other women filed out of her office, carrying our handbags and uniforms. The whole process was so quick, I never even had a chance to take off my hat and coat.

As we stepped into the afternoon sunshine again, we three linked arms and started giggling. Suddenly, I had a thought and stopped in my tracks, just missing the door as it closed behind us.

Ginny, forced to stop when I did, turned to me. "What?"

"How do we get home today? We can take the bus back to Upton Falls after our shift every night, but what about today?"

"Oh, don't worry, we'll be fine," said Ava.

"It's okay," said Ginny. "The matron told me they held the first-shift bus for the new recruits. We have to hurry, but they're waiting for us."

We ran to the bus and climbed on, laughing as we took seats. We did it; we had real jobs. We were going to have so much fun working together. I was excited and felt so much more like an adult.

"Can we go now?" A large woman, her hair still up in what I'd learned was the first-shift kerchief, pounded her fist on the back of the seat in front of her. "Some of us have ta get home to our kids, ya know." There was general muttering toward the back of the bus.

The bus started up, and we left the plant, heading back to Upton Falls. Ginny, Ava, and I put our heads together, talking quietly but unable to disguise our excitement.

"Were you nervous?" I couldn't help fiddling with the cross on the slinky chain around my neck. Helen's necklace certainly had been lucky for me.

Ginny nodded. "Absolutely. I thought Mr. Ward was kind of mean. I didn't want him to see how I was shaking."

"I thought he was a little pervy," said Ava. "Why did he have to look me up and down and make me turn around? He made me nervous."

"Me too," I confessed. "I kept wiping off my sweaty palms, in case he wanted to shake my hand. My mother told me to wear gloves; maybe I should have listened."

"He surely didn't try to shake my hand. I don't think he was all that keen to talk to me, even," said Ginny. "Maybe he didn't think I was as cute as you, Ava."

"Lucky me," said Ava.

I laughed. "Same for me. It sure didn't take very long. I spent a lot of time worrying about my first job interview, and I think I could have worn a bag over my head and still have gotten the job."

****

We parted company with Ava at the bus stop, as she lived on the other side of town. After Ginny and I walked to Ginny's house, which was closer to town than ours, I headed down the road on my own. It occurred to me that I could leave Jack's old bike at Ginny's every morning, before school, and have it to ride home in the evenings. Well, at least for as long as the tires held out.

I was thinking about the bike and my new job and how much money I would be making and didn't really notice the smoke until I started to cough. When I looked up and saw ash flying toward my face, I spun around, trying to figure out what was burning. Then I froze in place—the Lamberts' house was on fire!

I ran toward the wooden fence surrounding the yard, which had been painted white a long time ago. I kept searching for anyone else on the street as I made my way to the gate. Surely someone else had to have noticed the smoke by now, but no one seemed to be rushing toward the house but me.

"Fire! Help!" I shouted as loud as I could, but I wasn't even sure anyone was around to hear me.

Every breath was a mixture of smoke and heat. I

didn't see any of the family outside. I had to get close enough to figure out if anyone was home. "Hello, is anybody there?" I quickly but gingerly raced up the stone path to the front porch steps, which seemed removed from the fingers of fire, at least for now. "Hello? Hello?"

The fire itself was getting louder, the flames eating at the roof and crackling in the brisk winter air. Was that a voice? Was someone in there?

I turned back to the street, searching for any sign that someone else was coming to help, that the fire station had been notified. Why hadn't they sounded the siren?

"Help…"

I snapped around again, searching the nearest window, trying to verify I'd really heard someone; maybe it was just my imagination. The sound was so small, so soft.

Inside, I could see lots of smoke, but not much else. If there was someone in there, they wouldn't last for long. I guess I couldn't wait for someone else to come along. I reached and gave the knob a twist, but it wouldn't budge. It was locked.

Turning back to the window, I knocked on the glass. "Hello. Is anyone in there?"

A small, scared face appeared at the window. A child, no more than five or six, his eyes red and full of tears.

"Can you open the door?" I tried again, but the knob wouldn't budge.

He just stared at me, clearly frozen in place by his fear.

I had no choice; I'd have to break the window.

"Stand away from the window. Move away, so I can break the window. Don't worry. I'll get you out in a minute."

Running to the yard, I found a foundation stone that had fallen to the ground and grabbed it. I whipped it through the window as hard as I could, and the glass shattered. Smoke billowed out, stinging my eyes and lungs. Working quickly, I pushed the glass away from the sash, making the opening as large as possible.

"Okay," I called into the smoky darkness. "Come on, honey, I'll pull you out."

Where was he? Had I lost him to the smoke? I looked through the haze but couldn't see him. Maybe he didn't understand what I was going to do.

"Okay, I'll come in and get you." Without a thought to what I would do once I was in there, I climbed through the window. The heat hit me like a brick wall. The boy couldn't last in this inferno.

*Please, God, help me find him. Don't let me be too late.*

I couldn't see where I was going, but thankfully, I didn't have long to look. As soon as I took a couple of steps into the room, small hands grabbed my arm. Tears stung my eyes, but I grabbed his slight body, pulled him up, and turned back to make my way out the window, carrying the boy. I hardly had to hold on to him; I could tell he wouldn't be letting go of me. Once we cleared the window, I raced down the steps and into the yard, well clear of the house, and kneeled down to the ground.

Taking his tiny face in my hands and wiping off the soot, I looked him up and down. "Are you okay?"

He nodded, tears running down his cheeks. He

buried his face in my shoulder, but I pulled him away again, so I could see his face.

"Is there anyone else in there?"

He shook his head.

"You were home alone?"

Solemnly, he nodded and started to shake. I pulled him into my arms, his tiny hands clutching my blouse, the necklace, holding on for all he was worth.

I turned as I heard a fire truck approaching. I must have missed the sounds of the sirens while I was in the house, but I was enormously relieved to see the cavalry arrive. Standing up and carrying the boy, I went down the sidewalk, away from the burning house. I didn't want to get between the firemen and the fire.

Neighbors seemed to be pouring into the street now. Where were they all five minutes ago?

The boy clung to me, crying, hiccupping, shaking. Really, we both were shaking and clinging to each other. All I could do was hold him, rub his back, and whisper, "Everything's okay."

Thank God it was true.

"Lilly Walker? Is that you?"

I turned at the sound of my name to see Fire Chief Michaels heading my way. The volunteer firemen behind him were rushing toward the house, hoses and axes in hand.

"Yes, Chief. I was just walking home…"

He took my arm and led me to the seat of his truck, gently urging me to sit down. My little friend didn't budge or, frankly, even move, other than to burrow even farther into my neck.

"Are you okay, Lilly? Let's get the ambulance crew to take a look at you." He wiped some soot from the arm the boy threw around my shoulder. "And what about your friend here?"

"I don't know, Chief." Laying my cheek on the boy's head, I said, "Are you okay, honey? Do you want to tell Chief Michaels what happened?"

He just shook his head, not lifting it from my chest. I looked up at the chief.

"When I saw the smoke, I went to see if anyone was in the house. I heard a voice and saw this little guy in the window, so I broke it open and brought him out. He said there wasn't anybody else there."

"Was the door too hot to open?" Chief Michaels looked up at the house, where the front door now stood open.

"No, it was locked or jammed or something. I couldn't budge it, so I just went with what I could think of at the time. I had to get him out. He looked so scared."

Chief Michaels turned to speak to a firefighter who came running up to us.

"All clear, Chief. The fire's still not under control yet, but we didn't find anyone inside."

The chief turned to me. "That's because Lilly here rescued this little guy all by herself."

I shrugged. "I was hoping someone would come, someone in charge, but when no one even seemed to be aware of the fire, I…I couldn't just leave him in there."

The firefighter ran back to the house, absorbed in the work to be done. When the ambulance crew arrived, the chief walked over to speak to them, sent them in our direction, and headed back to the fire himself.

I felt like I was too tired to move, although my skin was still tingling from the heat and the smoke. I just held on to my unnamed shadow, and the tears started falling down my cheeks.

****

When I got home that evening, my mother looked ready to let me have it, because I was so late, but she seemed to think better of it when she took a look at me.

"Lilly, where have you been? What happened to your dress? Why are you covered in dirt? What's this bandage on your arm?" She came around the kitchen table and grabbed hold of my chin, flipping my face back and forth as if to get a closer look.

"There was a fire…" As soon as I started to tell my mother about it, tears filled my eyes again, and I sank into one of the kitchen chairs.

"A fire? What are you talking about? Are you okay?" Mom pulled out a chair next to me, calling to my father, "Earl, come here quick. Lilly's home."

Leonard and my father walked into the kitchen. Dad glanced over with a stern look in his eyes, took one look at me, and instantly softened. "What happened, sweetheart?"

I took a deep breath, trying to calm myself and release the vise grip my emotions had on my throat. "The Lamberts' house was on fire. I walked past it on my way home." I couldn't seem to stop the tears.

My mother put her arm around my shoulders, concern in her eyes. "Was anyone in the house?"

I shook my head. "The only one home was Johnny; he's five."

"The boy was home alone? Where were his parents?" My father pulled out a chair and sat.

Leonard was standing, leaning against the stove. "Did the firefighters get him out?" he asked.

Another deep breath. "No, I did. I was the first one there. No one else had seen the smoke yet. I saw him in the window, so…so I broke it with a stone and carried him out. He was so frightened." More tears.

Mom looked at Dad and then back at me. Now she had tears at the corners of her eyes.

"You walked into a burning house? All alone?"

"No one else was there, Mom! The house was full of horrid smoke. What could I do? I had to get him out." I took a gulp of air, which I seemed to be having trouble doing. "He was crying and scared and locked in…I had to help him. He was so frightened, he couldn't even tell me his name for half an hour. I got a scratch from the broken glass, so the ambulance workers bandaged it." I couldn't stop the tears now. I laid my head on my mother's shoulder.

"Oh, Lilly." She put her arms around me. "Of course you couldn't leave him. But you could have been seriously hurt; you could have died." Her tears started in earnest. "Oh, Lilly."

My father put his arm around us both, patting my knee with his other hand. He was usually a man of few words, not demonstrative in his love for his children. But even he had tears in his eyes.

Ruth came into the kitchen, followed by Clara, who was carrying Robert.

"Oh, no! What is it?" I looked up to see concern in Ruth's eyes. Clara pulled the baby closer to her chest; he squawked.

Leonard pulled himself up, walking toward the table. "Don't worry, gals. There's no bad news."

My father stood. "Yeah, everything is okay. Our Lilly here's a hero." He pulled the handkerchief from his back pocket and wiped his eyes. "She saved a little boy's life today."

Suddenly, he looked relieved, proud, and scared, all at the same time.

****

The following day, Ginny and I ran to the bus, nearly missing our ride to work. Ava was already on it when we got there.

"Ready?" Ginny linked her arm with mine as we stood in the line of other latecomers boarding.

"Ready." I climbed on the bus, and we took seats near the front again.

Mrs. Davis had told us it would be important not to wear jewelry on the production floor and that we would need to wear work boots, so we would be given a locker to keep our belongings in, while working, and to leave our coveralls and boots in when we weren't at work. I had worn the necklace that Helen loaned me yesterday, and got a funny look while waiting in line, but I wanted to be able to give it back to her on the bus.

Helen was already sitting in the seat behind us, so I turned to hand her the necklace, once everyone had filed past.

"Thanks so much for this. It worked; I got the job."

She smiled. "Congratulations. I had no doubt. This necklace hasn't let me down yet."

"That's a handy thing to have around." Ginny had turned in her seat and smiled at Helen. "It did more than get you the job, Lilly. Right?"

"Oh?" Helen attached the necklace around her own neck and tucked it under the collar of her dress.

"I guess so, Ginny." I couldn't help but blush a little.

"I should say so. She rescued a boy from a burning house yesterday."

"What?" exclaimed Helen. "What happened?"

I explained to her about the Lamberts' house fire and seeing Johnny through the window.

"You went into the house? Are you daft?" Helen was shaking her head.

"I know," said Ava. "Who does that?"

I couldn't really answer, but Ginny jumped in. "She pulled that little boy out and neither one of them was seriously hurt. I'd say that necklace is incredibly lucky."

"There wasn't anyone else around, so I couldn't leave him in there. It was over in less than a minute."

Helen smiled. "You were frightfully brave, Lilly. Good for you."

I nodded but was too embarrassed to say more.

Helen seemed to understand and changed the subject. "So, you're on blue shift with us, then?" Helen said as she pointed to the blue kerchief Ginny had tied around her neck.

"Yes," I answered. "Do you like the work?"

Helen cocked her head. "I guess so. I like having something to do and to be able to help the war effort. As I said, Billy, my husband, is over there. I like thinking that one of the engines we build will bring him home."

Like so many women these days, she looked a little forlorn talking about her Billy. It must be hard to be married and separated from your husband.

"Do you have any children, Helen?"

She snorted. "No." Shaking her head, she said, "I've been taking care of kids forever, and I'm not in any hurry to have my own."

"Lucky you," said Gladys, one of the women sitting behind Helen. "At least you don't have to worry about who's watching your young'uns while you're working. My ma is sick today, and I had to scramble to find someone to watch my kids."

Several of the women on the bus were nodding in agreement.

Another woman from the back of the bus was nodding. "Yeah, last week, I had to leave my youngest ones home with only my nine-year-old to watch them after she got home from school, as my sister had to work late and wasn't there before I had to catch the bus."

I couldn't help but think of Mrs. Lambert, on the first-shift bus.

## Chapter Nine
## Ruth

*Dear Jack, my love,*

*You'll never guess what Lilly did this week. In addition to getting a job at Nichols Motors, she rescued five-year-old Johnny Lambert from a fire. She broke a window, climbed in, and brought the boy out. We're so proud of our "heroine." Apparently, Johnny was alone and locked in because his babysitter couldn't make it, and Mrs. Lambert is working at Nichols Motors now, so she had to leave him home. His ten-year-old sister locked him in when she went to school so he wouldn't wander off. Thank God Lilly found him. Apparently, a lot of women at work are having trouble getting someone to watch their kids while they're at the plant. We need women in the workforce to make up for the men who have gone to war, but if they are going to go to work, there has to be some kind of reliable day care for their children. I can't imagine leaving a five-year-old child of ours at home alone, but some women don't have the family support we do. Lilly and I have been discussing it. There must be some solution…*

****

"I think we can make it work if we can get the cooperation of the church and the town." Lilly, Mom, and I were sitting together at the kitchen table before Lilly left for school. She was so busy now, between school and work, I hardly had time to talk to her.

"I know some of the women can leave their kids with their mothers, but not everyone has that option," said Mom.

"I think most of the women on second shift said they can get someone to watch the kids, whether it's their mother, sister, or friend, but it's the women on first shift that really have trouble, especially since even teenage babysitters aren't available during the day." Lilly told us she had heard a lot of discussion on the bus about the fire, and most of the women had an opinion about the day care problem.

"What if you and I went to see the mayor about starting a day care, Lilly?"

"Why me?" She shook her head. "I don't even have children."

"You're the local heroine. I think they'll listen to you." I couldn't help but wink at her. "If we could get one of the churches to give us some space for it, we could probably find someone to run it. Maybe we could see if Pastor Robbins would meet with us and the mayor."

Mom stood, taking her coffee cup to the sink to rinse it out. "I think it's a great idea, girls. Something like what happened with the Lamberts can't happen again."

"I'll go with you, for what it's worth," said Lilly. "I think it's a great idea, and I bet Pastor Robbins will say yes. The church basement sits empty all week anyway."

Lilly stood and gathered her books for school.

"I don't see how they can say no." I grabbed her breakfast dishes and said I'd take care of them. "If the mothers pay a small amount for each child they put in the day care, and bring a lunch for their children, we can use that money to pay someone to work there and buy supplies and whatever else we might need."

Lilly kissed Mom's cheek and headed out the door.

"I think that sounds like a good plan, Ruth," said Mom. "It would help so many people."

I grabbed my lunch, my book bag, and my coat, and ran out to get to school myself.

After school, I called the mayor's office to set up an appointment for Lilly and me to meet with him. Given our school and work schedules, I had to ask him to meet with us on Saturday morning. Once he set a time, I called Pastor Robbins, and he quickly agreed to meet with us all. He was curious to hear about Lilly's experience at the Lamberts' house and was impressed with her heroics.

****

Lilly and I met with the mayor and Pastor Robbins on Saturday. Everyone agreed that the day care was a wonderful idea and definitely needed. The only thing was, both the mayor and Pastor Robbins insisted that I be the one to run it. I loved the idea of helping the war effort in a more concrete way, but I wasn't sure this was the path for me.

My job was important to me; my students needed me. But I'd gone into teaching to make a difference, and the day care would certainly do that also. The kids at school wouldn't be in jeopardy if I didn't help them, and these preschoolers were. I agreed to set it up and get it running.

The mayor said he'd help in whatever way he could, and Pastor Robbins agreed to allow us to have the day care in the church basement. Everyone agreed that working mothers needed a way to be sure their children were safe, in the wake of the Lambert fire. Mayor Keeler said he would talk to the local businesses to try to get us donations. He would also contact Nichols Motors so they could tell their first-shift employees about the service. I was going to be swamped.

As we walked home from the church, Lilly said, "I want to invite Helen to come to dinner tomorrow. She's one of my co-workers, the one who loaned me her lucky necklace the day I got the job, the day of the Lamberts' fire. Do you think it'll be okay with Mom?"

"Sure. Doesn't she have any family?"

"She lives with her in-laws, the Andersons. She married Billy over in London and then came here to wait for him to come back after the war. I don't think she and her in-laws get on too well."

"That's too bad. I remember Billy Anderson left to fly planes for England before we were even in the war. He's a little older than Jack and me, but he's a nice fella. I heard he had to give up his American citizenship to join the RAF."

"Wow," said Lilly. "He must have really felt strongly about fighting the Nazis to give up being an American in order to do it."

"Yeah, I think he did. Also, he couldn't wait to fly planes. He'd been flying for the local crop dusters as much as he could. He's crazy about it."

"Well, Helen seems lonely, so I think she'd enjoy coming to dinner. I'm not sure she has much fun."

"I'd love to hear about her experiences in England and how she got to Upton Falls. Does she have any children?"

Lilly shook her head. “No, and she told me she’s not sure she ever wants any.”

Interesting. “I wonder what Billy thinks about that. I bet his parents aren’t too happy about it.”

## Chapter Ten
## Helen

"I'm heading out for the Walkers' house now."

"Fine."

That's all Mabel had to say. They always seemed happy to be shot of me.

As I followed the directions Lilly gave me, I passed by the house that had burned. I still couldn't believe Lilly pulled a child out of a burning house. My hand flew instinctively to my necklace. I guess if this necklace could save that young woman from the Blitz in London, it made sense it could save a young boy from a fire here in the States.

As the sprawling white farmhouse came into view, I was struck with how comforting it looked. There was a tall oak tree in the front yard, and the porch wrapping around the house looked like arms open to me in welcome. I could see a porch swing, and rocking chairs flanking the green front door. To the right of the house, there was a big black car and a beat-up-looking truck in the gravel driveway. Behind the cars, I could see a barn and some other outbuildings.

I'd never been to a farm before, and it reminded me of Camilla, who had volunteered for the Women's Land Army and was now on somebody's farm near Kendal in the Lake District. I could understand her wanting to get out of London, but I had to smile when I thought of her plowing a field or feeding pigs.

Lilly must have seen me coming, because she walked onto the front porch as soon as I reached the bottom of the steps.

"I'm so glad you came, Helen. Come on in."

Lilly was a sweet girl, but I felt a little edgy about meeting her family. I hadn't been doing such a brilliant job of getting the Andersons to like me, and I was related to them.

"Thank you so much for inviting me." I followed Lilly into the big old farmhouse, pasting a smile on my face. I was honored Lilly had invited me to lunch, or rather, she had told me that, on Sunday, it was called dinner, but I was worried I'd make a fool of myself. Feeling fairly peckish after the long walk from town, I couldn't help wondering what the delicious smells were.

As we walked into the parlor, several people rose from their seats. The room was warm and had a lovely fire going in the stone fireplace.

"Everyone, this is Helen. Helen, this is my mother and father, Earl and Julia Walker, and my sister-in-law, Ruth. Sitting next to Dad is our hired man, Leonard Kelp. My grandparents live next door, and they'll be joining us soon."

Mr. Walker stood and extended his hand. "Welcome." He was a tall man with brown hair that was going gray at the sides. His face was fairly wrinkled, obviously from lots of time in the sun, but his smile was warm, and his eyes were kind.

"Thank you for inviting me."

Mr. Kelp stood and nodded at me. "Nice to meet you, ma'am."

I nodded back. “Thank you.”

Mrs. Walker and Ruth both smiled and nodded. “We’re happy to have you,” said Ruth.

Mrs. Walker gestured to the sofa. “Please have a seat. Dinner will be ready shortly.”

Mrs. Walker was a short and slightly plump woman with soft brown hair shot through with plenty of gray and pinned up in a stylish, if matronly, fashion. She was wearing a brown dress covered in small pink and white flowers. Her warm smile made me feel welcome.

I took a seat, trying not to take up too much room on the sofa. Lilly and Ruth sat down next to me. The room was warm and smelled faintly of lemon and wood smoke. A wedding picture hanging over the mantel looked like it could be of Lilly’s parents. The wallpaper was a pale cream color with small brown and yellow flowers. In addition to the sofa, there were two stuffed chairs, a wooden rocker, and some small side tables. While not as posh as the Andersons’ parlor, it had a friendly and inviting feel to it.

A tall blonde woman entered the room carrying a sleepy toddler. She took a seat with him in the rocker in the corner.

“Helen, this is my sister-in-law, Clara, and my nephew Fred,” Lilly said.

I nodded, “Hello.”

Clara smiled. “Hello.” Her voice was soft and mellow.

“Clara’s married to my oldest brother, Will. They have another son, Robert, who’s only five months old. He’s napping.”

I smiled and nodded at Clara.

Ruth turned to catch my eye. “Lilly tells us you’re from London.” Ruth was an attractive woman with her chestnut brown hair swept up in a victory roll.

“Yes.” I didn’t think they needed to know what part of London, although maybe coming from the East End wouldn’t mean as much to Yanks.

“Do you still have family there?” asked Mrs. Walker.

“Yes, ma’am. My mum and youngest brothers were evacuated to the country, and my sister joined the Women’s Land Army, but my father and the oldest three of my brothers are still working in London.”

“How many brothers and sisters do you have?” asked Lilly.

I always hated this question. “I’m the oldest of twelve.”

“Twelve!” exclaimed Mr. Walker. “What a large family for the city. We usually see families of that size on farms hereabouts. It helps to have more hands to carry the load.”

I didn’t want to go into more of an explanation or invite other questions about my parents, so I looked down at my folded hands in my lap.

Ruth seemed to get the message, as she moved on to another topic. “I understand you’re married to Billy Anderson. Did you meet him in London?”

I couldn’t stop myself from smiling. “Yes. We met at the picture show one Sunday. We’ve been married for about a year and a half.”

“Ruth and Jack, my brother, have been married about a year and a half, too, although Will and Clara have been married for several years.” Lilly smiled. “I was ever so happy to finally have sisters.” She put her hand on Ruth's.

"What date did you two marry?" asked Ruth.

I stopped to think; it seemed like yesterday. "We got married on August first last year."

Ruth laughed. "Amazing! Jack and I were married the same day."

Lilly's grandparents arrived and, after introductions, we all moved into the dining room. The wallpaper in that room had small blue flowers and green swirls on a white background, coordinated with the white trim. The table was huge, and Mrs. Walker was just setting out a lovely meal, with potatoes, gravy, and carrots—and wherever did they get that amount of beef?

"Everything looks delicious. Thank you so much, Mr. and Mrs. Walker."

"Please," said Mrs. Walker, "call us Earl and Julia." She put a slice of beef on my plate and started passing the veg.

"All right, then. You've put together a terribly smart dinner, Julia."

"We're luckier than many," Earl said. "Living on the farm gives us more access to vegetables and potatoes, although we do sell most of what we grow."

Even as we all started to tuck into the meal, the questions kept coming.

"When did you move to Upton Falls, Helen?" Ruth was seated on my right.

"I was fortunate enough to be able to sail with my employer's children to Canada, where they have relatives. We arrived in Halifax in November. I spent a little time getting the children settled in Montreal and then got a ride to Upton Falls on Pearl Harbor Day, actually."

"I'm sure the Andersons were glad to have news of Billy," said Julia. "After he left for England, Mabel was simply beside herself."

"They didn't actually know Billy and I had gotten married. His letter telling them to expect me arrived later than I did." And they still hadn't forgiven me for that.

"That must have come as a big surprise for them," Julia said.

"I'm terribly grateful that the Andersons took me in." Although it would have been nice if their home felt as inviting as this one did.

****

The meal was delicious and the company was lovely. Apparently Ruth was a fan of baseball, the all-American pastime, and was excited about something called Opening Day. Lilly didn't seem too interested in sport, however, and shared stories of our work and our colorful co-workers. The men seemed to mostly discuss planting crops and work on the farm. Julia asked me questions about London and the Andersons, but Clara was quiet and focused on her children. Once dinner was finished, with some fantastic canned peaches for dessert, I really enjoyed helping Lilly and Ruth with the cleanup. It took a lot of effort to get Julia to let me help, but she finally conceded and went to the parlor to work on her knitting.

"So have you heard from Billy lately?" asked Ruth. "I write to Jack nearly every day, but his letters are few and far between."

Lilly laughed. "There's no way Jack could keep up with you, Ruth. You're a letter-writing machine."

I turned away, putting two plates in the cupboard. "Actually, I got a letter from Billy yesterday."

"Lucky you," said Ruth. "Was he able to give you any idea of where he is or how things are going?"

I picked up another plate to dry and turned away, avoiding Ruth's gaze. Just at the perfect moment, we heard the baby cry.

"I'll help Clara with the baby. You gals keep gabbing." Lilly headed up the stairs.

"So, Helen, what did Billy have to say? I mean, not the personal stuff, but any news from the front?"

Cowering a bit behind the cupboard door, I mumbled, "I haven't had time to read it yet." I had no idea who I could get to read me Billy's letters now. I couldn't ask Mabel or George, could I? I hated not knowing what Billy had to say.

"Wow, what restraint you have, Helen," exclaimed Ruth. "I steal away as soon as a letter arrives from Jack, to savor every word he's written."

I touched the letter in my pocket.

"Do you want some privacy to read it now? I can certainly keep busy in the house."

"No, thank you." I turned to face her, but kept my gaze fixed on the floor. "I'll find some time later."

Ruth walked closer to me, placing her hand on my shoulder. "Are you sure? We won't think it's rude. I always feel like I'm seeing a bit of Jack, if only for a moment, when I see his handwriting on a letter. I love reading about everything that's happening."

She seemed so nice, but I didn't know how to explain that, even though Billy's handwriting touched me the same way, it was the words themselves that were a blur to me. The Smith-Burtons' cook had read me Billy's letter in Montreal so many times, I'd memorized it. I could pull it out and remember what it said, almost as if I was reading it myself.

When I finally looked Ruth in the eye, she gasped and pulled me into a hug. She must have thought the fear in my eyes was for Billy's safety more than my own fear of my shameful secret being discovered.

"Oh, no, Helen. It's not bad news, is it?"

"No, well, I don't think so." It was driving me balmy to have a letter and not know what it said, but that was my problem to deal with.

"Are you afraid to open it?"

Sure, let her believe that. I just nodded.

"I don't think you'd get bad news in a letter written by Billy, but if you're worried, I could open it for you. Do you want me to do that?"

At least she would be able to see what it said. "Yes, please. I should like that."

I handed Ruth the letter, already a little wrinkled from being held so tightly in my hand, and watched her slide it open. She was vigilant not to tear the thin onion-skin paper and quickly scanned the first of the two pages.

"Oh." She looked at me, a bit embarrassed. I couldn't believe Billy would write anything too racy, but it might be too personal, especially given that we'd only known each other for a couple of hours.

"If you're not comfortable reading it, I understand." I reached for the letter, but she held tight.

Ruth looked me straight in the eye, her smile kind and gentle. "Oh, Helen…would you like me to read the letter to you?"

I couldn't hide the slight gasp. "I…uh…no, really,

I'll read it when I get home." Again, I reached for the letter.

Ruth grasped my hand in hers, still holding the letter in her other hand. "The first thing Billy wrote is that he hopes you found someone to read the letter to you and that maybe his mother would do it. I'd be honored to do that for you, if you'd like."

I closed my eyes; turned my head. How could I be so stupid? I shouldn't have let her open the letter. I'd been so anxious to know what Billy had to say that I didn't think. Of course he'd be worried about who was going to be reading the letters to me now.

Ruth put her arm around my shoulder, speaking quietly. "There's nothing to be ashamed of, Helen. Many people have trouble reading. I'd be happy to read Billy's letter to you, if you'd let me."

I nodded, desperate to hear what Billy had to say. She knew my secret now anyway.

"Let me just tell Lilly we're going to take a walk." Lilly was just coming down the stairs with little Robert.

"All cleaned up now," Lilly said, as she carried the baby into the kitchen.

"Helen and I are going to walk a bit. I told her I'd show her the garden."

"Have fun," said Lilly, nuzzling her nephew. His little hands waved like a windmill.

Ruth grabbed two wraps hanging in the mud room, gave one to me, and led me onto the back porch. I was relieved that she hadn't mentioned anything about the letter; I didn't want everyone knowing my problems.

We took a quick walk around the yard and climbed to the side porch. After we settled in a pretty porch swing, pulling the wraps more tightly around our shoulders to repel the early spring chill, Ruth pulled Billy's letter out of her pocket.

*Dear Helen,*

*I don't know who you'll have gotten to read you my letters now, maybe my mother, but I hope this one finds you well and safe in Upton Falls. I know my parents will welcome you and be happy to have you as part of the family. They are a little stiff and formal, but they won't be able to resist you any more than I could.*

*So have you made any friends? How do you like sleeping in my old room? In my old bed? I can't wait to come back home and find us a place of our own.*

*Things are going well here. Me and my little Spitfire are making quick work of all those Jerries across the water. Now that America has joined the fight, I'm sure we'll see a speedy end to this war. I can't believe it's been six months since Dave was killed when his Defiant was shot down. There aren't many of us Americans left in this unit. Luckily, the rest of us are too ornery to die.*

*I ran into your brother Eddy last week, and he said your dad heard from your mum and the little ones in the country and they are well, although your mum really doesn't want to stay out there. She wants to come back to London, but the teachers that arranged her evacuation are very stern about her staying where she is. Really, not many of the mothers got to go with their children, so I hope she'll stay where she is. I think your dad would like her to come back, but she's safer where she is. Eddy said they haven't heard from Millie, but I remember you saying if she could get away, she'd never look back.*

*If you can, please try to get your picture made. I*

*would like to have a picture to keep with me. Besides, my buddies are sick of hearing about how beautiful you are and need to see for themselves. As soon as you can find someone to help, please write to me. I can't wait to hear how you like Upton Falls and my parents. Anything you can tell me about home and your daily life there will help me on the cold lonely nights. I'm so glad you were able to get out of London, but I really miss having you here with me.*

*Take care and know that I am thinking about you. See you in my dreams,*

*All my love, Billy*

By the time Ruth had finished reading the letter, I couldn't control the tears running down my cheeks. It was so hard not to be able to write to him every day, as Ruth did her Jack, or re-read the letters he sent to me. Billy was the first person to ever love me and make me feel cherished, and I ached with missing him.

"Thank you so much, Ruth."

She handed me the letter, which I folded carefully back into the envelope and held to my heart.

"I'd be happy to help read your letters any time, or help you write one, if you want to."

"That'd be lovely. I have to get a picture made, so I can send it to him. Although if he shows his mates the picture, they'll think he's a bit daft talking about his 'beautiful' wife. I am many things, but I've never been beautiful."

Ruth laid her hand on mine. "But to Billy, you are. That's what love is, isn't it? I'm sure Billy is beautiful to you."

"Right, well sure, you've seen him, then. I don't think any woman could look at that face and not say how pretty a chap he is. The day we met at the pictures, I couldn't believe he came up to me and started talking. I could hardly utter a word. He looks so frightfully smart in his RAF uniform." My cheeks grew warm just thinking about it.

"I feel the same way about Jack. I mean, he's not a pilot; he's in the army. But I can't wait for him to send me a picture of him in his uniform. He's so handsome, even when he's just back from milking the cows." She giggled, and I found myself doing the same.

"Well, I appreciate your offer to write my letter to Billy. I know he thinks his mum could help me, but she's not too keen about me. I could never admit to her that I…well, that I can't read. She already thinks I'm not good enough for Billy. I'd hate for her to know I had to leave school when I was eight and never learned to read or write properly."

Ruth reached out and gave my hand a slight squeeze.

After a few silent moments, we both stood and started toward the back door, but Ruth put her hand out, stopping me in my tracks. "Would you like me to teach you to read and write better, Helen? I'm a teacher."

"Oh, I don't know. I would hate for you to waste your time on me. Besides, I really don't want everyone to know about this."

She turned to me, leaning in close and whispering, "No one needs to know what we're doing. We could tell anyone who asks that I'm teaching you to sew."

"I should like that, but I'm busy every evening except weekends. And Lilly told me you're going to be running a day care during the day for the kids of working mothers. I don't want to take too much of your time. You've got enough on your hands."

"Why don't you say you're volunteering at the day care, and you can come to the church after lunch, before you catch the bus? The kids nap after they eat, and we can work together there. I'll bring some needles, thread, and material, just in case any of the mothers come by."

I just had to give her a hug. "Do you think that would work? I'd be ever so grateful, Ruth. Do you think I could really learn? It's not too late?"

She linked her arm through mine, and we entered the mud room on the back of the house. "Of course it's not too late to learn…to sew, Helen. I'd be happy to teach you." Ruth winked at me just as Lilly appeared.

I couldn't stop smiling all the way back to the Andersons' house that afternoon.

# Chapter Eleven
## Ruth

"Okay, let's wash our hands, and then we can get everyone's sleep rug out, and I'll read you all a story before nap time." I was starting to get a rhythm going at the day care. "Mrs. Anderson, can you help Bobby and Mary put away their dishes?" Helen had become indispensable help, especially at lunchtime.

"Off you go now, everyone. We want this place spit-spot before the stories begin." Helen helped the two preschoolers to pack up their lunch bags and place everything near their jackets before finding a spot on the floor to unroll their small rugs and settle for story time.

Helen was turning out to be a natural with the children and a huge help to me. I wasn't sure that, alone, I could handle so many children. Some of the mothers dropped off their preschoolers with older children when they went to work. Even once the older ones walked off to school together, we had twelve children under five, including two babies. Without Helen's help, I'd have been sunk.

Whether it was because of Helen's height and strong build, because she'd had years of experience as a nanny, or just the way she had of talking to the youngsters, the children never put up a fuss for her. She was a valuable asset, especially at lunch and nap times.

I hoped the reading lessons were enough thanks for all her volunteer hours.

Once the story was done, the older children were tucked under their blankets for a short rest, and babies Tommy and Marion had been snuggled into their crib, Helen and I sat at the small table with her readers. Fortunately, she'd had enough schooling when she was young to learn her letters and numbers from sight. The issue was putting them together to form more than the easiest words and sentences.

"Thanks so much for convincing Johnny to give up his argument for no nap. I know he's one of the oldest children here, but I think they all need a short break in the afternoon."

Helen smiled. "As do we."

I chuckled. "So true." I picked up my sandwich and had a bite. Her reading lesson was also our lunch time.

We worked for thirty minutes, between bites of our lunch, on basic phonics and how to sound out words. Helen was determined and improving quickly. "I'm impressed. You've obviously found time to work on this at home."

She smiled tentatively. "I don't want the Andersons to find out that I can't read, so I stay up and practice after I get home. They are both sleeping by then, so I can sit at the kitchen table and go through everything I've learned."

"You're making real progress."

"Thanks, Ruth. You don't know how much this all means to me. If I can get good enough to read Billy's letters on my own, and write back, I won't have to worry about his parents finding out my secret."

"Do you think it would bother them?" I couldn't

see how Helen's misfortune could be counted against her.

"I had to leave school when I was eight, to help my mum with all the babies." She looked down at her hands in her lap. "I was embarrassed that my mum kept having babies even though we had no room for them and couldn't feed the family we had. It's not like we were different from many of the families in the East End, but having to leave school, not knowing how to read or write properly—it just made everything worse for me."

My heart ached a bit for the young girl who had been so ashamed and embarrassed. "Did your brothers and sisters help out much?"

"Not really. I was the oldest, and the next three were boys, so my dad said they should be working as soon as they could and had to stay in school long enough to get a decent job. My sister Camilla—I call her Millie—is the only other girl. She had to quit school to take over when I went to work for the Smith-Burtons."

Helen worked diligently at forming the letters we'd been practicing, her strokes still hesitant and shaky.

"How old were you when you left home?"

"Sixteen."

I was surprised. "And you lived with the Smith-Burtons?"

She met my gaze, smiling at my concern. "It was the best place I'd ever seen, never mind lived in. I had my own bed in my own room on the third floor. It was small, but it was all mine. There was always enough to eat, and it was warm in the winter, so I couldn't have been happier. The Smith-Burtons were wonderful to me, and the head housekeeper took me under her wing and helped me to fit in with the staff. I wasn't too happy to still be taking care of children, but I was glad to get out of my parents' apartment. The only one I ever missed was Millie."

I found myself shaking my head. I couldn't help picturing the young woman she had been and the conditions she must have left at home.

"You were so brave. I'm not sure I could have done the same, Helen." When I looked at Helen, her gaze was fixed on her pencil, but I could see her cheeks were slightly pink. "Now, back to work." She looked relieved to move on. "Let's put these letters together, and you tell me what the word would be."

She worked diligently on her reading and writing, just as she did everything. Lilly had commented on Helen's work at Nichols Motors, how she put her head down and got more work done than nearly anyone else on the line. She was no stranger to hard work and didn't resent it at all.

"You're good with the children here. Are you anxious for Billy to come home and start your own family?"

She shook her head slowly. "I can't wait for Billy to come home, but I don't know if I could ever be a proper mother. I would hate to have children only to resent the fact that I was spending my life taking care of them. I've never really done anything else."

"Well, not until you got the job at Nichols Motors, right? Are you enjoying that?"

She seemed to think about it a while, resting her chin in the palm of her left hand. "Well, I like the way the other women look at me, as if I matter, and I like that they want to know what I think about something sometimes. And I certainly like the paycheck. I'm saving most of it so we can get a house of our own when Billy gets home." She cocked her head. "The actual work is not stimulating, I have to admit. And the men that work there…" She shivered. "Nichols could only hire those too old to be drafted if they didn't already have a job, or the 4Fs, who seem to be angry all the time. I don't know if it's because they couldn't join up or because everyone knows they didn't make the cut. They worry me a bit."

"Have you had a run-in with anyone in particular?"

Shaking her head, she frowned. "The old chaps don't really bother us, but the younger ones are pretty cheeky. I've heard a couple of the blokes be frightfully rude to some of the girls, but I think my size frightens them a bit."

I put my sewing down. "That's just what Julia was worried about when Lilly started working there. She's young and naïve about men. She couldn't seem to understand her mother's worries, but I know Julia is concerned."

"I guess the job is not all I thought it would be, although I like the feeling of knowing what I'm doing and being able to do it well. It's nice to be respected for my work, and knowing that I'm helping the community is an added bonus."

That sounded like a teacher to me.

****

The next Monday, when Helen arrived early at the church, I could tell she'd been crying. Dread filled my heart, and I could hardly bear to ask.

"Oh, Helen. Is everything all right? You haven't

heard bad news about Billy, have you?"

She shook her head, dabbing her handkerchief in the corner of her eyes. "No," she croaked out. "Nothing like that."

Her voice sounded like crushed rocks. She must have been crying for hours.

I put my hand on her back and could feel her catch her breath. Tears started to flow down her face.

"What is it, Helen? Please, sit down. Let me help you."

I pulled out one of the children's chairs for her. If she hadn't been so upset, it would have been somewhat comical to see her large frame folded onto the tiny chair. It took a few minutes and a glass of water for her to be able to pull herself together enough to speak. "I have to find a new place to live. I can't stay there anymore."

"At the Andersons?"

She just nodded, her eyes still swimming in tears.

"What happened?"

Helen took a couple of deep breaths. "They…they found my reader. Billy's mum, Mabel, she caught me practicing."

She pulled out her handkerchief and indelicately blew her bright red nose.

"You mean Mrs. Anderson figured out you were just learning to read? Is that what's upsetting you so?"

Helen nodded. "She…she laughed."

"Laughed?"

Again, her eyes filled with tears. "It was horrible. She actually sneered at me. She said she'd known all along that I was not good enough for her William. That I must have tricked her son into thinking I was pregnant for him to agree to marry someone as ugly as me. And that, since I obviously wasn't pregnant, she would see about getting our marriage annulled and have me deported back to London. She can't wait to get me out of her son's life." The tears flowed freely now. "Can she even do that?"

Helen's chest heaved. I couldn't imagine how Mabel Anderson could be so cruel to someone as kind and gentle as Helen. I sat next to her and put my arms around her shoulders, pulling her into a hug. She laid her head on my shoulder and just sobbed.

All I could do was rub her back and wait for the tears to subside. After several minutes, she eased back, pulled out her handkerchief, and blew her nose again. I got up and went to the ladies room to get a cool cloth and handed it to her. Once she was calmed down again, I sat on the tiny chair next to her and took her hands in mine.

"No one can get your marriage annulled but you or Billy, so don't you let her frighten you. We both know how much Billy cherishes you. The only one who might be out of his life is her, when he hears about this." I was so mad I could spit. Helen was one of the kindest people I'd ever met and deserved better.

"Oh, no. I don't want Billy to know. He's got enough to worry about over there. I don't have to tell him, do I?"

"You don't have to do anything you don't want to do, Helen. If the Andersons can't see how special you are and how lucky Billy is to have found you, they don't deserve you in their lives."

She put her arms around me again and gave me a grateful hug.

"Now, how about you pack up your things at the Andersons after work and move into our house?"

She startled. "Oh, I couldn't do that. You're kind, but there's no room for a big old thing like me. I already packed everything." She nodded toward the cardboard suitcase I'd failed to notice near the door. "I'm going to find a boarding house. I'll have to use my wages to cover the costs, so it'll mean less money saved for when Billy comes home, but I'll get by."

I shook my head. "Don't be ridiculous. You're moving in with us. We'd love to have you. You're wonderful with Robert and Fred, and I'm sure you'll be a big help around the house. Lilly will be happy to give you her room. She sometimes sneaks in to sleep with me as it is. I think she worries about Jack and Will, and feels lonely and anxious. So she'll be happy to move into my room."

I pulled Helen to her feet and gave her a quick, firm hug. "Go ahead and tidy up your face before the children arrive. It's all settled. You can't live with people who humiliate you and treat you like that, even if they are supposedly your family. And I won't have you moving in with a bunch of strangers. You're part of our family now."

She nearly started crying again, so I steered her in the direction of the ladies room to pull herself together. I was still seething and wanted to go give Mabel Anderson a piece of my mind. But the children had started arriving, so I put my emotion away for later and plastered a smile on my face.

## Chapter Twelve
## Lilly

"That dress looks terribly smart, Lilly. All it needs is this to complete the outfit." Helen, who had been leaning against the bedroom doorframe, stepped into the room and handed me her lucky necklace.

"I can't take the necklace, Helen. I don't need it for graduation; I've already passed everything."

"That was a surprise to no one; you're too clever by half to be working on the line, you know." She grasped my shoulders, turned me around so I faced the mirror, and draped the necklace around my neck. "But I want you to wear the necklace with that dress. Not because it's lucky but because it looks so nice and I want you to have a wonderful graduation and a fun night of celebrating."

My senior prom had been cancelled; another casualty of the war. Not that there were many boys left to dance with anyway. But Helen and Ruth had decided I needed to celebrate, so they convinced me to go to the Red Cross dance hall in Beacon Heights tonight, after graduation. Mom had agreed and even gave me a little pin money and told me to enjoy myself. I had to admit I was excited about it; I hadn't been dancing in the longest time.

After Helen clasped the necklace, I adjusted it so that the small silver cross fell perfectly above the neckline of my pale blue party dress. True, the dress used to belong to Ruth, the light azure a perfect match for her eyes, but Mom had been able to let out the hem and take in the waist, to accommodate my taller height but smaller frame. I think it looked nice, even with my brown eyes, and it made me feel pretty to be able to dress up for a change.

I turned and hugged Helen. “Thank you so much. I agree—it looks lovely. I’ll be sure to give it back to you tomorrow.”

“Just have fun today.” She turned and left me to finish getting ready.

When Helen moved into our house, she quickly became part of the family. I loved having another “big sister” around, and Fred doted on his new “aunt.” Helen was good with both boys, always able to bring a smile to Fred’s face and coax out Robert’s little baby giggles. She had even volunteered to stay home with the boys so Clara could come to my graduation today, but Clara insisted they could come with us. It was going to be a memorable day, and night.

I arrived in the kitchen just as Ruth was opening a new letter from Jack. We tried to give her privacy—he was her husband, after all—but we were as anxious to hear from him as she was. After she read it through, she looked up, concern in her eyes.

My father put down the newspaper he was reading. “What is it, Ruthie girl? Is everything okay?”

Ruth swallowed. “He’s fine and sends his love to us all. He wrote this nearly three months ago, but it took longer to get to me because he got shipped out. He can’t seem to be more specific than that, but he says they are on the ground and in the fight.”

My hand instinctively closed over the cross hanging around my neck.

Ruth stood and offered the letter to my father, willing to share Jack's private thoughts with all of us.

"Yep, well, I'm sure he's glad to finally be able to be in the thick of it, to use the training he's had. I'm glad he and Will are in the same unit, that they're together over there." Dad's words were brave, but even I could see the worry in his gaze. He walked to my mother, gave her the letter to read, and put his arm around her shoulders. When she finished, she passed the letter to me.

*My love,*

*By the time you get this letter, I will have been on the ground in the European Theatre of Operations for a couple of months already. I can't give you more information about where I'm headed, but know that I am relieved to finally be in the fight. I will try to keep you as updated as the Army censors will let me, but know that we are doing what we joined up to do.*

*Even over here, we find time to goof around. The guys in my unit are mostly swell guys. When we get time off, we play cards—you'd be amazed how few guys have heard of Euchre—and toss a ball around, when we can find one. We swap stories and pictures of the gals we have back home. Will and I trust these guys and know they'll have our backs, just as we have theirs.*

*Thanks for sending me the latest picture of you. I miss you and kiss your picture every night before I fall asleep. I know how corny that sounds, but there's nothing like being far from home to make you realize what's important. And that's you and the life we'll have together when I get home.*

*Please tell Lilly how proud I am of her for saving that little boy's life in the fire. She's grown up to be a swell gal, especially considering what a pill she was when she was little. Ha, ha. By the time you get this letter, the new baseball season will be in full swing, so please send me an update on how it's going for the Pioneers. The little sports news we get over here is limited to the Dodgers and the Yankees, nothing about our little local teams. Give everyone my love and know that I think of each of you, and especially you, every night. I pray that we can whip those Jerries fast and get back to you soon. Your loving husband, Jack*

It felt good to know that Jack was proud of me, when I was the one who was proud of him for volunteering to serve our country. We all missed Will and Jack terribly, but it helped to hold Robert, who looked so much like his daddy, kiss his sweet baby head, and think of the day that my brothers would come home. I couldn't help but feel a little pang of jealousy at the love Jack showed for Ruth. Not that I didn't love her too, but I wanted to find a fella who would feel that way about me. Hard to do with them all away fighting a war.

****

When Ruth, Helen, and I climbed down off the bus in Beacon Heights, I was having trouble containing my excitement. It wasn't going to be exactly like a prom, but it would be fun to get a chance to dance with some of the soldiers before they shipped out. I was hoping that Ginny, Ava, and some of my other girlfriends could come, but Ginny said her family insisted she stay home for a big family dinner to celebrate her graduation. Ava said she might come, but I didn't see her on our bus. I would have plenty of fun with Helen and Ruth anyway.

"Do you think we'll get asked to dance much?" I asked as we walked into the dance hall. I wanted to have a fun night and not think about the war for a change.

"I should think you'll be wearing those shoes right through tonight, if you're not careful, my girl," said Helen. "You look smashing, and these young men won't be able to keep their eyes off you."

"As long as it's only their eyes," said Ruth, with a wink.

I couldn't help but giggle. "If they don't touch me, it'll be hard to dance with them."

"Just watch yourself, my lovely." Ruth was smiling, too, but I could tell the warning was serious.

When we walked through the front doors, there was a check room on the left, so Helen took all our coats to the clerk, returning with a ticket stub.

"Why don't we find a table?" With Helen leading the way, Ruth took my arm and we walked into the huge hall, toward the dance floor, which was surrounded by small tables with mismatched chairs. The bandstand was on the opposite wall, and we could hear the band warming up already.

"You're going to dance tonight, aren't you?"

Helen chuckled. "Of course, ducky. Just because we're old married ladies, it doesn't mean we'll leave these young chaps with no partner."

I looked at Ruth. She hadn't been out socially without Jack since they were married. "Oh, yes, I'll dance. We'll give these boys a gay old time before they ship out."

"I want to have some fun. I haven't been dancing since before the war started, and I spent most of my senior year working and knitting socks. I think I deserve some fun."

We found a table, and Helen said she'd go get us some punch, but before she could even drop off her handbag, a group of five G.I.s encircled the table.

"Ladies, you're looking lovely tonight," said a young guy in an Army uniform. "We're hoping you're here to dance." He smiled at Ruth and then me, but seemed taken aback by Helen's height. She towered over him by half a foot.

Ruth took a seat, crossed her hands in her lap, and smiled sweetly up at him. "Of course we're here to dance, once the music starts. In the meantime, I think we'll get some punch."

Three of the guys ran to the refreshment table to get us punch. Once I'd taken a seat, I looked up at the fifth man, in a naval uniform, and was struck by how handsome he was. He was tall—not too tall but definitely taller than me—with crystal blue eyes and wavy dark hair under his crisp white hat. When he looked at me, he immediately pulled off his hat. "Sorry, miss."

"That's all right. Why don't you have a seat?" I motioned to the chair next to me.

He seemed nervous; I could see his Adam's apple bobbing up and down. But he sat in the chair next to me, rolling his hat between the thumb and forefinger of his left hand.

"Hello." I extended my right hand. "I'm Lilly Walker."

He took my hand like it was made of spun glass,

hardly leaving an impression in my glove, but I could feel a tingle right through the fabric. “Nice to meet you, Miss Walker. I’m Seaman Paul Babcock.”

What a nice name to go with the handsome face. “Nice to meet you, too, Seaman Babcock. How long have you been in Beacon Heights?”

He seemed to blush a little. “I got here a few days ago. I just joined up, so I’ll be shipping out to Great Lakes Naval Base in Chicago in another week or two, as soon as my orders come through.”

The band members, warming up their instruments in earnest now, were dressed in formal black suits. A woman in a silver sequined dress, who must have been the singer, stood to the side, and the master of ceremonies came to the microphone.

“Thank you all for joining us tonight. Please enjoy the refreshments provided by our local branch of the Red Cross and put on your dancing shoes, as our wonderful band is ready to go.”

He swept his left arm around toward the band and walked off stage as the music began with Glenn Miller’s “In the Mood,” one of my number-one favorites.

Seaman Babcock stood up, tucked his cap into the back of his waistband, and held out a hand to me. “May I have this dance, Miss Walker?”

He was so cute, how could I say no? “I’d love to.” I put my hand in his, and we walked to the dance floor. Once he pulled me into his arms, I wasn’t sure there was anyone else left in the room.

****

Paul and I danced together all night. We dispensed with “Miss Walker” and “Seaman Babcock” rapidly during our first dance, as it felt too intimate not to use our first names. Every time someone tried to cut in, I refused and Paul danced us off in the opposite direction. We didn't talk much; it was hard to be heard over the music anyway. But, boy, did we dance.

Finally, when the band took a break, Paul asked if I wanted some fresh air. He took my arm, and we walked out onto the porch surrounding the hall. The cool air felt good after all that dancing. Even with all the other couples on the porch, it was finally quiet enough to be able to talk. I thought we'd be awkward, but it was as if I'd known him my whole life.

"How old are you, Lilly, if you don't mind me asking?"

"Eighteen. I just graduated from high school today."

"Well, congratulations. I finished early so I could join up as soon as I turned eighteen a few months ago."

We walked along the railing, finding a quiet, fairly dark corner of the porch with a bench.

"Why the navy? My older brothers, Will and Jack, joined the Army right after Pearl Harbor. My friend Helen's husband is in England, flying with the RAF."

He looked down at his shoes, still a shiny black. "I've always loved the water. I grew up here in the Finger Lakes, over on Keuka, and have been sailing and swimming nearly as long as I can remember. I couldn't imagine joining any other branch of the military. My ma says I have water on the brain."

I chuckled. "Were your parents upset that you enlisted right away? I got sort of mad at my brothers. I mean, we live on a farm, so they wouldn't necessarily have been drafted, at least not right away. I just didn't think they needed to go so soon, especially since the oldest, Will, and my sister-in-law, Clara, just had a baby."

Paul looked into my eyes. I could drown in his. "I bet they would have been drafted, Lilly. Even farmers will have to go, if there are any women, old men, and young boys to take their places. Everyone has to do their part. My parents knew I would be drafted anyway, so they understood why I didn't want to take the chance of ending up in the Army or something. It had to be the Navy for me."

"I took a job at Nichols Motors, building aircraft engines. My parents were not in favor of it, but I wanted to be independent, to do more than simply grow vegetables and knit socks."

"Good for you, Lilly. I'm so impressed with all you gals who have volunteered to take on these war jobs and who are keeping the home fires burning, as they say. It gives a fellow something to look forward to, coming home."

I instantly saw a picture of Paul returning home, of waiting for him at the door, with a fire burning in the parlor and a baby on my hip. It made me smile.

He leaned closer to my face. "What's that smile about?"

"What do you want to do after the war is over? Have you given it much thought?"

He shook his head. "Not really. We don't have a family farm or anything to tie me to my hometown. I just want what every guy wants, I guess. A nice little house, a wonderful wife, kids, the whole picture. That sounds so normal. I think it's what we're fighting for, the right to that simple kind of life."

I couldn't hide the tear in my eye. "That sounds perfect, Paul."

Before I knew what had happened, he leaned in just a couple inches more and placed the lightest, softest kiss on my lips. Even though I'd never been kissed before, I knew this was special. But he pulled back as quickly as he started.

"I'm so sorry, Lilly. I shouldn't have—I mean, I meant no disrespect. You're obviously a nice girl, from a good family. I'm…I'm sorry. I just couldn't help myself."

I did the only thing I could do to stop him; I kissed him again. He seemed surprised at first, but then he pulled me close, and I didn't want to ever let go.

Eventually, he pulled back, straightened his tie, and guided me to my feet. "Let's take a walk."

"I should tell Ruth and Helen, so they don't worry about me. And I'd like my wrap, as it's getting a little cool."

"Of course, what was I thinking? Let's just duck inside, let them know we're going to walk along the bank overlooking the lake, and we'll pick up your wrap." He took my hand, and I couldn't feel anything other than his strong fingers holding me, making me warm, keeping me safe.

We found Helen at the table, pink cheeked and fanning herself. "Frightfully warm in here, isn't it?"

"Yes. We just came in from the porch; it's much cooler out there." I turned to Paul. "Paul, this is my friend Helen Anderson. Helen, this is Seaman Paul Babcock. We're going to take a walk along the cliff. Can we have the coat check ticket so we can get my wrap?"

Helen dug it out of her purse and handed it to Paul. "Why don't you wait here, Lilly, while I get your wrap?" I told him which was mine and had a seat next to Helen.

"Well, he's mad about you, isn't he?" She smiled.

"I wouldn't go that far," I said, "but he's awfully cute, isn't he?"

"Paul, is it?"

"Yes, Paul Babcock. He just turned eighteen a couple of months ago and immediately joined the Navy. He's ever so sweet."

"And?" She gave me a most amused look, raising her eyebrows.

"What?"

She just sat there, smirking at me.

"Okay. He kissed me."

"I knew it. He has that dreamy look in his eyes. I knew he'd fallen for you already. What did you do when he kissed you?"

"I was surprised, but when he stopped, I kissed him right back." I could feel myself blushing.

"Oh, so you fancy him as well, then? Right." She had a big smile on her face. "Shall I tell Ruth you've gone out for some air?"

"Would you, please? I thought I'd see her, but there's such a crush in here."

"She's been dancing her feet off, but the last I knew, she was chatting with some of the Red Cross volunteers. I'll tell her. We'll be leaving at about midnight, Cinderella. Don't make us come looking for you." Helen winked at me as Paul returned with my wrap. He handed Helen the coat check ticket and took my hand.

"Thanks, Helen. I won't be late."

I could have sworn I heard a low whistle behind us as we headed to the door, but it must have been the band.

****

Paul and I walked, hand in hand, along the bank overlooking the still, dark lake below. It was a pleasant night in late June, but it definitely had cooled down. I couldn't stop myself from shivering, but that gave Paul an excuse to put his arm around me.

We talked about everything. His family, mine, his high school friends, my girlfriends, even my job. We talked about our dreams for the future, automatically combining them with no hesitation or discussion. I never knew I could be so comfortable around a man, especially one I was attracted to. It felt like he knew what I was thinking before I said it. He talked about the Navy and his hopes for after the war. He wanted to make a difference, to help save the innocent and beat the bad guys. It was simple and sincere and sweet. He melted my heart and reformed it in his likeness.

After some more wonderful kissing in the shadows, when I lost my head and sense of time, Paul came up for air and said it was nearly midnight. I had told him that Helen and Ruth would be waiting for me.

"Let's get you back before they send out a search party." He wrapped his arm around my shoulders and pulled me close. I loved the way I fit perfectly against his side, snug and warm. I snaked my own arm around his waist and leaned my head on his shoulder as we walked back to the dance hall.

When we saw Helen and Ruth waiting outside the door, Paul stopped and turned me to face him. "I know this is crazy, but I'm in love with you, Lilly."

"I love you, too." It might be quick, but it felt right.

"I don't know how long I'll be in Beacon Heights before I get shipped off to Chicago, but I want to spend every minute of it with you."

"Me, too, Paul, me, too."

He looked at me like he wanted to eat me up, and I liked it.

"Marry me, Lilly. I know we just met and we're young and it's too soon, but it's right. I feel it in here." He touched his heart, and then got down on one knee. "Will you marry me, Lilly Walker, and make me the happiest man alive?"

My eyes filled with tears. I dropped to my knees and threw myself into his arms. "Yes, Paul, yes. I'll marry you."

I kissed his cheek, his chin, his nose before he cupped my cheeks in his palms and took my lips in a deep, soul-scorching kiss.

"And the sooner the better."

## Chapter Thirteen
## Ruth

"Why do you have to rush into this?" Lilly had met Paul on Saturday, gotten engaged, and would be married in less than a week. Even during wartime, this seemed awfully quick.

"Well, we don't know how long he has before he gets shipped out, so why wait?"

"Because you hardly know each other," I said. "He seems like a nice young man, but maybe you could get engaged, write letters, and get married after the war. You could get to know each other through letters."

"No," pouted Lilly. "I love him, he loves me, and we want to be married. Who wants to wait until after the war? That could be ages." Lilly was wearing her mother's wedding dress, which Mom was attempting to hem, but she sounded more like a six-year-old than a blushing bride.

"Besides, Paul wants to get married. He wants a wife waiting for him at home. We fell in love at first sight, just like in the movies."

She could write him letters and wait for him at home without getting married. As it was, I had a long list of soldiers and sailors waiting for letters. While Lilly had been meeting the love of her life at the Red Cross dance, Helen and I had danced with so many young men I could hardly remember them all. They seemed so young, even though most weren't that much younger than I was. They were scared of going off to fight, and possibly die, in a foreign place far from home.

It broke my heart to see the fear and loneliness in their eyes, so I had agreed to write letters to them so they could get mail and know someone in America was thinking of them. Every soldier deserved to get mail, whether or not he had a wife or sweetheart waiting for him back home. I'd get the children at the day care to draw pictures to mail, too. I'd even invited a couple of the soldiers to join us for church and brought them back home for Sunday dinner afterwards.

"Okay, fine. If you really love him, I'm happy for you. I will pray that Paul comes back to you safe and sound, and we can all get to know him better after the war."

Once Mom was finished pinning the hem, Lilly slid out of the dress and came to kiss my cheek. "I knew you'd see it my way, Ruth. It's just going to be the best wedding ever."

The wedding was set for Saturday morning, a week after the Red Cross dance that had brought Lilly and Paul together. Several of the neighbors offered their precious sugar to allow us to make a wedding cake for the happy couple.

I walked into our bedroom on Saturday morning to see Lilly admiring herself in the mirror.

"You look beautiful. The dress turned out perfectly."

She turned to face me, and I could see she was worried about something.

"Thank you, but..." She held her bare foot out

from under the wispy hem of her dress. "I can't wear my work boots or my ugly walking shoes. With leather so hard to come by, I couldn't find any pretty shoes to wear, even if I could afford them."

She was right. Leather was reserved for army boots and military equipment these days; there were no frilly dress shoes to be found. But I had an idea, so I rummaged around in the bottom of my closet for a moment and pulled out a shoebox from the back.

"What about these?" I opened the box to reveal the pretty bedroom slippers I'd gotten from a college friend as a bridal gift.

"Bedroom slippers?"

"Sure, why not?" I walked to her, crouched down, and held each slipper so she could slide her feet into them. "They look elegant, and they've hardly been worn. I think they're perfect."

She turned back to the mirror, holding the hem of the dress up slightly to look at both feet at once. "You're right. They're lovely. Thanks." She turned and gave me a quick hug.

"Those can be your 'something borrowed.' Do you have something old, something new, and something blue?"

"Well, the dress is old, of course, and my nylons are new. I've been saving them for a special occasion. I asked Mom to find at least one blue flower to put in my bouquet. And I have two somethings borrowed, as Helen loaned me her necklace again. I was wearing it when I met Paul, and that was certainly the luckiest night of my life."

She handed me the necklace and turned so I could fasten it for her. She looked happy and even incredibly young. War made everyone grow up fast, but I was worried what it might be like for Lilly when Paul returned from war. Hopefully, he would return.

****

After the wedding ceremony, we had a small reception in the side yard. The bride was lovely in her altered dress and borrowed slippers, and the groom looked handsome in his Navy whites. I walked over to them, carrying Robert, who'd just woken up from his nap.

"Congratulations, Paul, and welcome to the family." I kissed Paul on the cheek, happy to see the excitement on his face. Robert reached a hand toward him, and Paul captured it, placing a kiss on the baby's knuckles.

"Thanks, Ruth." He nodded. "I wasn't sure Mr. and Mrs. Walker were going to let me steal away their darling girl, but she's all mine now." Paul slipped his arm around Lilly's waist.

"They couldn't tell me no, not once they saw how much I love you." Lilly smiled up at her husband. They were both so young and happy; it almost hurt to look at them. Hopefully nothing would happen to mar today's happiness once Paul was sent overseas.

"I hope we'll have time to get to know you better before you ship out, Paul. Any idea how long you'll be in town?"

"Not long, I imagine. Certainly not long enough." He kissed Lilly's cheek, and she giggled. "My first stop will be the Great Lakes Naval base in Chicago for training, and then who knows where."

"Paul and I are staying at the Lakeview Motel in Beacon Heights tonight. It will be so romantic." Lilly blushed just a bit.

"Well, Helen says she will gladly move in with me if you two want to stay in her room after tonight."

"That sounds swell, Ruth. Thanks," said Paul.

I moved on to give others the chance to wish the happy couple well. I prayed Lilly and Paul would have many years together.

Helen was standing near the cake table, pouring punch for guests.

"It's a proper party now, isn't it? Lilly and Paul look terribly smart. They'll have lovely babies someday."

I nearly choked on my punch. "They're still babies themselves, Helen. Let's not rush things."

"You never know what's going to happen, Ruth." She chuckled and looked to the porch, where Pop was sitting on the porch swing. "How are Julia and Earl holding up?"

I looked at Lilly and Paul, saw Leonard kissing the bride and then shaking Paul's hand. Even Leonard had on a jacket and tie for the big day, although he looked uncomfortable.

"You've seen how they spoil that girl. I love Lilly like my own sister, but they've given her everything she wanted, and she's grown up to expect life to go her way. They didn't want her to marry so young, but they couldn't refuse her anything, even this."

Mom walked over to the happy couple and herded them to the rose trellis at the side of the yard so Pop could take their picture.

"Let's make a picture of the whole family, Lilly." Mom nodded toward Clara, who went to find Fred. I carried Robert to the trellis, filling in next to Paul. Once

Clara had a handle on Fred, she stood next to me. Mom and Pop stood to Lilly's right, after giving the camera to Leonard.

"Oh, wait, where's Helen?" Lilly looked around. "Helen, we need you. We're making a picture."

Helen seemed genuinely surprised, and plastered a tremulous smile on her lips and walked over toward Clara. "This is a family picture, Lilly. I don't belong in it."

"Don't be silly, Helen. If you hadn't convinced me to go to that dance, and loaned me your lucky necklace, Paul and I might never have met. You're family now."

Helen didn't say another word, but I could see a bit of moisture in her eyes as she smiled for the camera.

****

Long after Lilly and Paul had said their goodbyes and we'd cleaned up from the party, I sat at my desk to write to Jack. He would be surprised when he heard about Lilly's short courtship and hurried wedding. He was quite protective of his little sister, so hopefully he and Paul would get along well after the war.

I pulled out his latest letter to re-read before writing mine.

*My love,*

*As always, thank you for your wonderful letters and the drawings from the kids. I shared them with some of the guys in our unit. And the pictures of the family are great. I can't believe my father has gotten so handy with a camera. Who would have guessed? I see a bit of what might be his thumb in the bottom of the shot, but I'm grateful to have it anyway.*

*Things here are dull, until they're not, of course. I can't tell you much, but we are in Northern Africa now, and it's hot. I remember complaining how hot it was for the 4th of July in Upton Falls, but if this continues, it'll be like a furnace here by then. You have my permission to poke me if I ever complain about snow again.*

*I won ten dollars playing poker last night. I don't know if it's because I've been playing Euchre and Pinochle since I was a kid, but I've taken to poker in nothing flat. It's one of the only ways to amuse ourselves in the evening. Even Will gets in on it, although he still prefers Gin Rummy. We're bored, until we're not. In fact, if you ever get a chance to send me a book, I'd be in heaven. It doesn't much matter what it is. It's just it would be nice to have something to read during my down time. I have no idea when it would catch up with me, or how much it would cost you to send, but I promise it would be much appreciated. Never thought you'd make a reader out of me, did you? I guess war changes us all.*

*I can't believe how much Fred and Robert have grown. I take out my pictures before lights out, when possible, just to have your face be the last thing I see before I fall asleep. I like seeing you in my dreams and thinking of the babies we'll make some day. Never mind the fun in making them. Ha, ha.*

*How goes the day care? What a great idea to help out the working mothers. You're a natural to run it. And don't worry, I won't let on to Helen that I know about your reading lessons, whenever I get to meet her. I love that you're helping her, and convinced her to move in, but not surprised. You always want to help anyone who needs it, like you did with Leonard. We'll probably have to add on to the farmhouse to make room for all the people you bring into our home, but I love you even more for it.*

*Thanks, too, for all the baseball updates. I'm glad to hear our Elmira Pioneers are having a good season, although I wish I was there to see it for myself. We'll have to make plans to take in a few games once I get home.*

*Well, I have to stop here. Lights out in five minutes and, if I want to get to the latrine, I need to go now. (Sorry to leave you with that mental picture. Ha, ha.)*

*Kiss my mother for me, and imagine me giving you some kisses and hugs, too. I miss you more than you can know and am always your loving husband, Jack*

****

After the newsreel I saw last week of General Eisenhower and the troops in North Africa, I had a better mental image of where Jack was, although I'm not sure that helped me feel any better. After all, Helen knew where Billy was flying out of, if not exactly where the planes were headed, but it didn't make her worry less. When part of your heart is thousands of miles away, it doesn't really help to know what it looks like there. You just want them to come home. Now it was Lilly's turn to find that out.

## Chapter Fourteen
Helen

"Again, Miss Anderson. Pretty please, read it again."

I couldn't refuse Kurt, especially since he didn't seem to mind the halting way I read. Ruth had to convince me to start reading to the children, but of course she was right. I was getting better at reading, and the children never asked why I didn't read faster or had to sound out some of the words. They just loved the stories.

I shouldn't have had favorites, but there was something special about Peter, Kurt, and Marion Blumenthal. Especially little Kurt. He was three and climbed right up into my lap as soon as I arrived at the day care each morning. I used to stop in just before lunch to help Ruth manage feeding the bunch, and then we'd work on my reading lessons after they lay down for a rest. Ever since Judith Blumenthal started dropping her children at the church, I found reasons to be there earlier every day.

After the fifth time through *Uncle Wiggly and the Peppermint*, I sent the children to wash up for lunch.

"You're getting much better, Helen. Can you feel it? I'm so proud of the progress you're making." Ruth was putting the children's lunch boxes out on the little table, so I pulled up chairs.

I laughed. “I think I know that book by heart now, so it hardly counts as reading.”

“Oh, it does. And part of learning to read is learning how much some stories never get old. I have books I’ve read over and over because I enjoy them so much.”

“I don’t know if I’ll get to that point any time soon, except with children’s books, but now that I’ve asked Billy to print his letters to me, instead of his sloppy handwriting, I am getting better at reading them myself.”

She smiled at me. “I knew you could do it.”

“You’re too kind, you are. It’s all to do with you and your teaching. Even giving me a chance to practice here, with the children. It helps a lot.”

Tommy started to fuss in his basket just as the children started to take their places at the table. “Let me get him. I’ll change his nappy and get his bottle. He probably wants his lunch.”

Tommy and Marion were easy babies, compared to my little brothers and the Smith-Burtons’ children. The day care children were well-behaved, most of the time, and I enjoyed being here more than I thought I would. There were times, when I found myself holding Marion, smelling her sweet baby head and feeling her warm weight in my arms, that my thoughts wandered to what it would be like to have Billy’s baby to hold. I still didn’t want a houseful of children, like my mother, but I was definitely warming to the idea of one or two.

Once he had a clean nappy, Tommy was only too happy to settle on my lap and take his bottle. He stopped every few moments to look up at me and smile, nipple still in his mouth, and milk dripping down his chin. Sometimes he'd reach up and grab one of the curls that had escaped my lopsided victory roll.

After the children were down for their rest, Ruth and I settled at the small table with our own lunch pails, and I got to work. Ruth was mending Earl's good shirt for church while I worked on a new letter to Billy. When I finished, Ruth read it over for me.

*Dear Billy,*

*Hello again. Work is going well and helping at the day care is fun. Peter Blumenthal drew me this picture last week, so I thought you'd like it. As you can see, he made me about ten feet taller than everyone else in the room. My head is hitting the bloody ceiling! The child thinks I'm a giant. I guess I am to them. Kurt says he wants to grow up as big as me someday.*

*I won't ask for what you can't tell me, but how are you? It sounds like most days are either dead dull or frightfully crazy. Do you ever get to go out? Go round a pub or to a Red Cross dance? I don't want you meeting a new love, like Lilly did, but you have to be able to let off steam with your mates now and then.*

*I'm writing this letter myself, with Ruth helping me, of course. So I'm going to keep it short, as it's hard work to find the right words. I'm getting better reading to the children and figuring out your letters. Stay safe and come home soon. Love always, your Helen*

Ruth handed the letter back to me. "He's going to love the picture Peter drew of you."

"If his mates see it, they'll think he married a big old cow. And Billy's so smart, so handsome, whatever does he see in me?" Somehow the drawing brought back all those old feelings.

"As you would say, he's mad about you. I can tell

from his letters that he loves you completely and thinks you're beautiful."

That made me laugh. "He's not so daft as that! I'll admit that he really does love me, although I'll never truly know why. I'm a lucky girl."

"And he's lucky to have found you, Helen."

I heard Kurt cough in his sleep, but when he didn't wake, we went back to work. I was carefully addressing the envelope to Billy.

"Did you hear that Henry Blumenthal is in North Africa? Judith told me when she dropped the children off yesterday. She'd just had a letter from him." Ruth concentrated on her mending.

"It must be hard for Judith, with no family nearby, to be alone with the children when she's not at the plant." I didn't have any real family here either, until I moved in with the Walkers. But then, I didn't have children to take care of.

"She says the day care really saved her. She's exactly the kind of working mother we aim to help. Before she brought the children here, she would farm them out on neighbors, but it's hard to rely on others to watch your children. She told me she would probably have gotten fired for having to miss work if Nichols Motors weren't so desperate for good help."

Lilly came rushing down the stairs to the basement, doing her best to rush quietly by the sleeping children.

"Did you hear about Cindy Douglas?" She was out of breath, like she'd been running.

"Hello to you, too, Lilly," said Ruth, somewhat sarcastically.

"Yes, yes, hello. Sorry, but I just heard the news from Ginny and thought you'd want to know."

Lilly sat in one of the tiny chairs at the table, pulling in close between Ruth and me.

"What news?" I couldn't imagine that anything about Cindy Douglas would have to do with me, as I'd only met the woman a couple of times in the locker room at work as she went off shift and I came on.

"She died."

"What? Who died?" Ruth put down her mending and lowered her voice.

"I told you, Cindy Douglas. Ginny heard it from her neighbor, who heard it from one of the girls who works first shift with Cindy."

"Shhh…" Ruth tried to get Lilly to speak more softly. "I don't want the children to hear about this."

"Sorry," Lilly whispered. Ruth and I leaned in to hear her better. "Apparently, Cindy got pregnant and didn't want the baby, you know, with her husband off at war for nearly a year now."

"Did she die in childbirth?" Last time I saw the woman, she surely didn't look pregnant.

"No," whispered Lilly. "She paid someone to get rid of the baby and, well, I guess things went badly, and she died. Can you believe it?"

Ruth leaned back in her chair, pressed her hand to her face and then looked at Lilly. "That poor woman. Did she have any children?"

"No, and apparently she wanted to keep it that way." Lilly's voice took on an unattractive sneer.

Ruth pressed her hand on Lilly's arm. "Don't judge, Lilly. Have you no compassion? The poor woman died, simply because she didn't want to have a baby."

"Then she shouldn't have gotten pregnant in the

first place. She was running around on her husband, and that's what she gets for it." Lilly shook off Ruth's hand and raised her voice.

I tried to lower the volume again. "This sort of thing happened often when I was growing up. A lot of families had too many children to feed and couldn't bear to bring another into the world. Sometimes they went to a proper doctor or midwife for help, but more often than not they had to turn to some woman with herbs and knitting needles. Those stories usually ended badly, and often the women died. It was terrible."

"Married women would try to get rid of babies they made with their husbands?" Lilly sounded shocked.

"All the time, Lilly. Apartments in the East End were tiny and cramped, and many people had little or no money. My whole family of fourteen lived in a two-room flat, with a shared bath down the hall. It's not a nice place to raise a family, especially one so large you can't afford to feed them all."

Ruth sighed. "You don't know what someone is going through, Lilly. Try to be more sympathetic. People have all sorts of reasons for what they do that we can never understand."

Lilly looked a little ashamed. "Well, it is sad that she died. I just think if she'd been faithful to her husband this wouldn't have happened. Now he has to get a letter from someone telling him his wife is dead, and what happens if he finds out how she died? How will he feel knowing she made a baby with someone else while he was off fighting a war?"

We all nodded. Her husband would probably be devastated, and there was no real way to protect him from that.

"Hopefully they don't send him all the information now, and there's a chaplain, or the Red Cross has people he can talk to." Ruth sadly shook her head. "He doesn't really need the details until he comes home, after the war, if ever."

"I just feel bad for her husband, that's all." Lilly had sobered and was much quieter when we left to walk to the bus to work.

## Chapter Fifteen
Ruth

"I'm worried about the Blumenthal children." Helen got ready to leave for the bus. "This is three days in a row they've been missing from day care. That likely means Judith has missed work as well, and Matron won't like that. I'd hate for her to lose her job."

"True. I'll stop by the house on my way home today and see what's up. Maybe Judith or the children have been ill. It must be hard not having family in town. I'll see if there's anything they need."

I said goodbye to Helen and Lilly, who had stopped by to pick up Helen on her way to the bus. Later that afternoon, after the children had been picked up, I headed out the door.

When I stopped at their house, I noticed a small pile of mail on the front porch. I couldn't help but wonder where they all might be, as there didn't seem to be any lights on in the house.

I knocked on the door. "Judith?" No response, so I knocked again. "Judith, it's Ruth Walker, from the day care. Are you there?"

I could hear something rustling inside the house, but still no lights. I knocked once more and finally saw Kurt's pale little face peering at me through the curtains at the sidelight window next to the intricately carved maple door.

"Kurt, honey, it's Mrs. Walker. Is your mother there? Can you let me in?"

He just stared up at me, his lower lip trembling, his eyes glistening with the start of tears.

"Let me in, please, Kurt. I want to talk to your mother."

Peter's face appeared behind Kurt, looking just as frightened.

"Please open the door, Peter. It's Mrs. Walker. I'd like to see your mother, make sure everyone is all right."

He waited a moment or two and then clicked open the lock and pulled in the heavy door.

I walked into the dim doorway, which led directly to the dining room. The parlor was on the left, and a door across the room had to be the kitchen. No lights were on anywhere on the main floor, so I set down my handbag and reached for the light switches.

While Peter was standing near the door, Kurt had backed up and was crouching under the edge of the dining room table. Marion was crawling under the table and headed for the stairs that ran up the far right wall.

"Where is your mother, Peter?"

"She's up in her bedroom still."

Still? "Is she sick, Peter?" The house seemed to be a bit messy, but raising three young children and working full-time was a lot to handle.

"I don't know. She won't come out of her room."

I walked over to the stairs, gently turning Marion from the bottom step. "Why don't you take Marion into the kitchen for a snack, Peter, and I'll go talk to your mother? Do you think that would be all right?"

"We don't have any snacks left. There's nothing to

eat." Kurt crawled out from under the table to peek up at me.

"Okay. I'll go talk to your mother while you boys play with the baby. You can help Peter watch your baby sister, can't you, Kurt?"

Kurt nodded at me, his large brown eyes solemn, but didn't say a word. Peter picked up the baby, and the three headed into the parlor, where I could see some toys strewn about.

At the top of the stairs, I saw a bathroom straight ahead, with two bedrooms to the left and one to the right, on the back of the house. The door was closed, so I guessed I would find Judith there and knocked.

"Judith? It's Ruth Walker. May I come in?"

When she didn't answer, I gently turned the knob and pushed the door inward. There was a pale light coming from the south-facing windows, but the room was in shadowy shades of gray. Judith sat on the edge of the bed, wearing a beige day dress and brown shoes. Her hair was flattened on one side, as if she'd just woken up. The bedclothes were askew and wrinkled, as if she'd been sleeping on top of the bedding.

"Judith?" She didn't react, so I walked toward the far side of the bed, trying to catch her gaze. Her eyes were swollen and puffy, her skin drawn and gray in the dim light. I leaned over the dressing table and switched on a lamp. The light must have surprised her, as she turned toward me, but still she didn't speak. I wasn't sure if she was ill, but she definitely wasn't herself.

"Judith? Are you ill? Is everything all right?" I sat on the stool in front of the dressing table so I was facing her. I hoped seeing me would bring her round.

Instead, she merely stared out the window, a

handkerchief clutched in her left hand. She sighed but didn't speak.

"I came to see if you need anything. We've been missing the children at day care this week. Will you be bringing them by tomorrow morning?"

Silence, again. Was she was having some kind of mental breakdown? She didn't react to my words or my presence and, if Peter couldn't get through to her either, there had to be something terribly wrong.

I looked around the room again, now that the light was on, and saw a wad of yellow paper sticking out from under the edge of the bedding, near Judith's feet. I leaned over to pick it up.

As I started to open the crumpled paper, I realized what I was holding. My breath caught. A telegram. I had to force my shaking hands to open the paper enough to see the four black stars and read the terse communication.

THE SECRETARY OF WAR DESIRES ME TO EXPRESS HIS DEEPEST REGRET THAT YOUR HUSBAND CORPORAL HENRY R. BLUMENTHAL WAS KILLED IN ACTION ON FIFTEENTH SEPTEMBER IN TUNISIA…

The telegram was dated October 2, 1942, so she had received it on Friday.

"Oh, Judith." I moved next to her and placed my hand on her shoulder. Judith turned her head to look at me. My gaze met hers, but she was nowhere to be found in her empty eyes. It was as if she'd disappeared completely.

I wrapped my arms around her, but she sat stiff and still as a board, so I let go.

I heard a noise in the hall and saw Kurt peeking

through the crack of the door.

"Come, Judith. The children need you. They're hungry." I put my hand on her right elbow, trying to get her to stand, to get her moving toward her children. She was like stone. She wouldn't move or speak.

"I'll go down and fix the children something to eat. Why don't you freshen up and join us in the kitchen. Wouldn't you like some dinner?"

I walked to the door. "Let's go downstairs, Kurt. I bet you're ready to eat." He took my hand and looked only briefly back toward his mother. I had no idea when she'd last made her children a meal.

When we got to the bottom of the stairs, I saw Peter playing with Marion in the parlor.

"Let's find something for dinner, children."

It looked like Judith hadn't been in the kitchen for days. The cupboard doors were hanging open, there were uncooked noodles and grains of rice on the floor, along with what looked like scattered flour, and dirty dishes on the table, in the sink, and on the floor. As I made my way, carefully stepping over dishes, food, and children, to the pantry, I found that the shelves in there were mostly empty. What had these children been eating for the past five days?

I found a loaf of bread in the refrigerator and cut some slices to make sandwiches. I opened a can of Spam and mixed it with mayonnaise, celery, pickles, salt, and pepper, and spread the mixture on the bread. I put the sandwiches on plates for the boys and cut one into tiny bites for Marion after I plopped her into a high chair. There wasn't any milk, so I gave them small cups of water and waited for Judith to join us. To no avail. When they finished the sandwiches, I buttered some bread and gave that to the boys.

"Peter, did your mother tell you why she was feeling so ill? Has she come out of her bedroom at all?"

Peter shook his head, his mouth stuffed full of bread.

After the children gobbled down their food, I walked to the table by the front door, picked up the telephone receiver, and called Mom. We'd gotten the farm on the telephone only a few years earlier, and it was valuable in situations like this.

"Hello?"

"Hello, Mom. It's Ruth."

"Ruth, dear. Is everything all right?" She was probably expecting me home by now.

"Not really. I'm at the Blumenthal house. The children haven't been to day care all week, and I came to check on them." I sighed. There was no easy way to handle a soldier's death, especially when talking to a soldier's mother or wife. I whispered, so the children didn't hear. "It's Henry, Mom, Mr. Blumenthal. Judith received a telegram last Friday. He's been killed."

"Oh, no. God rest his soul. How is Judith handling it? Is there anything we can do to help? I know she doesn't have family here, or, you know, a church…"

The Blumenthals were the only Jewish family in town. "She's not handling it at all, Mom. That's why I'm calling. I think I need to bring the children home with me, at least for now. She's pulled completely into herself and won't speak or leave her room. I think the kids have had to fend for themselves. They're hungry and dirty and scared."

"Oh, the poor lambs. Of course bring them home with you. Let's get them fed and cleaned up. They can sleep here tonight."

"Exactly what I was hoping you'd say, Mom. Thanks so much. I just couldn't leave them here. Judith is in a bad state." Bringing the children to the farm would be the first step, but I didn't think Judith could even take care of herself, as she was right now.

"I'll try to get Judith to come, Mom, but she won't speak. I don't know if I can get her to understand."

"Let's take care of the children tonight, and I can get to work on helping Judith tomorrow. Perhaps Pastor Robbins can help us round up some volunteers to make meals, clean the house, or even just sit with Judith. I'm sure the church ladies will step up, even though she doesn't belong to our church."

"Great idea, Mom. We'll be home as soon as I get some clothing together for them. I just made them sandwiches, but they'll probably still be hungry. Thanks so much for your help with this."

We rang off, and I left the children in the kitchen while I ran upstairs to throw some clothing in a bag. When I finished, I walked back into Judith's room.

"I'm going to take the children to our house, Judith, with your permission. I think they would enjoy a night on the farm. Why don't you come with us?"

She didn't turn her head, or move or speak. I hoped she heard me, at least. Just as I turned to leave, I noticed the telegram I had smoothed out and left on the dressing table was wadded up again and lying on the floor.

I touched my hand to her shoulder and gave it a light squeeze. "See you tomorrow, Judith."

When I got to the bottom of the stairs, the children were sprawled out on the floor, playing with trucks.

"Well, children, I spoke to your mother, and we decided that you three can come home with me tonight. Won't it be fun to have a sleepover at our farm? My nephews Fred and Robert will love having friends come for a visit." Hopefully my animated tone was hiding my worry.

Peter nodded in agreement, but Kurt said nothing. "Let's go, kids." I carried Marion outside and put her into the pram that was parked on the front porch. I picked up the children's clothes and my pocketbook, and then took Kurt by the hand while Peter pulled the door closed behind us.

I led our little band home, hoping that some hot food, warm baths, and clean beds would help prepare the kids for the bad news about their father.

****

Shhh…" As soon as Helen and Lilly walked into the kitchen, I held one finger in front of my lips. They weren't used to seeing me waiting up for them when they got home from work.

"What's going on?" Lilly set down her handbag and walked to the sink to rinse out her lunch pail.

Helen was hanging her coat on the hook by the kitchen door. Now that fall was fully here, the nights were getting crisp and cold.

"Peter and Kurt Blumenthal are sleeping on blankets on the floor of your room, Helen, and Marion is in with us, Lilly. I didn't want you to step on them when you went upstairs."

Helen walked quickly to the table, where she put down her lunch pail and touched my arm. "Why are the children here? What has happened?"

I pulled out a chair and sat, motioning to them to

do the same. I told them about my visit to the house and the telegram.

Helen gasped. "That poor family. I knew something was amiss."

"Poor Judith. I can't imagine what I'd be like if anything happened to Paul. What will she do now?"

I took Lilly's hand in mine. "I hope none of us ever has to find out what we'd do if we got news like that."

Helen nodded and stood. "I don't know what she'll do now. They don't have any family in town, but she said she and Henry grew up in New York City, so maybe they have family there. What did Judith have to say, Ruth?"

"She said nothing at all. I couldn't get her to speak or even look at me, really. It's like she's disappeared, like she's died inside." I could feel the tears in the corners of my eyes. "Those poor kids have been fending for themselves since Friday, from what I could see."

Helen's spine stiffened. "Those poor dears. I'm glad you've brought them home, Ruth." She set her lunch pail on the table. "If I was still living with the Andersons, I don't think I could bear to be in their house if anything happened to Billy. I don't know where I would go. But"—she paused, looking me straight in the eye—"I don't have any children to think about. What is Judith thinking, ignoring her children? She's lucky nothing happened to them."

"I'm worried about her, Helen. I can understand that she's devastated, but I don't think she's told the children what's happened. I'm not sure she's even spoken to them since she received the telegram."

Helen pulled out her chair and sat down. "It sounds

like she shut down. She doesn't want to believe it's true, so she's pretending it isn't. I saw this more often than you would expect during the Blitz. A parent who'd lost their child or a husband who'd lost his wife—they just went on like it never happened, because they couldn't deal with it."

"I think the children will be staying with us for a while. She can't take care of herself the way she is, never mind the kids. Mom called Pastor Robbins, and he asked the women of the church guild to help. Many of her neighbors belong to our church. The women are lining up to help with cooking, cleaning, and even just to keep an eye on Judith."

Helen nodded. "That sounds like a good idea. This small town is good at pulling together in a way no London neighborhood ever could be. When Billy used to tell me stories about growing up here, the thing that impressed me most was the feeling that everyone watched out for their neighbors."

"I'm exhausted, so I'm going up to bed, and hopefully we can get things straightened out in the morning. I think tomorrow will be a long and difficult day."

Lilly and Helen bade me good night and got busy cleaning out their lunch pails and packing tomorrow's dinner as I climbed the stairs.

****

"But where is Momma?" Little Kurt climbed up on Helen's lap at breakfast on Wednesday morning of the following week.

Lilly was feeding Marion, and Peter was sitting in the chair by Helen, digging into his oatmeal.

"Yeah, when are we going home?" said Peter

through a mouthful of food. He'd been weepy at bedtime last night; they all were missing their mother and knew something was wrong. Helen had calmed him by bringing Peter and Kurt into bed with her. I wasn't sure how much longer they would be willing to stay with us, without their mother.

"Your mummy has work today, you know that, but we'll have fun at the church, right?" Helen set Kurt down in the chair to her right. "Why don't you tuck into your oatmeal, old thing, and then you'll be ready when it's time to go to the church."

Kurt giggled. "Old thing! I'm not an old thing. You're so silly."

Helen took her dishes to the sink. I sidled up next to her and whispered, "Will you take the children in and open the day care today? I'm going over to see Judith this morning. When I spoke with Mrs. Robbins last night, she said Judith has returned to reality. It's taken several days and a lot of time with the church ladies, but she seems ready to go back to being a mother."

Helen snuck a glimpse over her shoulder and turned back, whispering to me, "I don't know. I wouldn't want to leave the children with her unless we're sure she's able to take care of them. Tell her that if she needs me to, I could always stay with them for a few days."

"You're so kind, Helen. I'll check in and see for myself how she's doing and will tell her of your generous offer and see what she thinks."

We stood shoulder to shoulder, or rather, my shoulder to Helen's rib cage, at the sink. "Whilst I can't imagine how I'd react if I got a telegram like hers, my heart really aches for these little tykes. It's almost as if they've lost both their parents."

I nodded. "Hopefully they'll get their mother back today."

Helen turned to the table. "Well, my lovelies, it's time we get this kitchen cleaned up, spit spot, and then we'll take our coats and lunches and march off to the church. Kurt and Peter, you run along and get your coats, and Marion's, and I'll get our breakfast washed up. Off you go, now, old thing," she said, turning to look at Kurt again, giving him a little wink.

He fell off his chair in a fit of giggles. "Old thing! You think I'm some moldy old shoe or sumpin'?" After he disentangled himself from the chair legs, he and Peter galloped to the mud room for their jackets and boots.

Helen smiled. "They are wonderful children, really. I hope she's brought herself round by now. They need her."

After rinsing out the dishes, Helen picked up Marion and bundled her into her jacket, while Lilly cleaned up the table. With Marion in the pram and the boys racing around like pups, Helen and Lilly headed off down the back steps to herd the children to the church.

Hopefully Judith would be ready to bring the warmth of her children's love back into her house. While they'd be sad about their father, they were young enough to move past it, if Judith was able to do the same.

# Chapter Sixteen
## Lilly

"Wow! I can't dance another minute. I need a break, okay? I'm going to sit and drink my punch." I flopped down in the chair next to Ginny, whose face was bright red.

"I'll be back when you're done with your punch, okay, doll?" The young G.I. I had been dancing with ran off toward the punch bowl. If I could avoid making eye contact with another Joe, I might be able to catch my breath.

I elbowed Ginny, chuckling. "He can call me 'doll' all he wants, but I'm still a married woman."

"Sometimes I wish I were, too," said Ginny. "Some of these guys get a little pushy."

"Well, that's not really anything new these days, is it?"

Ginny wrinkled her nose. "Are you talking about Harold?"

I shivered and nodded my head. "Among others. Some of those guys at the plant are disgusting. They are old enough to be our fathers, but that doesn't stop them from hooting and whistling and making all kinds of crude remarks at us."

"If my father ever heard them…" Ginny grimaced.

"Don't I know it. This is just what my parents were worried about. Good thing the Matron keeps them in line. These soldiers are nothing like them. Most of them are polite, even when they find out I'm married."

"Ruth's really invested in these Red Cross events, isn't she?" Ginny gestured toward Ruth, who was working behind the refreshment table.

"Yeah, it's like she's everybody's sister. She talks to these guys and serves them punch and cookies, but if they say they don't have family or a sweetheart back home, she offers to write them letters, to keep their spirits up. I don't know how she keeps up with all the letter writing. Never mind the ones she brings home for Sunday dinner. She just can't do enough for them."

"Like your mom, with the knitting," said Ginny.

I nodded. "Yeah, she makes me knit whenever I have a night at home. I don't know if soldiers are excited to get hand-knit socks, but she says we have to do our part. Frankly, writing to my own husband is more up my alley."

"I should think sending your husband off to the Pacific should be enough of a sacrifice for you. Never mind that we're spending our youth, and breaking our nails, making aircraft engines. Who would've thought?"

Another young man swooped in and took Ginny's hand. "Aren't you just the prettiest little thing here tonight?" He nodded to me. "No offense, of course."

I smiled. "None taken."

Still holding Ginny's hand, he said, "It's a crime for a beauty like you not to be on the dance floor. Let me redeem you. Come, dance with me."

Ginny was laughing so hard that she didn't fight him as he tugged her to her feet. "Okay. I have to admit, that's a new one. Let's go."

They'd only gotten a couple of steps from me when

Ginny ran back and bent down to whisper in my ear. "This one's a real cutie. Don't wait up for me." She ran back to her dance partner with a big smile on her face.

I watched them swing into the crowded dance floor and disappear. I was starting to cool down when a couple of sailors stopped at my table.

"Good evening, beautiful," said the tall one.

I held up my left hand.

"Mrs. Beautiful, then." He chuckled. "How about a dance?"

The shorter one pulled out a chair, spun it around, and sat down, his legs straddling the chair back. "The night is young, and so are we. Let's make the most of it."

I sighed. "I just sat down, guys. Give me a few minutes to rest and drink my punch, and I'm sure I'll be up for more dancing."

They nodded, said they'd be back, and moved on. Just then, I felt a hand on my left shoulder and jumped.

"Whoa. It's just me." Ruth dropped into the empty chair.

"Sorry. I didn't see you. I'm taking a little break. How are things going at the refreshment table?"

Ruth smiled. "Good. It's a busy night. I think several units are supposed to ship out this week, so the boys are trying to fit in all the fun they can."

"I had to sit for a while. I'm tired, and my feet are killing me." I reached down and eased my right foot out of my shoe. "I wish I could find some new shoes." I showed her the hole in the bottom of my shoe. "I tried covering this hole with cardboard, but I'm getting an awful blister. And there's a matching hole, and another blister, in the other shoe."

"I know. Even if we had enough ration coupons, we couldn't find any decent shoes to buy."

Helen spun by, dancing with a pimply-faced soldier at least six inches shorter, who couldn't seem to keep his eyes off her bosom.

I put my shoe back on and crossed my arms over my chest. "It's bad enough that I have to keep wearing the same old tattered dresses until they literally fall off me. And then Mom just picks them up, stitches or patches them, and slips them back into my closet. I'm so tired of it all."

"Now, Lilly. As tough as these little hardships are for us, think of the sacrifices our soldiers are making. And think of Judith and her children. We don't really have it that bad, do we?"

I swear, sometimes Ruth had a way of speaking to me in my mother's own voice. You'd think Ruth was her daughter instead of me. I loved Ruth, but I didn't need my mother nagging me on my evening out.

I rolled my eyes. "I do my part, Ruth, you know I do." I could feel my temper rising. "I work at Nichols, knit those silly socks, help can all those vegetables, and, even worse, I sent my husband off just days after we got married. I'm sorry Henry got killed, but we're all making sacrifices for this war, and I'm tired of it."

"Calm down, Lilly. There's no use getting upset. It's frustrating, but there's not much we can do until the war is over."

Suddenly, I stood up.

"I'm tired. I'm going home now."

"Oh, don't be mad."

"I'm not mad. I'm tired, and my feet hurt, and I don't want to dance anymore."

"I'm on duty for another hour, Lilly. Why don't you give these soldiers a little more of your time, like Helen is, and then we can leave at midnight?" Ruth stood, obviously assuming I'd agree.

I shook my head. "No. I'm going now. I don't want to wait another hour. Ginny told me not to bother waiting for her, so I'm going."

Helen walked up to the table, breathing heavily. "Going where?"

"Lilly wants to go home now, but I'm trying to convince her to stay until midnight and we can walk to the bus together."

"Maybe Helen wants to leave now, too." I knew she'd had a letter from Billy tonight. Maybe she'd want to rush home and work on her reply.

"Actually, I'd really rather stay. If I go home now, I'll just worry about Billy."

Ruth placed her hand on Helen's arm. "Is everything all right?"

Helen nodded. "Oh, yes, he's fine. He's just been transferred to a U.S. unit now, the Eighth Air Force, instead of the RAF Eagle Squadron he was in. He's got a new crew and is flying a new plane, so I'm just a little worried about him. He sent me a picture."

Helen pulled a photograph out of her pocket. It showed Billy and his new crew standing in front of a big plane with the name "This Above All" painted on the side.

"Nice, but what's with the name of the plane?"

"All he said was that it was already named before he joined the unit. I'll have to ask him what it means. Anyway, I can't do anything but worry about him, so I'd just as soon take my mind off it, at least tonight."

"So stay for another hour, Lilly, and we'll all go home together."

I knew I was being stubborn, but I just wanted to go home and feel sorry for myself. Why did everything have to be so hard? "No. I'm tired, and I'm going home. I'll catch the bus now, and you two can come home on the later one. I'll see you in the morning."

"It's dark out there, chickie," said Helen. "Do you have a torch?"

"You mean a flashlight?" I picked up my handbag. "Even if I could fit one in this bag, it's not like we've been able to buy batteries for weeks now." I turned to walk away.

Ruth put her hand on my arm. "Wait, Lilly—please. I'll worry about you."

"You could always take my necklace, to give Ruth peace of mind." Helen made to remove it.

"You keep it, Helen. You're worried about Billy, and he needs your luck more than I do. I'm taking the same bus that we take all the time, and I'll pick it up at the plant, like always. I'll be fine."

I turned my back on their protests and headed for the cloakroom. Maybe I'd write to Paul again tonight. He'd understand. I passed several G.I.s on my way out who tried to sweet talk me into another dance, but I kept pushing toward the door. I was tired of this whole night.

Once I made it outside, the cold air was a welcome change, and I didn't even put my coat on for a few minutes. The music from the dance died off quickly, and the cold night seemed hushed.

The bus stop was across the street from the entrance to the Nichols Motors parking lot, so I walked down Second Street from the back of the dance hall toward Front Street, where the parking lot was. While shift change should be happening within the next half hour, the street and parking lot were deserted at this point. I guess I'd never noticed the street lamps in the parking lot weren't working. When we left work at the end of second shift, we all walked down to the bus together and were too busy talking to care about the dark. On my own, however, the dark seemed overwhelming. I blamed the darned war for the lack of proper lighting, along with everything else.

As I approached the back corner of the parking lot, I felt a hand roughly grab my arm, causing me to drop my handbag, and felt a hot, sweaty hand clamp over my mouth. I struggled, trying to pull myself loose, furious that some bum would grab me. I couldn't shake his hand off, so I stomped my foot down on his toes, and he yelped, but his grasp held firm. He pulled me toward the small area of trees and bushes on the back edge of the parking lot. Nobody came out here even in the daytime, never mind at night.

I kept struggling, trying to pull away, trying to get free. This couldn't be real. My mouth was dry, and I felt tears fill my eyes. I tried to scream, but his hand never moved from my mouth, even when I tried to bite it.

"Stop fighting, girly." His voice was harsh and coarse and filled me with dread.

Before I knew what was happening, he had thrown me to the ground, and my head hit hard enough that my vision blurred. It was so dark, I couldn't see anything anyway, but since he'd removed his hand from my mouth, I took a deep breath and was about to scream when he backhanded me across the face.

No one had ever hit me before. I was as shocked as I was hurt, and it really hurt. I couldn't seem to get a grasp on what was happening. How this could be true? He shoved something into my mouth, and I gagged.

He had dropped to his knees over me. He was wearing a dark hat and had a scruffy beard, but I couldn't see much else. He put his hands on my upper arms, pinning me to the ground, even as I continued to struggle. I tried to get my feet under me, to no avail, so I started kicking out with my feet.

"Stop it," he said in a deep, evil whisper. "Stop your kicking, or I'll knock you around a bit more."

That voice was familiar. I felt both queasy and like an electric current went through my body. I couldn't stop shaking and wanted to scream, but I was gagging on the nasty bit of old wool he'd stuffed into my mouth.

He braced his left knee on my thigh, putting so much weight on me that I cried out behind the gag. With his right hand, he pulled apart my coat, ripped my dress, and grabbed my breast through my slip. The rough squeeze hurt so much that, again, I cried out. He simply laughed.

"Not so high and mighty now, are ya?" His low chuckle made my flesh crawl. This couldn't be happening; it mustn't be real.

He slid up the hem of my slip and tore off my underpants, burning the flesh of my legs with the torn elastic. My legs started kicking again of their own accord, and he made good on his promise to hit me again. I bit down on the gag and felt a trickle of what must be blood slide down my left cheek.

"Stop fighting me, bitch!"

He flopped down on top of me, his hand between us working down his zipper. I started to cry in earnest, unable to believe this was really happening, that no one had come to save me. I couldn't swallow the lump in my throat.

Shaking my head back and forth, I cried, "Nooo," behind the gag, and he laughed again.

"You'll like it, just wait 'n' see. You pro'ly never had a real man. Don't know what you're missin', bitch."

I barely had time to register the cold and the pain, to realize what he was doing, when, as quickly as it began, it ended.

And yet…everything had changed.

He stood, placed his left foot on my stomach, and stared down at me. "Don't think of calling the cops, bitch. Everyone knows you asked for it."

I would never forget that voice, or what I could see of his face.

He turned and ran, and I couldn't move, couldn't even speak. I lay there, stunned and battered, mentally curling into myself, trying to make myself believe it had never happened. How could it? This wasn't my life.

Finally, I pulled the dank, wet glove from my mouth and tossed it away. I gingerly sat up and looked down at the tatters of my dress. Even my mother couldn't mend it this time. My mother… Oh, God! I'd have to tell my mother what happened. How could I tell Paul? How could I tell anyone?

I'm not sure how long I sat there, but I finally realized no one was coming to rescue me. Nothing would change until I stood up and started moving. As much as I hurt, it didn't look like I was bleeding, at least not down there. I pulled my slip down and tried to wrap the bits of my dress back around me, although the tatters hung down my scraped and battered legs.

I had just about made it to the bus stop when I heard a car coming. Panic raced through me; if he was coming back, I wasn't going to be sitting there waiting.

I spun around, holding my hands out in front of my face. I wasn't sure how I'd fight back, but I couldn't live through that again.

A truck pulled into the parking lot, one that looked suspiciously like my father's truck. But when a man climbed out, it wasn't my father at all.

"Lilly? Is that you, girl?"

"Leonard?" I dropped my arms, wrapping them around my own waist.

Leonard walked up to me and, as much as I didn't want him to know what had happened, I couldn't stop the tears that came pouring down my face.

"Now, see here, what's the matter?" He looked me up and down, worry creasing his brow. "You're bleeding, child. What's happened?"

The words were stuck in my throat, caught by the lump of tears and shame and fear. I fell into his arms and thanked God that he caught me. He patted my back and held on.

"You're safe now, Lilly. It's okay." He murmured into my hair, his solid, slight but strong frame giving me what I needed to hold on to, to hold me together.

I could feel him turning and saw that he was looking around the parking lot.

His gaze caught mine, and I tried to keep my voice from breaking. "He's gone. At least, I think he is." I looked around, too. "I think he ran off as soon as he…as soon as he…finished."

After a few minutes more of just holding me, Leonard pulled back and looked me over again. He took a handkerchief from his pocket and dabbed at the corner of my lip. He didn't fuss, which would have brought on another rush of tears, but continued to give me his strong arm to lean on.

Without speaking, he put his arm around my shoulders and started walking us toward the truck. When he opened the door to help me climb in, I felt a wave of panic grip me. "Dad…"

"He gave me the truck earlier to come pick up the parts we need to fix the tractor. I stayed in town to meet up with an old buddy for a beer. I thought I might find you gals at the bus stop after your night at the dance hall."

I was glad not to have to face my father yet. What would he think of me?

Leonard helped me into the passenger side of the truck, closed my door, and climbed into the driver's seat. We pulled out onto Front Street, made a couple of turns, and left Beacon Heights behind us. We'd been driving for about five minutes when Leonard finally spoke.

"Do you need the doctor?"

"No. I'm fine."

He sighed. "You're far from fine, Lilly, but you will be." He stared straight ahead. "Do you want to stop at the sheriff's office? Maybe you should talk to the police?"

"No! No! I can't!" That was the last thing I wanted to do. I couldn't bear for the whole town to know what had happened.

"Okay, okay, now. Calm down. We'll go straight home, then."

We drove on for a few more minutes before he cleared his throat. "Do you know who it was?"

I closed my eyes. Even in the dark, with the hat and beard, through the haze of my tears and my fear, I would never forget that face. I swallowed the lump in my throat. "I know."

He nodded, still not turning to look at me.

When we came to a wide section of the road, Leonard pulled the truck to the side and stopped. He finally turned and looked at me, his expression both so gentle and so strong, I couldn't look away. "When you're ready, you tell me who did this to you. I know you're hurting now, but you need to remember that none of this is your fault. You did nothing wrong, child. The man who did this to you is an animal. He hurt your body, but don't let him hurt who you are. Inside. You're stronger than you know, and you can survive this. Don't forget that none of this was your fault. It's all on him."

I couldn't speak, but as the tears slowly slipped from my eyes, I nodded. Leonard gently laid his hand on mine for the briefest moment and then turned back to the road and drove us home.

After Leonard pulled the truck up to the side of the house, he put it in park, came around the truck and opened my door, and offered his arm to me. I hadn't realized how sore I was until then, and I leaned heavily on him to get out of the truck.

"Let's get you into the house." He half walked, half carried me to the back door, helping me up the back stairs.

Although it seemed like forever since I'd left the dance, I realized it was too early for Helen and Ruth to be back yet. It looked like everyone else was sleeping.

I flinched when Leonard tried to help me take off my coat. "No, please."

"Of course," he said quietly. "I'll heat up some water. I expect you'll want to wash up."

"Yes." I walked straight to the bathroom.

"I'll leave the buckets outside the door here when the water is hot."

"Thanks." I closed the door behind me. I didn't want to wake the house, but I needed a bath, with the hottest water I could stand. I wrapped a towel around my shoulders while I waited for the water.

Once Leonard brought the hot water, I filled the claw-foot tub and climbed in. I washed, and washed again, unable to stop the tears or the shaking that wracked my body.

When the water had gone cold, I got out of the tub and picked up the towel. I turned to see my face in the mirror and gasped. Besides the faint red line of blood that still snaked down from my lower lip, there was a bruise already blooming on my left cheek. Add the puffy, red eyes of crying, and I scared even myself. No wonder Leonard had been so gentle with me.

Once I'd combed out my hair, I realized I had nothing to wear. I wanted to burn the rags that used to be my dress, the dirty slip, the tattered stockings. I sank onto the side of the tub, suddenly too tired to stand a moment longer.

I jumped when there was a knock on the door.

"Lilly?"

Oh, no, my mother! Her voice sounded so

tentative. "I'll be done in a minute." Did I sound normal enough?

"I have your robe, honey… Uh, Leonard said you might need it."

I couldn't bear the thought of the look I was going to see in her eyes, but already I knew I'd have to tell her what happened. I opened the door enough for her to hand me the robe. "I'll be right out."

I put on the robe and carried my coat, shoes, and the tattered remains of my dignity back out into the kitchen. I turned and saw Leonard sitting in shadows at the dining room table with a mug in front of him. Mom stood in front of me, her face a study in worry.

"Oh, Lilly." She walked tentatively forward, tears already forming in her eyes, but didn't wrap me in her arms, as I knew she wanted to.

"I'm okay, Mom." I walked past her to the mud room, where I set my shoes on the floor and hung my coat on a hook. I turned and put my pile of tatters into the burn pail and walked back into the kitchen. "It's not as bad as it looks." I tried to smile but failed miserably.

My mother stepped toward me again, her arms held out. I walked into her embrace, and we clung to each other as tears engulfed us both. I didn't have to say anything; she just held me and murmured that nonsensical mom-speak that always comforted me. When I'd cried myself out, yet again, she dropped her arms slowly, and I stepped back.

She coughed and wiped her face with her handkerchief, handing me her spare one. "Leonard warmed up some water; I'll make tea." She turned to the stove, pulled out a mug, and poured hot water. After adding a tea bag, she put the mug on the table and nudged me to sit. Before sitting herself, she pulled down the sugar jar, long banished from the table due to rationing, and added several teaspoons of sugar to my tea. "Here, the sugar will do you good. Drink up."

She took a seat around the corner from me, and we sat in silence, drinking our tea. Every few minutes, she'd put her hand on top of mine and squeeze. It felt like she was trying to will her own strength into me.

We were sitting there, still drinking our tea, when Ruth and Helen walked in. Ruth seemed to know, immediately, that something was wrong and took a seat next to Mom. Helen followed course, taking a seat next to me, and everyone sat in silence, waiting.

"What happened?" Ruth looked from Mom to me, surely able to see the bruises, the cut, and the heartbreak on my face.

Mom took my hand again. "Lilly was attacked."

Ruth and Helen gasped in unison, and Helen put her arm around my shoulder. Mom continued speaking before they could say anything more.

"Leonard found her and brought her home. She didn't want to see a doctor or go to the police, right, Lilly?"

Everyone looked at me, and all I could do was nod. My voice was lost in my shame.

Helen softly hugged me tight, tears in her own eyes. "Oh, Lilly. I'm so sorry. I should have gone with you."

Ruth, agony showing on her face, spoke up. "I'm so sorry, Lilly. If we'd gone with you when you wanted to leave, you would never have been alone. I feel sick that we left you to walk by yourself."

I shook my head. "Please…don't. It's not your

fault."

Ruth stood and walked around Mom, kneeling down at my side. "No, and it's not your fault, either. The only fault is on the man who did this to you."

"I know, I know." I wiped my face and took another sip of tea.

"Did you recognize the bloke, Lilly? Do you know who it was?" Helen leaned in, looking me in the eyes.

I nodded, but couldn't find any words. Once I spoke his name aloud, there was no going back. It would change everything, and I wasn't sure I was ready for that. If my parents knew who'd done this, they'd make me quit work, which didn't actually sound too bad right now. If my father went after him, I was afraid of what might happen. Once the truth came spilling out, I couldn't stop what might happen next.

"Lilly, dear. If you know who did this to you, please tell us. You don't have to talk to the police, but your father could talk to them for you. This man needs to be held accountable for what he did to you." My mother looked so much older and smaller than she ever had before, it just broke my heart.

"Your mother's right, Lilly. He needs to be stopped before he does it to someone else." Ruth had that "savior of the world" look on her face. Just that fast, I'd become one of her causes.

I looked at Helen and saw in her gaze an understanding that Ruth and my mother didn't have. I could tell she'd seen things this terrible before, even if it hadn't happened to her. She had seen the bad side of people in a way that those of us who'd always lived in Upton Falls never had, at least, not until tonight.

She knew that I saw it and spoke from that place.

"If you let it, Lilly, this will eat you up from the inside out." She took my hand in hers. "You don't want people to know. I understand that. And no one outside this house has to. But if you can't share it with those of us who love you, you let it pull you away from your family in a way that you can never get back. Don't give him that power, Lilly. Call him out for what he's done to you, and you take back your power."

I nodded to Helen, tears in my eyes once again. That was just what I needed to hear.

"It was Hank Albert."

Ruth stood up. "Hank Albert? Who is he?"

But Helen was nodding. "That miserable old goat from the maintenance crew at Nichols. He's a pig, he is."

"You work with this man?" asked Mom.

I cleared my throat, trying to keep the incessant tears at bay. "He's 4F due to some deformity of his foot. I think it's made him bitter. He's always nasty, but not just to me. He acts that way to all the women."

Helen agreed. "He acts like he's all that, but he's quite crass. He loves that he's one of the few men there, working with all those women, so he always calls us crude names, makes indecent remarks, and whistles. He's even put his hands on some of the girls, although management would never admit to it."

Mom stood up, walking to the sink with her mug. She turned and looked back at Helen. "What are they thinking over there, letting a man like that work with you women? They should have fired him."

I was waiting to hear my mother say that this was exactly what she had been worried about when I asked to get this job, but she didn't. And from looking at her face, I realized the thought must not have even occured to her.

Suddenly, I felt exhaustion hit me like a wave that nearly pulled me under. My mother knew in an instant and said, “I think Lilly needs to get some sleep. This has been hard on you, honey, and your body needs a chance to heal. Let’s talk about this in the morning.”

Helen and Ruth murmured their agreement, and we all headed up to bed. I thought I heard the back door slam shut as I climbed the stairs, but I decided I must already be dreaming.

## Chapter Seventeen
## Ruth

When I came down to breakfast the next morning, I joined Mom, Pop, and Helen, who were wordlessly gathered around the table with mugs of coffee. Clara had Robert in his high chair with some cold Cherrioats and his bottle and was helping Fred with his breakfast. I picked at the oatmeal Mom had served up, too tired to be hungry. Lilly wasn't down yet, and I hoped she was still sleeping, although if anyone in this house got much sleep last night, other than the children, I'd be shocked.

Mom moved quietly to the table, placing her hand on Pop's shoulder. "Tell her, Earl."

Pop looked down at his hands, tightening them around his mug. "That Albert fella, he's dead."

I inhaled. "What? How do you know?"

His gaze met mine. "Leonard overheard Lilly last night, when she told you all who…uh, who hurt her. He drove back over to Beacon Heights."

I gasped. "What did he do?"

"Good for Leonard," said Helen.

Shaking his head, Pop said, "No, Leonard didn't do anything. He wanted to, I could see that when he told me about it. He's grown fond of Lilly, thinks of her as family. He couldn't get past how she looked when he found her. He was out for blood when he went over there, looking for that fella. But when he found him staggering out of Harvey's Grill, he didn't have to lay a finger on the guy. Once Albert caught sight of Leonard, who probably looked like the Angel of Death, the guy ran like hell in the opposite direction. Leonard said he hadn't even gotten that close when Albert ran right in front of a train."

I nearly dropped my mug. "He's dead?"

Pop just nodded, but Mom spoke up. "The Lord works in mysterious ways, Ruth."

"Fancy that," said Helen, taking a sip of her coffee. "Leonard did us all a favor, he did. Even without laying a finger on the bloke, he made him pay for what he did to Lilly."

"I'm glad Leonard didn't do anything he might regret." I couldn't help but picture Leonard going after that vile man with a shotgun.

"What did Leonard do?"

We all turned to see Lilly standing at the bottom of the kitchen stairs. My heart ached at the sight of her face, covered in ugly bruising. Mom got up quickly and went to her, putting her arms around Lilly's shoulders and walking her to the table.

Pop cleared his throat. "Leonard didn't do anything, honey."

"No," Lilly said, as she pushed away the coffee mug Mom had placed in front of her. "Tell me."

Mom spoke in her soft "don't frighten the horses" voice. "Hank Albert is dead, honey. Leonard saw him get hit by a train last night."

Even her bruises paled. "Leonard saw him? How did Leonard see him get hit by a train?"

Mom sat in the chair next to Lilly, taking Lilly's left hand in her own. "Leonard drove back to Beacon

Heights last night, after he heard you say who attacked you. But when that Albert man saw Leonard, he ran away and ended up running right in front of a train. It wasn't Leonard's fault. It was God's justice, Lilly."

Her shoulders sagged. Lilly said, "I don't know that God had much to do with anything that happened last night, Momma." Although her eyes filled with tears, Lilly wiped them away and straightened up. "At least, with that man dead, no one else ever needs to know what happened."

Pop stood up, put his mug in the sink, and walked to where Lilly was sitting. He put his hand on her shoulder, leaned down, and kissed the top of her head before he strode to the mud room, got his coat, and went back out to the barn.

Robert was busy eating in his high chair. Fred had finished his breakfast and was already climbing down from the table. The rest of us were busy thinking, not eating, but quiet.

Mom placed a bowl of oatmeal in front of Lilly. "I'm not hungry, Mom."

"You need to eat, honey. Your body is healing, and you have to keep up your strength."

She pushed the bowl away. "Just the same, I'm not hungry." She stood up, gingerly. "I'm going to go clean up and then write a letter to Paul."

I stood. "Do you think you might need a little more time to think through what happened before you try to tell Paul about it? You don't want to alarm him more than necessary when there's nothing he can do for you all the way from the Pacific." I could only imagine what a letter like that would do to Jack's morale. Paul deserved to know, but Jack would hate being far away when I needed him.

Lilly turned to look at me. "I'm not writing to Paul to tell him what happened last night. I am writing because I owe him a letter and I want to wish him a Happy Thanksgiving. There's no reason he ever needs to know about this."

"Lilly, you should tell him," Helen said. "That's too big a secret for you to have from your husband."

Helen was right. A secret like that would be awfully hard on a marriage.

"I don't have to tell him, and I'm not going to, Helen. There's nothing to be done about this. It's over, and I want to move on."

She picked up her coffee and took it with her up the stairs.

I shook my head, looking from Mom to Helen. "Maybe she just needs some time to think about this."

"I hope you're right, Ruth," said Mom. "I'd hate to imagine Paul coming home and not knowing why his wife is in so much pain."

Lilly might think it was over because Hank Albert was dead and no one outside our home knew what had happened. The problem was, Lilly knew, and she wasn't going to be able to forget about it just because she wanted to.

****

*My darling Ruth,*

*By the time you get this, I am hoping that we have gained some important ground here in Northern Africa. We have been promised a feast for Thanksgiving, but we have a major push on first. Of course I can't give you specifics, but know that, despite the long days and sore feet, we are making a difference here, and it's the only thing that can even start to make up for being away from you.*

*I'm lucky that we stopped long enough to be able to write to you—we have been moving fast. But the more ground we cover, the sooner this damn war will be over. Fred and Robert are going to need a little cousin to play with, or a dozen of them, so we have some serious work to do. Ha, ha.*

*You are the best morale boost there is for me. Thank you so much for all your letters, and pass along my thanks to Mom and Lilly, too. They really keep me going. I think you're great to write to all those soldiers you meet at the Red Cross. Even if you're my wife, not theirs, any letter from home is welcome. I've handed out some of the pictures your day care kids drew, and you'd be surprised how many of the guys are carrying those pictures along with them. It really means a lot to us all to know that you're all pulling for us back home. But no one loves getting letters from home any more than me. Even when I don't get a new one, I just pull out some old ones and read them over. It's almost as good as being able to talk to you, hold you, kiss you—well, it's not quite as good as that.*

*I think it's great that you have started bringing some of the G.I.s home for Sunday dinners. That may be the last home-cooked meal they have for a long time. I miss those dinners so much, even though I never really thought much about them before the war. It was just part of the week, church followed by chores and Sunday dinner. I appreciate it all the more now that I haven't tasted a good roast chicken or salt potato in months. I can't wait to come home.*

*Well, I'm going to try and get some rest before the*

*war starts getting noisy again. Goodnight, darling, and know that I love you more than anything,*

*Your Jack*

****

I'd reread the letter so many times in the past few weeks. This was our first Thanksgiving apart. I was glad to hear Jack was going to get a chance to celebrate, but I wanted the turkey he ate to be the one his father shot along the back tree line yesterday. I wanted him here, helping Lilly and me pluck the pin feathers. Not that he would do that if he were here, but the thought of it made me smile.

"What are you going on about, Ruth?" Helen was at the sink, peeling potatoes. At least the farm provided us with plenty of potatoes. We'd had to pool our rations tickets, trade potatoes with the O'Briens down the road for some extra sugar and eggs, and get creative with what we were able to scrape together, but at least the potatoes were real.

"She's been smiling like that all day. Maybe she's going round the bend." Lilly elbowed me, and I chuckled.

Once the last of the blasted pin feathers were out, I picked up the slippery bird and carried it to the sink. After giving it a quick rinse, Mom and I arranged the turkey in the roaster pan with some oil, salt, pepper, and herbs from last summer's garden.

"In she goes," I said, sliding the roaster into the oven and closing the door. The pumpkin pie was already out and cooling in the pie safe. Mom was a wizard at adapting recipes, so even with the limited ingredients, it would be delicious.

Lilly took the plates, napkins, and silverware into

the dining room to set the table. Helen watched her leave and then turned to me, whispering, "How do you think she's doing? Has she spoken to you about how she's feeling?"

I shook my head. "I asked her, but she said she's just tired, again. She's trying to act more upbeat because she really loves holidays, but she's definitely down."

"Well, I'm worried about her. Whenever she's not at work, she's sleeping. We had a neighbor, back on Hackney Road, who got the blues so bad after her last baby she wouldn't get out of bed for most of a year. She just kept getting worse and worse, until one night, when her husband and children were sleeping, she walked out of the house and into the Thames. It's scary stuff, it is. I don't want Lilly to fall down a hole that we can't pull her out of."

Mom nodded, wringing her hands. "It's been just over a month. I'm sure she'll snap back with a little more time."

I put my hand on Mom's shoulder. "She might not snap back on her own, Mom. We have to find a way to bring her out of her pain. Let's try to find something for her to get excited about."

"What are you thinking, Ruth? And how can I help?" Helen cut the potatoes and slid them into a pot of cold water.

"I'm going to ask her to take over more responsibility at the day care. I want to get more involved with the Red Cross. They need help organizing blood drives, running programs for troops before they ship out, and welcoming home injured soldiers. I feel like I can really make a difference there, help build the morale of the young men before they ship out. Maybe Lilly will feel the same way about the day care if she takes more responsibility for it."

Helen nodded. "You know I'll do what I can, as well."

I smiled at Helen, realizing how much more open and confident she was these days. Her reading and sewing lessons had really brought out so much more in her. The Andersons had no idea what they were missing. Picking up some glasses, I headed for the dining room.

"Can you help, before I drop these?" I balanced eight water glasses in my arms. Lilly rushed forward to grab a few.

"Thanks." I stopped at the head of the table. "Hey, it looks great in here." Lilly was folding the linen napkins to look like turkeys and had arranged some candles and a selection of leaves and acorns down the center of the table. She'd placed portraits of Jack, Paul, and Billy in front of three of the chairs. "You're really good at this."

She beamed in a way I hadn't seen her do in weeks. "Thanks. It's nothing."

"No, really. This is lovely, and I'm sure it will boost everyone's spirits. Even though we can't be with everyone we love this Thanksgiving, you've reminded us that they are close in our hearts and we have many things to be thankful for." I put down the rest of the glasses and gave her a quick hug. "You're truly thoughtful, Lilly."

She blushed but seemed pleased. "Everything smells so good in the kitchen, I wanted to make it feel like a celebration."

As I placed the glasses before each plate, I turned to her. “I was hoping I could talk to you about something. It’s a bit of a favor.”

She kept arranging the cornucopia centerpiece. “Sure. What do you need?”

“I’d like to take on more responsibility with the Red Cross. Even more than the dances, they need help running blood drives and gathering supplies to send to the troops. I really feel like I can make a difference there, helping soldiers before they ship out and those who have been wounded and shipped home.”

She stopped and looked at me. “But what about the day care? You’re already helping the war effort there.”

I pulled out a side chair and sat. “I know. But lately I feel a stronger pull toward the Red Cross work.”

Lilly chuckled. “I understand.” She shook her head. “You love kids and are a great teacher, but at your core, you want to mother everyone. You can’t bear the thought of our boys going off to war without knowing those of us left behind are cheering them on and, even if they are strangers, we’re waiting for them all to come home.”

“I don’t know…”

She sat across from me. “Think about it, Ruth. You convinced Dad to hire Leonard and move him into the shed and include him in family meals, because you hated to think of him without work or a home. You invited Judith and her children to Thanksgiving dinner today because you couldn’t bear to think of them alone on the holiday so soon after Henry’s death. You take names and addresses from all those soldiers at the dances who have no family or sweetheart to write to them, sending them letters and drawings every week, inviting many to church and Sunday dinner. All because you can't stop yourself from mothering them."

I tilted my head. Did I want to mother the world? No. "It just makes me feel better to tell these boys they aren't alone, to help them in small ways that show they are important."

She shook her head, smiling. "As I said…"

I held up my hand. "With the Red Cross, I can help build up the blood supply, to help wounded soldiers, and collect other supplies."

"Okay, okay." She chuckled. "So what do you want me to do?"

"Would you take on more responsibility at the day care? I'd like for you and Helen to open and run it every day, until it's time for you to catch the bus. I'll volunteer with the Red Cross in the mornings and work through mid-afternoon, then come back to the day care to take over when you gals have to leave. I know it's a big commitment on your part, but you're usually there helping out already. We'd only need a little more of your time."

"Have you talked to Helen about this? She might be the better person for the job. She's a natural with the kids."

"Yes, and I told her I was going to ask you. She said she'd help, but I wanted to be sure it was all right with both of you before I confirmed anything with the Red Cross. I feel so pulled to help there, and I know you two will be great with the children."

"Okay, then. I'll do it."

I stood, but stopped before heading back to the kitchen. "You think you'll be feeling well enough? I know you've been exhausted lately."

"I'm sure the kids will help take my mind off my problems. They are always good for that." She smiled as she stood up. "I'll be fine. Don't worry."

As we walked back into the kitchen, I wasn't sure if she was reassuring me or herself.

****

"You gals have certainly outdone yourselves," said Pop. He pushed his plate away and took one more sip of his coffee. "I haven't said this in recent memory, but I couldn't eat another bite."

Everyone chuckled.

"Well, it wouldn't have been much of a feast without your turkey, Earl." Mom smiled at him, a twinkle in her eye. "And, of course, those great Walker potatoes." It warmed my heart to see such affection between them, after all these years. I hoped Jack and I would be just as happy when we'd been married thirty years.

General murmurs of agreement around the table. "It was dee-licious," announced Kurt loudly, to everyone's amusement.

Judith tried to quiet him, but Helen smiled down at him. "You're right, Kurt. Everything was wonderful. You Yanks really know how to give thanks. I shan't be peckish again for days."

Kurt and Peter giggled at "peckish." Again, Judith tried to quiet the boys, but Mom interceded. She turned to Fred, Kurt, and Peter. "Do you boys want to go outside and play in the snow?" The three jumped up from the table, nearly spilling their chairs to the ground. Mom laughed. "Wait! You have to make sure it's all right with your mothers."

They stopped like little angels, despite the

remnants of dinner on their shirtsleeves and faces. "Can we, Momma?" They almost spoke in unison.

Judith smiled a tired smile. "After you finish your milk, yes, but then wash up and put on your coats, hats, mittens, and boots. And don't track any mud or snow back into the house."

Clara nodded, too. "Show the boys where the sleds are, Freddy, and make sure you keep your hat on."

The three little boys thundered away, and suddenly it felt as if they'd sucked all the air from the room when they left. Marion and Robert were still picking at their food, and the adults took a collective deep breath.

Helen laughed. "Wow, they are busy."

Judith nodded. "Yes, they love your farm. I'm sorry they're so loud, though. And thank you all so much for including us in your holiday."

"We love having you all here. I'm so glad Ruth was able to convince you to join us." Mom put her hand on Judith's arm. "And don't worry about the boys. Fred is thrilled to have someone to play with."

Smiling, Helen said, "Yes, I think it makes the holiday more fun to have you all here. It's my first Thanksgiving, and it seems like a great holiday to me."

"I wasn't sure what kind of Thanksgiving dinner I could pull together for us at home. Besides it's so much better to be with a wonderful family like this."

Pop was having a quiet conversation with his father and Leonard at one end of the table, probably about farm business. Helen and Grandma Walker started talking knitting on the far side. I looked around and smiled, enjoying the group we had brought together to give thanks with us. Robert was covered in mashed potatoes and yams but seemed to be getting some of it into his mouth. He looked up at me and smiled, orange slop oozing down his chin. He reached toward Marion in her high chair, and she laughed. My gaze fell on Jack's picture in front of me, and a tear came to my eyes. He would be enjoying this even more than I was. I physically ached for him to come home.

Everyone lingered over coffee and pie. Mom had done an incredible job making both the apple and pumpkin pies taste almost as good, although not quite as sweet, as normal. I relished the chance to just sit back and watch these people who were so important to me. Despite everything, we had a lot to be thankful for, especially since many of these people were new to our table. I was hoping that Jack got the Thanksgiving dinner they'd been told about.

The next thing we knew, the boys were thundering across the front porch, and the door flew open with a crash. Judith jumped up, already lambasting the boys about muddy footprints.

Peter jumped out of his boots and ran into the dining room, bypassing his mother's grasp and stopping in front of Pop, with Kurt and Fred right behind him.

"Where's the fire, young man?" Pop chuckled.

Breathless, Peter spoke to the whole table, his gaze flying to each of us in turn. "The Union man is here. We saw him. He's coming up the driveway. Come, quick."

A chill instantly enveloped me, with shivers running down my arms. The Western Union man. A lump formed somewhere between my heart and my throat. I could see everything around me slow down. Helen didn't move, nor did Lilly. The news would be life-shattering for at least one of us.

Judith went to Peter and wrapped her arm around his shoulders, ushering him into the living room. Tears were already streaking down her face, the memory of her own worst day fresh in her mind. Leonard stood and walked to the front door, while the rest of us remained frozen in our seats. No one spoke, and I couldn't bring myself to look at anyone. Fear had a hold on me in a way that had my heart racing. Only Robert and Marion made any noise at all.

We heard the door close and waited. I was afraid to move or even look up. Helen reached over and took my hand, each of us holding on in fear. I reached for Mom and she for Lilly, making a chain of hope, unable to escape our anxiety.

When Leonard stepped into the room, the temperature dropped. I looked into his eyes and felt the world tilt as I tried to rise. He nodded slightly, tears in his own eyes, and my heart shattered. "Jack…"

Helen's arms encircled me, lowering me back into my chair.

Leonard walked to me, placing the hated yellow envelope in front of me. I looked down, almost unable to pick it up, but I couldn't stand the obscenity of it lying in front of Jack's picture.

As I held the envelope, my cold fingers shook, and the delicious feast I'd consumed threatened to come back up, but I slid my index finger under the flap and forced the reluctant glue to give way. I inched the telegram out of the envelope and couldn't stop my eyes from scanning the type, seeing the four black stars, even as the bottom dropped out of my world.

DEEPEST REGRET… KILLED IN ACTION… MOROCCO…

I couldn't move or take my gaze off the silent death knell in front of me. I could see movement and hear cries around me, but the world folded in on itself and everything went black.

## Chapter Eighteen
## Helen

"Can I talk to you for a moment?" Lilly pulled her chair in close, whispering her words to me.

"Of course, love. What's on your mind?" We were sitting at the small card table in the church basement where we ate our lunch, whilst the children had a little lie-down.

Her eyes instantly became red, but no tears flowed. She seemed to struggle with emotion, took a deep breath, cleared her throat, and then pushed on.

"I don't know what to do, Helen. I…I can't talk to Ruth, not now. It's only been a few weeks since Jack's death and she's still in mourning. But this is just too much. I don't think I can put it off much longer."

I sat still, waiting.

She lowered her voice even further, so that I had to lean in to hear her. "I think I might be pregnant."

A single tear ran down her cheek. I reached out and squeezed her hand.

"Oh, Lilly. Are you sure?" I knew she'd been sluggish and not herself ever since she'd been attacked, but I hadn't considered this possibility.

She nodded. "What am I going to do?" Raising her hands to cover her eyes, she leaned forward on her elbows and shook her head. "No one outside the family knows about the…well, you know. What will everyone think of me? What will Paul think?"

She clasped her hands together, as if in prayer, leaning her head on her crossed thumbs. "Today should be our six-month anniversary. Instead of celebrating with me, he's somewhere six thousand miles away. Isn't that hard enough? But now…a baby?" She shook her head, trying to keep her voice low. "I can't just write him a letter and say, 'By the way, I'm going to have a baby, but don't worry, the father is dead.' "

Wrapping my arm around her shoulders, I pulled her close. "I'm so sorry, love. This is unfair to you."

She cried in earnest now. "It's more than unfair. It's obscene. How can I possibly have that man's baby? What will I do, Helen? I just can't bear it."

I let her cry. What could I say? It was unfair and awful, and it might scare Paul away. He didn't know about the attack. Lilly had been adamant that he never needed to know, at least not while they were so far apart. They'd hardly had a chance to get to know each other before they got married, hadn't really had much time to make a baby of their own. The child of a rapist would be hard for the strongest marriage to survive.

"Have you talked to your mother about this yet?"

She shook her head, still against my shoulder. "I haven't told anyone else. Mom is worried about Ruth and still so sad about Jack herself."

When Ruth fainted on Thanksgiving, Earl had carried her to bed, and she slept for fourteen hours. The next day, she'd hung the black flag in the window and jumped into her life again as if nothing had happened. In the weeks since, she had hardly slept at all. During the days, Ruth entrusted the day care to us and spent hours devoting herself to the Red Cross and the needs of other women's husbands, as she put it. In the evenings, she devoted herself to helping around the farm, unwilling to fall apart, wearing herself out. After everyone went to sleep at night, Ruth was up late writing letters to all the soldiers she'd met. She'd even recruited other volunteers to join in her letter-writing campaign. We had soldiers and sailors at dinner every Sunday. She seemed to be consumed with the idea of keeping them all alive, as if that could somehow make up for Jack's death. I was worried she was working herself to an early grave.

But poor Lilly.

"We can speak to your mother tomorrow before we come here, if you'd like. If you want me there. Or I can head out early, open up the day care on my own, and leave you some privacy."

Lilly sat up, nodding and wiping her face on her handkerchief. "Okay. I think it would be easier if you're there too. But what am I going to do, Helen?" Her sad eyes looked up to me, the weight of the world crushing her.

"What do you want to do, Lilly?"

She shook her head slowly. "What do you mean? What I want is to not be pregnant with that man's baby. That's what I want." She started to raise her voice. "Do you have a magic wand to make that so? Do you think that lucky necklace of yours is strong enough to undo what happened to me?"

I took a deep breath, putting my hand on her arm and squeezing slightly until she looked me in the eye. "There are ways to end a pregnancy that have nothing to do with my necklace or luck of any kind. Do you want to think about that option?"

Lilly started to answer but seemed to stop herself, fresh tears filling her eyes. "Oh."

I nodded. "It's possible, but it can be dangerous, as you surely remember."

"You're talking about Cindy Douglas, right?" Tears streamed down her face.

"Yes. That's the woman who died trying to get rid of a baby, isn't it?"

Lilly's hands covered her mouth, and she bent at the waist, laying her head on her knees, her shoulders shaking. I put my hand on her back, rubbing slowly.

Finally, Lilly looked up, her eyes red, her face ravaged. "Oh, my God. This is what she went through, isn't it? She had to choose to have a baby that wasn't her husband's or risk her life to get rid of it."

I looked down, thinking of the women I'd known, growing up, who had died or been severely injured making that choice. It was so unfair to Lilly, to any woman facing that kind of decision.

She touched my arm. "I understand what you and Ruth were talking about now. She made her choice and paid for it with her life." She took a deep breath. "Oh, that poor woman."

I wrapped my arm around Lilly's shoulder. "You don't have to make up your mind now, Lilly. You can't wait too long, but you should probably take some time to think about it."

Lilly sat back up, pulling away. "No," she shook her head. "I already know. Whatever Cindy felt was right for her, I know what's right for me." She looked down, visibly swallowed, and then looked me straight in the eyes. "I'm having this baby. I couldn't kill this child, who did nothing wrong, just because the father was a monster. I can't do it."

I nodded, reaching out to hold her hand.

"Well, if you're going to have a baby, then you'll have a baby." She looked surprised and more than a little cross at me. "You're right, none of this is the fault of that baby. Nor is it your fault, and it's not Paul's fault. It's just the situation you find yourself in, and yes, it's terribly unfair, but we have to deal with what it is."

I smoothed her hair with my palm and left my hand on her back. "We can come up with something to tell the nosey-nellies. We'll just have to give it some thought. And you've got about six months to figure out how to tell Paul."

"I can't…"

I nodded. "You can, and you will. He loves you, Lilly. You've not done anything wrong, and he'll understand that. He'll be angry for you, not at you. Give him some credit there, love. The chap's mad about you."

Her shoulders sagged; her breathing hitched; the tears continued. Life is hard sometimes, and even nice girls from good families aren't exempt.

I rubbed her back a bit. "We'll talk to your mum, and then you can tell Ruth. Even though you're all still mourning Jack's death, the promise of new life might be just what everyone needs." I reached back and unhooked my necklace, then fastened it around Lilly's neck.

She gave me a quizzical look.

"It can't hurt, right? I think you deserve a little extra luck right about now."

As her crying stopped, Lilly pulled herself up and wiped her face again. She sighed. "I'm going to give my notice at Nichols."

I thought for a moment and then nodded. "Good idea. It's safer for you and the baby here, and given Ruth's long hours with the Red Cross, it makes sense for you to take over altogether."

She straightened. "You'll continue to help, won't you?"

Smiling, I said, "Of course, for whatever it's worth."

She looked me straight in the eyes. "You say you don't like taking care of other people's children, but you are a natural, Helen. The children love you, and not just Peter and Kurt. You are so patient and kind with them, and you have a great way of making them laugh."

I couldn't help but look away. Of course I made them laugh. They'd surely never seen a woman as large or clumsy, never mind one who talked funny. "It's probably just the years of child-minding I've done, between my own brothers and sister and the Smith-Burton children."

"Children can always spot a fake, Helen. They know you really care about them."

I touched my hand to my cheek; my face felt warm. "I never said I didn't like children. I just got tired of doing nothing else."

Lilly nodded.

"Never mind about that. Right now, we need to concentrate on what's best for you and your baby. You can give your notice at Nichols tonight and then talk to your mum tomorrow morning. You can decide when and what to write to Paul, when you're ready. You'll see, everything will work out."

****

*April 30, 1943*
*My dearest Billy,*

*I hope you got the package I sent by now. I know you can use the extra socks, new shirts, and underpants, as you call them, and hope you enjoy the chocolate, and the pictures Kurt and Peter drew for you. They love to pretend to be you in your plane, pretending to shoot Nazi planes from the skies. I don't reckon this is the best children's game, but I don't have the heart to make them stop. At least you get some colorful pictures of planes to share with your mates.*

*Judith seems to be doing pretty well with her children again, although poor little Marion has had a bad cold for days. Judith is still sad, of course, but she brings the children to day care every day before she heads off to work. She has even become friends with some of the neighbors who helped when Henry was killed. The family is healing.*

*All is as well here as can be expected. Lilly is healthy but still hasn't written to tell Paul she's pregnant. She acts like she won't have to tell him, although she can't possibly believe that. At least she seems to be more excited about the baby these days. She's getting much more comfortable with the babies at day care, which can only be a good thing.*

*She's frantic at the moment, though, as she's misplaced my "lucky" necklace. I loaned it to her for a little extra courage in telling her parents about the baby, but somewhere along the way, she took it off, and now she can't find it. I'm sure it'll turn up—otherwise it wouldn't be so lucky, now, would it?*

*I'm still worried about Ruth. She puts everything she has into helping at the Red Cross, keeps frightfully busy, and hasn't really mourned Jack's death. She's wearing herself out and hardly sleeping. The only time I see her sit still is when we sit down to Sunday dinner, usually with half a dozen young men she's brought home. She wants them to have a good home-cooked meal with the family before they head off to war. I know she feels useful at the Red Cross, and I'm sure she's helping a lot of people, but I don't think she's properly come to terms with Jack's death.*

*Work is fine, thanks for asking. I'm glad to be able to contribute to the household earnings, especially as meat, oil, petrol, and even lard are becoming so much harder to buy. With Ruth constantly bringing any lost soul home for a meal, we need every last penny, and rations card, we can get.*

*I dream about the day you come home and can't wait. Please keep yourself safe for me. All my love is forever yours—Helen*

****

"Are you two ready to go?" Ruth came down the stairs to the kitchen, where Lilly and I were sitting at the kitchen table. The three of us had plans to go to town together to pick up the ham for tomorrow's Easter dinner, which Julia had ordered two weeks ago. We'd saved up as many rations tickets as possible to make this a nice holiday celebration.

"Are we ready? We're waiting for you, slowpoke." Lilly laughed, getting slowly to her feet. She was conspicuously pregnant these days, although she still had nearly two and a half months to go before the baby was due.

"Ha, ha," said Ruth, as we grabbed our pocketbooks and jackets and took off down the back stairs.

Julia opened the back door, leaning out. "Don't forget to stop at the O'Briens' house for more eggs on the way home. I called, and Minerva will have them waiting for you."

"Okay, Mom," Lilly called back. "We won't forget."

Lilly held her arms out, leaning her head back as we walked down the driveway toward town. "It's finally a warm day. I thought winter would last forever."

"You're right. The sun's smashing," I said. "I can't remember the last Saturday that was sunny and warm."

As we made our way through town, we headed first to the drugstore to check a few things off our list. I was looking for foot powder to send to Billy, who had asked for it in his last letter.

"Why don't I save us some time and run to the market for the ham while you two shop at the drugstore?" said Ruth. "I'll meet you back here."

"Okay," said Lilly, reaching for the door handle as Ruth took off down Second Street.

As Lilly pulled open the door, her friends Ginny and Ava rushed out the door, nearly running into Lilly.

Lilly hadn't seen much of her friends since she'd stopped working at Nichols after her attack.

"Oh, hi, girls. It's nice to see you." Lilly smiled a hesitant smile, holding her pocketbook in front of her pregnant belly.

"Lilly," said Ginny. "How are you? I haven't seen you in so long. How's the day care job?"

"It's good…" Lilly started, but was interrupted by Ava.

"Oh, my God, Ginny. She's pregnant!" Ava was almost yelling and blocking the doorway.

I motioned to the side. "Ladies, why don't you step to the side so people can get through the door?" I thought about offering to do the shopping for Lilly, but based on Ava's attitude, I didn't want to leave Lilly alone with her friends.

Ginny looked at Lilly, first her face and then her belly. "Oh…"

I put my hand on Lilly's back, hoping she could feel my support.

"The day care is going wonderfully, Ginny, thanks for asking. I love it there."

"How could you cheat on your husband when he's off at war?" Ava shouted. I noticed some of the passersby were slowing down as they walked near us.

"Ava, please lower your voice. You're making a scene." Lilly spoke softly and slowly, her voice somehow sounding thinner.

Ava stepped back, moving farther from Lilly and me. "You're the one creating a scene, Lilly. You're married, remember? Your husband has been gone for what, ten, eleven months?"

"It'll be a year in July," said Ginny, softly.

"Well, he's been gone longer than you are pregnant, that much is clear." Again, Ava was shouting, her lips curled back and her expression one of triumph and hatred at the same time.

"That's enough, Ava," I said as I wrapped my arm around Lilly's shoulders. I was trying to get her to back up and turn around, anything to get away from Ava.

Ginny stepped forward, closer to Lilly. "Are you okay, Lilly?"

Lilly just nodded, her eyes already rimmed in red.

"Why haven't I heard from you in so long? I thought you were mad at me."

Lilly shook her head, unable to speak.

Ava laughed—scoffed, really. "She hasn't been mad at you, Ginny. Don't be stupid. She's been spending her time with some man. Someone who isn't her husband; the father of that baby."

Ava turned her back to Lilly but continued to berate her.

"My mother won't allow me to associate with the likes of you anymore, that's for sure. Come on, Ginny. Let's go." Again Ava laughed, but it was a horrid sound.

"You need to leave, Ava. Lilly does not deserve to be spoken to like that." I took a step toward Ava, but Lilly put her hand out, drawing me back.

"It doesn't matter, Helen," she said sadly.

"Come on, Ginny!" Ava was shouting at Ginny now, but Ginny didn't move.

"Go, Ava. I'm not going with you. Just go." Ginny didn't raise her voice or confront Ava, but her calm, cool tone of voice was compelling.

"You can't be serious, Ginny. Don't you understand what she is? What she's done?" Ava turned back, venom nearly seething from her gaze.

Ginny turned, standing between Lilly and Ava. "Go, Ava. And don't say another word."

Ginny turned, took Lilly's arm, and walked with her into the drugstore. Ava seemed to want to follow, but I crossed my arms over my chest, staring down at her, blocking the doorway.

She said "Hmphf," turned, and stalked away.

I was so angry I was shaking, but I took a deep breath and tried to calm myself before I went into the store.

Ginny and Lilly were sitting at a small table near the soda fountain. Lilly had tears in her eyes when I approached, but they were both quiet.

"Are you okay?" I looked from Lilly to Ginny and back.

"Yes, I'm fine."

Ginny reached out and placed a hand over Lilly's hand. "I'm so sorry, Lilly. I can't believe she acted like that. I thought she was your friend."

Lilly looked at Ginny, as a tear escaped down her cheek. "No, I guess she's never been a real friend, Ginny. Not like you."

I left the two of them alone and went to pick up the items we needed. I'd have to tell Ruth what happened, if Lilly didn't, but there wasn't much any of us could do to protect her from the remarks of people like Ava. Lilly had insisted no one should know about her attack, so she had left herself open to innuendo and gossip.

When I'd checked out, Lilly and I started to the market to find Ruth, while Ginny went on with her shopping. As soon as we were alone, I put an arm around Lilly's shoulders, squeezing slightly before releasing her.

"Are you okay?"

Lilly nodded but hesitated before speaking. "I guess I shouldn't have been surprised that somebody said those things to me, although I never expected it to be Ava."

We walked along the street, talking softly. "I'm sorry she was so cruel to you, Lilly. You know you didn't deserve that attack."

"I know," she said, her voice strained. "I don't want Ava to know what happened, or anyone else, for that matter, but I guess I was hoping I wouldn't become such a topic of conversation."

I smiled sadly, shaking my head. "You have to know how naïve that sounds, right? It's a small town, and people are going to know you're pregnant. They're going to speculate on who the father is. It's just human nature."

Her eyes grew red again, but she didn't cry. "I know. If it was someone else's life, I'd probably be right there with Ava, wondering what the story was. I guess it took an awful thing happening to me for me to grow up and learn to give people the benefit of the doubt."

I linked my arm through hers. "Ava is immature, but luckily you have a good friend in Ginny."

She smiled up at me. "And in you, Helen."

I looked up, and Ruth was standing in front of us. "Is everything okay?"

I took the heavy ham and gave her the bag from the drugstore. "Lilly's just had a bit of a row with Ava."

Ruth fell into step next to Lilly. "What do you mean? What happened?"

I started to answer, but Lilly held up her hand. "We ran into Ginny and Ava, and when Ava realized I was pregnant, she said several mean and heartless things about me and my baby."

Ruth stopped, pulling Lilly into a brief hug. "Oh, honey, I'm so sorry. I know people can be cruel, but I wouldn't have expected it from one of your friends."

"Former friend," said Lilly. "But at least Ginny

was kind and told Ava to leave us alone. She didn't ask me any questions, although I could tell she was wondering about…the father. But she kept her questions to herself."

Ruth nodded. "Good."

We continued toward the farm, Ruth's arm linked with Lilly's, and Lilly's other arm linked with mine. I had never had girlfriends like Ruth and Lilly before, and I was grateful to have found them.

****

"I think Robert caught that bug Freddy has," said Ruth. She was standing in the kitchen, holding Robert in her arms, swaying back and forth and jiggling him. I hadn't expected anyone to be up when I got home from work.

"At least three of the children have been out sick every day for the past week." I walked to the sink to clean out my lunch pail. "And even still, probably another two or three should have stayed home as well, but the mothers have no one to stay with them. This is no summer cold. It's got to be something more."

"He's so hot, poor baby. Clara just couldn't get him to settle down, so I told her I'd try. She's got her hands full with Fred. Every time I think Robert's finally going to sleep, the cough wakes him back up."

I walked to the baby, placing a kiss on the crown of his head. "He does feel warm." I looked into Ruth's bloodshot eyes and placed the back of my hand on her forehead. "And so do you. I think you need some rest, too, Ruth."

"I'm fine; just tired. I feel so bad for the kids."

Robert suddenly lifted his sweaty head, looked me in the eye, turned away, and laid his head on Ruth's other shoulder.

"I know, but you have to take care of yourself before you're too sick to get out of bed yourself."

She nodded, leaning her cheek on the back of Robert's head. "I told Clara I was going to see if I could take him into bed with me; maybe we'll both be able to sleep."

"Why don't you sleep in my room? I'll share with Lilly while you two are sick."

Ruth looked exhausted but grateful. She nodded and whispered, "Thank you," as she started to climb the stairs.

I followed them upstairs to gather my nightgown, robe, and clothes for the next day from my room, hoping they would sleep late in the morning. Unfortunately, it didn't work out that way.

Less than four hours later, I woke from a deep sleep, disoriented and anxious. It took me a moment to remember that I wasn't in my own room. I realized what had awoken me sounded like crying coming from the base of the stairs. I slipped from bed, sliding my feet into my slippers and grabbing my bathrobe. Lilly's side of the bed was already empty.

When I got to the bottom of the stairs, properly awake, the sour smell of sick struck me first, with an overlying whiff of menthol. I heard crying and moaning, both soft and weak, and saw Lilly run from the bathroom with a basin and towels.

"Oh!" She nearly stopped in her tracks at the sight of me, but then started bustling across the kitchen again.

I fell into step behind her, following her into the mud room.

"What's wrong? What can I do to help?"

"They're both so sick," she motioned with her head toward the bathroom. "It's much more than just a cold. This must be influenza."

"Oh, no."

There had been an epidemic of influenza in the county last year, leaving a couple of children and one elderly woman dead.

Lilly cleaned out the basin, and I pulled fresh towels off the pile of clean laundry. "How can you be sure?"

She turned to me, a grim expression on her face. "Mom said she thinks this is the flu. She was one of the women from church who helped nurse old Mrs. Matthews last winter when she got influenza. Robert is as weak as a lamb from vomiting and diarrhea, and Fred is having trouble catching his breath. Even Ruth is pale, shivering, and sweating, but she won't stay in bed and let us tend to her."

While Lilly took the fresh towels and clean basin into the bathroom, I stayed in the kitchen and put water on to boil, for both laundry and tea. Even if Ruth wasn't able to keep it down, if we had influenza in the house, Julia, Clara, Lilly, and I would need something to keep us going.

I set a tub of linens to soak and started cleaning up the kitchen. Growing up, whenever one of the kids got sick, they all did. At least until I became a frightfully serious cleaner. Mum used to yell that I was wasting my time, but it seemed to me that the more time I spent cleaning crockery, sinks, cutlery, and linens, the less time I spent cleaning up after sick children.

Eventually, Julia came out of the bathroom

carrying Robert, who lay limp and listless in her arms. She carried him to the old wooden rocking chair, singing softly. Lilly supported much of Ruth's weight as the two walked from the bathroom to the sofa in the parlor. The faintest gold and apricot rays of early morning sun began to stream in the windows, promising a better day than we'd had a night.

I carried a tray of mugs filled with tea and a plate with some dry toast into the parlor. After setting it down on the side table, I returned to the kitchen for a cool cloth for Ruth's head. She was still shivering, but her face was flushed and feverish. Robert was no longer flushed but sadly pale and pasty. Each breath seemed to take all the energy he could muster and caused such a rattle in his chest that it made my own lungs hurt to hear it. Clara came down the stairs, dressed for the day. Fortunately, she reported that Fred was through the worst of it and seemed to be coming round again. Clara grabbed clean linens and headed back upstairs to strip the bed.

Lilly covered Ruth with an afghan. I placed a mug of tea within Julia's reach and then picked up mine and followed Lilly back into the kitchen.

Lilly pulled out a chair and lowered herself into it, weariness and worry battling for purchase on her face. I sat across from her.

"Did you get any sleep at all?" Lilly had been asleep when I climbed into bed. I had no idea how long she'd been there, nor did I waken at whatever time she'd gotten up.

"Sure. I went to bed not long after Ruth put Robert down, around 9:30 last night. Sadly, he was so fussy he just couldn't stay asleep. But how did you end up in our bed?"

"Ruth was trying to get Robert back to sleep when I got home from work. When she decided to take him to bed with her, I sent her to my bed, so they'd be more comfortable and also so you'd have less chance of catching what they have."

"Thanks, but I'm sure I'll be fine. You're the one who has two jobs every day; you should go get some more sleep."

I smiled. I wasn't the pregnant one. "Thanks, but you need the sleep. You have two jobs too—running the day care and growing a person."

Lilly laughed, snorting out the tea she'd been in the midst of swallowing. "Okay, so we both need our sleep. And neither of us wants to get the flu. Which reminds me," she said, as she reached into her pocket, "I finally found your lucky necklace."

She held it out to me, so I took it.

"Right, thanks. But I want you to wear it. We definitely don't want the expectant mother to catch the flu." I took the necklace, stood, and walked around behind her to drape the necklace around her neck and fasten it.

She rested a hand on it. "Thanks. I'll take all the luck I can get right now."

I walked to the sink. "I'm going to start cleaning up, especially in the bathroom. I want to freshen up my room so Ruth and Robert can keep on sleeping in there. I think Clara has had her hands full with Fred and the bed linens." I filled a bucket with soapy water. "If you don't mind, when you go up to get dressed, if Ruth and Robert are still down here, why don't you open the window in that bedroom, get some fresh air in there?"

"Sure thing." She slowly pulled herself to her feet, handed me her mug, and headed to the stairs. When she put her foot on the bottom step, she turned back to me and whispered, "Do you think they'll be all right? I mean, we don't have anything to worry about, do we?"

As I walked toward the bathroom with the bucket, I stopped near Lilly. "Let's see what the doctor says, when he gets here. I think Ruth will be fine, but Robert worries me. He's so listless and pale, and he's been fighting this longer than she has. I hope the doctor has something for the little fellow to ease his breathing and quiet his cough."

Lilly nodded and turned, climbing the stairs. It would be lovely to say we'd nothing to worry about, but I'd seen too many sick children take a turn for the worst to ignore the dangers of influenza.

Once I'd scrubbed the bathroom, bedroom, and kitchen, I got myself dressed, ate a quick breakfast, and headed off to the day care with Lilly. It was going to be a long day, but I couldn't get Ruth and Robert out of my thoughts.

****

Over the course of the next two days, Ruth's symptoms got worse, but Robert's didn't seem to change at all. We had quite a time trying to get Ruth to stay in bed and rest, convincing her to let the rest of us take care of Robert. Clara also seemed to have developed a slight case of the flu, but fortunately she wasn't nearly as sick as Ruth. Julia and I tried to get them all to eat, or at least take a little broth. Clara was best able to keep food down, and Ruth tried, reluctantly, although she said her throat was so raw she had trouble swallowing. Poor little Robert just lay still and let Julia pour broth into his mouth, but he wouldn't take even a watered-down bottle anymore.

I did my best to keep the house as clean as possible, leaving Julia to mind the sick beds and Lilly to handle the cooking. I tried to help Julia as much as I could, when I was home, keeping pregnant Lilly away from the flu. When Julia was making breakfast for everyone, I went to check on Ruth.

"Good morning, luv. How are you feeling today?" I adjusted her covers, refilled the water glass on her nightstand, and helped her to a sitting position. She was still weak but seemed to be on the mend.

"This thing has really knocked me for a loop," she answered weakly. Suddenly her eyes filled with tears.

I sat on the edge of her bed. "Are you feeling worse? Should I call the doctor?" I handed her a handkerchief.

She shook her head and grabbed my hand, squeezing tight, but didn't seem to be able to speak.

"What is it, Ruth? What do you need?"

Finally, she blew her nose and looked up at me. "Being sick in bed, not doing anything, has given me too much time to…" She gulped. "To think about Jack." She cried in earnest now, so I wrapped my arms around her.

This was bound to happen. She had merely been putting it off, with all her volunteer work and helping everyone else. Lilly and I had been worried about her.

She leaned her head on my shoulder and sobbed. After several minutes, her tears began to quiet, and she sat up again.

"I know he's gone, and I thought I was dealing with it, but I guess I didn't want to cry for fear I would never stop."

I tucked the blankets around her and then handed her the glass of water. "You have every right to cry, Ruth. You've lost the man you love. I think you needed to cry, and you may need to cry some more, in order to get over the pain."

She nodded. "I was trying so hard to keep busy with the Red Cross and all my volunteer work and chores around here. It helped keep the pain at bay if I didn't have a lot of quiet time to think about him. But lying in this bed for the past few days, I've done little else." She crumpled the handkerchief with her fingers. "How am I going to live without Jack?"

I ran my left hand along her arm and took her right hand in mine. "You'll live, Ruth. That's all you can do." I couldn't imagine how I would go on if anything happened to Billy. "The work you're doing at the Red Cross is important, and it's good to be helping others. But you have to take time, even quiet moments before you fall asleep at night, to mourn your husband, even as you learn to go on without him."

She looked down at our hands and then ran her left hand over the top of mine. "I know you're right, Helen. I can't pretend I have nothing to mourn, and I can't keep myself too busy and tired to deal with my grief. Maybe trying to do that is why I got sick in the first place."

I nodded. "So now you need to get better so you can get back to the important work you've been doing, but also be gentle with yourself and realize that mourning Jack will take over sometimes. You'll have to take a break now and then and allow yourself to feel what you feel."

Her smile was as weak and sad as she was. "You're a good friend, Helen." She leaned back against her pillows, the tears obviously exhausting her again.

"Now, tell me, how are the kids and Clara?"

As I sat on the edge of her bed, I tried not to sit on her. "Clara and Fred are definitely better. I'd say Freddy is practically back to his old self. Robert, however, seems to have got the worst of the lot. The poor thing is weak and listless."

She sat up again in alarm but didn't have the strength to do anything more. "Has the doctor seen him lately? When was he here last?"

I gently pushed her back into her pillows. "Doc Lawrence says the listlessness is to be expected, but Robert should be fine. He says Robert's over the worst of it, and I pray he's right. I'm hoping Lilly doesn't get it. Between the four of you sick here and all the sick children at the day care, she'll be lucky if she doesn't come down with the flu herself. And she's so close to her time now, I don't think it would be good for her."

"True. Has she been feeling okay? I mean, she's not having any contractions or anything, is she?"

I shook my head. "Not that I know of."

Ruth nodded. "The baby is coming soon, so she's going to have to find a way to tell Paul about the baby. I can't believe she hasn't written him about this whole situation." Ruth adjusted her blankets and took a sip of water. "If he loves her as much as he says, he'll find a way to be there for her, to convince her it's not her fault."

"And to love this baby as his own." This was part of my prayers every night, but I hadn't dared to say it out loud before.

"Yes, for all their sakes, I hope he's man enough to be a father to this baby when he comes home."

Clara stepped into the doorway, a limp, pale Robert in her arms.

"Mom asked me to find you, Helen. It looks like Lilly is getting sick, and so she's hoping you'll finish making supper while Mom calls Doc Lawrence again and gets Lilly tucked into bed. Oh, and she asked if you would mind if Lilly is in your bed."

"Of course not." I jumped up and looked at Ruth. "Do you need anything before I go back downstairs?"

She shook her head. "I'm just going to rest a while longer, but don't worry about me. I'll come down if I need anything. I'm tired right now, but I'm feeling much better." She smiled at me as I moved to the door. "Just let me know what the doctor has to say about Lilly when he comes."

****

When Doc Lawrence got to the house, he took a look at Robert first, to make sure he was recovering as expected. Then he followed Julia into Lilly's room. I tried not to worry as I finished cleaning up from supper. I kept a plate hot for the doctor and made some more coffee. The flu was all over town, and he was busy.

When Julia and Doc Lawrence came back down to the kitchen, neither looked too worried, so I let out a deep breath and offered him some supper.

"Why, I don't mind if I do." He sat down at the kitchen table and took a long drink of the coffee. "Thank you so much. It's been a long day."

I turned to Julia, unable to wait a moment longer for an update. "How's Lilly?"

Julia smiled. "She doesn't have the flu, thank the

Lord."

I hugged Julia, releasing another deep breath. Then I refilled the doctor's coffee, turning back to Julia. "So, was she just tired? I told her she needs to let me take over more of the work at the day care. She's doing too much for a woman in her condition."

Julia put her hand on my shoulder. "According to the doctor, she won't be in that condition much longer."

I dropped the towel I'd been holding. "The baby? She's in labor?"

Doc Lawrence nodded, his mouth full of peas. "My, this is good." He swallowed. "Sorry about that, I didn't realize how hungry I was." He took a sip of coffee. "Yes, she's in labor, although it's still early on. I expect it will be well into the morning before that baby comes."

He turned back to his plate, humming slightly.

"What do you need me to do, Julia? Would you like me to go sit with her for a while? I haven't had any babies myself, but I certainly helped my mum enough times to be able to do whatever needs doing."

Julia nodded. "Thank you, Helen; that would be wonderful. I know Lilly would like to have you with her right now, especially with Ruth still sick and Clara busy with the boys. I'll call the midwife and let her know we're in for a long night. I'll come in when the midwife gets here, so you can get some sleep."

"I'll be fine, Julia. Why don't you rest for a while, and I'll come get you if it looks like the baby's coming quicker than we expect. I'm awake now anyway. I can rest later."

Julia stopped in the living room to let Earl and Leonard know what was up, and they walked the doctor out, once he'd eaten his fill. He mentioned that he had several more stops to make that night. It seemed that some people in town weren't recovering from this flu outbreak as quickly as the Walkers were.

I poured myself another cup of coffee, filled a pitcher with water to take upstairs to the various sick rooms, and popped into Ruth's room to fill her in on the impending delivery. After I brought her the happy soon-to-be news, I went back to my own room to sit with Lilly. And wait. There was always a lot of waiting when it came to babies being born.

## Chapter Nineteen
Lilly

"I can't do this anymore. I'm done."

"You can do it, Lilly. I know you can." Helen grasped my right hand in hers, reaching up to wipe the hair from my face with her left hand. "You're almost there, luv. Besides, you're wearing my lucky necklace. You can't go wrong."

"I'm not feeling too lucky right now, thanks."

Even with Mom and Helen cheering me on, I was never going to be able to do this. I was too tired after a long night with no sleep and a long day of hip-wrenching pain. Every part of me hurt, even my hair.

Poor Helen had no bed to sleep in, as I was spread out on hers, the green chenille bedspread folded on top of her dresser and the blankets bunched up at the end of the bed. Throughout the night, I'd alternately thrown the wrinkled white top sheet off and then pulled it back on. I wasn't comfortable in any way, including temperature.

No one told me labor was going to feel like I had plow horses tied to each hip bone, pulling in opposite directions. My back had exploded in pain, and I just didn't have any strength left. How did women do this over and over again? Why had no one told me it was going to be like this?

Mom walked in with clean towels and placed a

cool, damp cloth on my head. I shook it off just as soon as she did. "That's not helping," I barked.

"Sorry, dear." She took back the washcloth and dropped it into her lap.

I knew I was being unreasonable; I knew she was trying to help, but I couldn't stop myself. I just didn't have the energy to be polite or even pleasant. The child in my womb was tearing me in two trying to get out.

Another wave of agony came over me. I curled onto my side and started to scream. Again.

"Why don't you try getting up and walking a bit?" asked the midwife. I couldn't even remember her name at this point, but then, I really didn't care. She had arrived late last night, after Doc Lawrence left to tend to more flu patients. I knew she'd helped Clara deliver the boys, but I'd never paid much attention to her in the past.

She was efficient and professional, and I wanted to punch her in the face.

Once I could talk again, I glared at her. "Why don't you?"

Again, she was only trying to help, but unless she figured out a way to get this baby out of me sooner rather than later, she was no good to me.

"Lilly," she started, her voice so calm and quiet I wanted to slap her. "Many mothers find it helpful to stand or walk, especially between contractions. Why not let gravity help that baby of yours to move in the right direction?"

Gravity? Really? "So if I just stand up and walk, the baby will simply fall out?" I chuckled darkly and made no move to get up. "Why didn't anyone tell me that sooner? Here I've been lying in bed all night while my hips are ripped apart."

My mother looked like she wanted to scold me for my sarcasm, but I think I scared her a little. At this point, I scared myself.

Helen stood and turned toward the door. She called back to my mother. "I'm going to check on Ruth and the boys. Shall I make some tea as well?"

Must have scared her off, too.

Another wave of pain started low in my back. I rolled into a ball, as much as I could around my giant stomach, trying to find some way to release the sharp ripping across my hips. I pulled the crumpled pillow to my chest, holding on for all my worth.

Mom placed a hot water bottle against the small of my back, holding it in place while I was on my side. Not the worst thing she could do, actually, although mere hot water couldn't really hold a candle to blinding agony.

"Why don't you roll onto your back so we can see how far we've come now, Lilly?" The midwife eased up my pink flowered nightgown and reached her hand between my legs, sticking fingers into what should be a large, gaping opening by now.

Mom moved closer to the head of my bed, smoothing back my hair and leaning down to kiss my forehead. "Why is her back in so much pain, Lorraine? I don't remember feeling my labor in my back."

Lorraine? I had no clue that was her name.

"I think her womb is tilted back instead of forward, so the baby's head presses down on her back more than usual." The woman finally looked me in the eye. "It won't be long now, Lilly dear. It's almost time to push." She said it like we were waiting for a bus.

"How long is not long?"

"Well, I can't say exactly, as the baby is in charge here, but I shouldn't think it will be more than an hour or two before you have your sweet child in your arms."

"Oh, God," I screamed as another wave of agony shot through me.

Mom took my hand in hers. "Squeeze all you like, honey. Give some of your pain to me. I can take it for you."

We kept this up for what seemed like days: me screaming, Mom soothing, Lorraine chirping like some crazy bird. Breathe, rest, roll, move—she probably taught swimming in her spare time.

The door opened a crack, and Ruth poked her head in, keeping her distance. She was pale and still wearing her nightgown and bathrobe, but at least she was standing.

I met her gaze. "Are you afraid of getting me sick, or did Helen warn you that there's a beast in this room?"

She laughed. "No warning necessary—I can hear you in my room." She moved into the room a bit more, stopping at the end of the bed. "I'm sorry you're having such a rough time of it."

I tried to agree, to thank her, to laugh—something—but the pain opened up again, and I couldn't even catch my breath.

"Breathe, Lilly, breathe. Come on, we're nearly there." Lorraine was kneeling on the bed, at my feet, trying to keep my knees up and open. I did my best not to kick her off the bed.

"That's it, Lilly. We're almost there." My mother's hand would probably be broken by the time her grandchild arrived. She never pulled away, though.

Once I was released from the contraction, the next one started up. I couldn't stand it one more minute. I dissolved into tears. "I can't do this anymore." I turned to my mother. "I can't, Mom. I just can't."

Her face was just inches from mine now, her soft blue eyes willing her strength into me. "Yes, Lilly, yes, you can. You're nearly there, and you're doing so good. It won't be much longer, sweetheart."

I just stared into her eyes, trying to believe her, holding on for dear life. She'd lived through this three times, so she should know. I wasn't sure I believed her, but I wanted to.

Once I had a moment of rest, Lorraine checked me over again and declared that it was time to push. She arranged more pillows against the tall pine headboard, supporting my back, pulling me up to sit as high as I could.

"Okay, Lilly, when the next contraction starts, I want you to roll your head and shoulders forward and push with all your might. Let's get this baby out of there."

I thought about making a snarky response, but the next wave of pain had started. I screamed, Mom soothed, Ruth smiled, and Lorraine chanted. "That's it, a little longer, keep going, now rest."

There was nothing else in the entire world but the pain, the chanting, Mom's hand, and trying to push.

When the contraction eased, I leaned back against the pillows, only to have the next pain start instantly and pull me back up.

Over and over again.

"That's it, Lilly. Keep pushing."

At some point, Helen must have come back, as she was standing in the doorway, smiling at me. I felt like a circus sideshow act, but by now I didn't care who was watching. I just wanted this baby out of me.

I have no idea who said what, but the chanting and cajoling continued.

"I can see the baby's head."

"Your baby's nearly here, Lilly."

"Great job, Lilly. Atta girl."

Lorraine pulled out a stack of towels and spread them between my knees. "Take a deep breath, Lilly, as deep as you can, and give us one long, strong push, and I think the baby will be out."

I tried to take a deep breath, but my lungs seized in pain. I pulled out the last bit of strength I had, tears running down my face, rolling forward and pushing for all I was worth.

"That's it, Lilly! That's it. The head is out."

The pressure continued, the pain blinding, but I kept pushing.

"Good job, Lilly. Another deep breath. Keep pushing. There we are."

The pressure stopped suddenly, like the massive rubber band around my middle was snipped with shears. I fell back against the pillows, crying and gasping.

I looked at my mother, but she was looking at my feet, her eyes filled with tears.

"What?" I tried to push myself forward again. "What's wrong?"

I didn't hear any crying. If the baby was out, wasn't there supposed to be crying?

"What's wrong?"

Was there something wrong with my baby? I couldn't admit to anyone else my fears about this baby, about the man who'd fathered it.

Lorraine put her hand on my knee, looking deep into my eyes. "Congratulations, Lilly. It's a little lady."

Did the fact that she was born of violence somehow mean something was wrong?

A girl. Could I look at her and not think of the attack? Was she mine, or would she always be a reminder of him?

Mom looked at me. "A girl, Lilly. She's beautiful!"

"Let me see, let me see. Why isn't she crying?"

Lorraine held her up, slapped her back, and my daughter started to cry.

My daughter. My throat was so tight I couldn't speak. I couldn't see well for the tears in my eyes, but I held my arms out, reaching for her. I swallowed the lump in my throat.

"Let me hold her."

Lorraine wrapped her in a clean blanket and handed the precious bundle to me. I looked into the eyes of my daughter and felt all my pain and anger fall away. She was mine, all mine. And perfect.

"She's beautiful." I grasped her hand, and she curled her little fingers around mine. I felt the pull run straight through me.

Mom was crying; Ruth was crying; Helen was crying. Everybody cried, including my daughter. Especially me.

I opened the blanket, counted her tiny fingers and toes, and ran my hands all over her.

"She's incredible." I looked up at my mother. "She's beautiful, isn't she?"

Mom was full-on bawling now. "She is, Lilly. Just like her mama."

"I mean, she's perfect, right? She's my perfect girl." I closed my eyes, released a breath and sent up a little prayer of thanks. All I could see in her eyes was love and beauty and none of the darkness.

Mom leaned down and kissed my cheek.

"Thanks, Mom. I'm sorry if I broke your hand."

She chuckled through her tears. "I'm fine, honey. I'm better than fine. It was worth it all, wasn't it?"

I looked at Lorraine, who was still busy wiping, cleaning, pushing, prodding me. "Maybe Grandma can hold the baby now, while we deliver the afterbirth."

I handed my daughter to Mom, even though my arms felt lost without her. At least the delivery of the afterbirth was quick and much less painful than any other part of this process. While Mom held her first granddaughter, Ruth and Helen looked over Mom's shoulder, smiling and cooing.

Ruth took a step back, reaching for the door. "I'm going to go back to my room, so I don't spread any germs to this little beauty. Once I'm all recovered, though, I can't wait to get my hands on her."

Once Lorraine was satisfied that I was cleaned up, not bleeding, and relatively comfortable, she took the baby back from Mom.

"I need to weigh and measure her, see what we've got here. Do you have a name for this lovely?"

I'd been asked this question so many times, but hadn't been able to think of names. I had been so afraid of not falling in love with my baby, even though Mom and Clara told me I would, I guess I'd been afraid to think of a name or even consider what would happen once the baby arrived.

But as Lorraine handed me my daughter again, I looked down at her little face, smoothed down her wispy hair, and said, “Elsie May.”

Lorraine was preparing the birth certificate. “She’s a healthy seven pounds, two ounces. Elsie May. And the father’s name?”

I looked at Mom and Helen, a feeling of guilt pressing on my euphoria. I had to talk to Paul about this, and soon. Maybe I’d been wrong not to tell him about the rape.

It was too late to change that now.

I turned back to Lorraine. “Her father’s name is Paul. Paul Michael Babcock.”

****

Once little Elsie had her first bottle, which Lorraine said should be mostly sugar water, and my tender breasts were bound, the two of us had taken a little nap. Despite my thrill at holding my new daughter, the hours of hard labor, literally, had left me exhausted.

When I opened my eyes, I was surprised to see my father in the small wooden chair next to my bed, his head bowed over the baby in his arms, making cooing and soft, silly noises to her. Dad had always been sweet on me, but to see his big, strong hands stroking my daughter’s velvety head melted my heart. I couldn’t hide my smile when he turned and looked my way.

“She’s a beauty, sweetheart.” His voice was a little rough, and his eyes a little wet.

“I completely agree.” I pulled myself up, gingerly, to a sitting position. Sitting wouldn’t be much fun for a few weeks, according to Lorraine, but at least my back wasn’t breaking anymore.

"How are you feeling, honey?"

"I'm fine, or at least as good as can be expected, I think. I'm certainly much better than I was a few hours ago." I laughed.

"Yeah." He dipped his head, almost sheepishly. "You've always had a good set of lungs on you, girl."

It was my turn to blush. "Sorry about that."

He smiled. "Nothing to be sorry about. It's hard work bringing a new person into this world. And she's worth it, isn't she?"

"Yeah, she is."

Dad leaned over and handed Elsie to me and then leaned back. "Are you really okay?"

"I'm fine, Dad. Really. The midwife checked me over and said everything is as it should be. She'll come back tomorrow just to be sure, but she said all is well."

He looked down at his joined hands, draped slightly between his knees. "I don't mean physically, Lilly. I mean, you know, well, I just wanted to be sure you're okay with the baby and everything, and, you know, not blaming yourself or her for how she came to be in this world."

He slowly raised his head, looking me in the eye, his lips a sad, thin line.

I nodded. "Yeah, I'm okay. I wasn't sure how I was going to feel once the baby was born. I couldn't help thinking about the attack, about the fact that this should be Paul's baby and he doesn't even know about her. But once I held her in my arms, it all faded away. She's mine, she's beautiful, and I couldn't love her more."

A small smile formed on Dad's face.

I reached my right hand out and laid it on his

joined hands. "She isn't to blame for the man who hurt me, and he can't hurt anyone ever again, so I'm not going to waste any more time thinking about him. I understand that I need to write to Paul and explain about the attack, try to make him understand why I didn't tell him sooner, but mostly, he needs to see her face, to know that we'll be waiting for him when he gets home. I know he's going to love her, too."

Dad nodded but didn't speak.

"Maybe you could take a picture of me holding her, so I could send it to Paul? Not right now, though, as I must look a fright."

He chuckled. "Of course I can take your picture. I think that's a great idea, although you shouldn't worry about how you look. The glow of new motherhood makes you more beautiful than ever."

Dad leaned in, gave me a kiss, and stood. "There are several other people dying to get in here and have a turn to visit you and hold the baby, if you're up to it."

I adjusted the covers and smiled. "Absolutely. Bring on her admirers."

Dad walked to the door and opened it. No more than a moment later, Helen stuck her head in the doorway.

"Up for company?"

"Come on in." She took a seat, leaning toward the bundle in my arms, so I handed the baby to her. Helen's face broke into a huge smile, and her eyes teared up.

"She's lovely, Lilly, and looks just like you." Helen leaned down and kissed her little head. "I'm so happy for you."

I kept smiling—I just couldn't seem to stop smiling. "Me, too." I chuckled. "But I have to apologize. I was a terrible bear last night. I took over your bed and growled at everyone who came near. I'm sorry for snapping at you when you were being so nice to me."

She looked up, surprise in her gaze. "You don't need to apologize, Lilly. It was nothing; you were in pain. My mum used to curse up a blue streak when she was birthin' a baby. Don't give it a thought."

I chuckled again. I wasn't sure I even knew enough swear words to make up a blue streak, but I could believe labor would bring that out in a woman.

"And, by the way, Happy Anniversary." She smiled at me.

"Oh, my gosh, that's right. Paul and I have been married a year already!" I'd completely forgotten about that. "I wish we could celebrate together."

"We all wish that, don't we?"

"Hopefully 1943 is the year the war will end and everyone will come home safely. We'll have to have a grand celebration then."

Helen swayed back and forth in her chair, a natural baby-soother. Seeing Elsie in her arms made it hard to believe she didn't want children of her own. After a few minutes, she handed the baby back to me, leaving us to get some rest. Both my daughter and I had a long night.

My daughter. Who would've thought? It was only a little over a year since my eighteenth birthday, and now I was a high school graduate, a working, married woman, and a mother. This didn't fit the ideas I'd had for life after high school, my boy-crazy dating and dancing plans. But now that I had a man of my own and was decidedly girl-crazy over the beautiful bundle of joy in my arms, I realized this was so much better than all I had planned.

The war changed everything and everyone.

****

Elsie and I must have drifted off because, when I next opened my eyes, my mother was sitting in the chair where Helen had been. Mom was smiling and cooing and feeding Elsie, who was wrapped in a yellow blanket in my mother's arms.

"How's she doing?"

Mom looked up. "She's wonderful, of course. She started fussing a bit, but I wanted to let you get some more sleep, so I thought I'd feed her."

"Thanks, Mom. I am a little tired." I sat up and then swung my legs over the edge of the bed. "But I also need to use the bathroom."

I walked out into the hall and ran into Ruth, coming up the stairs with a cup of tea. She was still pale, and her smile was shaky, but at least she was on her feet.

"There's the new mama." She smiled, but kept her distance. "I'd hug you, but I don't want to risk getting you sick."

"Thanks. I certainly don't want that flu. How are you feeling?"

She leaned against the wall. "Better, thanks, although still a little weak. I'm definitely on the mend, though."

"Good. I'm going to go clean up a bit while Mom is feeding the baby."

Ruth stepped aside, clearing my way to the bathroom door. "I can't wait to be healthy enough to get my hands on her. Will is going to be so excited to hear he has a niece."

As I walked into the bathroom, I realized that, in addition to keeping my pregnancy from Paul, I hadn't written to Will or Jack about it, either. Now it was too late for Jack; he'd never have a chance to meet Elsie. My brothers were good guys and wouldn't have held any part of this situation against me, but I guess I'd been worried about telling them anyway. I'd been afraid to tell anyone about the attack, and ashamed, but now that Elsie was here, I knew that the people who loved me would love her.

I'd waited too long to tell Jack. I needed to write to Will. I couldn't wait a minute longer to tell Paul about our beautiful new daughter.

While Mom fed and changed Elsie, I got my stationery from my desk and started to write to Paul. I wouldn't mail it until I had a picture of me and Elsie to send, but I needed to wish him a happy anniversary and tell him about our daughter.

*Dear Paul,*

*Happy Anniversary, my love. I can't believe it's been a whole year since we met, fell in love, and got married, and nearly a whole year since I saw you. The weeks that we were together were the best of my life, but I wish we could be together to celebrate today. I miss you so much and can't wait to see you again.*

*We have more to celebrate today, and I apologize for not telling you about this sooner. I gave birth this morning—we have a daughter. As soon as I have a picture of little Elsie May to send to you, I'll put it in this letter.*

*No, I haven't been unfaithful to you—I would never do that. I love you more than I can say, and nothing has changed my love for you. In November, when I was walking to catch the bus home from Beacon Heights, after a Red Cross dance, I was attacked.*

*I was raped.*

*Leonard found me after the attack and brought me home. When he found out that the man who raped me was someone I knew from work, he went after the guy, but I guess Leonard scared the man so much that he walked in front of a train and was killed.*

*I'm not sad that he died, but I was so ashamed of what happened I just couldn't talk about it. I didn't want to tell you about it, especially in a letter—I just wanted to forget about it and pretend it never happened. But it did.*

*And by the time I figured out I was pregnant, I was so ashamed and afraid, and I didn't want to risk losing your love. Ruth tried to convince me to write to you about it, and I should have listened to her, but I just couldn't do it.*

*It's been hard being pregnant when everyone knows you've been gone and assumes I had an affair. Some people have been cruel to me about it, even my supposed friend Ava. I know I should have told you sooner, but I was a coward.*

*This morning, though, when the midwife put my beautiful daughter in my arms, I knew she was our daughter. I knew instantly that you would love her as much as I do. I know it's not easy to think of raising another man's child as your own, but don't you see, she's not another man's child. She's yours; she's ours. She'll never know another father—she doesn't have another father. She has you, and I know now that you are kind enough and loving enough to take her as your own. She's perfect, Paul, just beautiful. I can't wait for you to be able to hold her, smell her sweet little baby head, and watch her wrap her tiny little fist around your finger. I know you'll fall in love with her, just the way I did.*

*I know I'm asking a lot of you, taking a lot for granted, but you are such a good man, such a loving person, I know that you will embrace Elsie and claim her as your own. I never want her to know she was conceived in pain and violence—she's too perfect to be associated with anything so dark or evil. She will be the light of our lives and only bring us closer together, now that we are a family.*

*I'm sorry I wasn't brave enough to tell you about all this when it happened. It's not the way I wanted to say happy anniversary to you, but I can't think of a better gift to us both than Elsie. Please know that I think of you whenever I look into her angel face. She's already a part of you, and I know you'll love her from the first moment you see her.*

*I have to go now, my love, because our daughter is awake and needs me. Don't forget that I need you, as does Elsie, so please come home to us safe and sound. We'll be waiting for you.*

*All my love—Lilly*

## Chapter Twenty
## Ruth

As the summer of 1943 moved into fall, our hope that the war would end before the second anniversary of Pearl Harbor was fading quickly. More and more young men, and even older ones, were making their way through the Beacon Heights Red Cross facilities before heading off to the European or Asian front lines.

Once Lilly was back at the day care after Elsie's birth, I found myself spending more and more time working at the Red Cross offices. Beyond rolling bandages, helping with blood drives, and working the dances, I took on more and more organization and management functions. I even volunteered at the hospital, although I'd never make much of a nurse. While the hole in my heart from losing Jack would never heal over, pouring myself into helping our soldiers and letting them know that their sacrifices were valued, that people on the home front were thinking of them and cheering for their safe return, helped me to honor Jack's legacy.

"I've invited a couple soldiers to Sunday dinner again. I hope you both don't mind." Mom and I were washing the breakfast dishes while Pop sat at the table drinking another cup of coffee. Everyone else was getting ready for church. Mom looked up from the sink, a smile in her gaze.

"Of course we don't mind, Ruth. We're lucky enough to be able to share what we have with these brave young men, and both Earl and I enjoy meeting them and hearing their stories."

Pop sipped his coffee, nodding in agreement. "It's the least we can do for our troops."

I dried the fry pan with a dish towel and put it away. "I appreciate that. I know I've been bringing home a lot of strangers lately, but my heart goes out to these boys, whether they are frightened new recruits about to ship out or wounded veterans coming home after seeing horrors we can't even imagine."

Mom wiped her hands on her apron and gently touched my arm.

"Don't apologize for caring, Ruth. You have a big heart and that's why…why we all love you."

Mom turned her head, but not before I could see the sheen of moisture in her eyes. She hadn't mentioned Jack's name, but he hovered above many of our conversations these days.

Pop cleared his throat and placed his mug on the table. "Julia said that Judith Blumenthal and her children are coming out for dinner today. Who else is joining us?"

I picked up a plate to dry, breaking eye contact. "We'll see who shows up, but I've invited a couple of returning soldiers this week, along with a new recruit from Wisconsin." I carried a stack of dry plates to the cupboard.

"Matthew Wilson is a Marine who just got back to Beacon Heights last week after being badly injured in Guadalcanal. He has spent a long time in a hospital in California. I hope he'll show up, but I have my doubts.

He's pretty closed off. I had a hard time convincing him to say yes to Sunday dinner."

"Oh, the poor dear," said Julia. "Do you think he'll have to go back once he's recovered?"

I stopped at the table, leaning on the back of a chair. "No, he's been honorably discharged due to some type of permanent injury. It's hard to get him to open up about any of this. I first met him in the hospital, when he got shipped here a couple of weeks ago. I've been trying to talk to him every day, as he seems so lost, so when he was released this week, I almost had to beg him to agree to come to dinner today. I really hope he shows up."

"Let's be sure to introduce him to Leonard when he's here," said Julia.

Earl nodded. "Good idea. Leonard had a tough time of it when he got shipped home injured in the Great War. He'll likely be able to speak to this young fella better than the rest of us."

"That's wonderful." I grabbed my coat and headed toward the back door. "I'm going to go let Leonard know that Matthew is coming, hopefully. Just to give Leonard the heads-up."

If anyone could ease Matthew's transition back to life on the home front, it would be Leonard.

****

"Why don't you all have a seat here in the parlor until dinner is ready?" I ushered the three soldiers into the house. I was grateful to see Leonard waiting for us, as he had agreed to when I spoke with him before church.

Wilbur, the fresh young boy from Wisconsin, took a seat on the sofa next to Lilly, a sleeping Elsie on her lap, and across from Earl. They had him talking up a storm in no time. He seemed so young, especially in comparison to Matthew, who hung back against the wall by the front door. If Leonard hadn't made his way over to talk to the Marine, I think Matthew might have made a hasty retreat.

The two men stood near the window, talking in low tones. Leonard seemed to do most of the talking, but at least he was able to get Matthew to nod and join in every once in a while. Hopefully, Leonard would be good for Matthew.

"Why don't you have a seat here, Lieutenant Cohen?" I ushered the third man, a pilot, to the other side of the room, gesturing to a comfortable armchair next to the settee. I sat on the edge of the settee and was joined by Helen.

Jacob Cohen smiled. He hadn't joined us for church, as Wilbur had. "Thank you, again, to all of you. It's great to be back in the midst of such a warm family."

"Where are you from, Lieutenant?"

He looked at me. "Please, call me Jacob, Mrs. Walker."

"Okay, Jacob, as long as you'll call me Ruth. And this is our dear friend, Helen Anderson."

"And please, call me Helen."

"Deal. I grew up in Brooklyn. My family is still there, so I guess that's home, although I haven't seen it in a long time."

Judith came through the front door with Marion, while the boys raced past with Fred. "No running in the house, boys," she called after them.

"Hello, Judith. Please join us." I motioned to the

empty chair next to Lilly.

"I'm sorry for the chaos." Judith smiled.

"Not to worry. You know Fred is thrilled to see your boys. He loves having friends to play with."

Judith took a seat and pulled Marion onto her lap.

"Judith Blumenthal, this is Lieutenant Jacob Cohen, a genuine war hero recently returned from England. He's from Brooklyn. Jacob, this is our dear friend, Judith, and her daughter Marion."

They said their hellos, almost immediately followed by Helen's questions. "Where were you in England, Jacob? I'm from London, and my husband is flying with the Eighth Army Air Force over there."

Marion climbed off Judith's lap and toddled directly to Helen, who instinctively pulled the child onto her lap.

"No kidding?" He seemed genuinely surprised. "That's my unit. I was flying a B-17, the flying fortress. What's your husband's name?"

Helen sat up straight, pulling Marion close to her chest. "William Anderson. He flies a Mustang as part of the Eighth Fighter Command. He started as part of Eagle Squadron in the RAF but was transferred to the Eighth Air Force last fall. Do you know him?"

"Sure, I know Billy. He's a great guy and a terrific pilot. Those Mustangs and their pilots saved our bacon lots of times."

Helen couldn't seem to speak, but her eyes filled with tears. She rested her chin on Marion's head.

I tried to speak for her. "When did you see him last, Jacob?"

"Not long ago. June, I guess. Just before we got sent home on this bond tour."

Helen visibly swallowed, kissed Marion's hair, and then finally spoke. "And he was well? When you saw him, Billy was good?"

Jacob smiled. "Oh, yes, ma'am. Right as rain."

She seemed to relax a bit. "Thank heavens." Helen ran her hand over Marion's hair and then hugged her tightly, so tightly that Marion squirmed. "Sorry, love."

She turned to me. "What's a bond tour?"

"Why don't you explain, Jacob?"

Jacob leaned forward, his forearms resting on his thighs. "Our crew flew twenty-five combat missions in a flying fortress, which completed our tour. So the Army decided we should come back to the U.S. and travel around selling war bonds."

Judith drew a quick breath. "Wow, a bona fide hero. Congratulations, Lieutenant. It's nice to hear a story of success now and then."

Jacob blushed, leaning back against the couch. "Don't know about the hero part, ma'am. I was just doing my job, just like everybody else over there. We were lucky, and had good help, like Billy, protecting us so we could drop our bombs. It's definitely a group effort."

"Well, congratulations all the same, Jacob." Helen held out her hand, and Jacob reluctantly shook it.

"And how is the tour going? Are you in town for long?" asked Judith.

"Not long, ma'am. We're just in this area for a few days, while we speak at the hospital and at the Saturday night dance. People are buying bonds, for sure, but the Army wants us to sell more. This is an expensive war."

I nodded. "And it can't end soon enough."

After a moment, Judith looked back at Jacob. "So,

you're from Brooklyn, Lieutenant. What part? My…late husband and I moved to Upton Falls from Brooklyn."

"I'm sorry for your loss, Mrs. Blumenthal."

"Thank you, Lieutenant. Henry was killed in North Africa, not quite a year ago."

"My condolences, ma'am." He paused for a moment. "I'm from Flatbush, not far from Ebbets Field."

I perked up. "You must be a Dodgers fan, then, Jacob."

He chuckled. "In my neighborhood, there's no other choice. Are you a baseball fan, Ruth?"

Helen and Judith shared a laugh. "She certainly is, Lieutenant," said Helen. "She's barmy with it."

Jacob chuckled. "You Brits never seem to appreciate the game, isn't that right, Ruth?"

I smiled. "Definitely. Have you been to many Dodgers games, Jacob?"

He nodded. "I used to go whenever I could, before the war."

"I'm so envious. We have a Class A team in Elmira, the Pioneers. They're a farm team for the Dodgers. Jack and I, well, we were avid fans, but even so, we didn't get to go to many games in person. I, uh, I still listen to the Dodgers on the radio, of course, whenever I can."

"Sure, I heard of the Pioneers when I was in college. A bunch of us piled into a friend's truck and headed over to a game during study week my junior year." He seemed to smile at the memory.

"Where did you go to college, Jacob?" asked Judith.

"I was at Cornell University, over in Ithaca. When I heard we were coming to the Finger Lakes area on this bond tour, it felt almost like coming home again."

"Can you tell us any more about the type of missions you fly, or what Billy does?" Helen couldn't take her eyes off Jacob, as if he were a direct link to her husband.

"I'll tell you what I can, although the Army is pretty secretive about details."

Helen held up a hand. "Oh, no, I don't need specifics. I'd just like a general idea of what Billy is doing over there."

"Excuse me while I check to see if Mom needs any help in the kitchen." I stood, as did Jacob, and went to the kitchen. Mom, Grandma Walker, and Clara were bustling about with plates of steaming potatoes and vegetables. I could smell the delicious aroma of a chicken roasting.

"Is there anything I can do to help?" I snagged a green bean out of the serving dish on the table.

Mom stood at the stove, her gingham print apron over her brown church dress. Steam from the gravy cooking in front of her had turned a few wispy hairs around her face into soft corkscrew curls.

"Actually, you can tell everyone that it's time for dinner, dear."

I knew enough to get out of the way of the production line as the three women all grabbed platters and bowls, laden with food, and headed to the dining room. I stepped back into the living room and told everyone it was time to eat. However, I noticed that Leonard and Matthew had disappeared, so I stepped out onto the front porch.

Matthew was leaning against the railing, his arms crossed over his chest, while Leonard sat in one of the rockers facing him. While Leonard looked up when I came through the door, Matthew looked down at the floor.

"Dinner's ready, gentlemen." I looked at Leonard, motioning slightly with my head toward Matthew. I couldn't help but wonder whether Leonard had been able to get the young man to open up at all.

Leonard stood, smiling broadly. "We won't say no to that, will we, Matt? Those delicious smells have been teasing me through the open window for some time now."

Matthew looked up at me, briefly, and then back down. But at least he followed Leonard, who held the door for me as we went back into the house.

When I'd met Matthew at the Red Cross hospital, he'd been sullen and somewhat rude, but slowly, over time, I'd been able to get him to speak to me, although not much more than "yes, ma'am" or "no, ma'am." It had taken me more than a week of mostly one-sided conversation to get him to agree to come to dinner, and I honestly believed he said yes mostly because I kept nagging him and I'd happened to be there when he was finally discharged from the hospital.

He hadn't seemed happy about coming, but he'd said he didn't have any family, so I don't think he had anywhere else to go.

Everyone was finding a seat in the crowded dining room. Helen, Judith, Jacob, and Marion were seated at the card table in the corner, with Kurt and Peter right behind Judith at the main table, next to Clara, Fred, and Robert, and easily within arm's reach. Leonard,

Matthew, and I found seats on the opposite side of the table, next to Granddad and Grandma Walker. Pop was already seated at the head of the table as Mom walked in with a pitcher of milk, her apron no longer in sight. Lilly showed Wilbur to a seat next to Clara and took the last open spot next to Mom, with baby Elsie somehow sleeping through the chaos in her basket in the corner.

Our mealtimes were never quiet, but when we added friends, neighbors, and servicemen to the already crowded dining room, the noise level was sometimes deafening. The children were mostly well-behaved but young, and even more rambunctious than usual when they had friends next to them.

"Everything is delicious, as always, Julia." Leonard took the platter of chicken from me, as it made its way around the table for a second time, and held it for Matthew. "Don't pass up on seconds, boy. You're not likely to get cookin' any better than this."

Matthew took a small piece of chicken, nodding silently toward Mom. As all the dishes made the rounds again, I noticed Matthew loaded up on mashed potatoes and gravy, bread, and green beans. While the hospital food was probably better than he'd eaten in a long time, it couldn't hold a candle to Mom's home cooking.

"It must feel good to be out of the hospital, Matthew."

"Yes, ma'am," Matthew said, around a mouth full of potatoes. He didn't take his gaze off his plate of food.

Leonard's gaze met mine over Matthew's head. His nod seemed to encourage me to keep trying.

"Where are you from, Matthew? Did you grow up in this area?"

He still didn't look up, but seemed to nod. After a few more bites of dinner, he responded with what sounded like a muffled, "Elmira."

"Oh, wonderful." I tried to ignore the gravy running down his chin. "I was just talking to Lieutenant Cohen about the Pioneers. Do you follow baseball, Matthew?"

Finally, he raised his gaze a bit, looking at me somewhat quizzically. "Yup." With his fork still in mid-shovel, he asked, "Do you like baseball?"

Leonard smiled at me. "She sure does, boy. She's usually the first one to turn on the radio when a game is on, unless she's out volunteering over at the Red Cross. I never met a girl more excited about baseball."

Matthew moved the forkful of potatoes and gravy to his mouth, nodding, his gaze actually meeting mine. No more words were forthcoming, though.

****

After dinner, I watched Leonard walk with Matthew out to the barn, each man bearing a permanent, limping reminder of his war. Helen, Judith, and Marion headed out to the front porch with Jacob, taking advantage of the warm fall weather. Pop and Granddad settled into the parlor with Wilbur, Lilly, and baby Elsie. While Clara put Robert down for his nap and Fred, Peter, and Kurt raced around the outside of the house, I helped Mom and Grandma with the dishes.

"I'm so glad Helen had a chance to talk to someone who actually knows Billy. It's wonderful for her to hear about him and what he's doing over there." Mom had her arms elbow deep in sudsy water, with Grandma at her side, rinsing the dishes that Mom washed.

"So true." Grandma turned to catch my eye. "But it

looked like Judith was quite attentive to that young man, too."

I smiled. "It's good to see her so engaged in conversation with a man. Since Henry's death, I think her life has revolved around the children, her job, and the time she spends with us. She certainly hasn't met any other nice Jewish men in Upton Falls."

"Nor is she likely to, at least not until this war is over." Mom drained the dishpan while I continued drying and putting away the dishes after Grandma rinsed them.

"True." I snuck a peek out the kitchen window, looking for signs of Leonard and Matthew. "I'm worried about Matthew, though. He seems so angry and in pain."

"What do you know about his injury?" Mom stopped in the midst of wiping down the kitchen table and took a seat, looking up at me.

I put down the platter I was drying and sat next to her. "From what I learned at the hospital, Matthew was severely injured during the battle on Guadalcanal. Some type of explosive, I guess, which left him in quite a few pieces and killed several of his friends."

Grandma gasped and took a seat across from me.

"Because of the prolonged heavy fighting, he couldn't be evacuated for several days. He eventually made it to a ship that was able to take him to a hospital in California, but it was a long and painful journey for him and all the other injured soldiers traveling with him. He spent a long time in that hospital and was eventually sent to the hospital in Beacon Heights because it's near his home. He was just released this past week."

"Will he be headed back to the front?" Grandma asked.

"No." I checked over my shoulder to make sure we were still alone. "The head nurse told me that he has some permanent nerve damage in his right foot and leg. The Marines have issued him an honorable discharge because he's no longer fit for duty."

Mom crossed her hands on the table in front of her. "No wonder the poor boy is angry."

Grandma spoke up. "Leonard is just the man to help that boy. He had a hard war, you know, the last one, and it took him a while to adjust to his injury. He struggled to find work and make his peace with his life. I'm sure he can help Matthew, if the boy is willing to be helped."

I stood and picked up the platter, taking it to the cupboard to put away. "One of the main reasons I pushed Matthew to come to dinner today was I really hoped being around everyone, having a good meal, and meeting Leonard would somehow break through that hard shell he's erected around himself."

"He is a little prickly, isn't he?" Mom smiled a sad, thin smile.

"I'm glad Leonard took him out to the barn. Men communicate better when they're working side by side."

Grandma had a good point. Maybe Leonard would be able to get through to Matthew if he got Matthew to help him with the chores.

I went into the parlor in time to see Wilbur heading out to the front porch, so I followed him out. Apparently everyone, with the exception of Matthew and Leonard, had gathered out there while Mom and

Grandma and I were working in the kitchen. Jacob, with Marion on his lap, was asking Judith and Helen about their work at Nichols Motors.

"Aircraft engines. Really? Wow, I guess I have to thank you both for your excellent work. You women are making all the difference in this war." He smiled up as I took a seat in the rocker near the door.

Judith blushed and murmured, "We try our best."

Helen laughed out loud. "Frightfully kind of you, but it's been a learning experience, for sure. I didn't know up from down at the beginning. I like to think I'm doing my part to help Billy and all our boys in uniform."

"You're all doing a bang-up job. We'd never be able to fight the good fight over there if you women weren't going above and beyond in the factories over here. I had a buddy, a pilot, who was shot down over the English Channel."

Helen gasped but quickly covered her mouth.

Jacob realized how his words were affecting Helen, so he raced on with his story. "He was rescued by the Brits, thank God, and when he got back to camp, he had an incredible story. He was wearing a life preserver…"

"His Mae West, you mean?" interrupted Helen.

I turned to Helen with a quizzical look, and Jacob laughed. Judith couldn't take her eyes off Jacob's face.

"That's what they call a life preserver in the RAF," Helen explained.

"Oh, okay."

He looked back to Helen. "Yes, his Mae West. Anyway, it turns out the life preserver that saved him when he got shot down had the markings on it to show that it was assembled in the U.S. in the plant where his mother works in Nebraska…and it was made by his very own mother."

Everybody laughed.

Jacob turned to Helen. "Don't for one minute think you aren't helping Billy, and all of us. For all you know, you may have worked on the engine that is in Billy's plane or the one that saves his life or saved mine. It matters what you all do here, it really does. And because you run the day care that lets mothers build engines or assemble life preservers or whatever job they take on, you make a difference, too, Lilly. And Ruth makes a difference to the servicemen who stop at the Red Cross in Beacon Heights, either as they're shipped out or when they return home. I've watched you over there, Ruth. You're a real boost to morale."

I smiled. "It doesn't seem like much, especially compared to making the life preserver that could save someone's son, or building an aircraft engine that could send a bomber over Berlin."

Jacob shook his head. "It makes a difference, believe me. Before we left England, I met some women working for the Red Cross over there. They served coffee and doughnuts, talked to the soldiers about places back home, the girls they left behind, even baseball, and it helped steady the men before a mission, helped remind them what we're all fighting for. When we're so far from home, focused on our missions, it's easy to lose touch with life back home."

Clara came onto the porch, carrying Will's guitar. "Will this do, Wilbur?"

Wilbur stood and took the guitar from Clara. "This is great, ma'am. Thank you kindly."

"Are you a musician, Wilbur?" The boy's face lit

up when his fingers ran over the strings.

"Well, I don't know about that, ma'am, but I can pick out a tune or two. As long as you all don't mind a little cowboy music."

He played a few chords, adjusted the tuning pegs a bit, and started strumming. Everyone was focused on Wilbur, smiling and relaxing, as he started singing Gene Autry's "Back in the Saddle Again."

As we all sat there listening and in some cases singing along, I noticed Leonard and Matthew step into the barn doorway. I hoped they could enjoy the music from there.

## Chapter Twenty-One
## Helen

*My darling wife,*

*I was so happy to get your latest letter. I can't believe you actually got to meet Jacob. I'm jealous that he was able to sit on the porch, talking with you, and looking into your eyes. Never mind getting to eat all that great food. I can't wait to do all that, and more.*

*I know the guys on that bond tour are busy covering the country, but it's great that he's had a chance to visit a few more times. He and I had talked about his time at Cornell and how much he loved the Finger Lakes. I don't think he has much family in Brooklyn anymore, so I wouldn't be surprised if he settled down in the area after this is all over. Which can't come soon enough for me.*

*Now, don't get mad, but I have an idea I'd like you to think about. I've always known how smart you are, and even you can't argue with how quickly you learned to read and write. I found out from a couple of the younger guys who are working in the mess that they are taking a correspondence course that will allow them to graduate from high school. I know you wouldn't want to sit in a high school classroom with all those kids, but if you could take these correspondence courses, or even just the final test that they take before graduation, I'm sure you would pass. You could even think about college. Give it some thought, my love. I know you could do it, and it would give you the chance to do so many wonderful things, as well as being my wife, which is the most wonderful thing of all.*

*It sounds like Ruth has really taken her role with the Red Cross seriously. I'm sure she's a huge help to soldiers there, both the ones getting ready to ship out and the injured who are sent home.*

*I know this letter is getting to you around Christmas time, so please know that it holds for you all my love and best wishes for, as you say, a Happy Christmas. I only hope that we'll be together long before Christmas rolls around again next year. Think of me kissing you at midnight on New Year's Eve and know that I'm missing you.*

*Give all my love to everyone, including my parents when you see them. I'm sorry they didn't make you feel more welcome at home, but I'm so glad you found Ruth, Lilly, and the Walkers. I'm including a little something for my parents in the Christmas package I sent you, so please deliver it for me. I miss you and love you and think of you always—*

*Yours, Billy*

****

*Billy. Billy. Billy.* The chant kept time with my steps as I walked to the Andersons' front door. If I didn't love him desperately, I'd never knock on this door again. But they were his family and he was mine, so I raised my hand and tapped three loud knocks on the polished oak.

Mrs. Anderson pulled the door open, and the tight smile she donned for strangers changed quickly into the look of disinterested disdain I'd grown used to while

I'd lived there.

"Oh, it's you."

*Billy. Billy. Billy.*

I pasted a smile on my face; at least one of us loved her son enough to be cordial.

"Hello, Mrs. Anderson."

"What do you want? Have the Walkers kicked you out?"

She didn't open the door farther, didn't ask me in. But I could do this. For Billy.

I held out the package. Billy had sent it unwrapped but had asked me to wrap it nicely for his parents, which I'd done, although not apparently up to her standards, if the look on her face was any indication. At least wrapping paper wasn't rationed.

"It's a gift for you and Mr. Anderson. For Christmas…"

"I can see that, girl," she interrupted. "Although why you think we'd want anything from you, I can only imagine…"

I pulled myself up to my full height and put some of that long expanse of backbone into my voice. "It's from Billy."

"Oh!" She grabbed it out of my hands. "Why did he send it to you?" She turned toward the interior of the house, probably toward the study. "George, come quick. We have a package from Billy."

Mr. Anderson was at her side in a moment. He looked at me and then at the package in his wife's hands. "Helen?"

"Good afternoon, Mr. Anderson. Billy sent a Christmas gift to you two in his package to me and asked that I deliver it."

"That's wonderful, Helen. Thank you." He pulled the door open farther. "Won't you come in?"

The look he got from his wife, at least what I saw before she turned around, was not filled with the Christmas spirit. Whilst I didn't relish spending any more time in their home than necessary, I couldn't resist annoying her just a little.

I followed them into the parlor and took a seat on the wingback chair nearest the door. Mr. and Mrs. Anderson sat on the sofa. She clutched the present to her chest, eyeing me warily, as if I was trying to steal it rather than deliver it.

"So you've heard from Billy recently, then?" Mr. Anderson put his arm along the back of the sofa and tried to ease his wife back from the edge. Of the two of them, he had always been the more civil to me.

"Yes, I got a package yesterday. Besides his latest letter, there was a Christmas gift for me and this gift for you. He asked me to wrap and deliver it and to wish you a Happy Christmas. He sends his love." I touched my hand to my throat and realized I'd forgotten to put on my necklace. I should have known I'd need it here.

"How would you even know what he said? It's not like you can read, right?"

I took a deep breath and brought Billy's face to my mind. *I'm doing this for you, my love. Only for you.*

"Mabel, really," Mr. Anderson hissed.

"Well, we both know she's a low-class, ignorant, gold-digger. Somehow she got her hooks into our son, while he was alone and far from home. But I'm not fooled by her."

Mr. Anderson dropped his arm from the back of the sofa and sat forward.

"Helen, I'm sorry. You don't deserve that."

"What?" Mrs. Anderson sputtered.

"Actually, Ruth Walker taught me to read and write, so I'm perfectly able to read Billy's letters and give you his best wishes."

He smiled. "That's wonderful, Helen. Good for you."

I looked him in the eye, ignoring her as best I could, pasting a proper smile on my face.

"Right. Thank you, sir. The Walkers have been frightfully good to me, and I'm grateful to them, especially to Ruth."

"That's great, Helen." Mr. Anderson smiled. "Good for you," he repeated

All she could say was, "Hmph."

"Mabel, really. The girl is improving herself…"

She stood abruptly and walked to the other end of the room, turning back to face me from in front of the marble fireplace. "As well she should. As long as she's still married to Billy, she's an Anderson. I won't be shamed by our relationship to such an ignorant, uneducated limey."

As much as I wanted to stay calm and be respectful, for Billy's sake, I was starting to lose my temper.

Mr. Anderson's voice was low and soft, probably trying to calm his balmy wife. "She doesn't shame us, Mabel. She has a job at Nichols, making aircraft engines, for heaven's sake. She's contributing to the war effort."

Mrs. Anderson turned on him. "Is that what you want for your grandchildren someday, George? To see their mother come home from work in the middle of the night with grease under her fingernails? Billy graduated from a good college. He's a pilot and will get a good job when he gets home. He deserves better and so do we."

"Billy doesn't think so, now, does he?" I rose to my feet, finally losing my patience. "In fact, he thinks I could go to college myself."

"Ha!" She almost smiled, but it was a bitter and ugly look. "You never graduated from high school. You can't go to college, at least not in this country."

"Well, Billy says otherwise. He says there's a test I can take, to get my high school diploma. Once I do that, I can go to college. I can be whatever I want to be." At least, Billy believed that. I had to learn to believe it myself.

"Of course you can, Helen," said Mr. Anderson, a slightly panicked look on his face. He probably thought I was becoming as daft as his wife.

"What kind of job could you ever get?" Her tone was so vile, I couldn't ignore her.

"I could be a teacher." I didn't know where that idea came from, but it sounded good to me.

She walked closer to me, hands on her hips, her eyes narrowed and her face pinched. "Who would hire you to teach children? That's laughable. You never even finished school yourself!"

I crossed my arms over my chest. "I work as a preschool teacher now, and I'm good at it. The children love me and I love them. I'd make a cracking good teacher."

I turned to look at Mr. Anderson. "I'm sorry, but I have to go."

He stood quickly, following me as I rushed toward

the front door. "I'm sorry, Helen." He looked back toward his wife, who was hurrying after him.

"Don't you dare apologize for me, not to her!" She was nearly screaming.

"Happy Christmas," I told my father-in-law as I pulled open the door, stepped through, and closed it behind me. I couldn't get off that porch fast enough.

****

By the time I got home, my temper had cooled and I was feeling more than a bit ashamed. I shouldn't have let that woman get to me. Above everything, she was Billy's mother, and I had to figure out how to get along with her once Billy came home.

Ruth was sitting at the kitchen table when I came in the back door. She had a packet of papers spread across the table in front of her and turned when she heard me walk in.

"How did it go?" She gave me an understanding look.

"Worse than expected, actually. I let Billy's mum get under my skin, didn't I?" After leaving my coat and boots on the back porch, I poured myself a cup of coffee from the pot on the stove and sat next to Ruth.

"Oh, no. What happened?" Ruth leaned back in her chair, picking up her own coffee.

I sighed. How could I let it get so bad? "I told myself I was just going to drop off the gift, wish them a happy Christmas, and leave. I'm sure that would have been fine by Mabel, but Billy's dad invited me in."

"He always was the nicer of the two."

"I shouldn't have gone in, didn't plan to, but the look on her face, the fact that she was clearly angry with him for inviting me in, it just made me say yes. I couldn't help myself."

She chuckled. "That sounds normal to me."

"No." I shook my head. "I wanted to be better, to do Billy proud, not to make her hate me more."

"What did she say?"

"Oh, she made a smart comment about how could I read the letter, I was too ignorant to be their daughter-in-law, that kind of stuff. I should have just dropped off the present and left, but instead I told them that you'd taught me to read, that Billy thought I should take some test to allow me to graduate from high school and go to college, and then I'll become a teacher." I laughed. "How could I let her get to me like that? I know how she is, and normally, I can ignore her."

Ruth looked at me, head tilted to the left, smiling a somewhat startling kind of smile.

"What?" I didn't think I could handle a "you should know better" kind of talk right now. I did know better, and I was already disappointed enough in myself.

"That's a terrific idea."

"Sorry? I don't think it was a brilliant idea to lose my temper in front of Billy's parents. I have to figure out a way to get along with them—well, with her, really—and this was not the way."

She sat forward again, drumming her fingers on the table. "I'm not talking about losing your temper." She looked me in the eye. "I'm talking about you becoming a teacher. I think that's a terrific idea. You're great with children, they love you, and you have the kindest disposition of anyone I know, with just the right amount of discipline. Probably comes from taking care of your brothers and sister all those years. You're a natural."

Now it was my turn to laugh. “Right. I never finished school myself, so I’m the perfect candidate to teach other people’s children.” I shook my head. “I don’t think so. Never mind the fact that I couldn’t even get into a college without a high school diploma.”

Ruth took my right hand in both of hers. “You’re smart, you’re kind, and you really care about children. That’s what it takes to be a good teacher.” She pulled out her pad of blank paper from the pile on the table. “Now, what did Billy tell you about this test you can take, to get a high school diploma?”

As quick as that, my future job as a teacher started to become a reality. Ruth made things happen, not just for herself but for anyone she cared about. She would help make this happen for me.

****

Winter had us buried under a couple of feet of snow, making everything more challenging, especially given the increased rationing, which now included not only gasoline for the cars but coal and firewood. Luckily, Earl could still get some gas for the farm trucks, because the government wanted him to keep growing food and raising dairy cows, but it wasn’t enough to allow for use of the cars often. Growing up in London, I was used to walking everywhere I went, but I wasn’t used to the deep snow and bitter cold we had to walk through this winter.

By January of 1944, the war news didn’t seem to promise a speedy return of our men. Lilly hadn’t received a letter from Paul in months, not since she’d written to him of Elsie’s birth. She was beside herself, alternately certain he had been killed or that he was alive but planning to divorce her.

Billy's letters were purposefully vague, although I was lucky enough to get them fairly regularly. We saw on the news reels that the RAF had been bombing Berlin, and I was sure that Billy was in the midst of that. Crews shot down over Germany, though, would be lucky to ever come out alive. I'd taken to wearing my lucky necklace twenty-four hours a day.

Clara received a letter from Will, which was a couple months old by the time she got it, telling her that his unit had moved from North Africa to Sicily. From what we saw on the news reels, he had most likely moved on to mainland Italy by now, and the fighting there looked brutal.

We were all in a constant state of worry. All of us but Ruth, that is.

"Really, the more I learn about these Clubmobiles, Pop, the more I think this is what I'm meant to do."

Ruth and Earl were seated at the kitchen table when I walked in after work. It was strange for Earl to be up this late, never mind deep in discussion with Ruth. I'd heard the Clubmobile story already but was curious as to what Earl thought of the idea.

I went to the sink, cleaned out my lunch pail, and poured myself a glass of water. I always felt so greasy after a shift, as if the dust and grime got inside me as much as it got all over me.

"These women are on the front lines, Ruth. Do you understand how dangerous that will be? You'd be in the thick of the fighting, wherever they send you." Earl looked tired, sad, and older than I'd seen him look. He knew he was fighting a losing battle.

"That's where I can be the most help, Pop."

Earl looked up at me. "What do you think, Helen?"

My heart sank as I carried my glass of water to the table and took a seat. "When Ruth first told me about these Clubmobiles, these converted trucks delivering coffee and doughnuts to the soldiers on the front lines, it sounded mad. All I could think was why was the Red Cross willing to risk the lives of American women to deliver food, cigarettes, and chewing gum."

"Right," said Earl.

"But after Ruth told me about it, I wrote to Billy and asked him. I spoke to some of the injured blokes over at the Red Cross dances and even some of the young ones just shipping out. They all agreed, even Billy, that the sight of a young American woman, the taste of coffee and doughnuts, right in the thick of things, could do more for their morale and drive to win the war than a hundred letters from home. While I hate the idea of Ruth putting her life at risk, I can understand her desire to help in such a profound way."

"That's just it, Pop. I would be making a difference in the war effort in a way I could never do from here. My supervisor in Beacon Heights said that the Red Cross is recruiting a large number of women right now for this program, and that the women have to be at least twenty-five, college-educated with work experience, strong, attractive, preferably unmarried, friendly, and comfortable talking to soldiers. She said she'd write me a letter of recommendation because she believes this job is tailor-made for me."

Earl shook his head. "That does sound like you."

Ruth placed her hand over Earl's on the table. "Believe me, I hate the idea of leaving the family. I will miss each and every one of you every minute of every day."

Earl looked down at Ruth's hand on top of his and placed his other hand on top. "And we'll miss you, sweetie."

I had tears in my own eyes, as did Ruth.

"I love you all so much and, you have to know, I loved Jack with everything I have and everything I am." She paused, swallowed hard, and waited for Earl to look her in the eyes. "I lived for the dream of his return, of the babies we would have and the life we would live here on the farm."

Earl was nodding, I was crying, but somehow Ruth kept talking.

"I look at Fred and Robert and even little Elsie and see the beautiful Walker babies I had dreamed of having, and it breaks my heart. I ache with missing Jack and still cry sometimes at night, thinking about the life we had, and planned to have, together."

She pulled a handkerchief from her pocket and wiped the tears from her face.

"I feel pulled to do this, like Jack's hand is guiding me to this job. Working on a Clubmobile will be hard work, for sure, but it will give me the chance to make a real difference to the men on the front lines, the men like Jack and Will and Billy and Paul. If I can help someone else's husband or brother or son, just by giving them some doughnuts and coffee or listening to them talk about the girl they left back home, if that can help them to come home safely when the war is over, I know it'll be worth the sacrifices I have to make when I'm away from you all."

Even Earl had tears running down his cheeks now. He looked at me, and I nodded. We'd lost her.

She was leaving us; there was nothing we could do

to stop her, and we had no way of knowing if she'd ever be coming home.

## Chapter Twenty-Two
## Lilly

"Okay, I finally got Elsie to sleep, so what still needs to be done?" I stopped at the bottom of the kitchen stairs to catch my breath before jumping into the party preparations.

Grandma was standing at the stove, putting the finishing touches on her famous chicken and dumplings, if the delicious smells in the kitchen were to be believed. Mom and Clara were in the dining room, setting out the food that was ready. I could see Helen in the parlor, sitting with Judith and Jacob and several of the small children.

Everyone was so busy, no one answered. Finally, Grandma looked up and said, "Go ask your mother, dear. I think we're almost ready."

"Oh, Lilly, dear, you look lovely." Mom placed her hand on my arm as she looked me over. Given that this was as close as we'd had to a party in years, I had decided to wear the pale blue party dress I hadn't worn since graduation, the day I'd met Paul. It finally fit again. Maybe wearing it would be a talisman of good luck and I'd finally receive a letter from him. If this didn't work, I'd have to borrow Helen's necklace.

"Dear, can you help Helen entertain the guests as they arrive?"

I walked into the parlor just in time for the doorbell

to ring, so I kept on to the front door. When I pulled it open, I found several of Ruth's fellow Red Cross workers from Beacon Heights as well as some of the mothers and children from the day care.

"Welcome, everyone, come in." I took coats and directed guests to take a seat in the parlor. We'd moved the dining room and kitchen chairs into the parlor, so there were more places to sit than there was room to stand.

"Is Ruth here? Does she know about the party yet?" Betty, Ruth's supervisor at the Red Cross, had played a big part in getting Ruth's application for the Clubmobile program expedited and was enthusiastic that Ruth had been accepted, at least, so far.

"No, she's still out with my father. He told her she needed a new suitcase to take with her to Washington, D.C. He even told her he'd wait while she shopped for new shoes, if she can find any. I can't believe she didn't see through the ruse just from that." I chuckled. "My father hates shopping."

Within two weeks of Ruth sending off her application, letters of recommendation, and physical forms, she'd gotten a letter asking her to report to the Red Cross headquarters in Washington, D.C. for further interviews. They told her to expect to be in D.C. for at least two weeks and, if she was accepted, she would immediately begin two weeks of training at American University before being shipped overseas. Once she'd made the decision to apply, it seemed like the Red Cross couldn't wait a moment to take her away from us.

Judith had taken a seat next to Helen, while Clara was herding the children off to play trucks with Fred and Robert under the dining room table.

Once I'd let another large group of neighbors and church friends in, I took a seat on a dining room chair next to Pastor Robbins, who was sitting on the end of one sofa.

"How's that day care going, young woman? I hear good things about it."

The minister was a sweet older man who smelled of pipe tobacco and always had a smile on his face. He reached out and shook my hand.

"I have to say, Pastor, I really love working with the children. I wasn't sure I'd be good at it when Ruth convinced me to take over for her, but it's really rewarding."

"That's why it's going so well, Lilly." He released my hand and sat back against the sofa cushions. "How is your family dealing with Ruth leaving? It must be hard on all of you."

I looked down at my folded hands before taking a deep breath and looking him in the eye. "It's going to be challenging, Pastor. I know she believes she's supposed to do this, and that may be true, but we've already lost Jack. It doesn't seem fair that we have to risk losing Ruth as well." I couldn't keep the waver out of my voice, no matter that I'd promised myself I wouldn't cry today.

"Of course it isn't fair, Lilly. Nothing about this war is fair."

"I know, Pastor. I'll miss her so much. She's the sister I never had."

"She's always been destined for great things. Just look at the ways she's made a difference in this community, from starting the day care to helping at the hospital and with the Red Cross dances, and even bringing many of the departing and returning soldiers to church and home to buoy up their spirits. Your father said she had a hand in convincing him to hire Leonard Kelp, which thoroughly enriched Leonard's life. Now I'm given to understand that one of the injured soldiers Ruth brought to dinner here is living and working here also?"

I nodded. "True. Ruth saw that Matthew was hurting, more than just physically, from the battle on Guadalcanal. He's got a permanent injury to his foot and leg. Ruth introduced him to Leonard, and it has made a huge difference in Matthew already. Leonard convinced him to take the other cot out in the tack room, off the barn. I never hear the two men talk very much, but Leonard told my father that Matthew had struggled with being injured and with his memories of the men who would never come home, just as Leonard did in the last war, and the job is helping the young man work through his anger and battle fatigue. Ruth knew that Matthew needed help and that Leonard was the right man for the job."

"It's good of your parents to hire the both of them, especially in times like these."

I smiled, looking to where my mother and grandmother were standing in the doorway to the kitchen. "They're good people, my parents. Plus, I think it gives Grandpa the chance to slow down a bit without feeling like he's letting Dad down. It's a big farm to run without Will or Jack around to help."

"Well, it's a good Christian act, and I'm sure your family will be rewarded."

I folded my hands over my heart. "From your lips to God's ears, Pastor. If Paul, Will, Billy, and Ruth come home safely, it will be all the reward we ever need."

Just then, Grandpa came in from the kitchen. "They're here! I just saw the truck coming up the driveway."

I couldn't remember a time that our home was so full of people, but everyone wanted to say their goodbyes and wish Ruth the best. We didn't know if she'd go to the European front or the Asian-Pacific theatre but, selfishly, I hoped she'd head west rather than east. The thought that she had a chance of running across Paul somewhere in Asia made him seem just the tiniest bit closer to home.

Everyone grew silent. Mom was smiling and shushing people, but I could see the sheen of tears in her eyes from here.

"I was happy to help, honey," we heard Dad say as he pushed open the front door and held it for Ruth to enter.

She walked in, stopped in her tracks, and stared.

"Surprise!" The chorus of greetings overwhelmed her as everyone stood.

She dropped the package she had in her arms. "Oh!"

Dad sort of pushed her into the room, as she seemed to be shocked and at a loss for words. He put the new suitcase on the floor, picked up the package she'd dropped and set it on top of the suitcase, and placed a hand on Ruth's elbow, guiding her farther into the crowd. "Everyone wanted to have a chance to wish you well."

After a few moments of stunned silence, Ruth's surprised face broke into a huge smile, and she started hugging everyone near her. “Thank you so much,” she repeated over and over.

Ruth made her way around the room, speaking with everyone for a moment, giving out hugs and tearful goodbyes. Although she had only lived in Upton Falls for a few years, she’d become an important part of the community.

Finally, as the crowds began to thin, she came and sat next to Pastor Robbins and his wife.

“I’m sorry it’s taken me so long to get a chance to speak to you both, but thank you for coming.”

The pastor took one of Ruth’s hands in his. “We’re proud of you, Ruth. What you’re doing is important.”

Mrs. Robbins leaned forward a bit. “Can you tell us more about what you’re going to be doing? It’s not secret war work, is it?”

Ruth laughed. “No, ma’am. Definitely not secret. If I am chosen for the Clubmobile program, I’ll spend most of my time making coffee and doughnuts.”

“What exactly is a Clubmobile, dear?”

“The Army and Red Cross have put together this program where Red Cross workers drive converted Army trucks to combat units, near the front lines. Once the truck is parked, the women make coffee and doughnuts for the troops. Most of the trucks also have a Victrola and speakers, to play American music, and they offer playing cards, gum, and cigarettes.”

Pastor Robbins clapped his hands together. “Just like a roving corner store.”

Ruth smiled. “Basically. The job of the Clubmobile workers is not only to make the coffee and doughnuts but to talk to the soldiers, bring them a bit of America, and remind them of their wives, mothers, sisters, and girlfriends back home and why they need to win this war."

Mrs. Robbins held her hands to her heart. "You drive right up to the front? Isn't it terribly dangerous, dear?"

I'd asked Ruth the same thing, but she'd tried to convince me she wouldn't actually be at the front.

"The Clubmobiles don't go all the way to the front, Mrs. Robbins. So far, the program has been successful, and safe."

Pastor Robbins placed a hand on his wife's arm. "Don't worry, Jane dear. I'm sure the driver is there to protect them. Or do you have more than just one man with your team?"

Ruth shook her head. "Actually, the women drive and maintain the trucks themselves, so they'll teach me all that, assuming I get accepted into the program. The Red Cross doesn't want to use men on the Clubmobiles, as they have so many other things the men need to be doing. The women can handle it all on their own."

"Do you know where you'll go?" Pastor Robbins asked.

"Well, it could be England, Italy, India, an island in the Pacific, or anywhere else our troops are fighting."

"Oh, my," said Mrs. Robbins.

Ruth nodded. "Yes, it'll be an exciting experience. I'll send lots of letters home about what I see."

As much as she tried to redirect the conversation that day, several of our friends and neighbors seemed surprised by what Ruth hoped to do and where she would be doing it. I couldn't imagine going to a war zone to make coffee and doughnuts, but I could easily see Ruth doing it. The Red Cross would be crazy not to take her. I just prayed they'd return her to us when this was all over.

I jumped to my feet when Grandma came into the parlor holding Elsie. "She just woke up," Grandma said. "I changed her, but I think she's hungry."

I placed kisses on the feathery brown curls on the crown of Elsie's head and each of her chubby cheeks and then carried her back to the kitchen. She was eating solid food these days, so I sat at the table with her on my lap and started feeding her bits of cooked potatoes and chicken. While I was there, Mom came in the back door and through the mud room, stopping when she saw me looking at her. Her eyes and nose were red.

"Are you okay?" I'd been fighting tears all day, so I was praying there wasn't something more upsetting my mother.

Mom pulled a handkerchief from her apron pocket and blew her nose. "I'm fine, of course. I got so warm at the stove that I just stepped outside for a breath of air and realized how cold it is out there."

I looked my mother in the eye and put my best "don't lie to me, young lady" expression on my face. She'd caught me many times with that expression, and now that I had a daughter of my own, I was working on developing the look myself.

"Really? I don't think so."

Her shoulders sagged as she walked to the table and sat in the chair across from me, giving me a sad smile. "When did you get so smart?"

"You didn't get bad news, did you?" No matter what we did these days, that possibility was always hovering around us.

"Oh, no." She sat up a little straighter, shaking her

head. "No, nothing like that, honey." Her voice trailed off. "I…"

"You're just worried about Ruth. I get it. If she gets chosen for the Clubmobile program, we'll have another member of our family to worry about."

Mom looked down at the table, shaking her head slightly. "Actually, I feel pretty calm about the idea of her working in the Clubmobiles. I'm sure the Red Cross will accept her, they'd be crazy not to, and she'll be perfect at that job. She can talk to the boys about baseball and farming, and everything. I'm not worried about losing her, because I don't believe the Lord could be that cruel. I'll miss her."

That's when it hit me, too. Never mind being worried about her safety or amazed by her tales of the adventures ahead of her, I was going to miss her terribly. She was the sister of my heart, my friend, and Elsie's aunt. How would we get through the weeks and months, possibly years, without her?

"Me, too." My eyes did fill with tears this time.

"And," Mom continued, "I'm afraid she'll meet someone new, fall in love, and when she moves back home, it won't be to our house, maybe not even to Upton Falls or New York State."

I hadn't even considered that. "But she's too young to be a widow forever, Mom."

Mom shook her head. "I don't want her to mourn for Jack the rest of her life and never fall in love again. But if she worked here in town, or in Beacon Heights, the chances are she would fall in love with someone local. Over in England or India or wherever they send her, she will meet men from all over the world and, knowing how special she is, I have no doubt someone will propose to her. I'll be happy for her, when the time comes, but my heart aches at the thought of losing her."

I wiped off Elsie's face and carried her to the refrigerator to retrieve her bottle. Her little arms started waving in front of her as I carried her back to the chair.

Once Elsie was nestled in my arms with her bottle, I looked up at my mother. "I really hadn't thought that far ahead. I want to be happy for her because she is so excited about the Clubmobile program. But now my feelings are even more mixed. I'm going to miss her, I'm worried about her getting hurt, and I'm worried about her coming home and telling us she's marrying some man from Wyoming or London or Hawaii."

"Don't worry. I'll come here when I come home. This is my home, and you are my family."

We both looked to the doorway, where Ruth was leaning her right shoulder against the molding, her arms crossed over her chest. "Our guests have gone."

Mom jumped up and hurried to her. "I'm sorry, Ruth. I didn't mean to make you think we don't support your decision."

Ruth put her arm around Mom. "I understand. I will miss you all so much, too. Don't think I haven't thought this through, trying to decide if it's the right thing to do, since I have to leave everyone I love to do it. But it is; it's the right thing for me."

Mom turned and pulled Ruth into a full hug. "Of course you do, honey. We're so proud of you. I'm just being a mother, worrying about my kids. But I'll be fine." She pulled back, holding Ruth at arm's length. "Just be sure you write us long letters, telling us about the incredible adventures you're having and the people you are meeting."

I moved Elsie to my shoulder to pat her back.

"I will, Mom, I promise." Ruth walked over to kiss Elsie on the top of her head and ran a hand along my arm. "I'll miss you so much, Lilly, and little Elsie. You have to promise to send me pictures of this beauty as she grows."

I nodded, unable to swallow the lump in my throat.

When we lost Jack, I could actually see the pain Ruth carried around with her everywhere. For a long time after that, she threw herself into work with the Red Cross and doubled her war efforts, but she still carried the shadow of that pain.

But since she'd learned about the Clubmobile program, and especially since she'd turned in her application, the shadow had lifted. She hadn't forgotten Jack, I was sure of that, but she had a new purpose for living. We couldn't deny that this kind of work was tailor-made for Ruth: helping people on a personal level, bringing hope and cheer to the front-line soldiers. She wouldn't need to bring people home to give them comfort and food anymore. She was taking the comfort and food straight to them.

"That's a promise, Ruth. Elsie and I will write you often and send both pictures of her and drawings from the day care. The children will love drawing pictures for you."

She laughed. "Peter and Kurt Blumenthal already gave me some pictures to take with me." She pulled some out of her pocket.

"I saw you and Judith talking. How's she doing?" Elsie stopped eating for a moment and stared up at me. "When I've seen her at the day care, she's always in a rush."

Ruth nodded. "She's good. She still misses Henry, but I think she's figured out how to get on with her life. She even blushed a bit when she told me that she and Jacob have been exchanging frequent letters."

I smiled. "You may have given her a second chance at happiness, Ruth, by bringing Jacob into her life." I smiled down at my daughter. "After all, spreading happiness is what you do best."

Ruth leaned down and gave me a hug. I saw a telltale tear in her eye as she headed back to the parlor to help with the clean-up.

****

That next morning, a Saturday, we woke up to gray skies. The temperatures had dipped down again, and Dad said it felt like the air froze his nose hairs together with every breath. Ah, winter in the Northeast.

Ruth was catching a bus to Washington, D.C. mid-morning, so everyone had eaten breakfast early but they were still hanging around the kitchen. Even the boys must have known something was up, as they were playing quietly in the parlor, which almost never happened.

"Auntie Lilly?" Fred came wandering into the kitchen with something wadded up in his hand.

"Yes, Fred?" I wiped Elsie's hands. She loved to play in oatmeal almost as much as to eat it.

"Is this yours?" He handed me a wrinkled ball of paper. Something snatched my breath away. It felt like air mail stationery. Could it be?

I smoothed open the paper and stopped. "Where did you get this?" I tried not to snap at the boy, but my heart was thumping.

"I found it in my toy box. I saw the 'L' like Mama

showed me. See, it's an 'L' and L stands for Lilly, right?"

I couldn't quite process the fact that my letter from Paul had been in his toy box, but I pulled him in for a hug, despite his squirming. "Yes, L stands for Lilly, you smart boy."

He pulled himself free of my embrace but smiled at me before running back to the parlor.

My mouth was dry. When did he write this letter? When did it arrive? How did it get misplaced? What did he think of me?

Helen must have seen my growing panic. She stood and picked Elsie up out of her chair. "Why don't this little lass and I play with the boys a while so her mum can read that letter?"

I tried to catch my breath. I mumbled, "Thank you," and hurried upstairs.

Elsie was born on July 4th, nearly seven months ago. I had written to Paul about her that day and had never heard back. I'd written to him several times in these past months, always begging for a reply, for anything to let me know he was okay and still loved me. But I hadn't received one letter. Until now.

This letter was dated in September and postmarked in December. Had it been hidden in the toy box for two months?

*Dear Lilly,*

*I'm sorry I haven't written sooner. I'll admit that I didn't know what to say at first when I got your letter. I couldn't write back until I had a chance to get over how angry I was. Plus, we weren't in a place where I could write you back for a while, so I had to wait. But I talked to the chaplain and some of my buddies, and I think I've got my thoughts together now, so here goes.*

*I waited to cool down because I didn't want you to think I was angry at you. I'm not. I'm shocked, for sure, to find out you had a baby when I didn't even know you were pregnant. We never had a chance to even talk about kids before I shipped out. I mean, we're both pretty young ourselves. You haven't even turned 21 yet, at least, at the time I'm writing this, but who knows how long before you get it. Anyway, I guess I never thought about kids so soon.*

*It took me a while to figure out that I'm not only mad at the man that hurt you, I'm also mad at myself for not being there to protect you. And I'm mad at this war for keeping us apart, so I couldn't be there to take care of you, to hold you, and to see our daughter be born.*

*I'm so proud of you for being so strong. You amaze me. I don't know if I could have been so forgiving of a baby born from violence, if not for you. You see her as a part of you, a member of our family, a sweet innocent child not responsible for the man who hurt you. Because you see it that way, I can too. She's our child and just the first—surely we'll want to have more, right?*

*Thank you, and your father, for the picture of you and Elsie May—a beautiful name, by the way. Please send more.*

*I used to be fighting this war for you, but now I'm fighting for you and Elsie. To come home to the two beautiful girls in my life. I'm the luckiest man alive, so I know I'll make it home to you safe and sound. Elsie deserves a father who loves her almost as much as he loves her mother, so I'll do everything I can, every day, to make sure I come home safely to you both.*

*Think of me holding you, missing you, and loving you more than life itself, because that's what I'm thinking. Please send me more pictures, tell me what she learns to do, and tell me what your life is like these days. I live for you and Elsie and will love you both forever.*

*Your loving husband and father to our daughter—*

*Paul*

I could hardly read his writing due to the tears in my eyes. What had I done to deserve a man like that? I knew the answer right away. Nothing. I didn't deserve him. Paul was such a good man, clearly a gift from God, and I was lucky that he loved me, and my—or rather, our—beautiful daughter.

I was reading it through again, savoring each word, when I heard a knock on the door.

"Lilly?" Helen spoke softly.

"Come in." I folded the letter back into the envelope.

"Clara has the baby, as Ruth is getting ready to go." She saw the tears in my eyes. "Oh, no, love. Is everything okay?"

I nodded, emotion swelling in my throat again.

She sank onto the bed next to me. "Are you sure? Is it Paul?"

I took a deep breath and swallowed my tears. "He's fine. Actually, he's perfect."

"He just couldn't write sooner?" She knew how worried I'd been.

"The letter's from months ago, although there's no way to know when it got delivered. It could have been crumpled up in the toy box for weeks." I laughed. "But it doesn't matter." I took another deep breath, looking up into her eyes. "He loves me, he loves Elsie, and he can't wait to get home to his family and have more babies. He's incredible and wonderful and everything I could have hoped for in a man."

Helen wrapped her arms around me, and my tears started to flow again. I'd have a sinus infection before this day was over.

"I'm happy for you, Lilly. You had me more than a wee bit worried, I'm going to say."

I tried to pull myself together. "Okay, you said Ruth is getting ready to leave. We'd better get downstairs."

Ruth had decided that she didn't want everyone coming to the bus station to see her off. She wanted to say her goodbyes at home, so only Mom and Dad were going to drive her to the station after the rest of us saw them off.

I stopped in the bathroom to wash my face while Helen headed downstairs to tell them I was on my way.

When I got to the parlor, Ruth was crouched down with both Robert and Fred caught up in a big hug. Clara stood next to Ruth, and everyone else was gathered in the parlor, including Leonard and Matthew.

Ruth looked up, and when she saw me, she released the boys, who immediately started jumping and skipping around the room, chanting, "Auntie Ruthie, off to D.C." Clara just shook her head.

"Everything okay?" Ruth almost mouthed the words to me, trying to keep her voice low.

"Wonderful." I smiled and walked into her open arms. "Paul can't wait for more pictures of Elsie and wants me to write him about all the things she's learning to do."

Ruth hugged me tight and kissed my cheek. "I knew he was a good man."

She started to pull back, but I tightened my arms around her. "I'm going to miss you so much." I spoke into her hair as I buried my face in her shoulder. "Please write all the time, keep your head down, and be careful."

She nodded and promised to write every day, so I loosened my hug.

"I'll miss you too, Lilly, and Elsie, of course. I'm so proud of the wonderful woman and mother you've become. I love you."

Tears streamed down my face now. "I love you, too, my sister."

Next it was Helen's turn. She pulled Ruth into her arms, leaning down to hug her tight. "Thank you for everything you've done for me, Ruth. Because of you, I can write you letters and read the ones you send me. I'll miss you so much. Hurry home."

"I'll miss you too, my dear friend. And remember, you're going to find out how to take those correspondence courses or the high school exam, so you can graduate and apply to teaching colleges. I think you'll be a wonderful teacher, Helen. I love you and am proud of you."

"I love you too," said Helen, her eyes filled with tears. "Please keep your head down over there."

Ruth laughed. "We don't even know if I'm going over there. Right now, I'm only going to Washington, but I'll keep my head down there, too."

Helen and everyone chuckled. At times like that, you either laughed or you cried.

Ruth gave hugs and goodbye kisses to Elsie, Grandma, Granddad, and Leonard. When she came to Matthew, he awkwardly held out his hand. "Thank you, Ruth," he said simply.

"You're welcome, Matthew." She pulled him into a hug, and he held on tight.

Once everyone had said goodbye, at least two or three times, and Dad was standing at the door muttering, "We're going to be late," over and over, Ruth finally put on her coat, picked up her handbag, and walked to the door, with Mom at her heels. With one last look over her shoulder and a blown kiss, Ruth was gone.

How could life ever be the same?

****

Less than a week later, I was just walking in the back door when I heard my mother shout. I quickly dumped my boots and winter coat in the mudroom and carried Elsie into the kitchen.

Dad, Grandma, and Granddad were sitting at the table, with Mom looking over Dad's shoulder.

"What's the matter?" I rushed to the table to see them all looking down at a letter. Thank heavens it wasn't a telegram.

Mom turned to hug me, kissing Elsie and pulling the baby into her arms. "Ruth's first letter arrived. She passed her interview, got the job, and has already started her training."

"Wow." I pulled up a chair next to Granddad. "That was fast."

Dad nodded. "They certainly aren't wasting any time."

"So what does she say?"

Dad looked back at the letter. "She's officially a staff assistant with the American Red Cross at the rate of a hundred and fifty dollars a month, plus some kind of maintenance when she's overseas. She's been assigned to a room at American University with a roommate she seems to like. She says she went to the Pentagon to get vaccinations, including typhoid and tetanus, and is meeting girls from all over the country."

"And she's getting fitted for a number of uniforms," said Grandma.

"But she has to pay for the tailor herself," Mom added, a slight scowl on her face. "But at least the Red Cross provides her with uniforms. They gave her a long list of things she has to buy to take with her, like blouses, socks, gloves, stockings, and even four girdles. I hope they pay her first month's salary right away, as it's going to cost her a lot to get everything she needs."

"She sounds excited about it all," Dad said, smiling. "I don't think she'll mind buying what she needs, as it'll probably be hard to get any more supplies wherever it is they send her."

Mom pulled two envelopes out of her pocket. "She sent you and Helen letters of your own."

****

As soon as supper was over and Elsie was tucked into her bed, I dropped Helen's letter on her bed and then pulled out my own letter and climbed onto my bed.

*Dearest Lilly,*

*So much is happening every day, I can hardly find time to write about it all. Let me start by thanking you again for the going-away party. It meant so much to me to get a chance to see everyone before leaving town. Everyone made me feel special and loved and put me in the best spirits for my new adventure. So thanks for all you did to make it happen.*

*The girls I've been meeting here, everyone who has been hired by the ARC (short for American Red Cross), especially the other girls in the Clubmobile program, have been wonderful. These women are strong, smart, funny, and friendly. I feel like I've found another group of "sisters," which will make this whole adventure all the better.*

*Our training just began, but I was told there isn't much to it at this point. More hands-on training will take place once we get to wherever we're going. So far, we've mostly been warned about getting enough rest, maintaining our health and vigor, as the jobs involve a lot of physical strength, and to avoid kissing anyone. They have encouraged us to try our hands at ice-breaking skills, so we can put large groups of enlisted men at ease, such as card tricks, ping-pong, poker, and dancing. I figure I can always talk baseball with the boys, especially if I can get my hands on a copy of* Stars and Stripes *now and then, with sports news.*

*Our uniform fittings are quite amusing. We apparently get winter- and summer-weight uniforms, with skirts, which seems impractical for what I've heard about Clubmobile work. One of the instructors said if we get assigned to a Clubmobile in Europe, we get a different uniform over there that has pants and a warmer coat, as it gets pretty cold. The Clubmobile workers in India and the Pacific get lighter, tropical-weight gear.*

*My roommate, Charlotte, is a lovely girl from Iowa. She was also a teacher before she decided to sign up, so we have that in common. We sat with the girls in the room next door at lunch and dinner today, and they both seem great too. Renee is from Brewster, NY, and her father is in a concentration camp, although she doesn't know where. Eileen is an aspiring actress from Los Angeles. Everyone I meet has similar reasons for signing up—we want to do something useful.*

*We do look a bit like stair steps when we're together, though, as Charlotte is around Helen's height. She says she's five foot twelve, as she doesn't want to admit to being six foot tall. Eileen is easily five nine, and then there's me, at five five, and finally Renee, who's only five foot one but is a barrel of energy.*

*Between uniform fittings, training meetings, and shopping for everything we need before we go, the rest of my time in Washington is going to fly by. Once we're finished here, we'll get a train to New York, if we're headed to Europe, or a plane to California, if we're off to the Far East. As soon as I know which way I'm headed, I'll write. I think I'll even have a chance to call home before I get on whatever ship is taking me wherever I'm going. I'll try for a weekend day, in the hopes of catching more people at home, but my schedule is not my own and won't be for a long time.*

*In the midst of all this preparation, I sometimes find myself wondering if this is the right path for me. I will always miss Jack. If I still expected him to come home from the war, I never would have left and would still be dreaming of a house full of kids and life on the farm. That's the life I truly wanted and believe I would have been incredibly happy living. But, without Jack, I found satisfaction in helping other women's husbands, boyfriends, sons, and brothers as they headed off to, and returned from, this war. If I can help keep their morale up, remind them of the reasons we're fighting this war, maybe it will help them come home safely to their loved ones. I hope you all understand why I have to do this and believe, as I do, that Jack would want me do it.*

*Please, please, please, write to me often. As much as this is where I need to be right now, I miss you already. I'm enclosing my new address, good even once I leave Washington. It's supposed to follow me wherever I go. Kiss Elsie, Fred, and Robert for me, as well as Mom and Pop and everybody else. Keep up the great work at the day care and know that I am proud of the strong woman you've become. I'm sure Paul can't wait to get home to you, and he will be impressed by how you've grown and matured while he's been away.*

*Take care of you and your little beauty.*

*All my love—Ruth*

# Chapter Twenty-Three
Ruth

"Come on, folks. We're going to be late!"

And just that fast, I was transported back to Upton Falls, to Pop standing at the door, his hat and coat on, trying to hurry us all up before we were late to church.

My Clubmobile comrades and I, dressed in full uniform, stepped out of the bus and hurried to the *Queen Elizabeth* for our voyage to England. The impressive ocean liner stood at the pier, her great red smokestacks billowing.

These gals had joined when I did, trained with me, and traveled with me from D.C. to New York two days ago. We'd done a little shopping and sightseeing, and enjoyed some good food before we headed to the pier. Our bedrolls and footlockers were already aboard, so we didn't have to carry much with us through the crowds.

The four of us who had roomed together the last two days were joined by nearly forty other Clubmobilers headed to London. From there, who knew where we would all end up, but the Army wanted a large influx of ARC girls, which meant they had some plans in the works. Of course, there were eight ARC clubs in London alone, so we might end up going no farther than that.

"Can you believe this crush?" Neither Renee nor I

could see over the masses of military men surrounding us. I trusted that Eileen and Charlotte could see where we were headed and get us where we needed to go.

"Well"—Eileen looked back at Renee—"they told us the ship would be overfull, right? How many men will be on board?"

I looked up. "I think they said fifteen hundred officers, thirteen thousand troops, and the forty of us ARC girls."

"Gotta love those odds." Charlotte laughed.

I was the only widow among the Clubmobile girls I knew; everyone else I'd met was single. No one, however, had taken this job to look for a husband. From everything I'd heard in talking to the other girls, we all were there to help the war effort.

As we climbed the gangplank, we heard some whistles from below and a lot of cheering from the decks above us. I looked up and saw scores of young, pimply-faced boys waving and smiling at us.

We climbed to the upper decks for a better view as we pulled out of the harbor. Even though I'd grown up around water in the Finger Lakes, I'd never seen a ship this large.

We walked through a crowd of officers on the top deck and found a place at the railing. Charlotte squeezed in next to me. "What a view, right?"

We looked out over Brooklyn, with Manhattan in the distance and miles of glistening water around us.

"You've got that right." I steadied myself against the railing while I turned and twisted to see as much as I could.

"You okay there, Midwestern girl?" Eileen had taken to teasing Charlotte about coming from the plains after Charlotte let it slip that she'd never seen an ocean.

"Don't you worry, California. I'm doing just fine."

"I hope we don't hit terribly rough seas," said Renee. I was thinking the same thing and decided to eat only lightly the first few days at sea, just in case ocean travel didn't agree with me.

In our winter ARC uniforms, we all appeared pretty jaunty. Glancing along the rail, I saw a mix of women, mostly in their mid- to late-twenties, all fairly attractive and physically fit, wearing our uniform skirts and jackets of a dark blue-gray wool, with the ARC shoulder patch on our left shoulder, white blouses buttoned at the neck, white gloves, and the military-style matching cap. We looked a bit like nurses.

During training, we'd been lectured on our expected behavior and how we represented the ARC when dressed in our uniforms. Viewing this group, I thought we represented the ARC charmingly.

****

Once the ship got underway, which seemed to take hours, we made our way below, to Deck C, to find our cabin, which was barely bigger than the mud room back home.

"Let's not all try to stand in here at once," Eileen said. Not that we could.

There were four beds hanging from the side walls, two lower and two upper bunks. The aisle between them was just wide enough to stand in. A couple of tiny built-in bureaus and two small closets were what we'd all have to share. Opposite the closets was a tiny bathroom, but at least we would only have to share it between the four of us.

"Who's up for a walk on deck?" Charlotte grabbed

her handbag and worked her way back to the door.

"I'm coming," said Renee.

"Me, too." I grabbed my coat, left my bag on my bunk, and stood.

Eileen kicked off her shoes and swung her legs up on her bed. "I'm staying put for a while. I need to rest and refresh before dinner at the captain's table this evening." She tied her scarf around her hair and lay back, ready for a nap.

Charlotte, Renee, and I headed up the nearest stairs to the main deck, which was windier now that we were well at sea. All around us, we saw miles of gray-blue water dotted with ripples of white waves. We'd been warned that February was a cold time for a crossing, so we'd packed extra sweaters, scarves, and winter gloves. I was definitely going to need them.

Renee stopped to lean on the rail, looking to the east. I stepped beside her, standing silently.

"Are you okay? Feeling queasy?"

Her expression was sad despite the faint smile on her lips. "I'm feeling queasy all right, but not because of the waves." She leaned her right shoulder against me.

Charlotte huddled behind us, wrapping her arms around our shoulders. "What's up, gals?"

Renee took a deep breath and turned to face us both. "I can't help thinking about what is happening to my father right now, if he's even still alive." She looked back toward the horizon, her eyes glistening. "I can't get to Europe fast enough. We need to win this war."

I put my hand over hers. I couldn't imagine what she must be going through. It was worse, even, than knowing Jack was gone. At least he was beyond the harm of the Nazis.

We stood together like that for a few quiet moments before the first group of enlisted men approached us. They held back a bit, either sensing our mood in the moment or afraid to speak to us.

Charlotte dropped her embrace and turned to face the soldiers while Renee took the moment to pull herself together.

“Well, hello there, gents. Fancy meeting you here.” Charlotte laughed, and I couldn’t help but join in. The astonished look on the faces of some of the soldiers was comical. They were mostly all shorter than Charlotte, save one skinny young man in the back.

The dark-haired private in the front sauntered closer to Charlotte. “Hello there, Stretch. I’m Anthony.” He turned to Renee and me. “And hello to you ladies, as well. We heard there were girls on board, but we had to see for ourselves.”

The redheaded boy to Anthony’s left almost jumped up and down. “I told ’em, I told ’em. I saw y’all gettin’ off a bus at the pier. I knew you were fixin’ to get on the ship with us.” He turned to Anthony. “Our lucky day, i’n’it?”

The tall, blond private on Anthony’s right leaned back and punched the redhead in his right arm. “We’re going to war, idiot. It’s nobody’s lucky day.”

Several of the soldiers nodded to that. I looked over at Charlotte, who was talking to Anthony and several of the soldiers around him. Renee hovered between us.

“We’re heading to London with the Red Cross.” I spoke to the tall blond and the group around him. They all looked so young. “What unit are you all with?”

"We're joining the Twenty-Ninth Infantry Division, ma'am," said the blond. He stood at attention and saluted. "Private Martin Rice at your service."

"Nice to meet you, Private. I'm Ruth Walker, and this is my friend, Renee Abrams." I held out my hand and, after a brief moment of surprise, he dropped the salute, relaxed, and shook my hand and then Renee's.

I heard choruses of "me, too," from a number of soldiers standing behind Private Rice.

"Where are you boys coming from?"

"We're out of Virginia, ma'am," said Private Rice. "Where are you gals from?"

"We're both from New York, Private."

One of the soldiers behind Private Rice shouted, "I'm from New York, too. Well, the Bronx!"

I smiled. "I live in Upton Falls, a tiny town in the Finger Lakes, a long way from the Bronx."

Renee nodded. "I'm from Brewster, which is closer to the city. I've been to the Bronx, though, and love the zoo." She finally smiled.

I watched her talking about New York City, and cities in general, with several of the soldiers and suddenly felt she would be okay. Working with the troops would help her as much as she would be helping them.

We met and talked to all the soldiers in the group, but before long it was time to get ready for dinner. We were nearly frozen from the cold wind on deck and had to pull ourselves away to go get ready.

****

*February 19, 1944*
*Dear Helen,*

*Well, we've been on this ship for four days now,*

*and I can honestly say I don't think I'll ever want to take a transatlantic voyage again, except to come home. It's cold and dull, even with all these people on board. We can't spend too much time on deck because the weather has been wet, making it even colder, so I end up playing cards, reading, and talking to the soldiers on board as much as possible, and writing letters. I'm grateful to have you all to write to and look forward to getting letters from you once we've landed in London.*

*By the way, thank you, again, for all the advice on how to get around and what to see in London, assuming I have much time there. I doubt I'll ever get there again in my life, so I want to make the most of it. I will go see your father and brothers as soon as I have a chance, and be sure to show them the pictures I brought of us.*

*I'll also do my best to get to High Wycombe quickly, to see Billy and deliver your package personally. Of course, I don't know where we'll be going yet, but we have learned that Charlotte, Renee, Eileen, and I will be assigned to the "*St. Louis.*" The Army has converted 6x6 GMC trucks into Clubmobiles, with a doughnut machine, coffee urns, sink, and stove in the front. The back half of the truck has books, records, a Victrola and speakers, and folding bunks, in case we end up sleeping in the Clubmobile overnight. Learning to drive (on the "wrong" side of the road) and maintain these beasts will be our first order of business when we get to our training site. I can't wait—it sounds like fun to me.*

*Jacob Cohen came to see me in New York, just before we set sail. It was wonderful to see him. His bond tour continues—little did he know that being a war hero would turn him into an advertising campaign.*

*He says he's anxious to have a chance to visit Upton Falls again. He seemed embarrassed to talk about it at first, but with enough encouragement, he admitted that he visits as often as he can, to see Judith and the children. He made me promise not to say anything to Judith, but he's working up the nerve to propose. I'm so glad for all of them—they deserve to be happy. He thanked me for introducing them. He also promised to take me to a Dodgers game after the war. I'm going to hold him to it.*

*I hope that everyone is well and all is good for you at work and at the day care. Give my love to the family and know that I miss you so much. It will help me to see your family, your city, and, of course, Billy—that will certainly make me feel closer to you. Take care of yourself—Love, Ruth*

****

After six days at sea, the *Queen Elizabeth* landed, and we took a bus from the docks to the ARC headquarters in London. We had a couple of hours to unpack and get our land legs again before training began in earnest.

"Welcome, ladies." The ARC representative, Miss Harper, was a small, blonde woman, probably about forty-five. "The Red Cross appreciates your desire to help your country. You will find this is the hardest job you've ever had, but I'm sure you'll grow to love it. We do important work here, and you girls, the Clubmobile girls, will get a chance to see what's happening in this war from an almost front-line perspective. You will be meeting boats and trains, seeing troops that arrive and those about to leave, as well as those in combat. You will help thousands of American soldiers, reminding them what they are fighting for, and you will remember this experience for the rest of your lives."

I didn't doubt that one bit.

"Now that you've been assigned to your Clubmobile, we'll spend the next week training you on not only operating procedures for the coffee urns, doughnut machines, and other equipment on the Clubmobile, but also driving and maintaining your vehicle. You will be part of a Clubmobile group, which consists of eight Clubmobiles, a cine-mobile designed to show movies, two supply trucks, two pickup trucks, and a Jeep. These groups will be deployed just behind advancing troops, so it will be essential for you to drive and maintain your own Clubmobile, so that no soldiers have to be assigned to support our mission but can be instead focused on winning the war."

Advancing troops? I couldn't help but wonder where we would be assigned. Were we headed to Italy, where Will's unit was? I hadn't even had a full day in England yet, and we were already preparing to leave.

After a demonstration of how the doughnut machine worked, we all followed Miss Harper to the motor pool to get our first up-close look at a Clubmobile. What struck me was how many of the converted trucks were lined up. The *St. Louis* was ten trucks down from the demo one.

"Wow, it's small in there, isn't it?" Charlotte followed me out of the truck, and we stood in front, looking down the line to the *St. Louis*.

I smiled. "Yeah, despite how huge these trucks are on the outside, there won't be a lot of room inside when all four of us are trying to make coffee and doughnuts and serve the troops."

"I sincerely hope we don't have to sleep in those cots regularly," said Eileen.

Charlotte laughed. "You and me both. My feet will hang off the end."

"I like how the service window on the side of the truck opens up, so we can talk to the boys while we're cooking and they can come up to the window to get their coffee." Renee's mood had brightened by the end of our sea voyage. She seemed to be ready to fight the good fight, even though we'd only be fighting with the doughnut machine.

"That's it for today, girls," called Miss Harper over the group. "Tomorrow morning, we'll start at seven o'clock sharp in the auditorium, where you'll learn, in depth, about maintaining your Clubmobile and the equipment on it. After lunch, you will break into groups to learn how to drive these trucks. We want all of you to know how to drive and maintain the vehicles, although some of you will most likely become the regular drivers, while others will take on different roles." She held up her right hand, finger waving at us, "get some sleep tonight, despite the time difference. It'll be a long day tomorrow, and just the first of many."

Eileen looked at me. "Oh, boy. Sounds like fun."

## Chapter Twenty-Four
## Helen

I was so knackered by the time I walked in the door after work, I could barely find the strength to hang up my coat. Our production quotas had been raised, hours had been extended, and the pressure was on to increase production beyond anything we'd even come close to before. I was as keen as the next girl to produce as many engines as our pilots would need, but this new pace was killing us.

After I cleaned up and shut off the lights downstairs, I climbed the stairs as quietly as possible, hoping not to disturb anyone, especially little Elsie. Sweet as she was, she wasn't much of a sleeper.

When I opened my door and flipped on the lights, I had to stop myself from shouting in delight when I saw two air mail envelopes on my bed. I hurried to open Billy's first, fingering the necklace at my throat.

*Dear Helen,*

*I'm writing this in late February, but I'm sure it will be well into March, at best, before you get it. I hope it's starting to warm up again in Upton Falls by now, as I know March can be full of gray, frozen mud there. As you well know, over here, it mostly rains all the blasted time.*

*We've had a busy month making direct hits at the heart of our enemy. Everyone, even those of us who have been here the longest, feel a renewed energy to finally be striking significant blows to the Nazis, working toward winning the war. Of course, I can't tell you any specifics, but (I hope) I can say that we really feel the tides turning.*

*Ruth made the trip to see me at High Wycombe, and I couldn't have been happier to see anyone unless it was you, yourself. Even in her Red Cross uniform, she looked like a part of home and made the miles between you and me melt away. It wasn't as good as seeing you would have been, but the sight of her was such a boon to my spirits, such a reminder of my real life, and every guy here felt as if he had known her and her co-workers all their lives.*

*Thank you for the sweater, socks, food, and skivvies. Although the clothes are always appreciated, I was in heaven with the homemade cookies and breads. When did you learn to bake chocolate chip cookies? They were incredible. The guys in my barracks looked like they might murder me in my sleep for the cookies, so I did share a few, just enough to save my neck. Everyone says to tell you they love you, but don't believe them, they're a fickle bunch. Not me, though; I'll love you forever.*

*Anyway, Ruth and her Clubmobile girls were a huge hit. They drove the thirty miles from London in their doughnut truck, saying it was a good test of their training. They fired up the machines and served us coffee and doughnuts, with a side of Benny Goodman and Glenn Miller on the Victrola. It was great fun and a welcome relief after all the tense missions we've been on.*

*You seemed apprehensive about Ruth's frame of*

*mind, but she seems incredibly happy to me. Her co-workers are a great bunch of gals, and she fits right in. The guys in the unit really enjoyed their visit and many fell a little bit in love with the girls. I don't think the Clubmobile girls will be in a lot of danger, so don't worry about her getting too near the fighting. By the time she gets home, she may be ready to put Jack's death behind her and begin life anew.*

*Well, zero-five-hundred comes early, so I'd better get some sleep. I feel so close to you this week, wearing the sweater you sent, munching on the last of the banana bread crumbs, looking at the picture Ruth brought. I can't tell you how much that all means to me and how much more I love you every day. Know that we're all working hard to get home as quickly as we can. I can't wait for the day I can hold you in my arms again. All my love, forever yours—Billy*

It took me a few times through the letter before I could absorb everything he had to say, not that the handwriting was hard to read, but because I wanted to savor each and every word and the images they brought to my mind. I could never thank Ruth enough for visiting Billy, bringing him my package and a wee bit of home.

I'd have to thank Julia for teaching me to make the cookies, as well.

When I finally put Billy's letter down, knowing I'd read it many more times before the next one arrived, I picked up the second letter and was relieved to see Ruth's handwriting. We hadn't received any letters since the ones she wrote on the ship. She'd been in London for more than a month now, and I was frightfully keen to hear how she was doing.

*March 24, 1944*
*Dear Helen,*

*I'm sorry I haven't written sooner. I just sent off letters to Mom and Pop as well as Lilly, so you'll probably all get them at once, but this is the first time I've really had to write that I wasn't asleep in my chair.*

*In Washington, our training took place in a classroom and felt like a cross between high school and college. It was mostly about how to represent the ARC, how to avoid diseases (most of which I haven't got a chance of catching in London), and how to recognize different military insignia. Well, that's as far from what we've been doing here as could be.*

*Since we arrived, we've been mostly dressed in our "battledress uniforms" similar to the British soldiers, not only because they're warmer but also because they have pants. It makes no sense to wear a uniform skirt while training on the Clubmobiles. As if driving those trucks wasn't enough of a challenge, on the wrong side of these skinny English roads, we're also trained to maintain the trucks, including tires, and to use and maintain the equipment inside. After half a day with my head under the hood of the truck, I finally got a begrudging "good" out of the sergeant who was training us.*

*The men training us to drive and maintain these trucks weren't convinced that members of the fairer sex could understand the workings of an internal combustion engine, learn to double clutch, or even haul the fifty-pound bags of flour. I'm happy to report that the ladies of the* St. Louis *and Clubmobile Group A were up to the challenge. Even little Renee hauled that bag of flour like a pro, although she can't be much more than one hundred pounds herself.*

*Making the doughnuts is quite a job, as the doughnut-making machines are particular. We have a prepared flour mixture, add water, and knead the dough before putting it into the machine. It's interesting to watch the machine use high-pressure air to push out the doughnuts and drop them into the heated grease. The machine even automatically flips them over, so all we have to do is take them out, load them on trays, and feed the clamoring hordes.*

*Anyway, once trained and let loose on the English countryside, we were off to see Billy and the 8th Air Force. Don't thank me for going—thank you for asking me to go. Not only was seeing Billy wonderful, the reception we got at the base was exactly why I wanted to do this work. Yes, they loved the doughnuts, coffee, cigarettes, and chocolates, but more than that, they just wanted to talk to us. Of course, I talked to many of them about baseball, but even just trivial things like cooking, farming, and current events in the U.S. made them elated. I spent a lot of the time listening to the G.I.s talk about their hometowns, their families, the girl they left behind, and the like. I can honestly tell you that this may be the most rewarding work I do in my entire life.*

*Billy is wonderful. He is healthy and handsome and as happy as he can be when he's so far away from you. He was thrilled with your package and letter and talked about you endlessly. He is so proud of you for learning to read and thinks you should pursue a diploma and then on to college, which we both agreed on. He seems to have some close "mates," as they say over here, and the other officers and G.I.s seem to respect him. I'd forgotten how funny he is, but they all joke around a lot. I'm happy to say he has eyes only for you and can't wait to get back to you.*

*I'd better end here and get this in the mail, or you'll all start to worry about ever hearing from me. Please know there are some big things brewing here that I can't talk about, so if my letters become fairly sporadic, just know that I'm happy and working hard. I miss you all. Love, Ruth*

By the time I put both letters on my nightstand, it was the middle of the night, but I fell asleep with a smile on my face.

****

"Helen?"

When I turned at the sound of my name, I couldn't believe my eyes. What was George Anderson doing at the bus stop?

I nodded and tried not to scowl. "Mr. Anderson." I hardly ever ran into the Andersons around town, other than a chance meeting after church on Sundays, but I never felt intimidated when I was with the Walkers.

He walked up to me, lightly placing his right hand on my left elbow. "Would you mind if we spoke for a moment before your bus arrives?"

My heart started to beat faster. "Have you heard something about Billy?" Again, I reached for my necklace, which had become a lifeline to Billy.

"No, no." He held his hands in front of him. "I should have said so sooner. No, everything is fine. I just wanted a word with you."

I took a deep breath, trying to regain my bearings. "Okay."

He stepped away from the bus stop and the nosey ears of my co-workers, so I followed.

"I received a letter from Billy last week," he started.

I nodded.

"He's fine," he hurried to continue. "He told me about Ruth Walker's visit. I had heard she joined the Red Cross, but didn't know she would be located so near to Billy."

Again, I sighed and tried to stay calm. What was he on about anyway?

"Yes, Ruth is stationed in London, at least for now, and delivered a package to Billy for me."

"Yes, he told me. That was generous of her."

I nodded. "She's a kind person."

"Yes, well." He cleared his throat. "Billy wrote that Ruth also told him that you'd moved out of our house because, well, because of the way we'd treated you. He's livid with us."

I closed my eyes. When I opened them again, I met his gaze. "I'm sorry for that. I told Billy I moved in with the Walkers before, but mostly said it was for the company, since Lilly and I were working together. I had no idea Ruth would tell Billy anything more."

Slowly, he shook his head, his gaze dropping to the ground. "Don't apologize. We were unkind to you." He looked back up at me. "I didn't realize Mabel taunted you about being unable to read. Why didn't you tell Billy about that yourself?"

"You're his mum and dad. I don't want to come between Billy and his parents, and certainly not while he's away at war." I swallowed the lump in my throat. "I figured things would be different once he came home."

Mr. Anderson reached out and took my hand.

"You're very thoughtful, Helen. I'm sorry we didn't see that sooner, and that Mabel, well, that we didn't treat you better. Billy is lucky to have found you. I can tell by his letters how much he truly loves you."

I couldn't speak and fought back tears.

He paused, apparently sensing I needed a moment.

"Helen, Billy told me that not only did Ruth teach you to read and write, but you really are seriously thinking about college." He smiled. "That's impressive, and you should be proud of yourself."

"Thank you. Ruth is a wonderful teacher."

He nodded. "Billy talked about the idea of furthering your education."

Billy and I were going to have words. "Maybe. Billy thinks I could take some courses and pass a test that would get me a high school diploma."

"Yes, he told me. I don't know if he ever told you that I'm a trustee at the Cortland Teachers College. I graduated from there, back when it was known as the Cortland Normal School."

"No, he never mentioned that." I didn't really know what it meant either, but I could always ask Julia and Earl later.

"Well, I checked, and Cortland is offering correspondence courses for soldiers to finish high school and begin college, so I think I could arrange for you to be a part of that program, if you are interested in that."

"You would do that for me?"

His face reddened. "You're my daughter-in-law, the love of my son's life. I want to help you any way I can."

What a lovely thing to say, even though Mabel

surely didn't feel that way.

"Thank you."

The bus pulled up, and the other women started to climb aboard. "I have to go, Mr. Anderson. I can't miss the bus." As I walked to the bus, he reached out his hand and grabbed my arm.

"Would you mind if I talk to the appropriate people at Cortland Teachers College about you and determine what you need to get started?"

"That'd be…fine, sir. Thank you." How could I ask him not to tell his wife?

I turned and climbed on the bus and saw George staring at me as I climbed into my seat. I raised a hand and waved.

He waved back but waited for the bus to pull out before walking away.

"What was that all about?" Gladys nudged me from the seat behind.

"Oh, nothing," I said. "Just passing on a message from Billy."

What was Billy thinking, writing a letter like that to his parents? I couldn't bear the thought of his mother taunting me if I never passed the high school graduation exam. I could hear her snide remarks already. *Oh, Billy, what have you done?*

****

Over lunch at the day care the following day, I told Lilly about George Anderson's visit.

"Oh, Helen."

Lilly must have been able to sense my mood, as her expression was full of sympathy.

"I know." I sighed. "I'm sure Billy was angry when he heard how they'd treated me, and he probably wanted to let them have it."

"At least Mr. Anderson apologized to you."

I nodded. "In truth, he was never that bad to me. It was always her." I looked down at my sandwich and wiped my hands on my slacks. "I just couldn't tell him what she'd said. Nothing good comes from standing between a chap and his mother."

Lilly set down her water cup. "Billy loves you, Helen. He has a right to tell his parents off for the way they treated his wife, the mother of his future children." She smiled at me. "Besides, if George Anderson can help you get a high school diploma and get into a teachers college, that's a good thing, isn't it?"

I inhaled, trying to steady my voice and swallow the panic I was starting to feel. "It's not a good thing if it gives Mabel the chance to be beastly to me again, laughing at the idea of me passing the test, starting college, trying to be a teacher. I just couldn't bear that, especially if Billy found out about it."

My hands were shaking when I picked up my own cup to have a sip of water.

"Surely she wouldn't taunt you about that, now that Billy knows how she behaved before, would she?"

I shrugged. "She knows I didn't tell Billy about it last time, doesn't she?"

Lilly tilted her head, looking up at me. "Are you angry with Ruth for telling Billy? Or are you angry with Billy for writing to his parents?"

I had been trying to figure that out since yesterday. "I don't think I'm angry with either of them, really. I know Billy is trying to protect me, and he must feel terrible about the way his parents treated me, especially after telling me how great it would be when I was living with them, and how excited they would be to meet me."

An image popped into my mind of their faces, the first day, when I told them I was Billy's wife. Excited was not the word for it.

"Of course he's angry at how they treated you. He should have realized that when you moved in with us." Lilly's spine straightened with her outrage for me.

"I told him that I was lonely for people my own age and I hoped he didn't mind but it was more fun for me to be with you and Ruth and Clara."

She laughed. "Well, that much was true."

I smiled. "Yes, it still is." Sighing, I thought of Ruth telling Billy what really happened. "I'm not angry with Ruth either, not really. She's been frightfully good to me—well, you all have—and I guess I should have realized that she'd want Billy to know what really happened. She's become a little protective of me, even though I tower over her like a tree." I chuckled.

Lilly rubbed a hand on my back. "We're all devoted to you, Helen. You're part of the family now."

"Yes, well..." These Americans were always so open with their emotions. "Thank you, Lilly. You must know I feel the same."

"Hey!"

She made me jump. "What?"

"I was just thinking. Maybe, since you were wearing your lucky necklace, maybe Mr. Anderson never even told his wife about your conversation. Maybe she doesn't even know about his letter from Billy. Wouldn't that be great?"

I smiled. "That'd be brilliant. But I don't think I could be that lucky."

****

It was only three weeks later that I got a reply letter from Ruth, responding to my letter about my meeting with Mr. Anderson.

*April 25, 1944*
*Dear Helen,*

*I am so sorry if I hurt you by telling Billy the real reason you moved in with us and how his parents have behaved toward you. I've never been good at lying, so when he asked me about it, he could tell there was more to the story than I was telling him. I know it wasn't my place to get involved in what you tell your husband, and I'm truly sorry. I hope you can forgive me.*

*I'm glad your conversation with Mr. Anderson went so well. It sounds like he's on your side and inclined to help you. I had always heard he was a nice man, so the way Mr. and Mrs. Anderson treated you has always seemed out of character for him.*

*I truly believe you have greatness inside you, Helen. Don't let the interruption in your formal education limit your future—you would make a wonderful college student and a great teacher someday. I can see you at the front of a classroom so clearly in my mind. Do whatever it takes, including accepting help from whoever can help you, to make your dreams a reality.*

*I have to go, as we are packing up in another "hurry up and wait" move with the Army. I can't say what we are facing, but if you don't hear from me for a little while, don't worry. I miss you and everyone at home. This is a terrible war and can't be over soon enough.*

*All my love—Ruth*

*P.S. No, please don't send me your lucky necklace.*

*I have all the Allied armies in the European Theatre to keep me safe. You need to hold on to that as your lifeline to Billy. And it might come in advantageous as you move ahead with your education. Ha, Ha!*

## Chapter Twenty-Five
## Ruth

*May 1, 1944*
*Dear Family,*

*I'm addressing this letter to all of you, hoping that Mom and Pop will share it with everyone, as I hardly have time to write one letter right now.*

*You wouldn't believe the gifts that I have found the most useful here, well, all the censors will let me say about my location is that I'm "somewhere in England." Anyway, the writing paper, pens, and ink are essential, as you can see for yourself. If anyone is putting together a package to send me at some point, please send more, as well as more film for my camera. This is such an incredible experience, I'm so lucky you gave me a camera, Pop, as a going-away gift. I'm going to want to have pictures to remember this all by, not that I think I'll ever forget it. But the other gifts that have been most useful are the shampoo and perfume. It's hard to get rid of the smell of doughnuts and doughnut grease after a fourteen-hour shift slinging coffee and doughnuts for the boys.*

*More ARC girls are pouring into London and going through training. Charlotte, Renee, Eileen, and I are living in a Red Cross dormitory. It's the top floor of a lovely private town house, filled with rows of wooden bunks. We're only about a mile away from the Army mess, where we take our meals with officers and enlisted men, depending on the day and time we make it to meals. When we dine with the officers, it's dining, with place settings, napkins, and fine conversation. When we eat with the enlisted GIs, it's mess, out of our mess kits and cups, but the conversation is just as fine. We have to walk a delicate line between socializing too much with the enlisted or with the officers, and trust me, each group notices the amount of time we spend with the other.*

*Every morning, we make coffee and doughnuts, and then, in the afternoons, we drive out into the countryside and serve the units. While the men are happy for the food, they are thrilled to see American women. We put our records on, serve them from the side of the truck, and then talk, dance, play cards, and mostly listen to the men. Many want to show us their snaps of the girl back home, their baby, wife, sister, or mother, or even a picture of their house or car. Some men are all about flirting and trying to get one of us to agree to a date, but some, especially the younger men who are newer to the ETO, as we all refer to the European Theatre of Operations, confess their fears to us. It's a humbling role we have, being the symbol for everything they are fighting for over here, but also being a live, flesh-and-blood girl-next-door they can jitterbug with or try to steal a kiss from.*

*From the radio, and your letters, I gather that you have heard some of what is in the works around here, so I can say that things are ramping up for the next big move. Some time ago, the* St. Louis *was assigned to Clubmobile Group A, a unit of eight Clubmobiles, four small half-ton trucks, trailers for water tanks, generators, etc., and a supply truck. Each Clubmobile group is attached to an Army unit.*

*In the little down time that we can scrape together, we've been doing some sightseeing around London. Despite all the damage from bombing, it's still a wonderful place. We've been to St. Paul's, Parliament, Westminster Abbey, the Tower of London, and even seen Big Ben. It's a miracle St. Paul's has survived, as everything around it was destroyed. We've even become quite accustomed to the doodlebugs, Hitler's famous buzz bombs, which appear out of nowhere any time of day or night. When a couple of us have an evening free, we have our choice of handsome, uniform-clad escorts for dinner at a local hotel, followed by dancing. There are Americans everywhere in London, awaiting the next step, trying to squeeze every ounce of fun in that we can.*

*I don't know, and couldn't tell you, when things will change around here or what our specific location will be, but you can continue to send letters and packages to me at the same ARC address. Mail might get slower, but things will eventually catch up with me.*

*Know that I love and miss you all and think about you every day.*

*All my love—Ruth*

****

*July 2, 1944*
*Dearest Family,*

*Now that I am safely aboard the transit to the Continent, I can relay some of what's been happening the past couple of weeks. Talk about chaos! Our work in and around London has kept us running and given us a chance to see a lot of the English countryside, including some quaint little towns of literary fame. When we're not driving, making doughnuts and coffee, serving the troops, cleaning our Clubmobile, or stopping for supplies, I have been able to find some time for tennis, as well as dancing and carousing. I haven't played so much tennis since college, but it has been a great diversion. Once a couple of officers found out I played at Keuka, they have included me in as many matches as they and I have time for. At night, we Clubmobile girls can't keep up with all the invitations to dinner or dancing or nights at the pub. Some nights I'm so tired I really just want to take a bath, wash my hair, and write letters, but one of the girls always convinces me to accompany them out. It's exhausting, but I think it's been good for all of us, especially with what we now face.*

*By now, you have heard of D-Day and the valiant efforts our troops have been undergoing on the Normandy front. We had the privilege of serving many of the ships that left the English shores just before they left, when everyone was anxious and full of nerves and determination.*

*Sadly, we've also had the honor of serving many of the hospital ships that have brought so many of those same fresh faces back in some stage of injury or beyond. I can't even describe my feelings during these past few weeks as the numbers of injured and dead have skyrocketed. The news of the invasion forces has continued to come over the radio daily. The Allies have been cautiously optimistic, although I think everyone knows we're in for a long haul now, with fresh troops arriving daily. The gals of Clubmobile Group A have spent several days pulling together many details, from additional immunizations to physical exams, x-rays, and dental checkups, all part of the paperwork to get ready for our turn to go to France.*

*After a day of doughnut-and-coffee delivering, we were making the last of the day's supply runs when we received a telephone call instructing us to return to headquarters to prepare for departure to the Continent. All of us were glad to hear the news and beyond ready to go. All Clubmobile personnel were called to a meeting on June 27 in a crowded noisy meeting, made all the more chaotic by buzz bombs exploding nearby. At 8 a.m. the next morning, we were loaded into trucks and taken to Wimbledon, where we had parked our Clubmobiles. We all got into our respective trucks, to drive in a convoy to Salisbury. We were proud of the clean, shiny* St. Louis, *and I was at the wheel when we arrived on the beautiful plains surrounding Stonehenge, where we pitched our tents for the night.*

*The next morning, at 6 a.m., we were off to the official launching area at Southampton, where we watched our beautiful* St. Louis, *and the other Clubmobiles, be loaded onto the ships. We got our money changed, rations issued, and heard our final orders on British soil.*

*I can't adequately describe the lump in my throat as we passed the Isle of Wight and sailed out into the Channel on our way to the soldiers on the front. While the mood on the ship was certainly jubilant, I felt the conflicting pulls of excitement and satisfaction of finally being able to help the frontline troops and spur our men on toward the end of the war versus the real fear of what we would see along the way. So many young men had already been injured and killed, just in the past month, and I knew, probably better than many of the young, unmarried girls I was working with, how tragic war is for the people left behind. Strangely, I felt Jack's presence as I stood on deck, staring out toward France. It brought me a certain peace, a feeling that he knew I was there and approved. I can't say how much that mattered to me, and I'm so grateful that you all, the people I love most in the world, were so supportive of me.*

*This morning, when I awoke, I knew we hadn't arrived yet, but I hurried to dress and breakfast so I could go up on deck to see the beaches of France. We had time, so I figured I'd write this letter now, as who knows when I'll next have a chance to do so. I'll be following our troops as they make their way toward Germany now, which will mean the mail may take more time to reach me. Keep your letters coming, though, please, as they mean so much to me. And, Lilly and Helen, please send more pictures from the children. Both the gals I work with and the troops we serve love to see the drawings. They never fail to bring a smile to our faces.*

*Now I'm off to the next adventure. I miss and love you all—your, Ruth*

****

*July 4, 1944*
*Dear Family,*

*Happy Independence Day! It's ironic to be here, in Northern France, on July 4$^{th}$, as our troops are bringing independence to the French once again.*

*I don't have much time to write, but I wanted to give you a feel for what we found when we landed on Utah Beach. The beach still showed signs of the recent invasion. The huge craters left behind when bombs hit the beach will never disappear. Stranded ships and destroyed military vehicles sat abandoned everywhere. We had to navigate around the Germans' concrete pillboxes and foxholes, which made driving more of a challenge, in addition to the dirt and dust in the air. We had to have the windshield wipers on constantly just to see through the dirt. At one point, we drove past cages of Nazi prisoners waiting for transport across the Channel. It was chilling.*

*Once we made it to a real road, we started passing troops who seemed buoyed up by our very presence. I was driving at this point, so I slowed enough to talk to some of the men as we went by. They called out "Anyone from Missouri?" or "Who's from California?" Even the French men and women on the road stopped to watch us pass, shouting, "Vive la France!" and holding up their fingers in a V for victory.*

*It is humbling to see the smiles on the faces of these French women, old men, and children, standing amid the rubble, thanking us and giving us what little they have. They refuse to accept anything in exchange but are so happy to see us. I have never hated anyone, but when I see what the Nazis have done here, the destruction and blatant cruelty they wrought here, among these charming people, it's hard not to let hatred seep into my heart.*

*Anytime we had to stop to change drivers or wait for others vehicles to catch up, the French people rushed to us with water, cider, and wine, graciously greeting and thanking us. It's quite heartwarming to feel their love and respect, knowing that our boys are working hard to give them back their country, or at least this part of it.*

*Our first trip has been through the countryside and on to Cherbourg, which is pretty beaten up. We have to wear our helmets at all times in these areas, even though we are behind the front—never fear, my loves, I am not at the front, although we get pretty near. We sleep in tents most nights, or in our Clubmobile on cots, and do our laundry in pails. In fact, my unmentionables are drying on the bushes behind the tent right now. The cold dormitory in England seems like years ago now. I wash my hair in my helmet, trying to stay clean in the mud. And the food, if you can call it that, is often K rations out of a can, although we can sometimes find a little French hotel and get a hot meal. Not a one of us would eat another doughnut, not even on a dare!*

*It's true that this work is so much harder even than what we were doing in England. We can never be sure where we'll bed down each night. Sometimes, we have to quickly move out of an area that starts to take shelling. But when we pull up to a unit that has been fighting their way through shell craters and hedgerows for weeks, the smiles on the faces of those men make everything we're doing worthwhile. The commanding officers often tell us how much difference our visits make to morale. This is why I'm here, and hard as it is, it's wonderful.*

*I miss you all every day. All my love—Ruth*

*P.S. I'm ecstatic to hear that Judith and Jacob got married. Please send pictures.*

## Chapter Twenty-Six
Helen

When I came down to breakfast on Friday morning, Earl was sitting with Julia at the kitchen table having a cup of coffee. Summer is such a busy time on the farm, so he had already been out doing chores, even though I was just starting my day. They both looked up when I got to the bottom of the stairs.

"Good morning, Helen." Julia rose to get me a cup of coffee, despite that I motioned for her to stay seated.

"Good morning, Julia. Good morning, Earl. How are things looking in the fields this morning?" I made toast and took a scoop of oatmeal out of the pot simmering on the stove.

Earl smiled slightly and nodded his head. "The corn is getting tall, knee high by the fourth of July, you know. The potatoes look good, thank heavens, so I think we'll have a good harvest if the weather holds out."

I didn't know anything about farming before I moved in with the Walkers but had learned much from Earl, Leonard, and the whole family about farm life.

Leonard came in, looked from Earl to Julia to me, nodded, and took a seat next to Earl. Julia got another cup of coffee and handed it to Leonard.

"He run off again," Leonard said in low tones, his gaze on Earl.

"He'll be back," said Earl, shaking his head slowly.

"Yup." Leonard took a sip of coffee and looked up.

"Do you want some porridge, Leonard?" Julia rose to her feet again, turning to the stove.

"That'd be great, Julia, and I thank you." Leonard looked at me and nodded, his expression still solemn. "Matthew has a hard time, now and again, and needs some time alone."

"So he just takes off?" I only really saw Matthew at meals on the weekends, due to my second shift hours, and he was always so quiet.

Leonard tilted his head. "Yup. I don't begrudge him some time to himself, and all, but I'd sure like it if he tol' me when he was going to take off. Always leaves me wonderin' if he's lyin' hurt somewhere or sumpin'."

I didn't know what to say to that. Matthew and Leonard seemed to get along pretty well together, so I didn't realize that the younger man took off sometimes.

"He's still in pain. He's had a bad time of it," Julia said, as she put the bowl of oatmeal in front of Leonard.

"Did." Leonard ate a spoonful of oatmeal, nodding toward Julia in thanks. "It's good, Julia, thank you." He sat eating quietly for a moment.

"The war was hard on Matthew, and not just because of his leg." Leonard looked at me and Julia. "When Matthew got injured and was sent back to the field hospital, his unit was mostly wiped out." Leonard paused, looking down. "The boy lost all his buddies."

"I'm so sorry," I murmured. I couldn't imagine how Matthew could learn to deal with the horrors he'd seen and lived through during the war. How would the men coming home ever get past it?

"Yup. Sometimes it gets hard for him that he's alive on account of he was shot. He gets to thinkin' he should've died with the rest of 'em and somehow it's his fault." Leonard held his coffee cup in both hands, arms resting on the table. "He has a hard time livin' with himself just then, never mind bein' around other people."

Julia shook her head. "The poor boy." She clasped her hands together in her lap. "My heart aches for him."

Leonard nodded. "Workin' and livin' here is good for him, Julia. You're all helpin' him by lettin' him be here, but sometimes it gets to be too much for him."

Earl folded his arms over his chest. "He does good work, so he earns his keep."

Julia placed her hand on Earl's arm. "And you help him the most, Leonard. You spend a lot of time with the boy, let him move into your quarters. You're the reason he has a job."

Leonard slowly shook his head. "He's not so different from me, when I came home from the Great War. I wish I'd known you all then, worked out here during some of those dark years. You've helped me by lettin' me live and work here, too."

"Me, too." I nodded, looking from Leonard to Earl and Julia. The Walkers had helped me by bringing me into their family, folding me seamlessly into the family life. Ruth may have brought us to the farm initially, but it was because Earl and Julia were kind and honorable people that Leonard, Matthew, and I were made to feel a part of the family.

"It was Ruth," said Julia, her eyes glistening. "She could always see the good in people, and we were lucky she brought each of you home to us." Julia stood and turned to get more coffee, placing her hand on my shoulder as she walked past me.

Leonard ate his oatmeal, smiled at Julia when she refilled his coffee cup, and nodded. “He’ll be back. Just needs a little time.”

As we all sat eating, we heard Elsie’s baby babble coming down the stairs. She was quite a talker these days, although we didn’t know what she was saying.

When Lilly walked into the kitchen, carrying Elsie, Leonard’s eyes lit up. He got up and pulled the high chair to the table, next to him, holding it open for Lilly. Whilst Lilly turned to get Elsie’s breakfast, Leonard didn’t take his gaze off that sweet little girl. He’d become quite mad for Elsie, offering to hold her and play with her, making her giggle. She always made the same “ned, ned” sounds around Leonard, holding her arms up to him, smiling, and pulling at his cheeks, so it seemed like she fancied him, as well.

I took my dishes to the sink and dumped them in the wash basin of soapy water. As I stood at the sink, washing the breakfast dishes, my thoughts slipped to Billy, hoping that the view of the war from the window of his Mustang would not be as close up and bloody as what Matthew and Leonard had seen of war. I hadn’t given thought to the idea that the Billy who would come home to me might not be the same man I left in London. And while I’d probably also changed, I hoped that we would figure out how to be everything to each other again, after the war was finally over.

****

When I got home from work that evening, I was relieved to find no one was up. In the quiet, I rinsed out my dishes, packed my lunch pail for the following day, and made my way up to bed.

I'd spent much of the day distracted, my thoughts circling back to Billy and what he must be going through every day. How could this entire generation of men ever be expected to pick up their lives again and carry on as if they hadn't been through hell? While the Billy I knew and loved came through in all his letters, he rarely let me see any of the darkness he must be seeing every day. He didn't share any of the tragic, ugly bits that must surround him.

As I walked into my room, I decided to write to Billy, to ask him to send me a proper letter, to share what he really went through. I needed to know what he was dealing with to be better prepared when he got home. I loved hearing his humor in his letters, but I didn't want him to think he had to entertain me all the time. I could handle what he was handling and wanted him to know he could lean on me as well.

When I sat down to take off my shoes, however, I sat on a letter that was waiting for me on my bed. I hadn't heard from Ruth in several weeks, other than her letters to the family in general, so it was wonderful to see her handwriting waiting for me. Billy's letter could wait.

*July 10, 1944*

*Dear Helen,*

*I don't have a lot of time to write but wanted to let you know that I visited your family before I left England. When I got word that we weren't going to be in the area much longer, I wanted to be sure to find time to visit them.*

*Your father was gracious when I arrived and told him who I was and showed the picture of you, Lilly, and me from my bon voyage party. I also showed him the family picture from Lilly and Paul's wedding, and he was surprised to see you as one of our family. I told him how you're like the sister I never had and how you fit right in. He and your brother laughed at the idea of you on a farm.*

*I also met your brother Stanley. He moved back to London as soon as he turned sixteen, so he could get a job with your father. Your mother and Ernest and Clifford are still in the country but are going to be moving back to London presently, now that the troops have moved to the Continent. As you know, Millie is still in the Lakes district with the Land Girls army.*

*I gave your letter to Stanley, who read it to your father. He seemed elated to hear from you. He said that each of the older boys has gone off to war. I had no idea you had seven brothers serving in the British Army. Why didn't you tell me? Stanley seems anxious to get his chance to sign up, but I sincerely pray for all our sakes that the war is over before he turns eighteen.*

*Helen, I'm so sorry to have to share this news with you in a letter. Your father told me that your brother Joseph was killed in action in May. He was in the battle of Anzio. Your father wouldn't give me any details beyond that, other than to say that Edward and Albert were both injured but have recovered and are back in action. I'm so sorry for your loss, Helen.*

*I've been trying to figure out how to write to you of this since I saw them, and I'm sorry that I didn't write sooner. You've always been so private about your family, I wasn't sure how to tell you.*

*Stanley let slip that Billy had been there just the week before I was, although your father was pretty upset when Stanley said it. Apparently, Billy has visited a few times. Stanley was excited, as he hadn't see Billy in years, but your father shared with me that they'd all be in much worse shape if not for the part of Billy's pay that he has sent to them. They just weren't supposed to tell you about it.*

*I think it's wonderful that Billy has taken your family into his heart the way he has. You must be so proud of him. He's a good man. I hope you won't be angry that I told you about this.*

*Again, I'm so sorry about your brother Joseph. I wish I could go see your father and Stanley again, and meet your mother and youngest brothers when they return, but the ARC had other plans for me. If I ever get a chance to return to London on leave, I'll go there. Know that you are in my heart & I miss you.*

*—Ruth*

I burst into tears, unable to control the waves of sobs racking my body. I almost never thought of my brothers without resentment for being tied to them while growing up. I never had any time to myself or a chance to do what I wanted, including staying in school, because I had to take care of the boys.

But, Joey? In my mind, he was still a little boy. To think that he was gone… I couldn't stop crying. To think of him dying so far from home and Mum and Dad, so young, I just couldn't bear it.

After all these years of anger at Mum and Dad, resenting the boys, shutting out my family, I realized that they were part of me. Once I cried myself out, I picked up a pen and started a letter to Stanley. At least he would tell me how I could write to the rest of the boys.

I needed them to know I was thinking of them. That I really did care.

But then, when Stanley's letter was finished, I had even more to write to Billy about.

*July 31, 1944*

*Dear Billy,*

*I just heard from Ruth about her visit to my father and brother. I can't believe Joey is gone. I knew that most of the boys were serving but had no idea that Edward and Albert were injured or that Joey was killed. While I write to Millie regularly, and hear from her every now and then, I haven't kept in touch with any of the boys enough. I wrote home when I got to Upton Falls, and when I moved to the Walkers, and one or two quick notes since then, but nothing more. I haven't even written to Millie in months. I'm a terrible daughter, a terrible sister, and feel both saddened and ashamed that I carried with me anger at my family for forcing me to quit school to take care of my younger brothers and sister, for ruining my life.*

*No one ruined my life. I have a good life which will, of course, be better when you come home. And even though my childhood was not what I could have hoped it would be, it wasn't the boys' fault. How could I blame them for simply being born? I look at little Robert, Fred, and Elsie and realize how wrong it was to blame the children for any of it. Why didn't you ever tell me what a monster I've been?*

*And you, you've been a proper son-in-law, a saint, even. Whilst your wife has been horrid to everyone, you've been sending them money. Oh, Billy, how brilliant. What a wonderful man you are. Why didn't you want them to tell me? I couldn't love you more than*

*I already do, but I do respect and thank you even more for all you're doing for my family.*

*Even before I got Ruth's letter, I realized that you have been holding back in your letters to me. I love to see your humor, your outlook on life, and don't want you to stop being you. But you must be seeing more darkness, more of the terrible parts of war, than you are letting on. I got to thinking about what Leonard and Matthew have been through, and it made me think that not all your days are as rosy as you lead me to believe.*

*Please know that you can share everything with me. I don't want you to bottle up inside you the terrible things you see and think you can't tell me about it. I'm here for you to lean on, even if only by letter. Please use me as your crutch, even if just to let off steam, so that when you get home you won't have a part of you that you feel you have to protect me from or hide from me. I want all of you, good and bad, light and dark—I love it all.*

*I'll close now, so I can get this in the mail, but I want to thank you, again, for being the wonderful man that you are. I love you more than you can ever know.*

*Yours, Helen*

*P.S. Thanks to your father's help, I'll be preparing for the high school graduation exam over the next two months, with the help of some tutors at his college. If all goes well, they'll let me start there after the New Year. Imagine me, a college student! What a mad thought.*

## Chapter Twenty-Seven
## Lilly

*August 15, 1944*
*Dear Paul,*

*I've started this letter several times, but it seems like the war news has been rolling in, and I find I have to start over. So I'm sorry it's been a while since I last wrote.*

*Thank you for remembering our anniversary and sending the Chinese dress for Elsie's birthday. I'm enclosing a picture my father took of her in it, and she looks adorable. She's walking now (and falling a lot), and it takes nearly all 7 of us adults (9 with Leonard and Matt) to keep her from being covered with bruises. But she's wonderful and healthy and growing, so we're blessed.*

*Speaking of Leonard, you should see him with Elsie. He is taken with her, and it appears to be mutual. She toddles over to him whenever he comes into the house, and he sweeps her up into his arms. She giggles the whole time. It's adorable.*

*I'm sure you've heard about the D-Day invasion in France, but I bet you'd be surprised to hear that only a few weeks after the first troops hit the beaches, Ruth and her fellow Red Cross girls hit the shores with their Clubmobiles. Ruth is in the* St. Louis *Clubmobile, and it sounds like they aren't far behind the troops as they progress across France. I hope she's not too close to the front.*

*Clara got word about the same time that Will's unit made it to Rome. From everything we've heard on the radio, it sounds like heavy fighting on the Italian front, but he writes that he's well and safe. He hinted they might be moving soon, but that all is good. I hope he's not just saying that to keep Clara, and the rest of us, from worrying.*

*Just like I hope that you're not just saying all is well with you to ease my mind. I know you can't tell me details about the fighting in the Philippine Sea, but I hope you are safe and healthy. We saw a newsreel on the battle for the Mariana Islands, and it scared me. I don't want you to feel like you can't tell me what's happening over there, but I can't help wishing you were home already.*

*Helen got good news from Billy just before D-Day. He got a pardon from the U.S. government, so his citizenship has been reinstated. I always thought it was unfair for it to be revoked just because he volunteered to help the RAF before the U.S. officially got in the war, so I'm glad they won't have to worry about that when he gets home.*

*Everything is fine with us. The day care keeps me busy, even with Helen's help, but Elsie really enjoys being with the other children. After work, Grandma often watches Elsie for me so I can help Mom with putting up the last of the summer vegetables, as well as with mending and knitting. I think one of the things I'm most looking forward to after the war, beyond you, Will, Ruth, and Billy getting home, is being able to buy clothes and shoes again. There are only so many times I can mend and alter the same dresses over and over. Clara is busy with those active boys of hers, although Fred is in school now. I think he's a bit of a handful, as Clara has gotten a couple of notes home from the teacher. He's got a lot of energy and is too smart for his own good, but he's a sweetie at heart.*

*I want to get this in the mail, so I'll stop here. Keep yourself safe and know that Elsie and I send you all our love. Hurry home—*

*Love, Lilly*

****

The summer of 1944 rushed by in a blink of an eye. One minute we were reading about D-Day, and then it was July 4th and Elsie turned one, and then, before we knew it, Paris had been liberated, and we couldn't wait for Ruth's letter to give us an inside peek as to what was happening in France, or to hear from Billy, Will, and Paul, to know they were safe and to let us know what was happening with them.

Life in Upton Falls carried on as ever. Helen was busy at Nichols Motors on second shift but still indispensable at the day care in the mornings. I loved being able to bring Elsie to work with me, and she even had friends among the other day care children. Clara and I helped Mom and Grandma at home, as the summer harvest had to be canned, pickled, or preserved in some way.

They were busy with bread-and-butter pickles when Elsie and I got home from work on September first. I was looking forward to a quiet Friday night after an unusually hot day. Helen and I had plans to go to the Red Cross dance the following night.

I walked in the back door, carrying Elsie, much to

her dismay. Since learning to walk, that was all she wanted to do.

"How's the pickling going?"

Mom turned to me, wiping her hands on her apron. "We have several crocks ready to sit and stew for a couple of weeks, and then we'll be able to get out the canner and put them up for winter. I think this'll be a good batch."

"Hmmm, I love your bread and butter pickles, so I can't wait."

Clara walked to the table and retrieved the mail. "You and I got letters from Will today, Lilly. He must have had a couple of minutes to spare."

I took my letter in surprise. "Wow, I haven't had a letter from him in weeks. I'm glad he remembered me."

I went to the parlor and let Elsie loose on the toy box while I sat on the couch to read my letter.

*August 20, 1944*

*Dear Lilly,*

*I know you're probably mad at me 'cause I haven't written to you in so long, but I haven't been able to find a minute to do more than jot a quick note to Clara. We're on board a ship, about to land on the southern coast of France, so I can spend a couple of minutes writing letters before all heck breaks loose again.*

*Thank you for the socks and cookies you sent for my birthday. I got them about ten days ago, and both were great to have. You wouldn't believe how hard this war is on socks. And, of course, any and all food is welcome, but especially homemade cookies. I was the most popular guy around when they arrived.*

*I got a letter from Ruth that she has been shipped to France with the Red Cross. As much as I would love to have a chance to see her, I'm worried about her being so close to the front. Even though the Allies are making progress in liberating France, we're still a long way from winning this war. And, trust me, war really is hell and no place for a woman. I understand Ruth wanting to do her part, and I'm as happy to get a doughnut and coffee as the next guy, but I don't want her to see what I've seen, be where I've been, and I can't imagine it's any better in Normandy and Paris than it was in Sicily and Rome.*

*I doubt any of us could convince her to go home, but if you think of some way to show her she's needed on the farm, please do so. I'm worried about not only her health but her soul.*

*Whenever you get a chance to write, please send a picture of Elsie and the boys, and all of you. I miss home, my wife and kids, and my entire family so much. A lot of guys say they want to come back to Europe after the war, to see it all without a gun in their hands. I can't wait to get back to Upton Falls and never want to leave again. Everything I want and need is there, and I'll be happy just to sit on the porch swing with my wife and watch my children grow.*

*Take care of yourself and Elsie and give her a hug and kiss from Uncle Will.*

*Love, Will*

****

While I worried about Ruth too, Will was dreaming if he thought one of us could convince her to quit the Red Cross and come home at this point. Every letter she sent made it clear to us that she loved her work, no matter how hard or dangerous it was.

Clara walked into the parlor with Robert close on

her heels. Even though he was almost three, he was a great playmate for Elsie. He helped her pull out the box of blocks, and the two of them sat on the floor, happily playing together for a long time.

"Did Will have anything interesting to tell you?" Clara took a seat across from me on the sofa.

"Not much, really," I replied. "He really liked the cookies and the socks I sent, so I'll have to send more next time. It sounds like food is a big hit with his buddies." I smiled. I wasn't much of a baker, but having an appreciative audience like men at war gave me a good chance to practice.

"He's always had a sweet tooth." Clara held her letter in her lap.

"He also seems worried about Ruth. Did he mention that to you?"

Clara shook her head slowly, her lips pressed tightly together. "He's mentioned that to me in every letter since I told him Ruth signed up with the Red Cross. He never thought it was a good idea. I don't know why he thought we could talk her out of going, once she heard about the Clubmobile program."

I nodded. "I was just thinking the same thing. He wants me to convince her to quit and come home, like that's going to happen."

Clara smiled. "Ruth has never been the kind of woman to seek the easy way out of something. Even if Jack were still alive, she might have signed up for the Clubmobile program anyway. She needs to be there, doing everything she possibly can to help our soldiers."

I had never thought about it that way, but Clara was right. "I guess that's true. Jack and Ruth had their life planned for here on the farm, with lots of babies.

She thought she'd be content, even if she never taught school again, but I don't know if that's true, even if Jack hadn't died."

"That's the life Will and I have planned, and I can't wait for him to get home so we can live that life. He'll be happy working the farm until the day he dies, and I will be happy in this house, raising babies, making supper, canning vegetables, and all the rest." She crossed her arms over her chest, leaning back against the sofa. "I dream of that, and it will be all that I ever need, as long as Will and our children are in it. But, Ruth, she's got so much…I don't know, so much more in her. There's something about her that draws people to her, makes everyone feel better just by being near her. She needs to help people just the same as she needs air to breathe."

I laughed. "That's so true, Clara. She's like the pied piper. I swear, those boys she worked with at the Red Cross in Beacon Heights would follow her anywhere." I blushed, hoping Clara didn't think I was saying Ruth was loose. "I don't mean like a date."

"I know what you mean," she said, smiling.

"People just want to be with her, to do what she's doing, to talk with her. She's got so much personality, I suspect she is fantastic at this Clubmobile job."

Clara shook her head. "While she may be in danger, there's no one who could talk her out of doing the job she was practically born to do."

I nodded. "So true. Will's crazy if he thinks we could do that."

"He's worried about her. I think he's seen some terrible things and doesn't want Ruth to be exposed to any of that. But she's strong and kind and practical. I worry about her getting too close to the fighting, but I think she can handle the rest, ugly as it may be."

"I hope you're right." I put my letter into the pocket of my dress and sat down on the floor to play with my daughter and nephew, pulling each of them into my arms for a quick kiss before they wriggled away.

## Chapter Twenty-Eight
## Ruth

*September 10, 1944*
*Dear Family,*

*I'm sorry it's been so long since my last letter. We are busy every day and exhausted every night, so it's hard to find time to put words to paper. We're often attached to a large division, following them across France, and traveling between different camps and units, so every day is an adventure.*

*We left Paris at the end of August. I don't think I can describe the joy of the French when Paris was liberated. They're tired, starving, beaten, and battered, but not broken. They greeted us with cheers, gifts of onions, chocolates, potatoes, or anything they could offer. It was hard to take anything from people with so little, but we couldn't refuse them. They were so earnest in their need to express thanks to the Allies and to celebrate their freedom.*

*From Paris, we went first to Rambouillet, about thirty miles away, met up with all the Clubmobiles from Group A, and were billeted in a chateau on the stunning Rothschild estate. Given that most of us hadn't had hot running water or electricity for weeks, we were in heaven. It was wonderful hearing the adventures the other girls had been through. The food at the chateau was a welcome relief as well, including hamburgers, beans, apple pie, and a real orange for each of us. I was so happy to see fresh fruit.*

*While at the chateau, the mail caught up with us, and I can't tell you how happy we are to finally get our letters and packages. I had twelve letters dropped in my lap, as well as the most delicious, if somewhat stale, brownies and molasses cookies. They are heavenly, and I couldn't thank you more. I passed them around to the other gals, and the boys who help us in the Clubmobile, and everyone went crazy for them. Especially when accompanied by the bottles of champagne the boys got in exchange for some cigarettes. The powders, cream, and perfume are all wonderful, especially given we usually don't have a chance to shower.*

*When we left the chateau, we headed east, closer to the fighting. At one point, we were serving soldiers at the front right across a river from the Jerries. When we pulled up, the air was still filled with smoke from the shelling. The noise is deafening, and I will say, while this is the best thing I've ever done in my life, I hate war with a vengeance. Most of the time, we travel the roads that the military has just liberated. Recently, we were serving troops in a heavily mined area, and Renee watched as a boy, after picking up his coffee and doughnuts, wandered in the wrong direction and was blown up by a mine. As horrific as these kinds of sights are, we just have to keep working, as Renee did that day. There are other men to serve, and we cannot grieve too long, as callous as that must sound to all of you at home. I think Renee is able to see the big picture better than some of the other gals because of her father in the concentration camp. She doesn't speak of him often, but we know he's on her mind.*

*I often wish all American women could have this experience. We get to see the boys just before they leave for duty, and we see them when they have a few hours' relief from battle. They are dirty, tired, sometimes shell-shocked, but happy to see us. I know we help them, if only for a few hours, to remember the good and let the evil of war recede.*

*It's hard, though, if we see the same boys when we stop at one of the field hospitals, or worse, when we see the trucks out in a field retrieving the dead. While we've had to become accustomed to that fact of war, it's especially hard when it's a company we've visited.*

*I will have to sign off now. I'm so tired I'm practically asleep at the table. Know that I miss you all like crazy and will write as soon as I can. Please keep those letters and packages coming.*

*All my love—Ruth*

****

*October 28, 1944*
*Dear Helen,*

*Thanks for the pictures of Judith and Jacob's wedding. I had no idea when I brought him to the farm for dinner that they would hit it off so quickly, although I was secretly hoping they would. He seemed like a good, decent man, strong, kind, and smart, and I prayed that it had been long enough after Henry's death for Judith to be ready to recognize what a wonderful man Jacob is. He'll be good for her and the children, and she'll be able to help him over the wounds he must still carry inside him. What a wonderful match. I'll have to try to find something to send as a wedding present next time I'm in Paris, although who knows what I'll be able to buy.*

*We have been steadily on the move from one infantry camp to another. Our travels have taken us through many of the towns that were mentioned in the newspapers as German strongholds. Our troops have engaged in heavy fighting, and sometimes we are rolling in not long after the Jerries have pulled out. Even the worst storm damage we've ever seen can't compare to the condition these towns are in. Many buildings are gone, leaving only holes in the ground where the cellars remain, filled with the debris that used to be a house. We come across a few brick walls standing upright, but everything else looks like it was chewed up and spit out by the German tanks and guns and soldiers.*

*We camped with an Army unit in a large field one night, and the Jerries made a short visit, so we spent an hour in a foxhole, but then went right back to serving the boys. While in that camp, we were given access to the shower, which was a total luxury. There were about 15 of us women waiting for the men to finish. When it was our turn, we crowded into the tent, which was set up next to the river. Water is pumped from the river, heated, and then sent through pipes with holes strategically placed for everyone in the shower tent. It was pure heaven to be able to wash my hair and body without using a bucket.*

*Last week, we were camping outside a field hospital. We see many of the wounded just before they are either sent back to the front or farther back, if they need more care. Again, they are always happy to see us, even though we don't end up serving a lot of coffee and doughnuts at the hospital stops. Often times, the boys want us to write letters for them or talk to them about when we were last in the States. I have so much admiration for the work the nurses do. We work hard, but their work never ends.*

*The boys in the hospital were excited to tell us Bing Crosby and his troop of performers had just been there. We missed him by just a day! Everyone told us how down-to-earth and friendly he is, as well as how swell his show was. It lifts the spirits of the wounded to get a little special treatment, especially, I think, for the boys who are about to head back to the fighting.*

*Anyway, just after we pulled in and started to set up camp outside the hospital, a Piper Cub airplane circled over our heads and came to a landing in the field where we were setting up camp. The pilot hopped out and came running over, looking for hot doughnuts. He scared the stuffing out of us, as we were sure the front had moved and we'd have to evacuate. By way of apology for giving us a fright, he volunteered to give us a chance to see the front from the air. Charlotte declined, but I jumped at the chance. What a sight! The leaves are all changing, so the colors were beautiful, which is so at odds with the destruction we could see in every village and road along the way. We didn't stray over the Jerries, don't worry, but it gave me an appreciation of why Billy loves flying. Even the mud, which is everywhere these days, looks better from the air. Speaking of mud, I wish I'd brought my red rubber barn boots. They'd handle this mud so much better than my ARC-issued boots.*

*I'm glad you're moving ahead with your education. I'm excited to hear the results of your exam. Please write as soon as you know, although I'm sure you'll pass. What classes will you be signing up for in*

*January? Can you take a bus directly from class in Cortland to Beacon Heights for work? I'm sure Lilly is happy for you, and she'll likely have no trouble getting help at the day care. Maybe Ginny? Or a recent high school graduate? Don't worry about those kids. By the time you're finished with college, you'll probably end up being their teacher!*

*Well, I'm off to bed. We have to maintain strict blackout conditions, so as soon as we finish eating and cleaning up, it's lights out in the Clubmobile. That's why I have trouble finding time to write, either I'm traveling, working, eating, washing (me or the Clubmobile), or sleeping in the dark. Finding a few minutes to write is a challenge, but I'm always happy to read the letters that find their way to me.*

*Take care & good luck with your exam. Give everyone my love.*

*—Ruth*

****

*November 23, 1944*
*Dear Family,*

*Happy Thanksgiving! I hope you all are having a wonderful holiday. I am picturing you having another tasty wild turkey that Pop shot in the woods, with delicious mashed potatoes, sweet potatoes, last summer's peas, and hopefully some pumpkin pie. I hope you have a wonderful group of friends around the table, as always.*

*We were lucky enough to get turkey today because we bunked last night at a chateau near the Ardennes Forest with the officers, and they had a Thanksgiving meal in their mess. We were assured that the enlisted men got Thanksgiving too, even though we're in a hot spot right now. The officers said the enlisted guys get to rotate in for the meal in shifts, when they're not out in their foxholes or catching some sleep. We had plenty of wine and champagne to accompany our Thanksgiving dinner, as usual. Alcohol flows freely in a battle zone.*

*In England, we didn't get any liquor rations, but here, we get the same as the officers do, which is one quart of Scotch and half a quart of gin per month. Add that to the champagne and wine we sometimes get from the locals, and every night is a party night if you want it to be. Farther back east in France, the Army captured warehouse after warehouse of cognac and wine that the Germans had hidden away. Whether they were planning to drink it all or send it home for the Führer, who knows, but it made for quite a party when the troops discovered it. As you know, I've never been much of a drinker, so I rarely overindulge, but the men use it to get through their tough days.*

*I can't believe that it was two years ago when Western Union delivered news of Jack's death. I feel him with me so often over here. I see his smile, hear his laugh, even some of his bad jokes from so many of the men. When some of the soldiers talk to me about the girl waiting for them at home, it makes me smile to think that Jack might have spoken of me in the same way.*

*I often see an infantry soldier who looks so much like Jack from the back that I find myself holding my breath until he turns around. If you're worried that all this makes me sad or makes me miss him more, don't be. First of all, I couldn't miss him more. I will always love him. But seeing these men doing what he did, fighting for the same things Jack fought for, laughing and joking the way he did, actually eases the pain and warms my heart.*

*Speaking of warm, that's something we are short on these days. We've had quite a bit of snow already, and believe me, the Clubmobile starts to feel like a wind tunnel when the back door and service window are open for us to serve the troops. You'd think the doughnut machine, hot oil, and hot coffee would warm up the place, but the floor stays as cold as ice. This area of France is definitely colder than England was, so we're lucky we got a gift from some of the men. We now have long, fur-lined coats that the Germans stole from the Russians but left behind in retreat. They are huge, but the added warmth will be indispensable as we progress through this winter.*

*I'm going to have to close now, as I'm being called. Apparently the officers have found a large room, on the interior of the chateau, that has no windows, so we can safely indulge in some after-dinner entertainment. They brought our records and Victrola in, so we'll have some dancing and champagne, of course. Sort of like singing for our supper, I guess, except we'll be dancing.*

*My Christmas list includes warm clothes and food, any kinds you can send. Canned tuna was a treat, as are all those baked goods. For that matter, some bobby pins would be greatly appreciated, especially by those who have to look at my hair. Ha, ha. And letters. Lots of letters. Please keep 'em coming, with pictures, too. I'm enclosing a couple we had taken recently, showing Charlotte, Renee, and me working the Clubmobile. Eileen was out on a date with her fiancé. Yes, she came all the way to France to fall in love with an American.*

*But anyway, you can see how healthy we "Doughnut Dollies" all are, so don't worry about me.*

*All my love, Ruth*

## Chapter Twenty-Nine
## Lilly

I rushed into Woodward's hardware store on Main Street, carrying Elsie, and was grateful for the wave of heat that enveloped us. I stamped the snow off my boots and pulled off Elsie's pink winter hat. Clara, Fred, Robert, and Mom followed behind me. As we crossed to the back of the store and climbed the wide, maple stairs, Bing Crosby was crooning "I'll Be Home for Christmas" on the radio.

Ever since I was a kid, I couldn't resist this place. On the day after Thanksgiving, Bob Woodward removed the rope that usually prohibited customers from accessing the second floor of the hardware store. At the kick-off of the Christmas season, the attic space was transformed into Santa's workshop. The store didn't sell toys any other time of the year, but from the Friday after Thanksgiving until December 24th, the stuff of children's dreams filled this attic, with tinsel wrapped on the railing heading up the stairs and white paper snowflakes tied by string to the ceiling.

As always, we'd started the day with the town Thanksgiving parade. Santa arrived by fire truck at the end of the parade, and we'd followed him to Woodward's, where Santa now sat in an oversized red velvet chair. A long line had formed of children waiting to give Santa their Christmas list.

"There he is! There he is!" Fred and Robert sang in unison, while they jumped up and down.

Clara pulled off their gloves and hats and tried to smooth down their hair. "Shhh. Calm down. You have to use your manners while you wait your turn."

Mom held onto Robert, while Clara took Fred in hand and pulled them into the line. Helen came running up the stairs to join us. She had borrowed Dad's camera so she could take pictures of the children sitting on Santa's lap.

Elsie was fussing in my arms, trying to climb down and get her hands on all the brightly colored boxes surrounding us. I picked up a wooden horse from the display near us to entertain her while in line.

"This is all such fun for the children," said Helen, looking around the room. "They do a great job of decorating this attic to look like the North Pole."

We inched ahead in line. Strings of lights and red-and-green garland were draped around the ceiling and windows, and an artificial Christmas tree stood in the corner, near Santa's chair, and was decorated with colorful ornaments and threads of silver tinsel.

I felt a tug on my skirt and looked down. Robert's big brown eyes stared seriously up at me.

"What is it, honey?"

He furrowed his brow, looking so much like his father deep in concentration, and said, "how can Elsie ask Santa for a present when she can't talk yet?"

I smiled. He was always such a quiet child, a deep thinker. "I don't know, Robert. Do you think we should ask Santa for her, tell him something we think she'd like?"

He rubbed his chin with the thumb and forefinger

of his right hand. “I guess that’s best.”

I nodded. “What do you think she’d like to get as a Christmas present?”

He looked around the room slowly, carefully evaluating the choices. “She might like a stuffed animal or even a Mickey Mouse.” He turned his head and then turned back, looking up at me. “I think she wants a doll, don’t you? Maybe a Raggedy Ann doll.”

I crouched down while Robert picked up a Raggedy Ann doll and showed it to Elsie. She reached for it, as she did with everything in the store.

Robert pulled it back. “No, no, Elsie. It’s not yours yet.” He put the doll back on the shelf, and I stood, Elsie’s gaze still following Robert and the doll. “But don’t worry, I’ll tell Santa that’s what you want.”

I could have sworn she understood him, as she stopped fussing and watched Robert when it was his turn to see Santa.

After Fred and Robert each had a chance to talk to the big guy, I put Elsie on Santa’s lap for a picture with all the children together. I was sure she’d start crying, but she was fascinated by his beard, tangling her fingers in the long white strands. Fortunately, it was the real thing, as she also started pulling but couldn’t pull it off. Poor Santa was a good sport, though, gently releasing her hold on his beard and turning everyone to face Helen and say “cheese.” He presented Fred and Robert each with a shiny new dime, and gave Elsie’s to me, so they could go across the street to the movie theatre and see the special holiday cartoons.

Clara and I herded the children around the toys and made our way back to the stairs. I turned to make sure Helen was with us but saw that she had paused for a moment, talking to Santa, and seemed to be giving something to him.

As we walked to the front of the store, I put my hand on her arm. "What's with you and Santa? Got a hot date for New Year's Eve?"

Helen burst out laughing, her whole body shaking with amusement. She always had the best laugh. "You caught me. I'm mad about Father Christmas, but don't tell Mrs. Claus. We're going out on New Year's, aren't we?"

Still laughing, she swooped Robert up into her arms as we crossed the street. "So what did you ask Santa for, young man?"

"I want a 'lectic train and an Army tank, just like Daddy drives." Robert's eyes shone with excitement and a child's dreams.

"He also gave Santa Elsie's Christmas list, like a good cousin." I smiled at him.

"Did you now? That's a good lad," said Helen.

Robert nodded. "Well, she can't talk yet, so I told Santa she'd like a Raggedy Ann doll."

I looked down at Elsie, and it almost looked like she was nodding, staring at Robert.

"Brilliant, my boy," said Helen, swinging him down to stand on the sidewalk in front of the movie theatre. She turned to me, lowering her voice to say, "I hope Santa grants my Christmas wish, as well."

Every one of us was hoping for a speedy end to the war. What a gift that would be.

Judith, Peter, Kurt, and Marion were waiting for us in front of the theatre. We planned to meet up for a fun day out, given that the plant was closed for the holiday, which meant that the day care was too.

While Mom and Clara herded the boys to the box office, so they could trade their shiny new dimes for movie tickets, Helen pulled three shiny dimes from her pocket and held them out to the Blumenthal children.

"Look what I found, just for the three of you," she said. Peter's eyes lit up, but he quickly looked from the dimes to his mother, waiting for permission.

Judith nodded. "Isn't that wonderful, children? What do you say to Mrs. Anderson?"

The three grabbed their dimes and wrapped their arms around Helen's legs. She'd become like a favorite aunt to the children. "Thank you, Mrs. Anderson," their singsong voices called out.

As they scrabbled after Fred and Robert, Helen laughed again. "I love to see the happiness a new dime can bring to their eyes."

"Thank you, Helen, although you shouldn't have. I was going to buy them a ticket." Judith smiled, despite her words.

Helen shook her head. "I traded some old dirty coins with Father Christmas, so they could have three shiny ones just like everybody else. It's not just Christian children who like cartoons."

Judith gave her a hug, and we all walked into the theatre. It was great to see how happy Judith was these days, since her marriage to Jacob, even when he was away on another bond tour. It had taken her a long time to act like she was alive again and finally recovered from Henry's death. She still talked to the children about their father, as did Jacob, and the kids were not shy about mentioning him, but the sadness seemed to have lifted. The whole family was healing, and it was a wonderful thing to see.

The older children enjoyed the cartoon, as well as the popcorn that came with their tickets, but fortunately Elsie nodded off on my shoulder during the show. She made for an armful when I stood up at the end of the movie, but Helen was kind enough to help me on with my coat and to put Elsie's arms in her coat, too.

"Why don't you and the children come back with us, Judith, and stay for supper?" Mom said as we started to walk back across town. "We have some wonderful leftovers from yesterday, if you don't mind having them again."

Judith smiled. "Your Thanksgiving dinner was delicious, but it hardly seems fair for you to feed all of us again today."

"But the children are having so much fun together," said Clara.

"Come on, Judith. If it makes you feel better, you can help with the knitting. Heaven knows you're better at it than I am," Helen said with a laugh.

Judith clasped her hands in front of her chest. "I know. I have some latkes and a delicious eggless sponge I made this morning. I can stop at my house and pick it up on the way to the farm. At least I can contribute something to the meal."

Mom nodded. "They sound delicious, Judith. I've always wanted to try latkes. Are they a special Hanukah recipe?"

Personally, I'd never heard my mother mention latkes, but I admired the way she had of making everyone feel appreciated and valued.

"Yes, adapted for rationing, of course. Same with the sponge. The children wanted eggs for breakfast on Wednesday, which used up our rations, so I decided I'd figure out how to make a sponge without eggs."

"Clever you, Judith," said Helen. "It sounds delicious."

She nodded. "I wouldn't go that far, but latkes are a traditional part of our Hanukah celebration. Now, more than ever, I believe it's important to keep our Jewish traditions alive and teach them to the next generation."

We all walked silently the rest of the way to Judith's house, with the children running circles around us on the sidewalk. We paused in the yard while Judith and Helen went into the house to get the food. Luckily, despite the chill and the thin covering of snow on the ground, the weather wasn't too bad for our walk to the farm.

When we moved on toward the farm, the children continued to race around us, sometimes stopping to throw snowballs or dropping down to make snow angels. Even without much snow, they found the fun spots. As always, we women fell into a group together, shifting Elsie among us, one or the other chasing after a runner or calling out to someone's child who'd drifted behind.

"Robert was sweet with Elsie at the store," I said to Clara. "He searched for just the thing he thought she'd want from Santa and, when it was his turn to give his list, he added, 'and a Raggedy Ann doll for my baby cousin Elsie, please.' It was adorable."

Clara smiled. She was a quieter presence in my life than Ruth ever was. While both were my sisters-in-law, they were so different. It wasn't that I didn't love Clara as much as I loved Ruth; she was just harder to get close to because she never said much.

"Well, every little girl needs a dolly, doesn't she?" Mom took Elsie in her arms, kissing her cheek.

When we all arrived at the farm, Helen and Judith stayed outside with the older kids while Mom, Clara, and I headed into the house. I fed Elsie her dinner, gave her a quick bath, and tucked her into her crib. She was exhausted from the fresh air and playing with her cousins. As I lowered the shade on our window, I noticed the four little boys clustered around Matthew, who was shoveling snow around the barn door. He was gentle with the children, even sharing a smile or two with them, but was still bashful around the rest of us. Leonard said Matt was coming along, so I trusted he was able to see the young man's emotional pain healing.

As I came downstairs, I heard Dad banging the back door, calling out, "Julia."

Mom, Grandma, and Clara were already working on supper, whipping the Thanksgiving leftovers, as well as some more vegetables and another chicken, into a sure-to-be-delicious feast for us all. Feeding sixteen for two days in a row, even if only four more than our usual crew, was a big accomplishment, but Mom always made it look easy.

"What are you shouting about, Earl?"

I entered the kitchen just as Dad hung up his jacket and came through the back door.

"We have a package."

"What?" Mom had her head in the oven, apparently checking on the chicken and unable to hear Dad.

"Dad says there's a package, Mom."

Mom stood, closed the oven door, and stepped over to the table, where Dad already sat, his pocket knife out and cutting through the tape and twine holding the brown paper.

"Well, now, Earl, who's it from?" Mom stood behind Dad, watching over his shoulder.

"Our girl Ruth, of course," Dad said with a smile.

"Oooh." Mom sank into the chair next to him. "What do you think she sent us?"

"One sure way to know, Julia." Once the tape, twine, and paper were off the box, Dad slid it to Mom.

Inside the box, Mom pulled out a stack of letters, setting them on the table. Next came wrapped gifts marked "Fred," "Robert," and "Elsie." At the bottom of the box, was a large envelope marked "Helen."

Mom picked up the envelope marked "Mom and Pop," handing the pile to me to distribute to Clara, Grandma and Granddad, and myself.

As she opened her envelope, she looked at the gifts. "What do you think, Clara? Should we give the boys their presents now or wait for Christmas?"

"Oh, let's save them for Christmas, if that's okay with you, Lilly. I'd like the boys to have a few things to open on Christmas morning."

I nodded. "Fine with me. Elsie's too little to know the difference."

Mom gasped, and we all turned to her.

"What is it, Julia?" Dad placed a hand on her arm.

"Oh…" She looked up at us all. "I didn't mean to worry you. Everything is okay." She dug out a check from the envelope. "It's just that Ruth sent us a check for $200."

Everyone murmured.

"She says she's been putting half of her pay each month in savings and half into checking, with the thought that she'd have more expenses over there. But it turns out, now that she's following the troops through France, there's practically nothing to spend money on, so she decided to send us all a check for Christmas. She wants us to buy the children lots of presents. She says she misses them terribly and wants them to believe there will soon be an end to this war and life will be wonderful again. We're to buy toys in addition to clothes or shoes or whatever practical things they need. Whatever we don't spend on the children, we're to use on each other, whether on gifts or whatever special holiday food there is to be had. She says: 'I miss you all so much and wish I could be with you this Christmas, so please use this little extra holiday money to celebrate in my absence. If God is good, we'll all be together by next Christmas.' "

Mom looked up from the letter, tears in her eyes, a sad smile on her face. Dad kneaded her right shoulder with his right hand and she placed her left hand over his.

She looked at me and winked. "It looks like there'll be a new Raggedy Ann in this house after all."

****

New snow had fallen overnight. I finished taping the box in front of me and picked up some twine. I handed the packaging tape to Mom, who handed it to Clara. Once Clara was done, she passed it on to Helen. We had a Christmas present assembly line going on, with each package going to a different part of the world.

"We're a little late in mailing these out, so I hope they arrive sometime close to Christmas." Mom printed Ruth's address in block letters on the package in front of her. "I think Ruth will be happy with the gifts we've put together for her. I bought several cans of shrimp, salmon, tuna, capers, and sardines, as well as a tin of crackers, a jar of peanut butter, a box of stationery, two pairs of wool socks, a package of bobby pins, and a soft new sweater. I even remembered to pack the film that Earl bought for her. I added in a tin of Grandma's molasses cookies and, of course, the sugar Christmas cookies we made this weekend. She should be set for a while."

I laughed. "Paul wouldn't be happy if I sent him wool socks, bobby pins, or a warm sweater." I carefully copied his address from his last letter. "I found him a couple of the paperback western novels he likes, some writing paper and pens, gum, mints, cigarettes, a new toothbrush, new boxer shorts, mosquito repellent, and, of course, both kinds of cookies. Just what every sailor needs in the Philippines."

Clara set down her pen and glanced down at Will's package. "Ever since Will's unit got transferred to Southern France in late August, the mail has been sporadic, at best. I keep writing every couple of days, and he keeps telling me he's not getting any letters. I hope this package finds him before Easter."

Helen smiled. "I'm sure he'll eat the cookies and wear the socks no matter when he gets them." She gathered up the brown paper, twine, and packaging tape and stored it away. "Billy is so thankful to get whatever I send him, I feel guilty that I don't mail more packages than I do. It's just so hard to find time to shop, never mind finding anything to buy that's worth sending. I think they'll all love the new pictures, though."

Mom nodded. "Ruth keeps asking about the boys,

and Elsie. I know she'll be happy to get the new pictures of the kids. I'm also including a few Judith gave us from the wedding and their honeymoon trip."

"I sent some of those to Billy as well," said Helen. "He will have fun showing them to the guys in their unit, as many of them know Jacob."

"Ruth should be proud of how happy Judith and Jacob look in those pictures, as the matchmaker." I smiled. "I remember the day she brought Jacob home for Sunday dinner and introduced him to Judith and the kids. I was watching Ruth watching them and could tell she was hoping something would grow between them, even from the beginning."

"I'm glad she did, then," said Helen. "Jacob is mad about Judith, and it has brought the color back to her cheeks and the sparkle back to her eyes. She carried Henry's shadow with her for so long after he was killed, it was like she wasn't fully alive herself anymore. She and the children deserve to be happy again."

I almost asked Helen when she thought Ruth would let go of Jack's shadow and be ready to love someone again, but stopped myself before I could hurt Mom's feelings. Ruth was her daughter as much as I was, but if Ruth remarried, I didn't know how Mom would feel about it. Especially if Ruth fell in love and married somebody from Kansas or California or somewhere far from Upton Falls. It was hard enough for me to think about it. I didn't want to upset my mother.

Helen and I had agreed to take the packages to the post office this morning to get them in the mail, so we gathered them up and got into our boots and coats. The layer of new snow would make the path into town a little slippery.

The back door banged shut just as I was retrieving my purse and two of the boxes from the kitchen table. I turned and saw Dad rubbing his hands together.

"Why don't I give you girls a lift to town? I need to go get a couple of parts for the tractor, at the farm supply store, so I can drop you at the post office."

With gasoline so tightly rationed now, we rarely used the car. Luckily, Dad was given extra gas to help run the farm machinery, so he could take us in the truck.

"That'd be wonderful, Dad." I leaned in and kissed his cheek. "Thanks so much."

Helen smiled. "Yes, thanks, Earl. I wasn't looking forward to the cold and slush."

We headed out to the truck, Dad taking one of the packages from each of us. He quickly got the heat running full blast to help warm up the cold bench seat, but I was still happy to have my hat and mittens on.

"So, ladies," started Dad, looking briefly at me and Helen. "Ruth sent a little extra money to me. Well, she actually sent a check to me in a letter to Leonard, so that Julia wouldn't know about it. She wants me to buy Julia something extra special for Christmas. Any ideas?"

Helen and I exchanged glances and shrugged.

"We could do some shopping while we're in town, if you'd like. You can go get your parts while we're at the post office and then you can meet us, after, to look at a few of the shops in town. What are you thinking about, Dad?"

He shrugged. "I don't know. I haven't had any extra cash to buy presents with in such a long time.

Over the past few years, your mother has had to be happy with scarves and gloves and a new roasting pan, and I only bought that because the bottom fell out of the old one. I'm not just sure what she'd like."

Helen leaned forward, looking at Dad. "Well, we could look at a new dress or hat, or some jewelry. Depending on how much we plan to spend."

"Hmmm," said Dad. "After you finish mailing your packages, why don't you two walk down to the five-and-ten, and I'll meet you there. If we don't see anything we like, we can move on."

I nodded. "Sounds good." Nothing like a little Christmas shopping, especially with someone else's money, to lift my spirits.

By the time we made it to the front of the long line of people mailing holiday packages overseas, Dad was already back from the farm supply store. He passed us as we walked out of the post office, pulled into a parking space on Main Street, and walked with us into the five-and-ten. A lot of people were out and about, despite the snow. The village workers had hung giant tinsel stockings and snowflakes on the street lamps, so the streets looked festive.

"So what do you think your mother would like, Lilly?"

We wandered around the aisles, and when Dad started to head toward the kitchen supplies, I pulled him away, sliding my hand through his right elbow.

"Let's see if we can find something special for her, not something she'll use to cook for all of us."

Dad nodded, blushing a little.

Helen stopped to look at some scarves. "Did Ruth say anything specific about the gift in her letter?"

Dad stopped. "Ruth said she wanted Julia to know how much Ruth misses and loves her and that Ruth wishes she could spend Christmas with us. I think she's feeling a little homesick."

Helen nodded. "As much as Ruth might love her work, and no matter how much good she is doing over there, it must be hard to face the idea of spending the holidays in a tent or on a cot in the back of that cold, dark truck. Especially when she's used to how warm and wonderful you all make Christmas."

Again Dad blushed. "We don't do anything special, Helen."

She touched his arm. "Earl, you do. Believe me. You and Julia have created a warm and welcoming home and a wonderful family. The holidays I've spent with you are magical in a way they never were when I was growing up."

Dad wrapped his arm around Helen, and it was her turn to blush. "You're part of the family now, Helen. And don't think you can forget about us when your Billy comes home. We expect to get a visit over Christmas even when you're the mother of eight and you and Billy are as ancient as Julia and I are now."

Helen laughed, and I could see, for once, no shadow of worry in her expression. She might never want to have eight children, but she looked like the idea of her and Billy having kids and raising a family was as precious to her as the idea of my family with Paul was to me.

We wandered by the jewelry counter, and Helen stopped to look in the glass cases. "What about one of these?" She pointed at something inside the first case.

"What" asked Dad, bending over the counter,

trying to see where Helen was pointing.

I scooted around the end of the case, leaning forward myself to see what they were looking at.

“There’s a lovely necklace,” said Helen.

While Helen was pointing out some pretty necklaces, something else caught my eyes. I put my hand on my father’s arm.

“Dad.”

He looked at me. “What?”

I pointed. “That brooch.”

In the middle of the display case was a lovely cameo brooch. It had delicate scallops of gold around the edges of a soft beige background and the pristine ivory silhouette. “That’s the one.”

Dad smiled. “You’re right, Lilly.”

Helen tilted her head, looking at me. “Am I missing something?”

I smiled. “My mother’s parents passed away before I was born.”

“Not long after Julia and I were married,” added Dad.

“Oh, I’m sorry. What happened?” asked Helen.

Dad slipped his arm around my shoulders. “There was an accident on their farm. The tractor fell over on Ezra and pulled over the wagon. Mercy had been riding on the wagon, helping bring in the corn, and she was thrown from the seat. They both were dead by the time a neighbor discovered them.”

Helen gasped. “Oh, how horrible.”

Dad nodded. “Julia doesn’t speak of them often, as it still can bring tears to her eyes. She has their wedding photo on the wall of our bedroom.”

I smiled. “And in that photo, my grandmother is

wearing a brooch just like this." I had to wipe from my cheek a tear that had escaped when I saw the brooch. It was perfect.

"Oh, I should like to see that sometime. I'm sure it's lovely."

"The best part is, Ruth even knows about it. One time I came into Mom and Dad's room with some clean laundry, and Ruth was there, asking Mom about the photo. My aunt has the original brooch, but I'm sure Mom would love one like it."

Dad just smiled and looked at me. "That's the one."

I called over a clerk, who rang us up and found a pretty little box for it.

"Mom will love it."

****

A couple of weeks later, Helen and I went into town to do some Christmas shopping. Mom and Grandma said they'd watch Elsie for me, so we took our time, even stopping at the drugstore for an ice cream, despite the snow and cold.

After Helen and I dropped our boots and coats in the mud room, we walked into the kitchen, which was empty for a change. We started to head upstairs, but stopped when we heard an adult crying in the parlor.

My throat went dry, and I felt rooted to the floor of the kitchen. I needed to go into the parlor to find out what was wrong, but I was terrified by what the answer might be. Was it Paul? Had something happened? Or Ruth? Or Will? Or Billy? It was hard to breathe when so many of our loved ones were in peril and bad news could be waiting in the next room.

Helen put her hand on my elbow, reminding me

that she was there. "We'd best find out what this is all about."

As we stepped into the parlor, I saw Mom and Clara huddled together on the sofa. One of those vile yellow telegrams was folded on the coffee table. I felt myself go cold, my fingers instantly numb, and couldn't form the words I needed to say.

Mom looked up, tears in her eyes.

Helen said, "Who?"

Mom handed Helen the telegram, which she held for us both to read.

DECEMBER 16, 1944
TO: MRS. WILLIAM WALKER
UPTON FALLS, NY

THE SECRETARY OF WAR DESIRES ME TO EXPRESS HIS DEEP REGRET THAT YOUR HUSBAND, SERGEANT WILLIAM WALKER, HAS BEEN REPORTED MISSING IN ACTION ON THIS DAY IN BELGIUM. IF FURTHER DETAILS OR OTHER INFORMATION ARE RECEIVED, YOU WILL BE PROMPTLY NOTIFIED.

ULDO THE ADJUTANT GENERAL

"Oh, no," I cried out, sinking into the armchair. Will? How could that be? The Lord couldn't be so cruel as to take both of my brothers.

Helen sat in the other armchair. "He's missing, only missing. We mustn't give up hope."

Clara looked up, her eyes red and puffy from crying. She used her handkerchief to wipe her face and nodded.

"Missing, in Belgium. I didn't even realize he was in Belgium." I couldn't wrap my mind around this.

Mom shook her head. "None of us did. Last we

heard, he was in the south of France." She had her arm around Clara, who looked too stunned to speak.

"Where are the boys?" Helen rose. "I can watch them."

Mom smiled, but it was a wan and weak expression. "Grandma has them out back. She told them they could have a snowball fight."

Helen went to the kitchen to look out the back window. While she was in there, I could hear water running. Probably putting the tea kettle on. The British always turn to tea.

I couldn't think what I should do, although it felt like I should be doing something. But what could we do, other than pray? Our helplessness and distance from our loved ones was one of the most frustrating parts of this war. We might join in the war effort, grow victory gardens, scrimp, re-use, go without, and even build aircraft engines, but we were still so far removed from what our husbands, brothers, friends, and even, now, sisters, were going through, it made our efforts feel futile at a time like this. Mom, Clara, and I sat in the parlor, no one talking or moving.

When Helen came back, she carried a tea tray, just as I expected, and her eyes were red. She probably felt, as I did, both worry for Will but relief that the news was not about her husband.

As guilty as it made me feel, especially because Will was my brother, I couldn't keep from thanking God it wasn't Paul.

The Christmas season, which had seemed so hopeful only a few minutes ago, was going to be subdued. How could any of us, especially Clara, pretend not to be worried sick about Will?

We would simply have to carry on, for the sake of the children. Sometimes, that seemed like all we did these days.

# Chapter Thirty
## Ruth

"We need to have everything packed up, as we'll probably be moved from Verdun tonight or tomorrow morning," Eileen said as we cleaned out the *St. Louis* from the day's runs.

"We never really unpack these days." I shook my head. After pouring out the remaining drips of coffee, I rinsed the urns and scrubbed them clean.

"I'm not sure how we could get out of here anyway," said Charlotte. "Since the breakthrough started yesterday, the roads have been clogged with convoys of troops coming and going from the front, wherever that is now."

I nodded. "I've seen way too many hospital trucks and ambulances heading away from the front over the past two days. Maybe they'll send us to some of the hospitals. It looks like there are plenty of wounded."

Renee stepped in the back door. "I just saw a truck full of Nazi prisoners go by. They always give me the creeps."

We hurried to get everything clean and strapped down so we could take the Clubmobile back to our current base in Verdun. Just as we got the engine started, the escort Jeep pulled up.

"You're being moved, girls. The front has moved again, and you're too close. The Army has ordered

Group A to pull back to Reims."

It was my turn to drive the *St. Louis*, so I followed the line of Clubmobiles, which in turn followed the Jeep, farther west, away from the Ardennes Forest, where the fighting seemed to be concentrated at the moment.

When we got to the abandoned school in which we were now billeted, we did our best to get set up in the second-floor room that had been turned into a dormitory. We'd moved so often, we were getting good at making any bombed-out, abandoned, or appropriated structure feel like home.

Our captain stopped in to give us our orders for the following day and tell us that the officers' mess was serving dinner at six-thirty.

"You were right, Ruth. We're stopping at three hospitals tomorrow, spread from here to Paris." Charlotte scanned the list she'd gotten from the captain.

"Paris?" Eileen perked right up. "We're going to Paris tomorrow?"

Charlotte laughed. "We're not going shopping, so down, girl. We have three stops to make, the last of which is in Paris, so we're going to have to stay there tomorrow night before we make the return trip through Troyes the following day."

Renee straightened up, hands on her hips. "Let's find the mess. I'm starving."

I had finished making up my cot, as had Renee and Charlotte, so we were waiting, as usual, for Eileen. She waved us off, saying she'd join us in the mess hall, so the three of us headed down to the temporary mess hall set up for officers and ARC girls.

"Hey, girls, come sit with us." A table of four

officers was flagging us down, guys we'd worked with many times.

"We'll just get our food first," said Charlotte, waving back.

We had our mess kits out and filed down the table to get our dinner.

"Is this actual beef?" Renee looked at the meat.

I nodded. "It looks like it to me." Somebody must have hit a cow along the road.

"Where did the Army get green beans? I'm so excited." Charlotte took extra vegetables, which was smart, as we didn't often have the chance.

After I filled my plate, I poured myself some coffee and walked to the table where Joe and the other guys were waiting for us.

"Well, hello there, Ruth. Where have you girls been hiding?"

I smiled and sat in the chair Danny held out for me. "We've been in Verdun for the past ten days, but we got kicked out of there in a hurry today."

Joe nodded. "Yeah, the Jerries are making crazy advances all through the forest near there. It's hard to fight what we can't see, so it came as quite a surprise."

Charlotte took the seat opposite from me, next to Pat. Eileen came scurrying over to our table before she even got her food.

"I just heard that Group F was caught in the retreat and one of the Clubmobiles was hit and destroyed. The *Arizona*."

"Oh, no!" I dropped my fork. "Was anyone injured?"

Eileen shrugged. "Nobody knows yet."

Eileen went back to the mess line, stopping first at

the table of girls from the *Lincoln* that she knew from training.

"No wonder we have a field hospital and two station hospitals to visit tomorrow on our way to Paris," I said.

Charlotte took a sip of coffee. "Those field hospitals are tough, as the men are so badly wounded. It's hard to know if we're helping or just in the way when we're there."

I nodded. "I know. At least the wounded at the station hospitals aren't as seriously hurt. I don't know if we'll have time to visit the general hospital in Paris, but those guys are in for the long haul, so I'd really like to stop there if we can."

Charlotte tore a corner off her piece of bread and waved it like a fork. "If it didn't get dark so damn early these days, we'd be able to fit more stops in each day. With the Army requiring us to be in by dark, it's tough to get done everything we need to do when sunset is so early."

Once Eileen had gotten her food and returned to the table, she ate quickly, as everyone else was nearly finished. Meanwhile, I looked around at the girls. "Let's try to get out of here as early as we can tomorrow morning, so we can have more time to spend with the wounded during the day." Even if mostly what we ended up doing was helping the men write letters home, and reading ones they'd received, I wanted to be as useful as we could on these hospital stops.

"Well," Joe said, a broad smile on his handsome face as he stood, "if you ladies are going to have an early morning, we'd best get to tonight's entertainment post haste."

As the tables were pushed to the side of the room, a lieutenant set up a Victrola from one of the Clubmobiles. To our delight, we found that a new collection of records had arrived from Special Services. Songs in the batch that were new to me included "San Fernando Valley," "I'll Walk Alone," "Milkman, Keep those Bottles Quiet," and "Spring Will be a Little Late this Year." These records had been made by well-known orchestras and performers for the Army, at no cost.

"I love the new music," said Eileen, as she danced by on my right with Dick, a captain with the Third Army.

I nodded, trying to keep my feet from being trod on by Butch, a second lieutenant from Cleveland. He was young and had arrived in Europe only two weeks ago.

"So you girls drive all over the countryside, delivering coffee and doughnuts?" Butch asked.

"Yes," I nodded, hoping for a faster song which would allow for less conversation.

"Wow, that's amazing. What a great service for the troops. How close do you get to the front?"

I sighed, thinking of Group F and the *Arizona*. "Sometimes too close."

"Where are you going tomorrow?"

I looked up at his face, "We'll stop at a field hospital here in Reims and then two station hospitals on the road to Paris."

He tripped but caught himself before he could fling me to the floor. "That's a long drive for one day."

I pasted a smile on my face. "We just go where they tell us to go."

I was thankful when Danny cut in and saved me

and my toes from agony.

"He's pretty green, isn't he?"

I laughed. "Well, he's young and enthusiastic."

Joe was a smooth dancer and always made our dances together fun. As the music switched tempo, he never missed a step and certainly never trod on my toes.

"Is this German offensive as bad as it sounds?"

Joe's face grew serious. "I'm headed to Metz. I was in Paris on administrative duty, but now I'm anxious to get back to my men. It's been a bad couple of days."

"Be careful, Joe."

He smiled again. "Are you worried about me, Ruthie?" He swung me in close, spinning us around.

"I'm worried about all of you, officers and enlisted alike. Don't go getting a big head, buddy."

"That's Lieutenant Buddy to you." He laughed.

While some of the Clubmobile girls had fallen in love, like Eileen, I had no expectation of finding love again so soon after Jack's death. Yes, it had been more than two years, and yes, I met some wonderful fellas here, like Joe. But my heart still belonged to Jack. Just because I'd accepted his death and moved on in my life, it didn't mean I was ready to move on in my heart.

The music and liquor flowed equally throughout the evening, but I finally had to drag myself and Charlotte away, knowing the morning would come early. Renee had already snuck out to bed, and I knew Eileen wouldn't leave until the party ended.

As Charlotte and I climbed the stairs, she put a hand on my arm, pulling me aside on the landing. She looked pale, and I was starting to think it wasn't from the exertion of dancing.

Her brow furrowed. “I heard about a Clubmobile girl from the *Arizona,* Mabel, do you remember her? She was injured and taken to a station hospital in Liege yesterday. Apparently, Group F got split in the retreat and the *Arizona* was in Bastogne when the German line broke through. Their driver was caught in the city when the Germans moved in and had to run out through machine-gun fire with a few other soldiers, just ahead of the advancing German tanks.”

“Wow.” I shook my head, covering my heart with my hand. “I can’t imagine what it must have been like for them. Is their driver okay?” Sometimes, depending on our assignment, we got a young soldier assigned to us as a driver.

“Yes.” We started climbing the stairs again. “But at some point, Mabel got injured, but I’m not sure how.”

“I’ll be sure to add her to my prayers tonight,” I said. It was hard to remember the names of everyone I wanted to include in my prayers sometimes, but I figured God would bless them all, nonetheless.

As we started up the stairs, Charlotte continued, “Apparently Group F was able to move five truckloads of G.I. mail out of Bastogne before they retreated. Those gals were really in the thick of it but came through like troopers.”

“Wow, that’s impressive. I only hope I would have done as well under those conditions. But tonight, I’m too tired to think about it.”

I stopped in our room to get my bathroom bag and headed back down the hall to wash up before turning in. When I got back to the room, Charlotte left for the bathroom, and I didn’t see anything more of her until morning.

****

Our first stop was at a field hospital in Riems, which was chaotic and overflowing. It was hard for Charlotte to find a place to park the *St. Louis* because the stream of hospital trucks coming and going was constant. We didn't stay there long but moved on to the first station hospital, where we could be of more use.

"Why don't Ruth and I take the rooms on the right side of the hall and you two take the ones on the left?" Charlotte was pushing a cart with an urn of coffee and plastic cups, plus a tray of doughnuts, some magazines, books, playing cards, cigarettes, and gum. I followed her into the first room of the hospital.

Renee and Eileen took their cart of supplies and headed off in the opposite direction.

Within a matter of minutes, casualties started coming in, a few at a time at first, and then one on top of another with great confusion. The hospital, which had the feel of a well-run clinic, was already busy and soon would be overflowing.

We parked our cart against the wall and started to make the rounds to the injured men in cots.

"Hello there, soldier." I stopped by, offering a doughnut to a young man in the first cot. He had one leg in a cast, held aloft over the cot with rope and a sling.

"Howdy, ma'am. You're sure a sight for sore eyes." He smiled and took a doughnut. "I'm Eddy."

"Well, Eddy, I'm Ruth. Where are you from?"

"Mississippi, ma'am. Have ya'll ever been to visit our sweet state?"

"Can't say that I have, Eddy." We chatted briefly, and then I moved to the next cot. "And what about you, soldier? Where are you from?"

He had a cast on his left arm, from armpit to fingertips, and a bandage over one eye. He looked at me with his uncovered eye, giving me a slight but pained smile.

"Missouri, ma'am."

I offered him a doughnut, but he said no. "A St. Louis Cardinals fan?"

"Yes, ma'am," he said, with a little more enthusiasm.

We chatted a bit about baseball, but he was obviously in a lot of pain, so I said goodbye and moved on.

I continued on from cot to cot, becoming sadder as I moved through the room. As nurses and doctors moved quickly through the rooms, I heard them saying to each other, over and over, that many of these wounded were so badly injured that they shouldn't have been moved, which must mean that the field hospitals were too full to take these additional men.

The doctors and nurses worked quickly and efficiently, but even they couldn't keep up with the continuous influx of wounded. We kept hearing trucks moving north and west throughout the day, and with the steady flow of additional casualties, it was clear something big was going on.

When Charlotte and I made our way to the last room in the station hospital, we found more men who had been brought in within the last day. As I started my rounds, I stopped dead in my tracks, and Charlotte bumped into me.

"Ruth? Are you okay?"

"Will? Is that you?" I hurried over to the cot at the

far end of the room, where my beloved brother-in-law was propped up, staring back at me.

"Ruth? How the hell did you find me?"

I ran to Will, looking quickly for injuries. Seeing that it was his left leg that was bandaged, I threw my arms around him and hugged him for all he was worth. He pushed me away, looked at my face, tears in his eyes, and pulled me back into a fierce bear hug.

"Ruth?"

I suddenly remembered Charlotte was there. I turned to her, at the same time not letting go of Will. "This is Will Walker, my brother-in-law. Jack's brother."

Charlotte reached out and shook Will's hand, although he wouldn't completely release me from his arms. "Nice to meet you, Will."

"Will, this is my good friend Charlotte. We work together on a Clubmobile, the *St. Louis*. It's out front."

"It's my lucky day, then, Charlotte, and I'm pleased to meet you."

Charlotte moved on to visit the other men in the room and gave me a chance to catch up with Will.

"What are you doing here, Will? What happened to you? When did you get here?"

He laughed. "Whoa, one question at a time." He adjusted himself in the bed but still held on to my hand. "My unit landed in southern France at the end of August, and we've been fighting our way northeast ever since. We made it to Bastogne last week, and then the Germans broke through that line on Saturday, the sixteenth. I was injured right off."

"How badly are you hurt?"

"Not too bad. I tore the shit out of the ligaments in

my ankle. I could hardly walk. The docs in the Seventy-Sixth General Hospital in Liege had to cut my boot off."

"I'm surprised they moved you to a station hospital from there."

"They were swamped, Ruth. It's bad. The snow and the forest really gave those Jerries the drop on us. A lot of men were killed or injured, and Liege was overrun with casualties. Things were crazy with troops in France and Belgium and the Jerries making quick work of our defenses. I got sent here on the next truck, because I'm apparently in for a long haul. I think I'll be sent on to Paris tomorrow."

I squeezed his hand. I couldn't believe my luck in finding him. I hadn't seen him since the day he and Jack boarded the bus for basic training, and it was so good to see his face.

"Did you get to send a telegram to Clara and your parents?"

"Not yet. I don't think I'll be able to until I get to Paris. Liege was chaos, and then, yesterday, the Germans bombed the hospital, those fuckers."

Before the war, I would have been surprised to hear Will use that kind of language, because he never did at home. Now, though, I'd grown used to it. Almost every enlisted man I met, and many officers as well, said the same or worse. War changed everyone.

"Oh, Will, I'm so glad you got out of there when you did. Can you imagine what happened to all those wounded when the hospital was bombed?"

I ran my hand up and down his arm, just happy to be able to touch him and know he was really there.

He shook his head, smiling at me. "I can't believe

how good you look, Ruth. It's been so long." He paused, his gaze filling with concern. "I still miss him so much."

I tried to swallow tears that filled up my throat. "I miss him, too, Will. It's hard, but I feel so much closer to him since I've been here. I mean, since we got transferred to France. I feel like he knows what I'm doing and approves, if that makes any sense."

Will's expression changed suddenly. "It doesn't make sense to me, Ruth. I don't think you should be here."

I was so surprised, I pulled back. I couldn't say a word.

"I wish you'd go back home. You were doing so much good there. Mom told me about the day care and the work you were doing with the Red Cross in Beacon Heights. Those men need your help too. And when this war ends, there will be a lot of returning soldiers who will need women like you helping them at home. It's too dangerous over here; it's no place for you."

I took a deep breath, folding my hands in my lap. "Has your unit been serviced by any Clubmobiles, Will?"

"No, I didn't see any in Italy or in the past few months that we've been in France. I think we've been moving too fast."

I nodded. "I wish you could see the faces of the men when we pull into a camp."

He almost snarled. "I can well imagine what their faces look like and what they're thinking." He released my hand.

I shook my head. "It's not like that at all, Will. These men are grateful that we're there. They appreciate the coffee and doughnuts, sure, and love hearing the music we play and dancing with us. But mostly they talk to me about their wives, girlfriends, their mothers or sisters, about their hometowns or jobs they left behind, what they want to do when they get back. We talk about baseball, not romance. I mean, I can't say none of them make passes—"

"Aha," he interrupted.

"No, let me finish. Yes, some of the men make passes, but nothing serious. They're generally good-natured about accepting rejection. The overwhelming majority of the men treat me like the girl next door. They're genuinely glad to see an American girl, mostly as a reminder of why they're here and what they're fighting for. It helps, Will, it really does."

He raised his voice, drawing the attention of several of the wounded men in the room. "I don't need a truck of American girls, risking their necks to serve me doughnuts, to remind me why I'm over here fighting." He crossed his arms over his chest. "It's a stupid and selfish reason for you to risk a bomb dropping on you. We already lost Jack. The family doesn't deserve to lose you, too, Ruth."

I staggered back. "Wow. That really hurts, Will. I can't believe you'd say that." Mom and Pop had never made me feel like I was selfish for joining the Red Cross. I knew they'd be sad if anything happened to me, but they didn't think the risk outweighed the good I could do.

I wasn't sure what more I could say. "I was hoping you'd be proud of me, or at least that you could respect what I'm doing. I honestly believe Jack would be supportive, if he were still alive."

Will looked down, not meeting my gaze. "I know it was rough on you when Jack died. But there's still plenty for you to do at home. They need you on the farm. Don't you see that?"

Tears filled my eyes. Had I been blind to what his family really felt about my leaving?

"I talked to your parents about this before I signed up. They both supported my decision and encouraged me to join the Clubmobile program. Why can't you see that what I'm doing here is important? It means something to the men, to the war."

He looked really angry now. "Of course my parents supported your decision. They're good people and they want you to be happy, even if it breaks their hearts or frightens them every day. If you told them you'd figured out how to join the Army and go fight the Nazis yourself, do you really think they'd tell you not to do it? No, they'd just stay silent and worry about you every minute, like they're doing now. That's a great way to say thank you for making you a part of our family."

I stood, unable to believe he could be this cold, this cruel. "It's my family, too, William Walker. When I married your brother, I became your sister and their daughter. You became my family, and just because Jack's gone that hasn't changed." I took a deep breath, trying to swallow the tears that were burning in my eyes. "And just because Jack died, it doesn't mean I died too, or that there's only one way to mourn him. I think of him every day and know that he would approve of what I'm doing. If you can't see it that way, you'll just have to learn to deal with it."

I stepped away from his cot, seeing that we had quite an audience by now. I turned back to face him. "I can see I'm not going to change your mind, and you'd better believe you're not changing mine. I'm glad you're not seriously hurt, Will. Be sure to send that telegram to Clara and the rest of the family when you get to Paris, as I'm sure they'll want to hear from you. But I have to get back to work because, despite what you think, what we do here is important and meaningful to the men that thank us every day for being here. If I don't see you again, once you make it to Paris, I wish you a speedy and full recovery. See you at home."

I turned and stalked away, my heart racing and my face burning. I walked right past Charlotte and the young man she was talking to. I couldn't be in the same room as Will right now and needed some fresh, albeit cold, air.

I grabbed my coat and stepped out the front door, sucking in huge gulps of air, trying to keep myself from screaming. I couldn't stop the tears that poured down my face. It was frustrating to cry when what I wanted to do was scream at Will.

I was excited and grateful to see him, hug him, and see that he was alive and safe. It was almost like a part of Jack was right in front of me. What gave him the right to say those things to me? How could he hurt me like that? I was in charge of what I wanted to do with my life, not him!

I stomped around in the snow, trying to ward off the cold seeping into my feet and release the fury that was boiling up my spine.

Did Mom and Pop think I was being selfish? Did Lilly or Clara? Was I indulging myself at the family's expense? Had I been blind to the burden my service was placing on my family?

I covered my face with my gloved hands and let the tears flow until I was shaking, gulping, and gasping.

I was still crying, although somewhat calmed down, when I felt Charlotte's soft hands on my shoulders. I turned into her embrace, more tears washing through me.

She held me, patting me on the back, until I wound down again. I felt sick, weak, and exhausted, as if I were recovering from a severe illness.

Eventually, I pulled back. "I'm sorry."

She shook her head. "Doll, you've got nothing to apologize for." She smiled a sad smile at me. "He was out of line. He had no right to say the things he said to you, brother-in-law or not."

I nodded, my throat too raw to say much. I used my handkerchief to wipe my face and nose.

"You should have heard how the guys around him laid into him after you left."

"What?"

She nodded. "Oh, yeah. They gave him hell. Told him he was an ass and had no right talking to a Red Cross girl that way."

I smiled.

"It was sweet, really. Several of the guys in the room were from units that had been visited by Clubmobiles several times, and they said what a difference it made to them. They told him how great it was when we pulled into the field or forest or wherever they were and started serving them coffee and doughnuts, giving out gum and cigarettes and even just talking to them. They said how it was like their sister had stopped in to visit. They told him if he couldn't see that you were making a sacrifice to support the troops, and that it mattered what you did, then he was a jackass."

"They said that to Will?" I had to laugh.

"They did, several of them. And worse. They apologized to me for their language, but I was smiling by then."

I put my arms around Charlotte again. "Thanks for telling me that." We turned and started back into the hospital. "It doesn't change what Will said to me, but it helps me remember this is not something I'm doing only for myself. It might have been a partly selfish choice to make, but it makes a difference to a lot of people."

Charlotte grabbed my arm. "That's horseshit, if you'll pardon my French. You are one of the least selfish people I've ever met. Will was out of line, and that's all there is to it."

"Thanks." We got our cart from the hospital and headed back to the Clubmobile to pack up. We had another hospital to visit.

"Has he always talked to you like that, Ruth?"

I shook my head. "No, not at all. I guess that's why it hurt. I've never had a cross word from Will in all the time I've known him. I mean, sometimes he and Jack would disagree about something, but nothing big. I've never heard Will talk to anyone like that before."

Charlotte patted me on the back as she stepped outside to rinse out the urn and then came back in to pack it away. "You know, Ruth, he may still be struggling with Jack's death, since he was with Jack when he was killed. Maybe Will can't bear the thought, you know, of losing you too. Don't think that I'm excusing him for the way he talked to you. I'm not. He was a jackass. But maybe there's more to it."

I nodded, considering this. "That's possible, Charlotte." I packed away the doughnut tray and secured our cart. "I'm not sure, but maybe he has a reason for acting the way he did. Maybe by the next time I see him, he'll have realized what an ass he was and will apologize."

"You can always hope."

Eileen and Renee came out with their cart and supplies and started loading everything up to get ready to move on. I stepped out, trying to calm myself, while Eileen rinsed out their urn. A nurse came running out to us, calling my name.

"Are you Ruth Walker?"

"Yes." I turned to her. "Do you need something?"

She nodded, placing her hand on my arm. "Yes, I need you to come back into the hospital, just for a moment."

"Is something wrong? We have to get to the next hospital, and we're under a time crunch."

"Please, just for a moment."

I followed her inside, anxious to leave again and get on the road. I needed to put some space between me and Will.

I stepped into the hospital, and the soldiers in the first room started clapping and hooting. Someone yelled "Hooray."

I looked at the nurse, and she motioned me to follow her. We got the same reaction when we entered the second room. I really didn't want to go into the last room, where Will was, but she pulled me along.

Will was sitting up in his bed, staring at me. The rest of the men in his room were clapping, hooting, and hollering, cheering for the Red Cross and Clubmobile girls. The nurse led me to Will.

"Okay, I got her here. The rest is up to you."

I stood at the end of his bed, and he motioned to the side, where I'd been sitting before. I hesitated, and he said, "Please," so I sat.

The men around us quieted down. Will took my hand, looking into my eyes. "I'm sorry, Ruth. I had no right to yell at you. You're a grown woman and can do what you think is best."

He visibly swallowed, as if he had to get it out as fast as he could. "It kills me that even though I was with Jack when he was shot I couldn't do anything about it. I feel so guilty I can hardly stand it, even though I know it was the fuckin' Jerries that killed him, not me."

I nodded, not knowing what to say. I could feel the tears burning behind my eyes.

"I'm scared, is all. I can't bear the thought of losing you too. But these guys gave me hell when you walked out, telling me what you Red Cross girls do over here and what a difference you make to everyone. Now I'm jealous my unit never got a visit, but I get why you're doing this."

He looked down at my hand, and then back up at my face. "Please forgive me, sister of my heart. You will always be a part of our family, and right now, I'm sure Mom and Dad would rather have you than me, given how I acted. I'm so sorry."

It was just as Charlotte had said. Fear and guilt were a potent combination. I felt a huge weight lift off my chest, but tears fell from my eyes again.

"Oh, God. Don't cry, Ruth, please. I'm sorry, I'm

so sorry." He looked panicked, and it made me smile.

I leaned in, wrapping my arms around him, and he squeezed me tight.

"Thank God. I was afraid you'd left and would be angry with me forever."

I shook my head, smiling. "No, I'm scared sometimes too, but mostly for you and Billy and Paul and all the young men we meet. I just want this war to be over."

He visibly relaxed, tears in his eyes as well. "Me too. I can't wait until we get back home."

He hugged me again, and I said a quick goodbye, as we were already running behind schedule. I promised to write to him, and he said he'd try to do the same. I walked out of that hospital smiling, hopeful, and much happier.

## Chapter Thirty-One
Helen

"I'll take it, or…rather, we'll take it." I tried not to blush as I looked at the stooped old man who'd shown Lilly and me the apartment, but I couldn't stop thinking about Billy.

Billy coming through the door.

Billy eating at the kitchen table.

Billy lying in the bed.

It'd been so long since we'd been together.

Ever since he'd written to tell me he had the eighty-five points he needed to come home, I hadn't been able to think of anything else.

"When do you want to move in, miss?"

"It's Mrs.—Mrs. William Anderson." I could feel my shoulders straightening as I said it. "My husband is due back from Europe any day now, so as long as it comes with this furniture, I'd like to move in today."

I looked over to Lilly, who was smiling and nodding. She could probably see what was in my thoughts.

"Is he going to be needing a ramp, missus? Lot of the men coming home can't handle the stairs, if you know what I mean."

I'm sure he meant well enough, but neither Lilly nor I needed to hear about the injuries that so many of our men were bringing home with them. We prayed daily that our men—and also our woman—overseas would come home to us safe and sound. We had no idea when Paul would be coming home, as the war in the Pacific didn't seem nearly as close to victory as did the one in Europe.

"That will not be necessary, thank you." And Thank God.

As soon as we had the keys, Lilly and I rushed home to pack my few belongings into the truck and return.

As I walked down the stairs, carrying all my worldly possessions, I heard Julia calling the men in for dinner. She turned to look at me, her eyes suspiciously red.

"You won't leave before we eat, will you?"

This woman had both mothered and befriended me, giving me love and making me part of her family. I could never deny her a thing.

"Of course not, Julia."

I walked to the back porch and set down my suitcase and boxes. While I was excited to settle the home I would share with Billy, I could still enjoy these lovely people around the dinner table.

After the blessing and the first passing of the food was complete, Earl cleared his throat. "So you're leaving the nest, are you, Helen?"

His smile calmed the nerves I'd been fighting. I didn't want them to think I was ungrateful for their love and support.

"Now, Earl, she's off to build a nest of her own, as she should." Julia smiled and winked, and I found breathing much easier.

"It's not too far, Dad," said Lilly. "And it's the

cutest little house. You know, the old Grimble place."

"It's very convenient to town and work, but not far from here, so I can come visit." I looked around the table, seeing smiles from everyone.

"Don't let Albert Grimble take advantage of you, girl. That was a nice house in its day, but it needs some work." Earl took a drink of his coffee. "Make sure you have Billy check the roof and get after Albert if it's not up to par."

"I will, Earl. Thank you." I looked to Lilly and Julia. "I hope Billy likes it. It was really the best place we saw."

"Billy will be happy wherever you are, dear." Julia smiled, patting my hand with hers.

"Do you know when he's due back?" Leonard looked up from his meal.

I shook my head. "Not exactly. His letter said he'd be shipped home as soon as there was room on a New York-bound ship, but he couldn't be sure when that would be. Even though the war isn't over, and they're still shipping replacement soldiers to Europe, a lot of the men have gotten enough points to come home. Billy said there's a lot of traffic going back and forth, so he may have to wait a bit to get out of there."

Clara looked up. "I'm so glad he's coming home, Helen. Safe and sound."

All I could think was, Don't jinx it, Clara. He's not home yet.

After dinner, I hugged everyone and shed a few tears before saying a proper goodbye and letting Earl drive me to the new house. Lilly volunteered, but Earl insisted that he wanted to take a look at the place and make sure it was safe before leaving me there.

"Helen."

I was almost unsure Earl had spoken, as his voice was so soft.

"Yes?"

"You know we think of you as our own daughter now, don't you?" Emotion showed in his voice, which was rare for him.

I couldn't help but smile, although my eyes misted a bit. "Thank you, Earl, I do. You and Julia, well, all the Walkers, couldn't have been any kinder to me. I can't thank you all for getting me through this war. I would have been miserable anywhere else."

He nodded, staring straight ahead at the road. "I know Billy will be as happy to see you as you are going to be at his return." He glanced briefly at me, a smile in his gaze.

I nodded. "I hope so."

"Trust me, he will." Earl chuckled. "But if his mother gives you one moment of grief, I want you to remember that the Andersons are not your only family in this town. We couldn't love you any more than we do, and we won't stand for that woman treating you like you aren't good enough for the Anderson name. You hear me?" His voice had taken on a gravelly tone.

I took a deep breath, nodding my head and trying hard to keep the tears at bay. I reached out and put my hand on his arm as he pulled to a stop in front of my new home.

"Thanks to you, and Julia, Lilly, Ruth, and all your loving family, I don't think anything Mabel Anderson has to say to me will ever affect me the way it did when I first came to Upton Falls. You've given me the truly brilliant gift of love and confidence, and I know, now, that Billy and I are meant to be together."

Earl turned to look at me, the same dampness in his eyes that I couldn't keep out of my own. I reached across the seat and wrapped my arms around him.

When he pulled back, he took out his handkerchief and blew his nose. He looked back at me. "I'm very glad to hear that, girl. You are worth ten of that woman, in my book. Young Billy is lucky to have you waiting for him." He opened his door and got out of the truck. "Now, let's get you moved into this new house so you're ready for your husband's return."

****

Long after Earl had checked over the house, pronounced it sturdy enough, and headed back to the farm, I stayed up unpacking and setting up our house. I didn't have much, but the house came with all the basic furniture we would need. Billy and I could decide what else to buy once he was home. But Julia had sent me home with fresh linens for our bed and towels for the bathroom, so I cleaned and fussed and made it look as welcoming as I could. I would have to buy some fresh flowers to set out, just waiting for Billy to return.

I'd written him right away with the new address, but it seemed very unlikely that he'd get the letter before he got home. Or at least I was hoping he would be home long before the letter could make it to him. If he went to the Walker farm, though, they'd know where to send him.

Surely he'd also let his parents know his return was imminent, even though he couldn't tell us when he'd actually arrive. Whilst I'd spoken brave words to Earl, there was still a part of me that was anxious about how Mabel would react to Billy living with me, in this house, and not with them. Well, she didn't like me already, so it couldn't really make her like me less.

Once every inch of the house was clean and tidy and ready for Billy's return, I found I couldn't keep my eyes open a minute longer, so I climbed into our new bed. My last thought was what it would feel like soon when Billy was right there beside me.

I came awake with a start when I heard knocking at the front door. The clock on the bedside table read eight-thirty. Who could possibly be knocking at my new door at that time? Lilly had already told me to take the morning off from the day care so I could get settled in.

The knocking was insistent, so I grabbed my robe and slid my feet into my slippers. By the time I got to the door, I was quite annoyed by whoever was on the other side. I wrenched the door open and said "What..."

Before I could say another words, I was lifted off my feet, wrapped in a tight embrace, and being kissed for all I was worth. Billy!

The tears began in earnest.

"Billy?"

He didn't say a word. He just held me, gently swinging me back and forth in his arms, kissing every inch of my face, including the tears that leaked from my eyes. Before I knew what was happening, he lifted me in his arms and carried me over the threshold.

I didn't want to let him go but at the same time wanted to get a proper look at him. I placed my hands on either side of his face, holding it still so I could drink in his eyes, his lips, the color in his cheeks, and the scruff of his beard.

Slowly, he let me slide down his body, so that we

were facing each other but still joined.

He took a deep breath and nearly knocked me down with the sheer beauty of his smile.

"Billy." I didn't seem to be able to say more.

"Yes, baby, I'm home." He wrapped his right arm around my waist and propelled us into the sitting room. "Thank you for finding us a home of our own. I'm so glad to have you all to myself." He kissed me again, and I found that whatever I'd been intending to say was gone.

He sat in the wingback chair adjacent to the fireplace and pulled me onto his lap.

"But when, how…?"

I sounded like a bloody idiot, but I couldn't believe he was here.

"Just lucky, my love. I caught a transport that was taking some wounded men back stateside, and they had some empty spots, so I grabbed one. I had to help the nurses a bit during the trip, but it was definitely worth it to get back here as soon as I could."

I kept touching his face, unable to believe he was real. I hadn't touched that beautiful face for nearly three and a half years, and I couldn't get enough of it. He was leaner than when I'd seen him last, but he looked healthy and strong and all mine.

"I can't believe you're really here. It's like a dream." I smiled, ignoring the tears that continued to leak from my eyes.

Billy leaned forward and kissed my tears away. "Don't cry now, Helen. I'm home, and I'm never leaving you again."

That made the tears come even harder, but it must have convinced Billy I needed more attention. As if I weighed nothing at all, he stood with me in his arms and started carrying me through the house.

"You'd better tell me where the bedroom is, my love, unless this sofa is more comfortable than it looks."

I laughed and pointed him in the right direction. The sofa could wait for another day.

****

As the war seemed to drag on, everyone was anxious to get letters from Ruth, but no one more so than me.

*March 1, 1945*

*Dear Helen,*

*I'm excited to hear that Billy is on his way home—or may already be there by now. You must be walking on air. I'll be sorry you aren't living with us when I get home, but I can't wait to see you together. I couldn't be happier for you both!*

*I'm sorry you all were worried about Will being missing in action when he was safe in an Army hospital. I trust he explained that it was because the first hospital he was sent to was bombed just after he left, sent to a different hospital, and the records got destroyed. Anyway, he's recovering in Paris, although it will take some time before his left ankle is as strong as the right one. I saw him in the second hospital he was in and had a chance to see him again this past week, when I was in Paris.*

*Speaking of the hospital in Paris, guess who else I saw when I was there? Your brother Percy. It was the strangest thing. When I talk to the wounded men, I go to their bedsides and talk, ask them where they're from and such. We didn't know there were British soldiers mixed in with Americans until we started talking to them.*

*Anyway, when I was talking to one young man, asking his name and where he was from, he said, "I'm Percy Cole from London." I joked, "Well, my friend Helen is from the East End, and her maiden name was Cole. Maybe you know her." I laughed, but his mouth dropped open. He said, "Is her name Helen Anderson now?" and then my mouth dropped open. I couldn't believe I got to meet another of your brothers. He's fine, by the way.*

*He was injured in the battle along the northern end of the Ardennes Forest, while Will was injured down on the southern end. Anyway, Percy was shot, but don't worry. It was just a flesh wound in his upper thigh, and he'll be fine. It got infected in the field hospital, so they shipped him to Paris for recuperation, but he'll be up and about in no time.*

*He was excited to hear about you and impressed that you are now a college student. He said your other brothers are fine, last he knew, and that your parents and younger brothers are doing well at home. He sends his love and hopes that someday he can come to America to see you. I gave him your address so he can write to you.*

*As for me, I'm fine, as well. The fighting continues, but we are following the Army as they make their way across Germany, and I don't think this will last much longer.*

*We're moving so fast I'm usually serving doughnuts within M1 range of the enemy and driving, as one of the girls says, from "gun to gun" through mine fields and over roads that are no longer even roads. Don't worry, though. The Army takes good care of us.*

*I'm finding it hard to keep charity in my heart, though, as we drive through these German towns and see what good condition the German citizens are in, especially compared to the poor starving people of France. Even their fields look normal, as there's been little bombing here, by comparison. Is it wrong to resent them for the easy time they've had during the war when the occupied countries have been starving to death, dying in prisoner of war camps, or being arbitrarily shot? It was easier on our morale when we were the liberators, and people were so glad to see us, rather than now, when we're the conquerors.*

*And the rumors we hear about the concentration camps frighten me. I don't know how much you have heard about them, but I am afraid we'll discover the horrors are real.*

*We're so close to ending this whole mess, at least here in Europe, I wish Hitler would just surrender. The fighting seems unnecessary at this point. Let's hope it's over soon, for everyone's sake.*

*Give everyone there my love and hugs and kisses, especially the little ones. Hug yourself for me, too, and Billy, when he gets home. All my love—*

*Ruth*

****

*May 15, 1945*
*Dear Helen,*

*Well, it's finally over! Your VE Day celebrations in the U.S. were probably more exciting than ours here. It was so expected, day after day during that last week, that when it finally happened, it was anticlimactic, if you can believe it. I think everyone's worn out and overwhelmed. But at least many of the boys will be coming home soon. Unless they have to go to the Pacific.*

*When we got the news, we were glad there weren't many troops near us, as we were exhausted. We celebrated, although in a more subdued fashion than usual, as some of the men came to lure us out to parties. We decided we owed it to everything they had done to bring about the surrender. We had little liquor left, but we took out the cookies and other food we'd been saving and polished it all off in honor of victory.*

*We were stationed in Munich at the end of April, when the troops liberated the concentration camp at Dachau. No, I didn't go. One of the men I know well told me to stay away, and given what I was hearing, I decided he was right. I never would have been able to "un-see" it. Just listening to the soldiers talk about it and seeing the survivors has taken a toll on us all. The Army insisted the troops see the death camps and, as horrific as it all was, many said it reaffirmed why they fought this war, to stop those kinds of atrocities from happening.*

*Renee insisted on seeing the camp herself, to see if she could find out anything about her father. She didn't speak for a day after she came back. So far, she hasn't learned anything about her father's whereabouts, but she's trying to stay hopeful.*

*The poor people released from these camps, those who were able to survive it, mostly Jews, of course—they're barely alive. Walking skeletons, really. We wanted to be able to do something for them, but thankfully the Army is on it. One of the Clubmobiles was nearby as a camp was liberated, and the starving survivors rushed to eat the doughnuts, even though everyone, including the survivors, knew they would be sick. It's all terribly sad, but also incredibly maddening. Sometimes, all I can do is cry.*

*We continue to service the troops and travel the area, even though the war is over. It will be some time before anything changes for us. As long as the troops need us, we'll be here. I know some of the girls who have been here the longest will start rotating out. I'm even going to get a month of leave. I'm really ready for it, even if all I do is sleep for a month. I'm going to go back to London, as I don't want to spend my leave in Germany, and England will be more comfortable than France at this point. I'll probably travel back to Paris and then from there to London, but I'll let you know specifics when I get them. I hope I can get a lift in somebody's airplane, as it is safe now, with no flak to worry about, and I enjoyed the view from above. I'll visit your parents while I'm in London.*

*I'll write soon. Give my love to everyone.*

*—Love, Ruth*

****

*July 10, 1945*
*Dearest Family,*

*I know I said I'd stop combining letters, especially now that Helen no longer lives at the farm, but I'm short of time, so I'm sending this to Helen, but addressed to everyone, knowing that she'll share it with you.*

*I am writing this to you all from Paris. I got a ride here with a pilot I met when we were here during the Battle of the Bulge. Last week he was in Munich, and we happened to run into one another at the officers' club. I was thrilled to hear he was flying back to Paris, so I hitched a ride. I've been able to work at the headquarters here now and will officially start my month-long leave on July 24, when I head to London. My pilot friend was able to arrange a ride for me with a friend of his, who is transferring back to London then, so that's why I'm waiting another two weeks before starting my vacation.*

*Anyway, being at the Paris headquarters has its benefits. I have been able to sit in on some discussions of plans for the ARC Clubmobiles. Many girls have requested to be released, as they have served their time. The ARC doesn't need as many Clubmobiles at this point, as the occupation troops are no longer on the move, nor are they spread across Europe as they were when actively fighting.*

*So those of us still serving will be concentrated in Germany or in a few designated cities to service active troops in those areas. It doesn't sound like they will be moving any Clubmobiles or girls from the ETO to the Pacific, thank heavens. While I'm praying for a speedy end to the war in the Pacific, I don't want to start all over with a Clubmobile over there. I'm much happier to stay here, working with the people I know. So after my month of leave, I'll be back in service with Charlotte, Renee, and Eileen, as long as the ARC needs us, but no later than February of next year, as that's when our two years are up.*

*I hope I can get home for Christmas this year but will have to wait and see. It's a possibility, I'm happy to say, but we'd best not count on it.*

*Anyway, I'm glad that Will and Billy are home and*

*hope that Paul makes it home soon. It sounds like Will has a lot of therapy to do to build up his ankle to be as strong as it was before he was injured, but he can surely do that at home. You all must be so thrilled to have them home.*

*As hard as the end of the war has been, I have to say, again, how lucky I am to have been able to work for the ARC as a Clubmobiler. This was a privilege for me and gave me the chance to make a difference in the war effort in a way that was most meaningful to me.*

*I don't know if I'll go back to teaching when I get home. I may see if I can continue to work for the ARC in Beacon Heights or even the Veterans Administration. There will be a lot of veterans who will need services when they return, and I'd like to go on serving them. I think my experiences here will make me uniquely qualified to relate to the men and help them as they move forward in civilian life. I don't know exactly what I'll do yet, but I thought I'd talk to some of the women at the ARC headquarters in London while I'm there.*

*Anyway, I just want to thank you all for your support while I've been here. I know it put more work on your shoulders, especially Mom, Lilly, and Helen, so thank you for never making me feel guilty for choosing to come over here.*

*Thank you, again, for all the heartwarming letters and greatly appreciated packages you've sent me. You can't begin to know how much it meant each and every time I got something in mail call. It was like a little piece of you had come to visit me here, just when I needed you the most. Although don't think by saying this I don't want to go on receiving letters—I do!*

*As Will and I discussed when I saw him last, you*

*are all the best family in the world, and I am so lucky to have found Jack, and through him, all of you. While I'll miss him every day of my life, I can look back on our years together without pain now, because I know in my heart that he supported my decision to join the ARC and come to Europe.*

*So, thank you again. I love you all so much and miss you dearly. I look forward to seeing you, maybe at Christmas, but definitely by next February, at the latest. I still have work to do here, but know that you are all in my heart.*

*Now, before I get even mushier, I need to get back to work so I can go play in two weeks. I'll try to send a postcard or two from London, if I can make myself get out of bed to go buy some. Ha, ha.*

*All my love to all of you.*

*—Ruth*

****

*AMERICAN RED CROSS*
*July 25, 1945*
*TO: Mr. and Mrs. Earl Walker, Upton Falls, NY*
*Dear Mr. and Mrs. Walker,*

*It is with great sadness that we must inform you of the death of your daughter-in-law, Ruth Walker, yesterday, July 24, in France. Ruth was scheduled to start a month's leave but was killed when the small plane she was flying in crashed over the English Channel when they encountered a sudden storm. The pilot flying the two-seater was an excellent, experienced pilot. We hope you will be comforted to know that both Ruth and the pilot died instantly and did not suffer.*

*Ruth did her country and the American Red Cross proud every moment of her service. Her death is a tragedy, and the loss will be felt by all who knew her.*

*We will hold a funeral service for Ruth, at the Red Cross Hall at the 179th General Hospital in Rouen, as soon as her fellow Clubmobilers from the* St. Louis *can be flown in from Germany. Burial will follow at the temporary military cemetery in St. Andre.*

*We cannot express strongly enough our sadness at Ruth's passing. We will be forwarding you Ruth's personal effects and the balance of her bank account. Please accept our deepest apologies for your loss,*

*Sincerely,*

*Martha Barton, ARC Executive Officer, London*

# Epilogue

*May 8, 1995*

Helen entered the reception area of the banquet hall and stopped at the sign-in table, which was flanked by red-white-and-blue bunting. She took her name tag, searching the round tables for her seat.

"The tables are named for occupied cities in France that were liberated by the Allies," said the helpful young woman at the sign-in table. "The flags in the centerpieces honor each of the Allied countries."

Each table had gleaming white tablecloths, shining cutlery, and sparking crystal. The centerpieces were an arrangement of fresh flowers matching the colors of the small flag that rose from the flowers. She found her way to the table marked Rouen, which had an American flag and an arrangement of white lilies and carnations, red roses and poppies, and tall blue salvia.

When she'd decided to attend the fiftieth anniversary of VE Day, she didn't know what she was signing up for. She'd decided it was her final chance to visit Ruth's grave, plus she had added on one last trip to London to see her family. She was lucky her daughter and granddaughter were able to come with her.

As she entered the room alone, she found herself wishing that Ruthie and Irene had come with her to the dinner, but she hadn't been able to convince her stubborn daughter that Irene would have been perfectly fine here. Ruthie didn't give the child enough credit.

It was nice of the organizers to list not only Helen Cole Anderson on her name tag but also the name of the person she was here to honor. When she met people, they could see not only her name, but that she was here on behalf of Ruth Walker, ARC. She was embarrassed to be the only one there on Ruth's behalf.

There was a nice cocktail hour going on before dinner, but after the emotional trip to the cemetery, she was tired enough to want to sit for a moment. After taking a place, and a sip of water, she picked up the program to see what was planned for the evening.

"Mom?"

She looked up, and there were Ruthie and Irene standing in front of her. "You came?"

Her daughter smiled at her. Ruthie looked so much like Billy when she smiled that Helen's old heart warmed at the sight of her.

"Of course we came. You didn't really think I was going to make you go through this alone, did you?"

That's exactly what she'd thought. "No, not really. I'm just so glad to see you. Why don't you sit right here?"

Irene, dressed in a frilly pink dress that Helen hadn't seen in the child's suitcase, climbed up in the chair next to Helen, and Ruthie took the seat on the far side of Irene.

"Granny?"

"Yes, lovey." She looked down into Irene's beautiful blue eyes.

"Why are there so many old people here?"

Helen laughed, and Ruthie scoffed. "Irene," she

scolded. “It’s not polite to call them old people.”

“We are old.” Helen smiled down at the child. “Anyway, my love”—she took her granddaughter’s hand in her own—“this is a party to remember our friends and family from World War Two, which happened fifty years ago. So those of us who remember these people are frightfully old ourselves.”

“Okay, Granny.”

“Why don’t you mingle, Mom? I thought you wanted to meet some of the women Ruth worked with, maybe meet some of the men she served. How are you going to know who they are if you don’t introduce yourself?”

“I know, I know. I wanted to take a moment to gather my thoughts.” Or screw up the courage.

“We’ll hold down the fort here.”

“Okay.” Helen stood and walked toward a group of men and women wearing military caps of some kind. Surely they’d know something about the Clubmobile program.

As she approached, one of the women turned and smiled. “Hello.” She reached out her hand. “I’m Nancy Wilson, and this is my husband, Bert. And you are…”

Helen took her hand to shake. “Hello, Nancy, Bert. I’m Helen Anderson.”

“Did you serve, Helen?”

She smiled. “No, I stayed in the States, working at an aircraft engine factory.”

“A real Rosie the Riveter, then?” Bert smiled.

“Sort of. But, actually, I’m here to honor my dearest friend, Ruth Walker, who worked in a Red Cross Clubmobile. Did any of you know her?”

Nancy looked curious. “What’s a Clubmobile?”

Helen explained how the Clubmobile program worked, and they were both polite and interested but knew nothing of Ruth.

One of the other men in the group moved toward Helen. “Did I hear you say you’re here to honor a Clubmobiler?” He wore a beige Army hat with some type of silver bars on it.

Helen smiled. “Yes. Did you know any?”

He held out his hand. “Hi. I’m Danny Milano.”

He was a tall man, posture still erect, even though he had to be close to eighty. He had military-short gray hair and a warm smile.

“I sure did know some of those Clubmobile girls,” he said. “They were a lifesaver, I tell you. What fun it was when we got a visit from the Doughnut Dollies! They were such a boost to our morale, just to see a real American girl in the middle of a bombed-out field. It was wonderful.”

He turned and motioned to a woman, presumably his wife. She wandered over, slipping her hand through his arm. She wore a dark blue hat bearing a white circle with a red cross inside it.

“My wife, Betty, was in the Red Cross. Betty, this gal’s here to honor another Clubmobiler.”

“That’s great. What’s her name?”

“Ruth Walker, from upstate New York. Did you know her?”

Betty shook her head, looking at her husband, who shrugged his shoulders.

Helen tried not to show her disappointment.

Betty smiled. “Her name doesn’t ring a bell. Do you know what Clubmobile she was on? Which group she was in?”

"The Clubmobile was called the *St. Louis*, but I don't remember the group." Helen realized she should have looked over Ruth's letters before coming. She remembered the names of the three girls Ruth had worked with on the *St. Louis*, but that was pretty much all.

"There were so many Clubmobiles and so many girls. It was a wonderful program, but I'm afraid I didn't know everyone."

Betty turned and waved to a group of women who were at a nearby table. "These gals were all Clubmobilers, so maybe one of them knows your Ruth." The group of women approached, all wearing the navy blue hat with the Red Cross patch on it. Helen remembered seeing a picture of Ruth in a similar hat.

Betty faced the other women. "Hey, girls, this is—I'm sorry, I didn't get your name?"

She stepped forward. "I'm Helen Anderson, but I'm here in honor of my friend Ruth Walker. She was a Clubmobiler on the *St. Louis*."

Several of the women started talking to each other, and Helen could hear names such as *Arizona, Lincoln, Daniel Boone,* and *General Lee*.

A short, plump woman with a head covered in gray curls turned to the taller woman on her left. "Weren't you on the *St. Louis*, Charlotte?"

Helen turned to Charlotte and could see the tears in her soft brown eyes. She was nodding but hadn't said anything yet. This woman had known Ruth. Charlotte was still tall and striking, just as Ruth had described her, with a kind smile and soft waves of silver hair. Helen could see the resemblance to the younger woman smiling in some of Ruth's pictures.

"Charlotte, are you all right? Maybe you'd better sit down." Her friend directed her to a chair, and Helen quickly sat down next to her.

"Your Ruth's Helen, aren't you? The British war bride." Charlotte reached out her hand and placed it atop Helen's.

Helen smiled at her. "That's me. And you're Ruth's Charlotte. I recognize you from the pictures and letters Ruth sent. I'm honored to meet you."

Charlotte leaned forward, pulling Helen into her embrace. While it wasn't the same as having Ruth back, she could almost feel her friend beside her.

Betty and the other women were smiling and chattering about Ruth and the fact that Charlotte worked with her. Charlotte turned to her friends. "You remember Ruth, don't you, girls? She and I were together right from the very start. We were roommates, starting with the training at American University all the way through VE Day and beyond. Until the plane crash, that is."

Helen smiled and wiped a couple of tears from her eyes. "That's her."

Several of Charlotte's friends nodded, recognition dawning with mention of the plane crash.

The plump friend of Charlotte's placed a hand on Helen's shoulder and squeezed gently. "I'm sorry for your loss."

"I still think of her often," Charlotte continued. "My husband, Ardean, he's over there at the bar with some of the other husbands. Anyway, we went out to the cemetery this morning, to visit her grave. I was at the funeral and at the temporary cemetery, but I never came back once they moved her here. It was too hard, before, but I was glad to see her final resting place today."

Helen nodded, as she had felt the same way. She should have come before, but Ruth would have understood that she was too busy with Billy and Ruthie, as well as her work, her precious students.

"I took my daughter and granddaughter to the cemetery with me today, too, to see Ruth's grave. It's a lovely spot, especially with the sun reflecting off the water below."

Charlotte nodded. "We took our grandson to several of the beaches yesterday, covering old ground. He loved running up and down the sides of the bomb craters, still there after all these years. It looks so peaceful now, it's almost hard to remember how many young men lost their lives out there."

Helen suddenly realized Ruthie and Irene were standing behind her chair.

"Who are these beauties?" Charlotte held out a hand to Irene, who took it and stepped closer to Charlotte.

"I'm Irene, and this is my mother. Her name is Ruthie."

Charlotte looked from Irene to Ruthie to Helen and back. "That's wonderful. It's a pleasure to meet you both." A few tears escaped the corners of Charlotte's eyes.

Helen felt a wealth of emotion fill her. While the sadness of Ruth's loss returned, she was also proud of the life she'd made with Billy and their beautiful daughter. Helen wished they'd been blessed with more children, but it wasn't to be. Luckily, now she had Irene.

Some of the other women sat with them, filling in the table and pulling over more chairs. Soon they were introducing themselves. All had served with the ARC, mostly as Clubmobilers, although some had worked at stationary clubs in some of the bigger cities. A few remembered Ruth personally, but all remembered hearing about the girl who had died in the plane crash and was buried in Normandy. Ruth was one of only four women, and the only civilian, buried there.

It was wonderful to hear them share stories of their days with the ARC and the fun they had in the middle of the war, serving the troops, driving the trucks, going to dances, going on dates, and camping in the rain. As crazy as it had always seemed when Ruth wrote these things in her letters, telling them all what a wonderful experience it had been for her, these women were backing up Ruth's story.

Helen turned to Charlotte. "Do you stay in touch with the other women from the *St. Louis*? I think their names were Renee and Eileen?"

A sad smile crept over Charlotte's face. "Renee passed away fifteen years ago of breast cancer. She married a wonderful man and moved to Brooklyn shortly after we got back to the U.S. We wrote and spoke on the phone often over the years."

"Was she the one whose father was in a concentration camp?"

Charlotte nodded. "Yes, sadly. Renee tracked down his records a couple of years after the war. He'd been sent to Auschwitz. Almost no one got out of there alive."

They sat quietly for a while, Helen remembering all they'd learned in the years since the end of the war about the horrors of the camps.

Eventually, Charlotte looked up at Helen again. "You may remember that Eileen got engaged to an Army officer she met in France, Tom. They got married not long after VE Day, while we were still in Germany. She never made it back to Hollywood but has been living happily with Tom, their three children, and now at least seven grandchildren outside of Tampa, Florida since 1946. Ardean and I have visited Tom and Eileen many times, with our four children. Now our visits include our grandchildren, who also love to go to Disney World."

Helen felt sure Ruth would have been pleased to know her friends had found happy marriages and had children and grandchildren. She said as much to Charlotte.

Eventually, Charlotte turned to Helen, a sparkle in her gaze and a sweet smile on her face. "Ruth talked about her family all the time and read us many of your letters. I feel like I knew you all, at least for a short time. How is everyone? Catch me up on the past fifty years."

Helen smiled. "Well, we're all older. Lots of gray hair all around." She chuckled. "I'm happy to say I went to college, because of Ruth, and became a teacher. I loved every minute of the thirty years I taught in our local elementary school. After Billy and I retired, we traveled a bit, but he passed five years ago. At least I still have my beautiful daughter and granddaughter, as well as a wonderful son-in-law, so I'm blessed."

Charlotte smiled. "I'm glad you became a teacher. Ruth was certain you'd be a great one. She used to tell me how smart you were, how strong and loving.

Everything, she said, that you'd need to teach children."

Ruthie placed her hand on Helen's shoulder. "She was a terrific teacher, exactly for those reasons. She was everyone's favorite, and her former students always came to visit whenever they were in town. Many still do."

Charlotte dabbed at her eyes. "I'm so glad. Ruth would be proud of you."

Helen looked down at her hands, taking a private moment to thank Ruth once again for the gifts she'd given.

"What about Lilly? What has Lilly done with her life?"

Helen sent Irene to get her purse so she could share some pictures. "Lilly's Paul came home from the war, safe and sound, and fell in love with Elsie and she with him. He got a good job in sales, and they went on to have five more daughters. They still live in Upton Falls. You've never seen a happier man in all your life."

Charlotte laughed. Helen handed her the pictures of Lilly, Paul, and their girls, and she admired it.

"This was taken at Elsie's wedding. It was such a happy day."

Charlotte handed the pictures back. "And what about everyone else?"

"Well, first Grandpa and Grandma Walker and then Earl and Julia passed on, of course, but Will and Clara took over the farm. Will is able to work with his injured ankle, although it has always bothered him in the winter. Luckily, he's always had the hired man, Matthew, to help him. Will and Clara had another son after the war and named him Jack. The boys have taken over most of the day-to-day running of the farm at this point, but Will still gets out to the barn every morning, just to stay on top of things."

Helen pulled out more pictures. "These are from the Walker Farm Centennial celebration just a couple of years ago. One hundred years of family farming, right there in Upton Falls."

Some of the other ladies leaned in to take a look at the photos.

Helen turned to Charlotte. "Did Ruth ever talk about Judith and Jacob Cohen?"

Charlotte nodded. "Isn't Jacob the pilot who flew a Fighting Fortress?"

"That's him. Ruth invited him home for dinner when he was on his bond tour in about 1943. Anyway, she introduced Jacob to Judith, a war widow, and they eventually got married." Helen laughed. "She saw the match before they did. I teased her about it later on. Anyway, Judith and Jacob moved back to Brooklyn and had two more boys, in addition to the three children she had with her first husband. Jacob passed a few years ago, but they had a long, happy marriage."

"Thanks to Ruth," Charlotte said.

Helen nodded. "Thanks to Ruth."

"One of the boys, Kurt, moved back to Upton Falls after he graduated from college. He got married and still lives there."

"Mom's sweet on Kurt," Ruthie teased.

Charlotte looked up from the photos, a questioning smirk on her face.

Helen actually giggled. "I've always had a sweet spot for Kurt, I admit. And now, of course, I'm quite taken with his son, Henry. What a cutie."

"So, all in all, Ruth left everyone in pretty good

shape back in Upton Falls?"

Helen leaned back in her chair, fanning the pictures out on her lap. When she looked at the generations of family that Ruth had touched, she couldn't keep the smile off her face. Ruthie handed her a tissue.

"Ruth left us happy, healthy, and grateful to have each other. She left a hole in our hearts when she died, but she'd given us so much that she was never completely gone. Not really."

Charlotte and Helen joined hands, sitting quietly, remembering the friend they'd shared, the wonderful woman who had made so many lives better simply by being in it. That was a rare gift, one that Helen and all the others in the family were fortunate to have been given. Once again, her hand went to the lucky necklace at her throat. She'd been very lucky in her life, they all had, and they were grateful.

### A word about the author...

Barb Warner Deane was born and raised in the small town of Watkins Glen in the beautiful Finger Lakes area of New York. She graduated from Cornell University, where she met her husband. They married on graduation weekend, and she went on to get her law degree from the University of Connecticut.

Barb, her husband, and their three incredible daughters have lived in the Chicago area for the past twenty-five years, other than two years in Frankfurt, Germany and two years in Shanghai, China. She draws a lot of writing inspiration from her experiences and the incredible people she met as an expat. *On The Homefront* was inspired by a trip to Normandy, France with The American Women's Club of the Taunus.

After giving up the practice of law, Barb has worked mostly as a mom but also as a paralegal, bookstore owner, book merchandiser, travel writer, proofreader, writing consultant, high school media guru, and avid volunteer for the Girl Scouts, including a leader for five troops on two continents and for the American Women's Club in both Frankfurt and Shanghai. She has also been president of the Windy City Chapter of Romance Writers of America and a high school PTA president.

Barb is also a genealogy and WWII buff, loves to read, is a huge fan of *The Big Bang Theory* and Harry Potter, and is crazy for both U.S. and international travel. She and her husband are about to be empty-nesters; she's making plans to expand on her "Visited" list of 45 states and 37 countries on 6 continents.

http://www.barbwarnerdeane.com